"You love me, and you know it."

"Why won't you admit it?" he demanded gruffly, his lips moving atop the throbbing pulse of her neck.

"No, I don't. I hate you, and I will as long as I live," she answered automatically. But the breathless moan that followed her pronouncement belied her words.

Gray gave a low laugh. "Yes, you do, Tyler, but you don't have to say the words if you don't want to. Not when you'll prove different to me every night in our bed, just as you're going to do right now." He took her lips then, tenderly, hungrily, and they began their long, slow ascent to the very gates of heaven.

"I recommend FROSTFIRE with pleasure.... Entertaining and thoroughly enjoyable."
Karen Robards, author of *Morning Song*

"This is Linda Ladd's best book—in fact, it's one of the best books I've read in a long, long time. With this book I would rate Linda Ladd among the top writers in this genre."
Barbara Keenan, *Affaire de Coeur*

"FROSTFIRE is delightful and fresh. Linda Ladd's absolute best . . . A gem of a romance. I thoroughly enjoyed it."
Kathe Robin, *Romantic Times*

FROSTFIRE

LINDA LADD

AVON BOOKS NEW YORK

For Steve and Bev Ladd
   and Lucas and Katelyn

With a very special thank-you
   to those readers who have written
   with words of encouragement.
   I love to hear from you!

Linda Ladd
c/o Avon Books

FROSTFIRE is an original publication of Avon Books. This work has never before appeared in book form. This work is a novel. Any similarity to actual persons or events is purely coincidental.

AVON BOOKS
A division of
The Hearst Corporation
105 Madison Avenue
New York, New York 10016

First Avon Books Printing: April 1990

AVON TRADEMARK REG. U.S. PAT. OFF. AND IN OTHER COUNTRIES, MARCA REGISTRADA, HECHO EN U.S.A.

Printed in the U.S.A.

RA 10 9 8 7 6 5 4 3 2 1

1

February 27, 1871
Chicago, Illinois

"Tyler, I'm not at all sure we should go through with such an underhanded plot. You know I've had no experience with this sort of trick! Why, I've never done a fraudulent deed in my life!"

"I know, Etty, but I told you before, it's not really dishonest, not when it's him. You don't have to utter a syllable. Just stand there and look matronly and sincere, like always, and I'll do all the talking, I promise," Tyler MacKenzie insisted gently, her final words taking on a wheedling tone as she tried to calm the older, bespectacled woman standing beside her. Tyler knew that her dear friend Harriet Stokely, who was fifty-five, considered herself a good bit wiser in the ways of the world than eighteen-year-old Tyler. At the moment, Harriet did not look the least bit convinced, despite Tyler's reassurances.

Tyler sighed. Her small, high-heeled red boots made crunching sounds in the ice-crusted snow as she stamped her feet, trying to keep warm. The night wind was so cold! "Just remember I've done this sham before, lots and lots of times, and it always works like a charm. Anyway, we've got to do

1

it this way, because the Yankee must think we met him by chance. According to the *Tribune*, he's one of the fastest fellows in Chicago, so he's bound to pay me some notice if I act the coquette. You read the account of him and that awful artist woman yourself. She ended up deserting her husband and going back east because of him. I can have him eating out of the palm of my hand in no time at all, I know I can," she finished with a self-confident nod.

"Oh, Tyler, won't you please reconsider? You haven't tried any of these"—Harriet faltered over the distasteful words—"disgraceful conspiracies for months now, not since last summer when your uncle Burl was laid to rest in St. Louis. He was the mastermind, if you'll remember!"

Tyler knew Harriet would never condone her scheme, so she took a different tack, one she knew would appeal to the other woman.

"Etty, tonight will end our deceptions, just as I promised you. I mean it, truly. Once we get Rose Point back from Gray Kincaid, we can go there to live. You know that's all I've ever wanted. He owes it to me. Rose Point is rightfully mine."

Harriet detected the barely perceptible catch in Tyler's voice, and she sighed heavily in surrender. Shaking her head and grumbling a few more disapproving words, she tugged her gray squirrel cap down over her silvering dark brown hair. Lordy, she thought, vigorously chafing her hands inside her black woolen gloves, what a horrid night to stand about in the snow!

"Perhaps he's not intending to come around tonight after all," Harriet suggested, peering down the wide public mall and hoping desperately that she was right. "It's getting late. He usually passes this way by now. Mercy me, I'm becoming quite numb," she added.

"Please bear up, Etty. I'm not used to snow either," Tyler MacKenzie replied, shivering. "A brisk walk down to the end of the bridge would do you good, I suspect. He'll be along shortly now, I'm sure. He hasn't missed a night in five days. And, Etty, if you catch sight of him, and you're quite certain it's Gray Kincaid, stroll back toward me. That can be our signal."

"I declare, I don't know what ails you, child, to persist in such nonsensical and unseemly artifice now that Burl's gone," Harriet muttered, her cross words producing a frosty cloud that hung between them in the cold night air. But she lifted the front of her black wool skirt and picked her way gingerly through the gently falling flakes to the nearby bridge spanning the Chicago River.

Tyler watched Harriet sweep away, her huge hoopskirt cutting a wide swath along the three inches of new snow on the walkway. Then she thrust her own kid-gloved hands deeper into her soft ermine muff. Harriet was terribly old-fashioned about everything, especially her apparel. No matter how many times Tyler had cajoled her to lighten up her drab outfits and exchange her stiff crinolines for stylish panniers, Harriet had remained adamantly opposed. She was quite satisfied with her reliable hoopskirts, thank you. And plain black served her nicely, she had said, because after all, her husband and sons had been dead only five years, all sacrificed to preserve the Union.

Tyler shivered, raising the big, soft muff against her face to blow into the silky white fur. The resulting warmth helped to thaw her wind-reddened nose.

Now that it had grown dark, the low temperature felt even more severe. She had grown up in southern climes, and now it was peculiar to think that she had once considered it cold in Natchez, Mississippi, at Christmastide! This frigid Yankee town on Lake Michigan had seemed more like the North Pole to Harriet and her since they had arrived on the St. Louis–Chicago Express a week ago and begun their surveillance of Gray Kincaid.

Hatred seeped through her bones—hot, intense,

and oddly comforting in its familiarity. She had never laid eyes on her intended victim until her recent arrival in Chicago, and only then from a distance. But she knew him. She knew all about him. Stranger or not, he had managed to play a powerful role in her life, virtually destroying everything she loved.

Six years ago, when the Yankee bluebellies had descended like a plague on Mississippi, not only had Gray Kincaid commandeered Rose Point Plantation for his troops, he had also burned every bale of cotton, which had plunged her father, Colin MacKenzie, into bankruptcy. Tyler's throat constricted. Then her father had taken his life out of despair over what Captain Gray Kincaid had done.

Deep in her heart, an unhealed wound began to throb, bitterness and pain rising forcefully to crash over her mind like a giant, sluicing wall of water. She saw the dreadful scene again, so vivid and real that her fists clenched convulsively inside her muff.

She was twelve years old again, alone, padding barefoot down the silent halls of Rose Point as the midnight hour began to toll. She opened the door to her father's library just as he picked up his small, ivory-handled pistol. . . .

Determined not to relive the horror all over again, Tyler lifted her face to the sky, deeply inhaling the crisp, cleansing air.

Her moment of truth was at hand, she told herself. She was in Chicago, ready to wreak vengeance on the Yankee. Gray Kincaid now owned Rose Point, having bought it for a pittance after the war when it had been auctioned for nonpayment of back taxes. When she had discovered in the Natchez newspapers that he had recently put the plantation up for sale for ten thousand dollars, she had decided to come to Chicago and rook out of Gray Kincaid himself the money with which to buy it back. How fitting her plan was, because he would lose twofold and look the fool in the process. Once she had succeeded, she would never again need to resort to any of the illegal ventures and confidence games her uncle Burl had taught her when she had gone to live with him following her father's funeral.

"Where the thunder is he, anyway?" she grumbled as another violent shiver seized her. Every night Gray Kincaid had taken the same route over the Clark Street Bridge, directly past the spot where she now stood, then on to his big gray stone mansion a few blocks up on Lincoln Avenue. Why did he have to be late on the very night she'd planned to accost him? She hoped it wasn't a bad omen.

Tyler lifted cinnamon-brown eyes to gaze across the frozen river to the three-story white limestone building where Gray Kincaid's railroad offices were located. The howling wind made the fragile white flakes of snow dance in graceful cotillions—cotillions like the ones her father had hosted in the great drawing room at Rose Point when she was a little girl, before the Yankees and Gray Kincaid had ended their whole way of life.

"Come on, you damn Yankee," she muttered through stiff lips. A sudden gust of wind swept impudently beneath her heavy red velvet skirt, promptly raising an army of goose bumps upon her stockinged legs. She already had a head cold from this abominable northern weather, and if he didn't arrive soon, she and Harriet would both succumb to fever from standing out in the snow for three hours.

Tensing, she focused her eyes on a tall, heavily cloaked figure that had moved into sight, striding swiftly along the hump of the bridge. Her gaze darted quickly to Harriet just as the other woman turned and started back toward Tyler in their agreed-upon sign.

So he's come at last, Tyler thought triumphantly. She inhaled deeply, fortifying herself against the anxiety that always riveted her just before she first approached a mark. In control again, she started walking briskly across the icy sidewalk. Timing was everything. She must pretend to slip and fall just as he noticed her. Then she would feign a sprained ankle so he would feel compelled to carry her back to her hotel—or to his own house, if Lady Luck was smiling.

She continued at a reckless clip toward the bridge; then, when she was sure the big man could see her through the darkness and fast-falling snow, she acted, flailing her arms for balance as she went into an expert skid across the ice. Unfortunately, however, the pavement proved to be a good deal more treacherous than she had anticipated, and she went down hard, grunting as her backside hit the frozen ground.

But all thought of that pain fled as she slid off the narrow sidewalk and down the slippery incline toward the frozen river. She reached the ice and kept going, coasting a short distance from the shore until, to her unadulterated horror, a sharp snapping and crackling began in the ice around her. Terrified, she cried out for help, frantically grabbing for a handhold as her legs plunged into the frigid river, her heavy winter garments dragging her down.

At first Tyler felt nothing but the mind-numbing shock of the icy water rising over her legs and torso. Panic came next, and she began to scream and struggle. Almost at once, however, her feet settled into the cold muck covering the river bottom, sinking well past her ankles. She could stand, she thought joyously. Although she was up to her waist in water and surrounded by floating chunks of ice, the river was not swift enough to sweep her away. She turned, breaking through the thin crust of ice as she pushed toward shore as rapidly as she could in her heavy skirts, shivering uncontrollably.

"Over here, girl! Grab my cane, and I'll pull you out!" The authoritative masculine order floated out from the darkness of the bank only a few feet away from her. She knew instinctively that it was Gray Kincaid coming valiantly to her rescue, as planned.

Thigh-deep in the cold water though Tyler was, she was still practical enough to capitalize on the situation. For the past six years she had been taught to adapt, instantly and without hesitation. *Good or bad, make all things work to your advantage,* Uncle Burl had told her at least once a day.

"Help! Help me, please!" she cried, trying to sound more hysterical than she really was. She waved her arms with calculated show, all the while inching closer to shore.

Seconds later, she grabbed the solid-gold head of an extended ebony cane, and quickly and easily, her Yankee foe pulled her out of the water and over the broken ice, despite the weight of her heavy, waterlogged garments. She barely had time to blink before he had jerked loose the buttons of her fitted crimson velvet jacket and stripped it off her, then wrapped her tightly in his own fur-lined greatcoat.

"Not to worry, miss. I've got you now," he was saying quite calmly, as if he pulled half-frozen women off ice floes every night on his way home from work. Then Tyler felt herself being swung into a pair of strong, capable arms, and Gray Kincaid trudged with surefooted ease back up the bank to where Harriet stood, wringing her hands with anxiety. As Gray Kincaid spoke to Harriet, Tyler decided to pretend she was half conscious so he would feel compelled to take her to his house.

"She's had a fright, madam, but I daresay she'll recover quick enough if we can get her home to bed without delay. Do you live close by?"

Harriet was so overwhelmed and distressed by the accident and the limp way Tyler was hanging in the big man's arms that she could barely stammer out an answer.

"Yes, yes, we must get her home—to our rooms, I mean," she answered, her words garbled. For her life, she couldn't remember the name of their hotel—not with poor Tyler lying there in his arms, so white and still. "Oh, my goodness me, what's the

name of it? It's downtown, and it's got a fancy man-
sard roof, I do remember that, but I just can't think
of the name. Are you sure she's all right? She's not
moving."

"Yes, she will be, I'm sure. But come on, we'd
better take her to my house. We need to get her
warm. It's just down the street. Can you navigate
the ice on your own?"

"Yes, yes, I think so. But please, don't concern
yourself with me! Do hurry!" Harriet cried, rushing
after him as quickly as she could as he carried a
lifeless-looking Tyler down the sidewalk with long,
rapid strides.

Please, please, let Tyler be all right, Harriet prayed
fervently while she hurriedly picked her way along,
not at all sure the good Lord would be willing to do
anything about her plight—not after her participa-
tion in Tyler's wicked machinations. She had known
all along that she shouldn't have agreed to such a
devious scheme, and now look what had happened!
Tyler might die from exposure!

Five minutes later, Harriet was greatly relieved to
see the man in front of her turn into the back carriage entrance of a house. She followed him through
the tall, black-spiked gates, and farther up the drive
she could see carriages and sleighs parked in the
slanting squares of yellow light coming from the
front windows. She realized suddenly that a party
or soiree must be in progress in the stately mansion,
but hurried on as Gray Kincaid reached a wide set
of stone steps that led to a lofty rear porch sup-
ported by square pillars that ran across the back and
down one side of the house. An identical porch
stretched above them on the second level.

Gray Kincaid burst into the warm, well-lit kitchen.
His wild entrance and the way the door banged
loudly against the wall frightened three of his young
kitchen maids who were busy filling huge silver trays
with fancy canapés and sweet pastries. When he
barked out sharp orders that were unlike his usual

calmly uttered directives, the trio of servants nearly jumped out of their shoes.

"Joyce, Sally, quick, run fetch some blankets, and plenty of them, and you, Hildie, ready one of the guest rooms. And get one of Carly's warmest nightdresses. She fell through the ice! Hurry, dammit!"

Gray crossed to the wide cooking hearth where a fire flamed high and lowered his tightly wrapped bundle to the spotless brick floor. Carefully he unwound his coat from the girl's shivering body while Harriet moved close behind him, hovering over his right shoulder.

"Quick, help me get her out of these wet clothes," he instructed Harriet, pulling off one of Tyler's small, muddy slippers.

Tyler had been faking semiconsciousness, though the quaking of her ice-cold limbs was genuine. But as her Yankee prey began pulling off her wet, clinging wool stockings, she knew that she must do something before he relieved her of every stitch of clothing.

"Ooooh, oooooh," she moaned loudly, twisting from his grasp while she pretended to regain consciousness with a violent start. But he only held her tighter, his fingers moving deftly to the fastenings of her undergarments. In the twinkling of an eye, he peeled off her sodden petticoats and began working with a good deal of success on the soggy pannier and pantalettes underneath her skirt. Tyler began to panic. Was he really going to strip her stark naked? And with an efficiency that made her wonder how many other times he had undressed ladies? To Tyler's heartfelt relief, Harriet intervened.

"Please, sir! You must let me do that!" Harriet cried out in true matronly outrage.

"Don't be silly, woman. She's hardly more than a child. Help me with these blasted stays before she catches her death!"

Child, Tyler thought, bridling at the insult. But at least Harriet was attempting to stop him as he moved to pull off another of Tyler's stiff, muddy petticoats.

"Tyler is no child, sir. Please, you must let me attend to her."

"Is that her name—Tyler? And what is yours, madam? I assume you are her mother?"

Oh, no, no, no, Tyler thought, horrified. Now he knows my real name. But even that terrible mistake was eclipsed by other problems as Gray Kincaid began to massage her numb legs with a warm towel, so vigorously that Tyler wanted to slap him silly and scramble away.

Harriet was so shocked by what Gray Kincaid was doing to Tyler's legs that she could barely answer his questions.

"My name's Harriet. Harriet Sto—" she began distractedly, breaking off at midword. Oh, no, she'd already mentioned Tyler's real name! Tyler had insisted they both assume fictional names for their hoax.

Harriet's abrupt stop caused Gray Kincaid to let up on his energetic kneading. "I beg your pardon, but did you say Harriet Stowe?" He twisted around to survey her, surprise evident on his handsome dark features. "The abolitionist author?"

Not nearly as quick-tongued as Tyler was, Harriet panicked again.

"Oh—no," she stuttered nervously, face scarlet. "I'm not her. She's my . . . my aunt. And I'm Tyler's aunt, of course."

Oh, my word, Tyler thought in absolute disbelief, realizing she had to do something quick, before Harriet either revealed everything or succumbed to a fit of vapors.

She came upright into a sitting position, pushing both hands against the massive muscles of Gray Kincaid's chest, at the same time giving a wonderfully genuine-sounding scream of hysteria. As she had intended, her actions cut short Harriet's disastrous conversation with the Yankee. Unfortunately,

it also earned her a quick, brutal shake from him—
one designed, no doubt, to calm her, but which
instead sent the hairpins flying out of her heavy
auburn chignon. Just as quickly, she was enfolded
tightly in the man's embrace, his large palm gently
holding her head securely against his starched white
shirtfront.

"Hush now, you're safe. Your aunt Harriet is right
here. We'll take care of you."

A maid rushed in with an armload of blankets, her
wide eyes on Tyler's bare, blue-tinged legs as Gray
Kincaid wrapped several of the soft, warm quilts
around the poor, unfortunate girl. Without another
word, he scooped Tyler into his arms again and carried her up a narrow flight of back servants' stairs
that led to the second-floor bedchambers.

Harriet followed helplessly, so flustered now that
she didn't know what else to do. Upstairs, she scurried in Gray Kincaid's wake as he took Tyler down
a wide hall to a set of double doors which stood
open near the top of a massive mahogany staircase.

Chamber music wafted up the crimson-carpeted
steps, and Harriet caught sight of a crowd of guests
below before she entered the bedchamber where the
man had disappeared with Tyler. Inside, she found
the maid Gray Kincaid had called Hildie sliding a
long-handled pewter bed warmer between the sheets
of a high white four-poster draped with flowing folds
of purple silk. She approached as Gray Kincaid lay
Tyler down on the warmed sheets and then turned
to the servant.

"Did you get the bedgown from Carly's room?"

"Yes, sir. Here 'tis, sir."

"I'll leave it with you, then, Mrs. Stowe," Gray
Kincaid said, placing the soft white garment in Harriet's hands. "I believe there's a doctor in atten-
dance downstairs, a friend of mine. As soon as I
change out of these wet clothes, I'll ask him to come
up and check on her condition. She's reviving a bit
now, I believe."

"You've been so kind." Harriet said, breathless with ragged nerves, glad he was leaving, and even more relieved he was summoning a doctor. "I just can't tell you how grateful I am."

"It's a good thing I happened along in time to help," he answered absently, then turned to the maid. "You had best prepare the room next door for Mrs. Stowe." He returned his attention to Harriet. "I'm certain you'll need to stay the night. You won't want to leave Miss—I'm sorry, I don't believe you've told me your niece's last name. Is it Stowe as well?"

Harriet hesitated, chagrined to be in such a fix, but she had managed to regain a certain degree of reason. She fibbed the way she was supposed to, Lord forgive her.

"Lancaster," Harriet told him, since Tyler's uncle's name was the only thing that came to her. Her gaze slid guiltily away from his incredible bluer-than-blue eyes. "Her name is Tyler Lancaster."

"Well, Miss Lancaster—she is a miss, at her age, I assume?" Harriet nodded, becoming more uncomfortable as she became deeper embroiled in Tyler's plot. She listened while her unsuspecting host continued, obviously deeply concerned about Tyler's well-being. "Miss Lancaster will need to stay abed until the doctor can see to her. Is there need to notify anyone? Your menfolk are probably alarmed, since it's well past dark."

"I appreciate your concern, but there's no one. We're on a holiday here, just the two of us." Harriet answered quickly, most gratified that she was finally able to speak a scrap of truth.

"Indeed? At this time of year? I must say that surprises me. Most visitors prefer the summertime."

"I am just so truly appreciative," Harriet repeated.

"I'm afraid I must say good night to you now, Mrs. Stowe. I need to see to my guests. But if you should require anything, the servants will gladly attend to you. There's the bell cord, beside the bed."

He paused, looking solicitously into Harriet's worried face. "You appear very pale. Are you quite sure you're all right?"

"Oh, mercy sakes, of course," Harriet answered a little too hastily. "It's my poor niece we must worry about, Mr.—" Harriet suddenly remembered she wasn't supposed to know his name!

"Kincaid. Gray Kincaid," he said in a pleasant manner. "I think you had better put that gown on little Tyler there, then tuck her under the covers."

"Oh, yes, I will, at once."

"All right, then, I'll bid you good night."

2

"Can you believe our luck?" Tyler whispered softly, popping up in bed the moment the door closed.

"Luck?" Harriet parroted hoarsely, watching in astonishment as Tyler grabbed the warm white cashmere nightdress and slipped it over her head, then quickly wriggled out of the cold wet chemise underneath it. "Tyler! I thought you were unconscious!"

"That was just pretend. Couldn't you tell? But I can't stop shaking. I'm still so cold I'm about to croak. I was scared witless at first, but the river was real shallow where I went in. I could have walked out on my own if I'd wanted."

"You just about frightened me to death acting half dead like that!" Harriet scolded in a rare display of ire, her eyes kindling and her cheeks going pale.

"Forgive me, Etty," Tyler replied, looking the picture of remorse. "I truly didn't intend to worry you. Uncle Burl always knew when I was putting on an act, and I thought you'd see through it, too. But didn't it all work out just grand! I told you we needed to get into Kincaid's house, and here we are!" Tyler scrunched down deeper under the warm blankets, trying to control the shudders that still

15

racked her. "It'll just take a spell to warm up, and then we'll search the Yankee's bedroom."

"We'll what!" Harriet's brown eyes grew round behind her octagonal glasses. "I simply won't allow it, Tyler. We cannot do such a thing without someone seeing us! *He'll* see us!"

"Oh, pooh, no one will see. Not with all the goings-on downstairs. He's hosting a party, isn't he? And that means the servants will be busy with all the cooking and serving and such."

"Now listen to me, young lady. We can't just go creeping around in plain sight! Oh, gracious me, we'll get caught for sure!" Harriet leaned against the bed with a despairing groan, as if scandalized at the mere thought of such shenanigans.

"Oh, Etty, you just aren't used to tricking people yet. As soon as I get some feeling back in my legs, I'll show you how simple it is." Tyler buried her face in the warm flannel blanket. "I nearly fainted for true when you told him my real name," she said, her voice muffled by the bedclothes. "I was terrified you'd spill out everything so I threw a hissy."

"Well, that frightened me, too—when you screamed, I mean," Harriet muttered in reproach, finally thinking to remove her hat and hooded cloak. She arranged her wide hoops as she sat gracefully on the bed.

"You did pretty well, under the circumstances," Tyler praised her, reaching up to smooth back a strand of Harriet's hair which had come loose from its crown of braids during all the excitement. "Except for the part about Harriet Stowe. I nearly crowed when you said you were related to her. Why, Uncle Burl said that book of hers was what got all the Yankees stirred up so much about the Negroes!"

Tyler giggled at the absurd notion of being related to the famous writer. Then her face quickly sobered as she took both of Harriet's hands and squeezed them in silent appeal. "Things can still work out, Etty, because I intend to find a way to stay longer.

He seems eager enough to have us here, so we'll just accept his hospitality. He won't find out what we're after until it's too late."

"Perhaps he's not as bad as you think. He certainly appears a gentleman," Harriet felt compelled to say, earning a frown from Tyler. "Are you sure he's the culprit?"

"Of course I'm sure!" Tyler cried indignantly. "And don't go all softhearted just because he decided to drag me out of the river. He wouldn't have bothered if he'd known who I really was, and he'll be sorry he went to the trouble before I get through with him!"

"But how can you be sure it's him? The war was so long ago. You were so young then, and he's not that old either, probably barely into his thirties." Harriet chafed Tyler's ice-cold fingers.

"Oh, please, Etty, you must trust me. Uncle Burl told me all about him when I was a little girl—his name, where he lived, what he looked like, everything. He's the one, all right, and he deserves everything he's going to get. Oh, Etty, now that my feet are thawing out, it feels like thousands of little pins are sticking them!"

A tap on the door sent Tyler diving back into the pillows to feign unconsciousness, while Harriet lunged to her feet, thoroughly alarmed until she saw Hildie, Gray Kincaid's freckle-faced chambermaid, appear in the portal.

"The fire's burnin' next door, ma'am," she announced courteously.

"Thank you kindly, Hildie."

"If you have a need, you most likely'll find one of us down in the kitchen, ma'am. The master said we was to see to you right smartly if you ring." With that the girl bobbed a curtsy and left.

"There, you see?" Tyler said triumphantly. "They're all much too busy with their duties downstairs to bother with us." She shifted under the blankets, feeling much better now. "You will watch

at the door and see when the Yankee goes downstairs, won't you? Please, Etty? Then will be the
perfect time for me to snoop around.''

Harriet shook her head. ''This is nothing but mad-
ness, Tyler. Someone will see you. I know they
will.''

''Please, Etty, help me this one last time. If it
wasn't for him, Papa would still be alive and we'd
be together at Rose Point. I'll hate Gray Kincaid for
as long as I live.''

Harriet sighed, as usual unable to resist Tyler's
pleading, especially when she talked about her plantation in Mississippi—which was often. Harriet had
never known anyone who wanted to go home as
badly as Tyler, unless it was Harriet herself. But unlike Tyler, Harriet refused to let herself dwell on the
old, comfortable farmhouse in northern Missouri
where she had married and given birth to her four
sons. She could never go back there again. There
were too many torturous memories.

Reluctantly, she moved to take her post at the
door. She opened it a crack and peered into the corridor as Tyler rubbed her feet and legs to increase
the circulation. Moments later, she saw Gray Kincaid leave a room on the other side of the hall. She
watched him walk along the banister of the open
stairwell, from which one could peer down into the
vast foyer below. He had changed into dark evening
attire, and Harriet thought he looked extremely
handsome and elegant as he rounded the carved
newel-post topped by a statue of a Grecian maiden
holding a lamp.

''He's gone,'' she whispered to Tyler as he disappeared down the staircase.

Tyler threw back the covers, eager to get the job
done. She needed to find out as much as she could
about his railroad holdings. If he was like other
wealthy men, he would probably have a safe in his
bedchamber, and if not there, in a private office
somewhere in the house.

"Now you stay here, Etty, just in case someone comes upstairs."

Tyler arranged the covers as she spoke, pulling the bed drapes to obscure the interior of the four-poster.

"If someone does come, just keep him over by the door, and he'll never know I'm not in the bed. Look, those French doors by the fireplace must lead to the upstairs porch." She ran to peek out the silk draperies to make sure. "Yes, and I'll bet all the bedrooms lead onto it. It's always good to know all the exits from a room, in case something goes wrong," she said as she returned to the hall door. "Uncle Burl told me that plenty of times, so you better remember it, too."

"Oh, Lordy me." Harriet groaned.

"Don't look so worried," Tyler chided cheerfully. "No one's going to come up during the few minutes I'm gone. I've got very good instincts about such things. I wouldn't ask you to help, Etty, really, but it might be the only chance I'll have to find out where he keeps his important papers. Now where do you think he'd hide his safe?"

"His safe! You're not going to burglarize him, are you?" Harriet looked aghast at the notion.

"Not unless I have to. I'd much rather trick him into buying the fake stocks. But in any case, I'll only be taking back what he stole from my family. Now, which room is his?"

Moments later, Tyler left a harried-looking Harriet on guard in the doorway and tiptoed stealthily around the stairwell, looking like a lost ghost in her long white nightdress.

The entire upstairs was deserted, but the sound of stringed instruments and merry laughter rose from below. Feeling more confident, she turned the shiny brass doorknob and quickly entered Gray Kincaid's bedchamber. She stood motionless on the threshold, her chest heaving with fearful excitement. She drew in a deep breath as she let her gaze wander over the spacious room.

The gas had been turned low. The only other light was the crimson glow of banked embers coming from the black marble hearth in the adjoining sitting room. A curved dark blue sofa and matching wing chairs flanked the fireplace facing the French doors, which Tyler assumed also led to the upstairs porch. She took a step inside, unnerved by the silence, broken only by the slow, steady ticking of an antique case clock beside the door. The furniture was dark and massive, ebony perhaps, lost in the shadows looming along the walls. Everything was very austere and masculine, but at the same time tasteful and finely made.

Deciding she had better hasten to her task, she silently moved past the huge bed hung with maroon velvet to a highboy chest against the wall. She barely glanced at the wood-framed dressing valet over which Gray Kincaid had carelessly tossed his wet clothing. She was much more interested in what she might find in the chest of drawers.

A glint from the top of the chiffonier caught her eye, however, and she reached up to lift one of the small silver picture frames arranged on the glossy surface. Gray Kincaid stared back at her, alongside another man. Both looked to be well over six feet tall and wore the detested dark blue, brass-buttoned uniform of the Union Army.

Even now, years after the South's defeat, the sight of their fine Yankee attire filled her with bitterness. The gallant men of the Confederacy she recalled had worn threadbare rags and soleless boots. Her uncle Burl had sent them much of the money he and Tyler had accumulated during the years of conflict, and she would always take pride in their contribution. She shook away her anger over the war and focused on the young girl in the photograph, standing between the two bluecoats. She appeared to be around ten or eleven, and gazed into the camera with a bold, proud smile that was unusual in a girl of her age. A sister? Tyler wondered. Perhaps the one Gray Kincaid had called Carly, who owned the nightgown Tyler now wore.

Tyler put down the heavy frame and picked up the other ornate pictures one by one, finding several more photographs of the same three people, one before a fir tree hung with strands of popcorn and gay Christmas decorations, and a few of Gray Kincaid with other men. She assumed they were his business associates, since they stood in front of various locomotives and depot offices.

The last picture was an old daguerreotype, browned by age. It showed a pretty young woman sitting on a small bench beneath a leafy tree with a tall, dark-haired man behind her, his hand resting on her shoulder. Two small boys hugged her skirts, and she held a baby in a long white christening gown. The family looked rather poor and shabbily dressed, and she wondered if the two adults were Gray Kincaid's parents. She knew nothing of his life before he stole Rose Point.

She replaced that last frame, then slid open the top drawer, realizing she had wasted too much time on the pictures. She quickly but thoroughly searched each of the long narrow drawers, finding only neatly starched shirts, neckties, and handkerchiefs, all laid in precise stacks.

Disappointed, she moved to one of the few pictures hanging in the room, of a wild white stallion. But there was no safe hidden behind it, and to her chagrin, none behind the room's two other pictures either. Well, she would just have to search his office. That was where he'd likely keep all his business secrets. And the more she knew about her victim, the smoother her plan would go. Uncle Burl had always said so.

Her face set with renewed determination, she eased out into the corridor and nearly swallowed her tongue as she turned and knocked into Harriet, causing a violent swaying of hoops.

"He's coming up the steps! Whatever shall we do?" Harriet hissed hysterically, her dark eyes wild with panic behind her wire-rimmed spectacles.

Tyler's heart dropped to her knees as she saw the Yankee's broad back coming up the last turn of the steps. Within a few seconds he would round the stairwell and see them standing at his bedroom door. Tyler looked around frantically, but saw neither a convenient set of drapes nor a towering potted plant behind which to hide. Then her eyes went to Harriet's wide, voluminous black wool skirt.

"Etty, don't move. No matter what, don't move," she whispered. Harriet gasped in astonished shock as Tyler suddenly fell to her knees and ducked beneath the back of her hoop, sending it waving precariously forward.

"Oh, Lordy, Lordy—" Harriet croaked out in utter mortification and woe. She lost every ounce of color in her face as Gray Kincaid turned and caught sight of her. Her heart seemed to rise into her throat until it got stuck somewhere around her tonsils.

"Mrs. Stowe?" Gray Kincaid said, obviously surprised to see her. "Is anything wrong?" he inquired, striding toward her.

"I feel as if I might faint," announced Harriet with utmost honesty, then belatedly realized that was the very last thing she could do with Tyler crouched behind her wobbling knees.

"It could be that your niece's mishap upset you more than you first thought," he replied solicitously. "Please, madam, allow me to assist you to your bedchamber. You do look a little worse for wear."

"No!" Harriet cried as his hand closed over her elbow. "I mean, I don't believe I can walk a step right now. It's my heart," she improvised. "Yes, that must be it. I have a heart condition."

The tall man looked down at her, dark brows knitted in concern. "Perhaps I should carry you," he offered.

"No, no, I'm much too heavy for that," she said, then flushed, comparing the strength in his broad shoulders and immense muscular arms to her slight size.

"I assure you I can lift you, Mrs. Stowe," he answered, the corner of his mouth twitching with a hint of a smile.

"Oh, dear, but of course you can, silly me, but now that I think upon it . . . perhaps I had better just stand right here by myself for a very long time. Please, sir, don't bother yourself about me. Return to your guests, I really must insist upon it."

Harriet gazed at him hopefully, but Gray Kincaid gave a resolute shake of his head. "My dear Mrs. Stowe, you surely cannot expect me to go blithely on about my business, abandoning you here all alone when you feel so ill." Although studiously polite, his deep voice carried an uncompromising note. "Allow me to take your arm, madam, and I'll see you safely to your bed."

Harriet lurched noticeably as Tyler grabbed her ankle. Gray Kincaid frowned and reached out to steady her. Underneath Harriet's voluminous hoop-skirt Tyler was now pinching the back of Harriet's calf. Obviously, she wanted Harriet to let him help her to bed.

"Well, perhaps I *can* make it, Mr. Kincaid, if you will be so good as to lead me. But we must walk slowly, very, very slowly."

Oh, please, please don't let him see Tyler under my dress, Harriet moaned inwardly as Gray Kincaid's fingers closed firmly around her upper arm. She couldn't even imagine the humiliation she would feel if the well-mannered, elegant gentleman towering over her found a young, scantily clad woman cowering beneath her hoop! Barely able to draw a breath, she withdrew her handkerchief from her sleeve and pressed it to her mouth as they moved one tiny step at a time the short distance to her chamber. Perspiration broke out on her brow as her hoop bumped against Gray's leg, ballooning out behind her. Tyler jerked it back into place, and Harriet stopped, mopping her face, which now had taken on the color and sheen of a South Seas pearl.

"Try to hold on a bit longer, Mrs. Stowe, we're nearly there. You're as white as chalk," he added with concern.

"I'm sure I can make it by myself now," Harriet murmured as he leaned around to open the door for her.

"I really would feel better if you'd allow me to escort you to your bedside," he insisted, a trip which seemed to drag out to well over a day and a half. Never had Harriet been so ecstatic to merely lean against a bedpost. Her host stared down at her, still supporting her arm, and Harriet's face went from white to crimson as she felt Tyler slither like a snake from under her hoop to take refuge beneath the ruffled eyelet bed skirt.

"I really think you should have a good, long rest, Mrs. Stowe. The physician I mentioned was called away on an emergency earlier this evening, but I've sent word for him to pay a call on Miss Lancaster in the morning. He'll need to examine you, as well, I fear."

"Perhaps not, Mr. Kincaid. I'm feeling uncommonly improved of a sudden."

"I'm pleased to hear that. You do look a trifle better. The color is coming back into your cheeks." Gray Kincaid's extraordinary azure eyes searched hers. "And don't worry about your niece. I'll check on her on my way downstairs."

"No need," Harriet squeaked out. "She was sound asleep when I left her."

"I'll look in on her anyway," Gray insisted affably. "Are you sure you're all right?"

"Please, don't concern yourself. I'm quite myself again."

"Then I'll leave you now so you can rest."

Plagued by the heaviest foreboding she had suffered yet, Harriet watched him depart. He was going to find Tyler gone, and then what in heaven's name would they do? How could they ever explain what Tyler was doing in Harriet's room?

Before the door had closed all the way, Tyler scurried out from under the bed and raced to the porch, her white gown streaking behind her. She barely felt the frosty flagstones beneath her bare feet as she sprinted the few yards to the twin doors of her own bedchamber. She flung them wide just as Gray Kincaid knocked. She pushed the French doors shut behind her, then flew toward the sanctuary of the bed. Before she was three steps across the plush black-and purple Chinese carpet, Gray Kincaid opened the door. She froze where she was, and for one awful moment they just stared at each other in stupefaction. Then Tyler did what her uncle had always told her to do in a dire emergency. She grabbed the back of the chair beside her and prepared to fake a graceful swoon.

3

Gray Kincaid reached her very quickly, too quickly for her to fall all the way to the floor, so Tyler was forced to lean weakly against his big, sturdy frame. The shaking of her voice had more to do with her near discovery than any fainting spell.

"I—I heard a knock," she temporized as best she could, "but once I was up, I couldn't think where I was—"

Her speech faltered when, without a word, he leaned forward and swept her into his arms as he had done twice previously in the short time since they had met. Tyler, hoping the feel of her lightly draped body might convince him that she wasn't the child he had called her earlier, immediately looped her arms around his neck as he strode with her to the bed. Her plot depended on his being attracted to her.

"You shouldn't be up yet. You're not well," he told her, lowering her gently to the bed.

Tyler watched his face as he carefully drew the soft, downy comforter up over her. For the first time she got a good look at him, having had to keep her eyes closed during most of the rescue. With his black wavy hair and dark skin, he was handsome, she had to admit. His brows were slightly arched, his jaw square, lean, and clean-shaven. But his eyes riveted her gaze. Sky-blue with darker blue rings around the irises, they settled on her face, clear and penetrating, and filled with something—what was it? Worry? Wouldn't that be lucky!

"Don't be afraid. I'm the one who pulled you out of the river. Do you remember going through the ice?"

Tyler shook her head, making her eyes very round and guileless. "Only that I was so cold and afraid." She glanced around, as if puzzled. "Where am I? This isn't my hotel, is it?"

"No, I carried you to my house since I lived close by. And you mustn't worry about your aunt. Mrs. Stowe is resting right next door."

"I see."

Awkward silence reigned for several seconds, during which his piercing blue eyes roamed freely over her face.

"Are you warm enough now?" he asked; then, to Tyler's shock, he sat down on the edge of the bed beside her. For some reason, she was dreadfully embarrassed by such familiarity from a complete stranger, especially from her avowed enemy. Why, not even her uncle Burl had ever sat upon her bed when she was in it! She blushed, until she could actually feel her skin burning. Her unlikely reaction to his boldness surprised her. She never blushed!

"Why, yes, I'm quite comfortable now," she began, moistening her dry lips, and was further startled when he picked up her slender hand and held it sandwiched between his large, warm ones.

"Your fingers are like ice. I'll see if I can find another coverlet for you."

He released her hand, placed an equally heated palm against her cheek, then touched the back of his long, tanned fingers to her forehead, as if checking for a temperature.

"Your face is too warm. I'm afraid you might have a touch of fever," he announced. Tyler stared at him, thinking it wasn't fever, but humiliation. Just who did he think he was anyway? she fumed inwardly, then checked her ire. She shouldn't mind him touching her; that was what she had intended all along.

"I've summoned a doctor to see about you and Mrs. Stowe. He will probably call tomorrow morning, if he makes it at all. This storm is turning into a blizzard, I fear."

"Is Etty ill?" she asked, gazing at him with just the right amount of innocent concern.

"Frankly, I was worried about her a few moments ago. She nearly swooned outside in the hall and was acting peculiar. But as far as I know, she's resting comfortably now."

"Are you certain she's all right?" Tyler decided it would be wise to brace up Harriet's rashly concocted story. "She has a heart affliction."

"Yes, she told me. That's why I want Dr. Bond to see her. But don't worry. I made sure her weak spell had passed before I left her alone."

"I think I should go see her."

"No, you're not strong enough yourself. I'll have one of the chambermaids tend to you both from time to time throughout the night, if it would ease your mind."

"You're too kind, Mr. Kincaid," Tyler murmured, shyly lowering her lashes.

"How did you know my name?"

Tyler stiffened, but under her uncle's tutorage she had become adept at making up quick lies. They had practiced often when she had first come to live with him. He had made it into a game that was fun for a twelve-year-old child.

"Harriet told me when I first woke up. I recall her telling me that before she left, but little else. Isn't that curious?" She made a mental note to have Harriet back up that lie if Kincaid ever confronted her with it. "Wait, I remember now that she said you were very brave to save me the way you did." He'll like that, she thought smugly. Every man she had ever known enjoyed having his vanity stroked. Compliment, defer, disarm—how many times had Uncle Burl repeated that formula?

Gray Kincaid smiled, as she knew he would, revealing strong, even white teeth.

"I only pulled you to safety, Miss Lancaster. You were a very courageous young lady not to panic. Most women I know would have."

"Oh, no, you are too modest," she protested, filling her eyes with earnest adoration. "I owe you my life."

Tyler raised her gaze in time to see a glint of amusement in his eyes. Suddenly an alarm blinked in her brain. Perhaps Gray Kincaid was one of the few men who didn't value shy, retiring women with empty heads and vacuous smiles. She knew that most Southern gentlemen prized such qualities, but a few males she had met, especially among the Yankees, seemed to prefer a lively intellect in a feminine head. As far as Tyler herself was concerned, the modern-thinking men were the better of the two, even if they were more dangerous to scheme against.

"I must say I'm pleased to have happened along at such a propitious moment."

His answer was gracious, and as he finished, those vivid eyes she found so disturbing dipped to contemplate the softness of her lips. Inexplicably, Tyler was affected, but she hastily decided that the heat searing in her cheekbones was due to the thickness of the flannel blanket and nothing more. Well, at least he seemed to be taking more notice of her womanly attributes.

"There's a chill in the air," he was saying now, rising from the bed. "I better stoke the fire and get that blanket for you."

Tyler watched silently as he crossed to the hearth. He was taller than most men she had met, with shoulders broad enough to cause his tailor extra work, but he was not at all heavy. In fact, his large frame had a sinewy leanness, despite the bands of muscle that bulged noticeably under the fine black silk of his evening jacket as he bent to shovel fuel from the ornate brass coal hod.

She wondered what he did to maintain such an impressive masculine physique. Why wasn't he soft and pampered like the other rich businessmen she had swindled? Most of them had pudgy paunches and palms every bit as smooth as her own. But when Gray Kincaid had held her hand, his fingers had been hard, strong, and bronzed by the sun.

A sound from the doorway abruptly drew Tyler's attention from her examination of the Yankee's manliness. She was surprised to see a young girl enter the room and carefully draw the door closed behind her. She was pretty, about fifteen or sixteen, with blond hair coiffed in fashionable, elaborate puffs, braids, and a frizzled fringe of curls over her forehead.

Wondering if she should make her presence known, Tyler watched the young woman glide gracefully toward Gray Kincaid, who was still busily poking at the fire.

"Gray?" the blonde said softly. He jerked around, his dark face registering surprise.

"Betsy, what are you doing here?"

The girl twisted her lace handkerchief. "I realize it's frightfully forward of me to be in here with you, but I just had to talk to you alone."

"Is something wrong? Is your father ill?"

"Oh, no, don't concern yourself with Father. He's quite all right." She paused momentarily, then hurried on, as if she was afraid he would stop her. "I just want you to listen to me, please."

"Of course. Do you need my help with something, Betsy?"

"No, that's not it," the girl replied hesitantly; then her words came rushing out in a flood of emotion. "I love you, Gray, I really do. I have for the longest time, ever since that first day when you came to see Father on business.''

Tyler gasped. A declaration of devotion had been the last thing she had expected. And Gray Kincaid looked positively abashed, the expression on his handsome face almost comical.

''But, Betsy, you were only five years old when I met your father.''

''I know, but even then I knew I'd love you forever. Please, Gray, don't you love me just a little?''

Tyler began to feel sorry for the girl, but she wasn't sure if it was because poor Betsy loved a monster of a man like Gray Kincaid or because she had innocently avowed it to him in the presence of an unknown female. Tyler wished she could disappear and, for Betsy's sake, rolled over to face away from the couple, pretending she was asleep as Gray Kincaid said, ''Betsy, please don't go on. We're not alone.''

Even from across the room Tyler could sense the poor girl's shock. She kept her eyes closed, barely breathing underneath the bedclothes.

''Who is she?'' Hurt, humiliation, and fear mingled in Betsy's whisper.

''She's a guest,'' Gray hastily informed her, his voice low. ''She fell through the ice as I was passing the Clark Street Bridge tonight, and I brought her here. She's the one I wanted your father to see earlier.''

An awful silence descended, marred only by the hissing and snapping of the flames. Gray Kincaid spoke a moment later, evidently trying to reassure her. ''I believe she's been asleep for a while. She didn't hear what you said.''

No answer came from the lovesick girl.

''Betsy, I can't tell you how flattered I am by what you told me a moment ago, but you're so young. You haven't even had your coming-out season yet—''

''I'll be seventeen in just a few weeks,'' Betsy interrupted him, her voice trembling, "and Papa said I could have my debut then. He told you that last Friday when you dined with us, don't you remember?"

Gray remained silent for a moment, then said in a kinder tone, "You know how much I think of you, Betsy. But it's not that kind of affection. I've always considered myself an uncle or older brother to you. Believe me, sweetheart, someday the perfect man will come along—"

"Stop, stop," the girl whispered hoarsely. "I won't listen. You're talking to me like I'm a child, and I'm not! I love you!"

Tyler remained motionless, then heard Betsy sob and her skirts rustle past the bed. The door closed and the Yankee released a long-drawn-out sigh. When he spoke again, he was standing very close to Tyler.

"You can open your eyes now. I know you're not asleep."

Tyler did as bade, turning onto her back. Their gazes locked, and Gray Kincaid gave a small, sheepish shrug.

"I apologize for you having to witness such a private conversation." He ran his fingers through the thick black waves at his temple. "But I appreciate the sensitivity you showed for Betsy's feelings. It would have been worse for her if she had known you had heard our conversation."

"You were very kind to her," Tyler said in an attempt to win his good will, then realized with a start that she did admire the way he had handled the awkward situation. He had been gentle and considerate, not at all what she would have expected from a libertine like Gray Kincaid.

"Betsy's a sweet girl, and her father, Charles Bond, is one of my oldest friends. Our families are very close. I guess I should have seen this coming." He stopped, shaking his head. "But the possibility

never occurred to me. I had better go and find her.
Do you need anything else, Miss Lancaster?''
    "No, I'm just tired, is all."
    "Then rest well."
    "Thank you, Mr. Kincaid. Good night."
The Yankee smiled down at her for an extra moment, which Tyler took as an encouraging sign. After he was gone she lay back against the soft silk
pillows, a satisfied smile carving deep dimples in her
cheeks. What an odd course her scheme had taken!
Her carefully laid plans had gone amiss from the
beginning. Yet, despite her bad luck, she was actually lying in one of Gray Kincaid's guest rooms,
basking in his good will. And he liked her—she had
read it in his smile.

Despite all of Harriet's blunders, Tyler was in an
excellent position to entice Gray to buy the bogus
stocks she had had printed in St. Louis. But since
Gray Kincaid was a bachelor, propriety dictated that
tomorrow she and Harriet return to their lodgings
at the hotel, and that would make things more difficult. Why, she hadn't even discovered where the
Yankee hid his safe!

Her delicate brows drew together as she leisurely
stretched her arms and then laced her fingers beneath her head to contemplate the purple canopy.
She would just have to find a way to stay right
where she was without drawing the wrath of society
upon them. After a few minutes of intense reflection, she knew exactly what she must do.

If I have a sudden relapse, she thought, and I am
too ill to move, who will condemn the Yankee for
letting me stay until I recover?

Yes, she decided, her grin widening, in the morning she would be so deathly sick that even Gray Kincaid's doctor friend would be appalled.

She laughed softly, convinced her new plan would
work, and she turned on her side to stare at the
dancing shadows playing on the wall across from
the dwindling fire. She lay still for a long time, con-

tent and comfortable, then became too warm and kicked off the coverlet. Her mind raced over the details of her deception; she devised a Plan A and then a Plan B, just in case something went wrong. Uncle Burl had taught her to be ready for any and all unexpected exigencies. *Two plans are better than one*, he used to say, *and three are better than two*.

Time ticked on, measured by the gentle, hypnotic swaying of the pendulum of the ormolu anniversary clock on the bureau. Tyler tossed and turned, throwing off the rest of the bedclothes, barely aware that her body had grown increasingly hot. Her muscles felt stiff and achy, and each breath became a labored effort, as if she were imprisoned in a lead corset. She slept, but only fitfully. Long before Gray Kincaid's friends had bundled themselves up in fur hats and velvet cloaks and bustled out the door, Tyler writhed in the throes of a raging fever.

In Tyler's delirious dreams, she was a little girl again. The wide, shiny oak floors of Rose Point stretched out before her, and wavery, indistinct lights glowed out of a strange white mist. She felt frightened standing alone in the dim and eerie place, and she held tight to the toy snowscene her father had given her for Christmas. She started slowly down the hall, her bare feet peeking out beneath her long white nightdress. The polished wood felt cold underfoot, and somehow she knew she was all alone in the great plantation house. No one answered her forlorn cries or appeared from the strange fog to take her hand.

"Papa?" she cried, her voice shrill, her words echoing down the hall. She drew up in fear as Mammy Rose Marie suddenly loomed out of nowhere.

"Yo papa in de librar'. He waitin' fo yo dere, chile," came the heavyset Negress's familiar voice—but all different and spooky. Tyler quailed as the colored woman seemed to float toward her, eye sockets aglow. The apparition pointed to a blinding shaft of light coming from a doorway down the hall.

"No, I don't want to," Tyler cried, frozen with dread.

"Come on now, chile, come wid yo Mammy Rose Marie, or you be naughty and de jaybird'll come and peck yo eyes out and tell de debil on yo."

"No, no!" Tyler jerked, trying to get away as icy fingers settled on her thin shoulder. Then, somehow, she stood in her father's book-lined library. He sat behind his desk, and when he raised his head, the same strange lights flowed from his eyes, making the small gun he held in his hand reflect silvery glints.

Tyler tried to shut her eyes, but she couldn't make her lids go down, and for the thousandth time in her nightmares, she saw her father put the gun into his mouth and pull the trigger. She heard the shot, saw his head jerk backward, watched blood spray the chair behind him before he reeled forward, his forehead hitting the desk with a final thud.

"Papa!" she screamed over and over. But when she reached out to touch him, a different visage appeared, a handsome, dark face with evil, azure eyes that jolted her out of her horrible dream.

"No!" Tyler cried, lurching upright in bed, wide awake, her flushed cheeks damp with perspiration, her fever-weakened limbs trembling. She tossed her head around wildly, frightened eyes latching almost at once upon the same blue-eyed face that had sent her fleeing from her nightmare.

"You! I hate you, I hate you!" she cried viciously, pummeling her enemy's chest with both fists.

Tyler's unexpected attack on Gray Kincaid made Harriet, who was standing nearby, gasp in shock. She stepped forward in concern as Tyler fought Gray Kincaid, forcing him to hold her tightly against his chest.

"I hate you, I hate you. I'll hate you as long as I live." Tyler was sobbing, though now completely immobilized by his restraining embrace, and Harriet leaned down to help him calm the hysterical girl.

"Shh, hush now, Tyler," he was murmuring as he held her. "You've had a bad dream, that's all. Everything's going to be all right."

"I don't know why she's saying such things, Mr. Kincaid," Harriet began nervously. She was alarmed not only over Tyler's condition, but because she feared that Tyler's delirious words would lead him to discover the truth. To her relief, Gray only shook his head as he continued to hold Tyler comfortingly, his hand gently stroking her long, tangled auburn hair.

"No need to apologize, Mrs. Stowe. I've seen fever fits before."

Harriet twisted her handkerchief. Tyler had been lost in her fever since very early that morning, and Harriet was beside herself with worry. Yet the doctor had still not shown up.

As Gray carefully lowered Tyler back against the pillows, pausing to brush the damp curls away from her hot, flushed face, Harriet leaned forward to dab at the perspiration on Tyler's brow.

"I fear she's getting worse. Whenever will the doctor arrive?" she finally blurted out, her anxiety getting the better of her good manners.

"The doctor has come, madam, with the sincerest of apologies for his tardiness. The confounded snow and ice sent my coupé into the gutter. I had to walk the last three blocks."

A man of about sixty moved from the portal. His white hair was fringed thickly around his ears and the back of his head, but a bald spot shone from his pate. His face was pleasantly proportioned, with a reddish flush in his cheeks, whether from the wintry weather or natural coloring, Harriet knew not.

"Sorry to hear of your accident, Charles. You weren't injured, were you?" Gray asked, rising to shake the doctor's hand.

"No, but the trap was banged up a bit. I suspect

Willy is still digging the blasted thing out of the drifts, poor devil.''

Gray immediately led the doctor toward the bed. "She's been like this all morning, Charles. And she's been hallucinating, I think.''

"Well, stand back and let me have a look. Good morning to you, madam,'' the doctor said, placing a small pair of bifocals upon his large nose. He peered at Harriet and smiled, obviously approving of her point-lace cap and black silk morning dress with its dainty white collar.

Gray Kincaid quickly took the hint. "Mrs. Stowe, allow me to present one of my oldest friends, Dr. Charles Bond. Charles, this is my guest, Mrs. Harriet Stowe.''

"Not Harriet Beecher Stowe!'' Charles exclaimed heartily, still holding his well-worn, black leather bag.

"My aunt,'' Harriet replied lamely, chagrined to be locked into such a ridiculous falsehood. She blushed at her own deceitfulness.

"I'm a great admirer of your aunt's novels,'' the doctor exclaimed. "Why, I was so incensed by poor Eliza's plight that I nearly joined the army myself. If it hadn't been for my duties here in Chicago, I should have gladly traveled with Gray's unit to Mississippi.''

Not wanting to discuss the war or the merits of *Uncle Tom's Cabin*, Harriet quickly changed the subject. She reached out, worriedly taking Tyler's hand. "Will she be all right, Doctor? I'm very concerned about her.''

"Oh, I should think so,'' Charles Bond answered, turning his full attention to his small, restless patient. He felt her face, then bent to lay his ear to Tyler's heaving chest.

"I want to go home,'' Tyler muttered, tossing to and fro, her voice thick and barely coherent. "Please, let me go home, please, Papa needs me—''

The doctor patted Tyler's cheek reassuringly, but

his patient had already lapsed back into the haunting dreams that gave her no peace. "Poor child. Pretty little thing, isn't she?" Dr. Bond murmured, glancing at Gray, who nodded agreement. "She's burning with fever, and her lungs are congested. We'll have to make sure she doesn't develop pneumonia. But at least it's not the scarlet fever. Only yesterday, I lost a mother and both her children to that devil's tool. I take it she's the one you fished out of the river?"

"How did you know?" Gray asked, surprised.

"Betsy mentioned her last night when I returned home. Among other things," he added with a significant look at his friend. Harriet noted Gray Kincaid looked a trifle uncomfortable until the doctor spoke again. "Don't feel bad about it, Gray. It appears to me that you handled the situation in the best possible way. The little minx will get over it soon enough, I'll wager. Young John Mooney's been coming around of late. Of course, he says it's me he's visiting, but I imagine it's Betsy's company he really enjoys. I tell you, it's times like this when I wish her poor dear mother had lived to see her into womanhood. It pains me that Betsy's never had a gentle woman to influence her. Ofttimes she's as bold as a boy." He shook his head, sighed, then looked back to the sickbed. "There's not a lot more we can do for this young lady, except to keep her skin cool and moist. After the fever breaks, I'll give her a dose of belladonna, and she should be herself within the week. Do you want me to take her over to the infirmary?"

"May I stay there with her, Dr. Bond?" Harriet asked at once, but Gray spoke before Charles could answer.

"That won't be necessary. Both of you are welcome to remain here. It's still snowing, and the temperature's dropped. It would be foolhardy to move her." He turned to Harriet and added quickly, "If that arrangement is agreeable to you, Mrs. Stowe . . ."

"Why, I don't know what to say. We certainly appreciate your kindness, Mr. Kincaid, but I'm not sure it's proper, you being unmarried and all. People might talk—"

"Nonsense," he said. "The girl is very ill, and I won't be here anyway. I travel a good bit on business, and I'll be leaving for Louisville tomorrow morning. You'll be alone in the house for several days."

Harriet liked the sound of that, but she hesitated, looking down at Tyler's restless, fever-flushed face.

"I'm so grateful. We don't know a soul here in Chicago," she said with complete truthfulness. Gray Kincaid had been extraordinarily kind to them—so kind that she had to wonder whether he was really as terrible and cruel as Tyler had said he was.

"Then it's settled. Hildie will help you nurse her, and I'm certain Dr. Bond here will be good enough to visit often during her recuperation."

"Indeed, I will," the older man agreed with another appreciative glance at Harriet, which brought a rosy blush to her cheeks.

"I'll send my man for your trunks," Gray told Harriet. "Have you been able to recall the name of your hotel?"

"Yes, of course," Harriet answered at once, feeling thoroughly silly. "It's the Tremont House Hotel."

Gray Kincaid nodded. "I'll have your baggage here by teatime," he told her, and Harriet watched the two men leave, glad to be alone with her young charge.

She sat down beside Tyler, squeezing water from a thick white bath cloth bearing Gray Kincaid's gold monogram.

"I want to go home," Tyler muttered again as Harriet tenderly wiped her forehead.

Harriet bit her lip. ''Oh, Tyler, I know you do, you poor angel. That's what this is all about.''

Tyler tossed her head to one side, and Harriet's eyes went dark with sympathy. The girl was an expert at dissembling, but Harriet knew agony like this couldn't be shammed. If only she could do more to help, she thought despondently. Suddenly weary, Harriet closed her tired eyes, her melancholy mood summoning memories of those terrible times during and after the war.

She had been alone with her pregnant daughter-in-law then, fighting hopelessly to keep the farm going. She hadn't even known her beloved husband, Michael, was dead until a month after he had been buried haphazardly on a faraway battlefield called Bull Run. Many more months passed before she learned that all of her boys had been taken as well, dying lonely deaths on scattered, blood-soaked plains.

After that, God had taken Anne when frail little Cole was born, and Harriet had lost the farm. So she'd bundled up the consumptive baby and gone to St. Louis to look for work.

She met Tyler and her uncle Burl in a boarding-house there. The Southern girl immediately took the baby to her heart, helping Harriet tend Cole right up to the end. Then, despite her uncle's objections, Tyler had given Harriet a job as her maid.

When Burl Lancaster was shot during a poker game six months ago, Harriet had been only too glad to step in as Tyler's foster parent and friend. She knew Tyler's mother had died when she was too young to remember and that Colin MacKenzie had killed himself during the war. She'd heard Tyler call for her papa in nightmares many times before. And each time, her heart went out to the generous, orphaned girl. Tyler had her faults—which Harriet knew all too well—but she loved her like the daughter she had never had.

Tears sprang into her eyes now as she sat beside

Tyler. She couldn't bear the thought of losing another person she loved.

"Oh, Tyler," she whispered, clutching her hot hand, "you're not going to die. You have to get well . . . so you can go home to Rose Point."

4

Gray Kincaid sat motionless, his face pensive as he stared out the coach window. Tall, wind-sculpted drifts of snow edged bricked walls, spiked fences, and mansions alike, transforming fashionable Lincoln Avenue into a picture of white ocean waves. The gunmetal-gray sky hung low overhead as crystal flakes fell furiously, blown southward by the bitter, bone-tingling winds off Lake Michigan.

The temperature was low enough to freeze the river solid and bring the busy lakeside docks to a standstill. But Gray didn't mind the frigid weather, so glad was he to be back after spending the week at his Louisville office. While gone, he'd acquired Johnson and Sons of Cincinnati, making it possible for him to build his own railway sleeper cars—something he'd long been wanting to do. The venture would be a lucrative one, because it would enable him to send more expresses out west. Of course, with the constant threat of Indians and prairie fires such routes were risky to operate. But his brother, Stone, had done a good job repairing disrupted lines and had stationed their rail construction crew in Denver. Gray only hoped no unforeseen emergencies occurred in Colorado while Stone was in New Orleans visiting their sister, Carlisle.

Gray's mouth quirked slightly at the thought of
his little sister. To his surprise, he had missed her a
great deal during the past year while she had been
in the convent school in New Orleans. But he was
well rid of all the trouble she had caused with her
constant talk of Women's Rights, or Irish Rights, or
Negro Rights, or whatever other cause she felt
needed an extra zealous crusader. She meant well,
he knew, and she had helped many unfortunate
people with her tireless charity work. Grinning, he
remembered the time she had invited the entire Dor-
cas Society—one hundred women from twelve to
seventy—to "sew for the indigent fringe of society."
Unfortunately, a majority of them decided Gray
would be the ideal candidate for a husband, lover,
or son-in-law, forcing him to stay away from the
house for a week. He had taken refuge in his men's
club on Michigan Street.

But when Carlisle had nearly been arrested at a
blasted Woman Suffrage rally, he had had no choice
but to send her out of town for a time. He wondered
if she had simmered down and forgiven him yet;
she had been furious at first. Even more, he wondered how she had gotten on with the white-habited
nuns. It would be nice to have her back home in a
few months when she was graduated. It was unfortunate that she wasn't in residence at the moment
to act as hostess to Mrs. Stowe and Miss Lancaster.

Since Gray had left Chicago a week ago, his
thoughts had often turned to those two ladies. He
hoped the younger one had not succumbed to pneumonia. He knew better than to take that malady
lightly. He had seen too many men die of it during
the war—and of dysentery, fever, and the scalding
lead of Confederate bullets. He had seen a thousand
faces of death during those awful five years of conflict.

Not liking to think about the long, tragic war, or
of his part in it, he summoned up the vision of Tyler
Lancaster's beautiful young face. Thoughts of her

had often occupied him while he was in Louisville, even though he had shared most of his leisure time with Reva Marsh. She was settled comfortably in her own artist's studio at last, and happy now that she had escaped her overbearing husband and the strict dictates of Chicago society. He was glad he had given her the money to flee a life she found unbearable, regardless of the gossip he'd suffered when his part in her disappearance had been discovered.

Reva was a longtime friend and lover, but his passion for her had cooled long ago. Even with her warm, willing body in his arms, he had been inexplicably preoccupied with his young guest. So much so, in fact, that Reva had become annoyed with him and locked herself in her studio to finish her latest work.

Gray shifted, peering through the veil of falling snow, anxious to see Miss Tyler Lancaster again. Since he usually avoided entanglements with women her age, the intensity of his interest unsettled him. Sweet and innocent virgins were not the type of women who appealed to him. In fact, they were dangerous. He decided it was his bizarre first meeting with Tyler that intrigued him.

More than anything else, he remembered the way her slender body had felt pressed against his chest on the morning she had lashed out at him, her unusual reddish-brown eyes so bright with fever and her auburn hair so like silk against his arms. Some faint tinge of familiarity had touched him then, as it did now. But he was certain he had not met her before; she was a woman a man would remember.

By the time the hired conveyance rolled to a standstill in front of his house, he was even more impatient to see her. He reached for his tall beaver hat and black leather gloves, then tossed the driver a coin, the frosty ground squeaking with each footstep as he moved past the deep piles of shoveled snow to the front door.

Kicking his boots against the top step to remove the caked snow, he entered the vestibule. He hung his heavy overcoat on a massive mirrored coat tree standing beside the door, placed his hat and gloves on a shining oak table beneath it, then passed through the second set of doors leading into the foyer. He paused there, his attention drawn to the dining parlor, from which bursts of merry laughter rang out. He went to investigate, for a moment standing unnoticed in the open doorway.

The three diners were still chuckling over some amusing remark, but Gray barely noticed Charles Bond or Mrs. Stowe. His gaze fell solely on their young companion. She sat closest to the fire blazing in the hearth behind the table, and although her long hair was drawn up in a pink velvet net, the flames shone upon the wispy curls at her face, forming a bright coppery halo around her head.

Gray had certainly thought her lovely before, with her unusual and vivid coloring, but now she looked even more beautiful in her demure rose velvet gown, her cheeks slightly flushed from the heat of the fireplace, or perhaps from a lingering touch of fever. She didn't look as if she had been sick, and his wave of pleasure at finding her so much better shocked him. He had been more worried about her than he had realized.

Before Gray could step into the room, Dr. Bond caught sight of him and stood, his voice booming boisterously.

"Gray, welcome! By George, you've finally come home! I was beginning to think you'd forsaken us! Not that I've minded the company of your two delightful guests. These lovely ladies have certainly brightened the dreary winter days for me!"

Charles beamed through his horn-rimmed spectacles at Harriet Stowe, who fluttered her hands as if to ward away his compliment. But she looked pleased.

"Welcome home, Mr. Kincaid. I've been most

anxious to see you again," Tyler said, rising from the table with a truly angelic smile. To Gray's surprise, she moved gracefully to him in a whisper of velvet and satin.

"Indeed? Is something amiss?" asked Gray, most gratified by her warm reception.

She laughed easily, her eyes sparkling. "Of course not. I have just been eager to thank you for your warm hospitality."

"My pleasure, I assure you," he answered. "I must say you're looking very much better."

"She's nearly as good as new," Charles Bond said, slapping Gray's shoulder in affectionate good humor. "But we're prepared to watch over her closely for a while longer. We wouldn't want a relapse, hey?"

"No, we certainly wouldn't," Gray agreed, glancing at the enchanting creature, then berating himself for his reluctance to look away from her. He remembered his manners, however, as he reached the table.

"And you, Mrs. Stowe? No more palpitations, I hope."

"No, sir, thank you very much. I have gotten over all that."

Gray wondered if she really had. She still appeared as fidgety as the devil on Sunday. He rather liked her, though, which was surprising, since flighty women, prone to attacks of vapors, usually irritated him beyond reason.

"Will you be wantin' a place, sir?" asked Hildie from her post alongside the silver chafing dishes on the heavy walnut sideboard.

"No, thank you. I dined on the train scarcely an hour ago." He looked at the ladies. "But I will join you, if you don't object?"

Both women murmured assent at once, and Dr. Bond offered to move. "I've taken your place at the head of the table, I fear."

"No bother, Charles, keep your chair. I'd be honored to take this place beside Mrs. Stowe. If I may?"

"Of course, please do," Harriet acquiesced politely. Gray sat down, smiling over the candelabra at Tyler. He had chosen that particular chair because it gave him a perfect view of her. Gray's gaze lingered on her smooth oval face, and he was again moved by her beauty. Her eyes were her most striking feature because of their unusual color, the rich red-brown of cinnamon which reflected light in an extraordinary glow. Or was it the dimpled smile that made her so pretty?

Next Gray examined her pink lips, soft and full enough to entice any man to taste them. As she lowered her dark, curly eyelashes, forming feathery crescents against her cheeks, he suddenly realized his admiring scrutiny had embarrassed her.

"I do hope you righted your business affairs straight off," Charles was saying.

Gray forcibly shook off his fascination with the girl long enough to answer.

"A bit of extra time was required, but nothing major." He turned to Harriet. "My delay caused no inconvenience here at home, I hope?"

"Oh, mercy no. We have been treated like queens. And Dr. Bond called often."

"Tut, tut, my dear. Didn't we agree that you would call me Charles?" Bond gently admonished.

The inflection in his voice arrested Gray's attention, and a glance told him the good doctor was beaming like the morning sun and looking as if Harriet Stowe was a choice plum, ripe for picking. He hid his amusement, thinking it a good sign for his old friend to be smitten in the winter of his life. But Gray wasn't sure Harriet's nervous condition would allow the strain of having a beau. Content to let them carry on an old-fashioned courtship, he turned his attention back to Harriet's niece.

"And what about you, Miss Lancaster? Have you any complaints concerning my hospitality?"

"Only one, I'm afraid. Dr. Bond wouldn't allow me to leave my bed until this very day, when I was more than ready three days past. And a good thing it is that he let me come downstairs tonight, or I would have missed your homecoming."

Gray wasn't so sure that he wouldn't have preferred her in bed, perhaps in the soft, skimpy cashmere nightgown she had worn the last time he'd seen her. He chuckled inwardly, wondering what the shy little Miss Lancaster would think of his lustful inclinations. He lifted a fragile, long-stemmed goblet which Hildie had just filled with ruby-red wine.

"I got to thinking while I was away that I know very little about the two of you. All I've surmised thus far is that you are from the South," he remarked casually, noticing how Harriet stiffened beside him.

"Why, Mr. Kincaid, how could you possibly know that?" Tyler asked.

The girl was obviously surprised, and Gray hunched one shoulder in a small shrug. "I, too, resided south of the Mason-Dixon line for a time. Yours is a true Mississippi accent, I'd guess. Vicksburg, perhaps, or is it Natchez?"

Some emotion flared in Tyler's wide eyes, but before Gray could identify what it was, it faded.

"How clever you are, Mr. Kincaid. Mississippi was my home when I was very young. But I really grew up with Aunt Etty in Montgomery. Isn't that so, Aunt Etty? Have you ever been to Alabama, Mr. Kincaid?"

"I'm afraid not," Gray answered, observing the way Harriet Stowe's fingers fiddled with the heavy damask napkin on her lap.

Charles noticed her agitation as well. "Are you all right, my dear? You seem to have grown pale of a sudden."

As everyone looked at Harriet, she rested her hand over her heart. "Dear me, I do feel a bit peculiar."

"Why, Mrs. Stowe, I'm beginning to believe my

presence is the cause of your palpitations," said Gray.

His quip was met with an alarmed look from Harriet. But Tyler's low, pleasant laugh seemed to put the older lady at ease again, though Gray still thought she looked uncomfortable as if she had sat on a pincushion.

"Please, Miss Lancaster, tell me about yourself." Gray took a sip of wine, watching Tyler over the rim. "I'm especially curious as to why you and Mrs. Stowe chose to winter in our city. Most Southerners I know find Chicago closely akin to the Arctic wastelands."

He wanted her to tell him about herself, and he waited, trying to fathom just what it was about her that he found so spellbinding. As Tyler answered, he decided it was her soft fragility that made her so irresistible.

"I know this will surprise you, but we came here on business," Tyler informed him.

"Indeed? What sort of business?" Her revelation had been unexpected, but only added to his growing captivation.

"Actually, my brother sent me. He wants to build a railroad. You see, Aunt Harriet and I traveled here to seek out possible investors. When it comes to railway concerns, I'm sure you're aware this is the place to be."

"Well, I'll be hanged," Charles Bond declared. "If that isn't the most extraordinary coincidence I've ever been a party to!"

"Coincidence? Whatever do you mean?" Tyler's delicate brows arched questioningly.

"Why, Gray's quite the railway baron himself. He owns stock in five of the major rail lines out of Chicago."

"No!" exclaimed Tyler, transferring her attention to Gray, her eyes round with surprise. "Do you really, Mr. Kincaid?"

"Actually, it's six now," he answered. But despite Tyler's innocent expression, a tickling suspicion began to gnaw. Years of experience in negotiating with other people had taught him that few coincidences were true ones—not when it came to business deals.

"Oh, my goodness, now I suspect you'll think all this was some elaborate hoax just so I could meet you."

Harriet made some sort of strangled sound, but Tyler's teasing remark caused Gray to doubt his own distrustful nature.

"I might have," he answered affably, "if I thought a young lady as sensible as yourself would go to the trouble of throwing herself in an icy river just to make my acquaintance—especially when she could simply make an appointment with my secretary."

"But now that I know who you are, I suppose you're afraid I'll do that very thing," Tyler accused, her cheeks dimpling winsomely.

"On the contrary, Miss Lancaster. I *hope* you will."

"I wouldn't dream of making such a request of you now." She shook her head resolutely. "I'd be afraid that as a gentleman, you'd feel obligated since I am your guest."

Her remarks seemed sincere, and Gray had a feeling she could charm just about any male she chose into investing in her brother's venture. As unorthodox as it was to send a young woman as a representative, perhaps her brother was more astute than most.

"Tell me about your brother, Miss Lancaster. Am I to assume he lives in Montgomery with you?"

"Oh, no, Chase lives in Monterrey, Mexico."

Gray lowered the glass he was holding. "You're not talking about Chase Lancaster? The foreign minister to Benito Juarez?"

For the first time since Gray Kincaid had walked into the dining parlor, Tyler's composure was shaken. "Why, yes," she answered, chagrined by the slight stammer in her voice.

"Then here's yet another coincidence. I know Chase Lancaster well. We met in Mexico City a year ago."

Tyler was first appalled, then panic-stricken as her glib tongue deserted her in the face of the alarming complication. Apparently Harriet was affected similarly, since she suddenly choked on her wine and went into a paroxysm of coughing. To Tyler, the interruption was a godsend, because it gave her time to compose herself while both men jumped to their feet to tend to the poor woman.

She went to Harriet, too, patting her back until the fit gradually subsided. She was ready again when Gray resumed the subject, apparently much more delighted than she about his association with Chase Lancaster.

"Chase is a fine man. We became good friends during my stay, but I don't recollect him mentioning a sister. His hacienda is near Monterrey, you say? He invited me there for a visit, but I was unable to accept since I had to return home."

"What a small world we live in," Tyler said as brightly as she could, though inside she was truly dismayed at the news that Gray Kincaid was acquainted with Chase. He was her cousin, not her brother, Uncle Burl's son and the product of an unhappy marriage that had ended when Chase was eight years old. His mother had taken Chase to Mexico to live, and Tyler hadn't seen him since he'd visited them in Natchez during the war when he'd come to the United States to drum up support for Benito Juarez. Gray Kincaid probably knew him better than she did! Clearly, it was time to steer the conversation away from Chase until she had time to polish up her plot. She looked solicitously at Harriet.

"Aunt Etty, are you quite all right now?"

Harriet nodded, dabbing at her eyes and looking gray-faced and shaky.

Gray stood. "I believe we're all finished in here. Why don't we retire to the drawing room, where Mrs. Stowe will be more comfortable?"

"I quite agree," Dr. Bond said, assisting Harriet to her feet. Gray held out an elbow to Tyler, who, glad for a further opportunity to charm him, tucked her hand familiarly into the crook of his arm.

She put a good deal of feeling in her eyes as she gazed up at him, a little awed by his impressive height. She barely reached his chin, despite the high-heeled boots she wore. "I still feel a bit wobbly at times," she confided. "But you mustn't tell the doctor, or he'll put me to bed again."

"Your secret's safe with me. Here, lean on me, if you wish."

Tyler did wish. Her plans had taken a decidedly rocky course, and if Harriet didn't quit acting so anxious and apprehensive, the jig would be up for sure. The only bright spot in the fiasco was Gray Kincaid's definite attraction to her—she could sense it. She relaxed against him, and his arm went around her waist and drew her closer.

The private family drawing room was down the hall, a small, cozy chamber with forest-green sofas and rose-sprigged yellow wallpaper. Dr. Bond led Harriet to a low-backed divan facing the fire, but Tyler was glad when Gray chose a pair of deep wing chairs near the windows for them. They sat down across from each other, as Tyler racked her brain for a way to entice him back into a discussion of the stocks.

"Why don't you tell me about Chase's business?" Gray Kincaid suggested as if cued, and Tyler thanked her lucky star—which sometimes seemed to hover right over her head.

"I'd really rather not, under the circumstances. I wouldn't want you to feel obligated."

Something in Gray's expression seemed to mock her words. "You don't have to worry about that."

His answer gave Tyler pause. Gray Kincaid was a shrewd businessman, and she knew she must never underestimate him.

"Well, if you're quite sure," she answered. "But you must promise me you won't act interested just to be polite. I won't be offended in the least if you turn me down. I'm sure there are other railway men here in Chicago who'll see me."

"I promise," Gray agreed dryly, deciding she was probably already into her sales pitch. But he was willing to listen to what she had to say. He found himself examining her youthful face again and felt a rush of self-annoyance at his adolescent reaction. Her skin was the color of peaches, soft and creamy and so smooth that it was all he could do to stay his hand from reaching out to stroke the elegant curve of her cheek. Just as strong was his urge to pull away her velvet snood and release her silky hair. He was suddenly jealous of the idea that she would call on other prospective clients, who, he had no doubt, would be more than willing to invite her into their private offices and gaze into those beguiling, long-lashed eyes of hers.

"It's really quite simple. Chase raises cattle for the American market, and he needs a way to transport them north," she extrapolated. "That's why he's so keen to build a line from his hacienda to the Texas border. He doesn't have the capital to begin construction on his own. That's why he's willing to share the profits with investors. It's really a very good opportunity for gentlemen such as yourself, who have funds available."

"Unless the railroad fails," Gray reminded her.

"True," Tyler agreed. "But Chase thinks it will be a grand success. And I hope he's not mistaken, because he's putting most of my dowry into it."

Gray grinned inwardly, thinking she was one woman who wouldn't have to worry about a dowry.

Most men would pay her to marry them. Hardly immune to the spell she was weaving around him, he stared into her glowing eyes, warmed by her mere presence.

"How much capital are we talking about, Miss Lancaster?"

"Please, can't we be on a first-name basis? I'd hoped we'd become good friends before I left Chicago."

Or more than that, Gray thought. "I think that's a good idea, Tyler," he said. "How much?"

"Chase would like each investor to buy a block of stocks worth roughly one hundred thousand dollars," she answered quietly.

If Gray Kincaid was surprised by the large amount, he didn't show it, and Tyler knew she mustn't act too eager. "But let's not talk about Chase's business anymore." She turned her attention to Harriet and Charles, talking quietly together in front of the hearth. "Do you know what I think?" she asked, leaning toward Gray.

"No. What do you think?"

She lowered her voice to a bare whisper. "I think Dr. Bond's sweet on my aunt Etty."

"I think you're right," Gray agreed in the same low, conspiratorial tone. His teeth flashed white, and Tyler could not help but notice what a pleasant smile he had. "But how does she feel about him?"

"She told me she thinks he's the kindest, most honest gentleman she's met in a long time," Tyler answered truthfully. She didn't tell him that Harriet had also pointed out how wicked it was for them to draw him into their deceptions.

"Charles is old-fashioned that way."

Tyler had to laugh. "Aren't modern men good and kind?"

"What do you think?"

"I really don't know much about men. Chase is very protective of me."

"I don't blame him," he replied, his eyes lowering to contemplate her mouth.

A strange, giddy sensation reeled inside Tyler's stomach. She was beginning to understand some of the newspaper accounts about Gray Kincaid. She could easily see how a woman, especially one who didn't hate him as much as she did, might be taken in by his charm and handsome face.

Across the room, Harriet rose to take her leave, and Tyler decided she'd said enough in her first encounter with the Yankee.

"I suppose I should go upstairs with Aunt Etty. I've been worried about her. My illness has upset her. I've never seen her so nervous."

"Yes, I noticed that, too." Gray stood politely.

"Oh, yes, Gray, I nearly forgot," Charles said as the two couples met near the door. "I want you to come to the ball on Saturday next. It's to be a grand affair down at the Richmond Hotel. The proceeds will go to charity, and a goodly portion to the new wing of City Hospital. I've promised Betsy she can use the occasion for her coming out, so you really must attend, Gray. She'll be dreadfully disappointed if you don't."

"Of course I will. I'll bring my guests along with me, if they would do me the honor."

"That's a jolly idea, but I've beaten you to the punch with Mrs. Stowe. I'm afraid you'll have to make do by escorting her niece."

Tyler was pleased to see that Gray Kincaid didn't look opposed to Charles's suggestion. "If I'm strong enough by then, I think it sounds like a lovely evening," she said.

"I'm sure you will be fully recovered by then," Dr. Bond interjected amiably.

"Then we'll bid you good night, gentlemen," Tyler said, relieved when she and Harriet could finally escape into the downstairs hall. Answering Gray's questions about Chase had been more of a strain than she had expected.

As soon as they were out of earshot, Harriet hissed, "Tyler, I just can't keep up with this. I'm shaking so badly I can barely walk, and he knows Chase! Mercy me, they're good friends! He's sure to telegraph him! Then we'll be thrown in jail!"

"Hush now, Etty! You're all distraught over nothing. Chase lives in Mexico, and that's a long way from here. Gray has no reason to seek verification of my story. We've already discussed the stocks, and I don't think he's the least bit suspicious. Everything's going to work out fine."

"Fine?" Harriet repeated. "How can you say that? Your plot is a shambles!"

"Oh, pish," Tyler said, helping her agitated friend up the stairs. "You're just not used to hoodwinking people. Leave things to me."

Later, however, when Tyler was alone in her bed, she took Harriet's fears to heart, admitting she had a few misgivings of her own. Things had gone wrong too many times to ignore, and that usually foretold failure. On the other hand, the stock swindle was working so far. Gray Kincaid had seemed interested, had he not? He had seemed calm, relaxed, and self-assured. She wondered how he would feel once she tricked him out of enough money to buy back Rose Point, and left him looking like a fool. Too bad she wouldn't be around then to gloat over the expression such a scandal would leave on his handsome face.

She shivered suddenly, remembering the way he had looked at her. She vowed to move very slowly with him. She had first thought she would just try to make him want her, as she'd done to other men, but now she wasn't so sure that would be wise. He had a good deal of experience with women, which would make a serious flirtation more risky for her than him.

She had to convince him she was an innocent—totally out of reach romantically to anyone who wasn't interested in marriage. That would certainly

scare him off! According to the gossip sheets, there
was no end to the number of women who'd tried to
bag him for a husband and had come out losers.
Confident again with her new plan, she turned over
and snuggled into the pillows, and soon slept without a twinge of conscience.

5

On the night of Betsy's coming-out fete, Tyler made a final inspection of herself in the looking glass. She felt a bit concerned about appearing in public with Gray Kincaid. The nagging fear of being identified by a former victim plagued her, even though she and her uncle Burl had never come to Chicago to ply their trade. Earlier in the week she had endeavored to beg off, but the doctor had given her a clean bill of health, and after that, Gray Kincaid had insisted.

In a hurry, she positioned the little pannier under her draping lime-colored sash, then fussed with the various streamers and festoons adorning her green-and-white taffeta skirt. She rearranged the rosettes edging her neckline, which wasn't nearly so bold as some she'd worn. She didn't want to appear too daring; that would jeopardize the aura of innocence she was trying to project. She noted with satisfaction, however, that her décolletage did reveal enough of her bosom to be modestly alluring.

Her long auburn tresses were piled at the top of her head, and she picked at the short curls fringing her forehead, glad she had naturally wavy hair. She would hate to have to crimp them with hot irons and apply curlpapers at night the way Harriet did.

Turning slightly, she made sure that one long, silky lock streamed down her back, in the latest fashion. Since the affair was formal, she added several short ostrich plumes to her coiffure, sliding them down into her chignon. Pinching her cheeks for heightened color, she glanced at the clock as she pulled on her long white kid gloves. Five-thirty. Plenty of time to rifle through Gray Kincaid's private office.

She hadn't had a chance to do so during her illness, and since then either Hildie, Dr. Bond, or Gray himself seemed always to be hovering around her. But she still wanted to learn as much about Gray as she could, and she *was* slightly concerned that he might have telegraphed her cousin Chase, as Harriet had warned. If so, there would surely be evidence of it in his office.

The household staff had long since retired to their quarters because no evening meal was required, and a short time ago Tyler had seen Gray cross the upstairs hall and enter his own bedchamber. He would be dressing for the evening.

Harriet was already with Dr. Bond, having had tea earlier with him and his daughter, Betsy. Tyler had declined the invitation to join them, having decided that Harriet didn't need to know what she was up to—not after what had happened that first night. Harriet was a dear, an angel, but she was a failure of a fibber, bless her heart.

Tyler gathered her lustrous silk skirt in one hand and hurried to the door. She had a feeling that Gray Kincaid's home office would be a regular treasure trove of information about him and his business affairs. She stopped just outside her door to listen.

The house was as silent as death, the deep snow outside muffling all sound. The satin petticoats beneath Tyler's ten yards of rich taffeta whispered softly as she rounded the top banister to descend like a floating green-and-white cloud to the glossy oak floors of the hall below. The Yankee's private sanctuary was located beside the ground-floor entrance that opened onto the long downstairs porch. Tyler had no doubt she would find his safe hidden somewhere in that room.

The door was closed, and Tyler was prudent enough to take the precaution of tapping softly, just in case. No one answered, so she ducked inside quickly, swept her trailing gown after her, and pulled the door closed. The lamps were not burning, but a small fire still glowed in the hearth. Gray must have been working at his desk just before he came upstairs to change.

She looked at the dark, masculine furniture set against the walls, but the room was not quite as spartan as Gray Kincaid's bedchamber. Instead, it appeared a comfortable haven for a busy business-man, with deep, dark brown leather chairs and the lingering scent of pipe tobacco.

For one awful moment, the room reminded her of her father's library at Rose Point. Tyler shut her eyes and struggled to master a horrible, sick feeling in the pit of her stomach. A haunting refrain rolled through her mind like a tumbling boulder: the shot, the thud of her father's head hitting the desktop, his blood dripping from the ink-stained blotter where she had scrawled so many adoring notes to him as a child.

She wouldn't think about it, she wouldn't.

Setting her small chin firmly, she forced herself to concentrate solely on Gray Kincaid. He was the one who had caused her father's downfall and death. She hated Gray for what he had done to her; she hated him with every fiber of her being. Her anger fully rejuvenated, she glided across the carpet to the massive mahogany desk near the velvet-draped windows.

A clean white blotter lay on the shiny top with a set of intricately wrought silver pens and an elabo-rate silver inkstand. Early in her stay in Gray Kin-caid's house she had found that he insisted on neatness and order. It showed in the way he ar-ranged his private possessions and in the spotless condition in which his servants kept his home. A rack of pipes stood in one corner of the desktop alongside a corked glass container of tobacco. She sat down in the big swivel chair and slowly slid out the long middle drawer. Crisp initialed notepaper of the finest white vellum was neatly stacked inside, along with matching envelopes.

The four deep side drawers were her next goal, and she was delighted to find they contained files of Gray Kincaid's business transactions. She flipped quickly through them, recognizing the Yankee's small, neat hand. Frowning, she perused a few, finding that many were background accounts of business partners, with detailed notes about their past, including family history and personal habits.

The discovery brought Tyler up short. If he was prone to check out everything and everyone so meticulously, maybe he *had* already delved into her past. She and Harriet had been at his house for almost a fortnight. He would have had time. But as she examined the contents of the desk further, she found nothing to suggest he'd launched an investigation of her yet. Nonetheless, she would be foolish to take any chances. She had to convince Gray Kincaid to give her the money that very night.

She slid the last drawer back into place, annoyed that she had uncovered so little about the Yankee. She should have guessed that a man like him would not leave important papers lying around for just anyone to see. He would keep his valuables in his safe, and she looked around contemplatively, instinctively knowing it was close by.

Standing, she slid practiced eyes over the walls, her narrowed gaze finally settling on a gilt-framed picture of a sleek sailing ship with white canvas sails billowing against a cloudless blue sky. Her lips formed a confident curve as she moved toward it. A gentle tug released the picture's hidden hinge. In seconds the face of a small black-and-gold safe looked back at her. Tyler blew on her fingertips, placing them lightly upon the numbered tumbler, leaning close to listen to the low, sharp sounds. Click, click, click. Then Tyler smiled, slowly revolving the cylinder in the opposite direction.

Perfecting the art of safecracking had taken a good deal of time and practice, but Uncle Burl had been a patient man. She had not found a safe in years she couldn't open in a matter of seconds. One last turn of the tumbler and she was able to pull open the heavy door.

Tyler peered inside the small opening and removed several stacks of money. Her eyes widened as she realized she held close to one hundred thousand dollars in her hands. Just one of the banded parcels would buy back Rose Point, but that would be too easy. She intended to get the money in a way that would make Gray Kincaid look like a fool.

Behind the cash, she found a heavy black velvet bag. Suspecting it held jewelry, she loosened the drawstring and pulled out a long, delicate gold chain from which hung a large ruby cut into the shape of a full-blown red rose. Her mother's rose ruby. Heartsick, she remembered the day her father had taken it from a safe at Rose Point and told her he had given it to his wife on the day Tyler was born.

Tears filled Tyler's eyes as she emptied the bag into her hand, until all her mother's jewels lay in her cupped palm. These jewels were to have been Tyler's own someday, the pearls clasped with a gold rose, the silver bracelet set with garnet rosebuds, the rose emerald earrings—all sculptured by jewelers into unique rose designs because her mother had loved the flower so much.

A hard lump rose in Tyler's throat as she clutched the precious heirlooms to her heart. Her lips trembled, and she fought the desire to keep them.

"Damn him, damn him," she muttered, quickly stuffing the jewelry back into the bag and pulling the purse strings tight. She couldn't take anything yet, not while she was still in the house.

She shut the safe and spun the dial. Replacing the picture, she let the power of her resentment subjugate the hurt. As she turned away, however, a glint of gold from the table beside her caught her eye.

Tyler stepped closer, then picked up the heavy glass globe, turning it upside down and watching the white snowflakes captured inside swirl gently around the tiny yellow sleigh pulled by a black horse.

Colin MacKenzie's beloved face appeared inside her mind, smiling fondly, transporting Tyler back in time. Early one Christmas morning when she was only six years old, her father had cuddled her on his wide, comfortable lap and given her the crystal snowscene. She had loved it with all her heart, even more than the spotted pony and miniature phaeton he had also given her that day.

The toy was a small thing, but a never-forgotten token of her childhood, a precious, treasured memory enshrined in her heart. Rarely in the years since she had lost her father and home had she wept, but now the choked tightness in her throat could not be stifled. She sank to her knees, a forlorn sob escaping her.

It was hers! Damn him, damn him, it was her special gift from her father! And *he* had it! The Yankee had stolen it from her house, as he had stolen everything else she had ever loved! Tears of angry, long-withheld grief streamed down her face, and she clutched the toy close to her breast.

Upstairs, Gray slipped a diamond-studded gold sleeve button into place, then performed the identical task on his other cuff before plunging his arm into his black silk evening coat. In a hurry because he had worked in his office longer than he'd intended, he straightened the expertly tailored garment across his broad shoulders. He allowed himself an inward smile. He didn't want to keep Tyler waiting, although he knew she wasn't particularly keen on accompanying him to the evening's festivities. Since most women loved parties and dancing, her reluctance to attend the ball puzzled him. But her reaction wasn't any more baffling than everything else about her.

During the last week he had spent a good deal of time in her company and had been completely bewitched. Such strong physical attraction was a novel experience for him. In the past, he had been with many beautiful, accomplished women, but none of them had been a blushing virgin or left any lasting impression on him. Nor had he ever before found a woman he could imagine taking as a wife.

Since the war, he had been much too busy building his business and overseeing family interests for marriage to be anything but a vague probability in the distant future. However, with Carlisle away at school the past year, he had been without a hostess for the frequent social affairs a man in his position was obliged to give. Lately he had begun to entertain thoughts of finding a bride.

At nearly thirty-two, perhaps it was time he took a wife and produced an heir. Until now, no one had seemed worthy of serious consideration, but Tyler looked more suitable with each passing day. Young, beautiful, and innocent, she came from an excellent family with high political connections in Mexico City. He already knew her brother well, and respected both him and his political vision for a democratic Mexico. But he did find it peculiar that Chase had never mentioned a sister during Gray's month-long visit in Mexico City.

Gray suddenly grinned as he brushed a speck of lint off his sleeve and glanced around for his silver cigar case. Perhaps it wasn't so strange, after all. They had spent most of their days in meetings about possible American-Mexican investments. In the evenings, Chase Lancaster had introduced Gray to the beautiful courtesans of Los Angeles, the most fashionable bordello in the Latin capital. Now that he thought of it, it wasn't a bit surprising that they hadn't discussed their sisters. Carlisle's name hadn't come up either.

Having spent so much time with Chase, he did know that Chase would have made sure his sister was brought up properly and under strict supervision, as Gray himself had done for Carlisle. Yes, Tyler Lancaster might be the perfect wife for him, and the fact that he found her extremely desirable did not hurt. In any case, the idea was well worth pursuing.

A quick search of the room did not yield his cigars, and suddenly remembering that he had left them in his office, Gray threw his evening cape over his arm and strode downstairs. Tyler hadn't come down yet, so he walked toward his office. Opening the door, he drew up, startled to see Tyler huddled near his desk, her satin skirt spread out around her on the floor.

"Tyler, what are you doing?"

Gray took a step toward her, stopping as she jerked her tearstained face toward him, then looked quickly away.

"You're crying." Gray went to her, his first thought that she'd had a relapse. "What is it, Tyler? Are you ill?"

Gray was so close now that Tyler could smell the fresh scent of his spicy masculine cologne. She struggled to compose herself, but a bitter, agonizing streak of hatred gushed up inside her.

"No," she muttered hoarsely. To her dismay, an unwanted sob clogged her throat. She put a hand to her mouth to stifle it, angry at herself as Gray pulled a large white handkerchief from his inside pocket.

"Here, take this and dry your tears. Then tell me what's wrong. Maybe I can help."

You? Help me? Tyler thought savagely. You, who ruined my life? Without looking at him, she took the proffered handkerchief. He remained silent for a few moments while she fought for control.

"I'm sorry," she said finally. "I don't know what's wrong with me."

The glib lies that usually came so effortlessly were not to be had, and when Gray reached out to help her onto a wing-backed chair, it took all Tyler's willpower not to cringe from his touch. She wiped her tears as he leaned against his desk.

"What are you doing in my office?" he asked then, and Tyler realized she must pull herself together, and fast. Fear of discovery proved to be the best incentive.

When in trouble and afraid of being caught, stick to the truth as much as possible, came her uncle's oft-repeated instructions. *Give your pigeon as much truth as you can to throw him off guard.*

"I was looking for you," she told Gray, her mind racing. "But when I saw this on the table"—she gestured to the snow globe—"it reminded me of one I had when I was a little girl. It made me feel sad, and I began to cry. I don't know why."

Now perfectly calm and in control, she stole a quick glance up at him, then dropped her gaze immediately.

"I see," he said, his eyes going to the small glass snowscene Tyler held in her lap. "Would you like to have that one, then? If it reminds you of yours, you might as well keep it."

It *is* mine, Tyler thought furiously. "I couldn't take it," she began to protest.

Gray interrupted. "It's yours. I have no use for it. It's just a trinket I picked up for my sister during the war."

A trinket picked up in the war. A trinket that Tyler had thought about and longed for a million times since she had left Rose Point. She stared down at the globe.

Gray studied her face, wet with tears and so clearly full of pain. He wondered what childhood memory had evoked such anguish in Tyler Lancas-

ter. He suddenly felt a desire to comfort and protect
her. The strength of his feelings shocked him.

"Perhaps if you tell me about it," he suggested
gently, "it might make you feel better."

"Someday you'll know," she murmured, avoiding his gaze. Something in her tone provoked wari-
ness in Gray. He stared down at her bent head as
she shook the small round child's toy and was again
appalled by her effect on him. Before, she had
seemed young and happy, but this was a very different side of her. She was an enigma. A mysterious
aura enveloped her, as if she held secrets, secrets he
wanted to know. But her answer concerning the
snow globe didn't sit well with him. There was more
to it, and he meant to find out what it was.

"You said you were looking for me. Why?"

Instantly, Tyler knew he was dubious of her story.
She had heard that subtle change of inflection in
other victims' voices when her schemes were about
to go amiss. She had to throw him off again. She
stared at her lap, twisting the buttons on her glove.
If she had to come up with something to tell him, she
would turn the revelation to her own advantage.

"I'm afraid I have a dreadful confession to make,"
she murmured, very low. She raised her eyes, then
lowered her lashes quickly to make him think she
couldn't face him.

"Indeed?" Gray arched a dark brow. "How
dreadful?"

Tyler looked up at him. It was always easier to tell
if a man was swallowing her story if she could see
his eyes. "I'm afraid it will shock you and make you
hate me."

"I'm not easily shocked," he answered. A shadow
of a smile appeared, but his eyes remained keen,
intelligent, and watchful. Tyler knew she had to be
careful. She hesitated a bit longer, her nervousness
not entirely manufactured.

"Remember the first night we met, down by the
river?" she began slowly. When he nodded, she let

the words pour out of her in a guilty flood. "I didn't meet you by accident. I planned it."

She searched his face to gauge his reaction, but his expression did not change. He was the hardest man to read she'd ever tried to trick.

"I feel terrible about everything now," she went on, with wide, imploring eyes. "I shouldn't have done anything so deceitful. It was terribly wrong, but I wanted Chase to be proud of me. He treats me like such a child, and I wanted to prove that I could help him get investors."

Gray Kincaid stared silently at her, and Tyler gritted her teeth. He was not the least bit helpful. Most other men would be patting her hand by now and telling her not to worry her pretty little head about it. But no, Gray Kincaid just sat there and let her grovel. She hated him! Maybe it was time to burst into tears. That nearly always worked. But she had already been crying when he came in, she reminded herself, and all he had done then was hand her his handkerchief. How many hankies did she have to drench to earn his sympathy? She looked up, shocked, as he laughed suddenly.

"Are you trying to tell me you *did* throw yourself into the river just to get my attention?"

"Of course not," she snapped, almost revealing her true colors before she realized her mistake and went on in a shamefaced monotone. "That was truly an accident. I was only going to slip on the sidewalk so you would come to my assistance."

"And your little plot backfired?"

Tyler nodded. "Then, when you rescued me and rushed me here, opening your home and your heart to Harriet and me, I felt so awful and guilty. But I was too ashamed to tell you the truth. Today I realized I just couldn't go on deceiving you any longer. I abhor lies and dishonesty. I couldn't stand living with the guilt any longer, so I came down here to beg your forgiveness."

Gray remained silent, and she tried not to show her tense dread.

"Well, you *should* feel guilty. That was a stupid, childish stunt that nearly cost you your life."

He didn't sound exactly angry, but he didn't look particularly forgiving either.

"Anyway, it's hardly worth all these tears," he went on. "I daresay you learned your lesson, didn't you? Lying has a tendency to get people in trouble, and you found that out the hard way."

Tyler tried to look dutifully chastised. "Yes, I have certainly learned my lesson," she agreed tearfully, dabbing theatrically at her eyes. "And I wouldn't blame you if you weren't even interested in the railway stock now."

When he grinned, Tyler knew she had made a big mistake. To his ears, she had undoubtedly sounded much too eager.

"You want me to buy Chase's stocks in the worst way, don't you, Tyler?"

"Yes, I do. I want to show him that I'm not a child anymore, like he thinks."

"Then I wouldn't mention to him how you fell through the ice trying to deceive me."

"I knew you'd hate me if I told you the truth."

"I don't hate you, Tyler. But I don't like what you did either. However, now that you've told me the facts of the matter, I'm willing to forget it. And I'm still interested in your brother's railroad. Perhaps tonight after we return from the hotel, we can discuss it further. Is that agreeable?"

"Oh, that's wonderful!" Tyler said, inwardly triumphant. Men were so gullible. The hook was set, nice and deep, and soon Gray Kincaid would be flopping on the bank like a big fat mackerel.

Gray's smile was indulgent. "All right. It's about time for us to leave. Would you like to go upstairs and wash your face first?"

Tyler nodded, and as she left him to climb the stairs to her room, she felt relieved that her scheme was nearing fruition. He wasn't suspicious of her any longer, at least she didn't think he was. But an odd guilty feeling began to rise inside her, which struck her as absolutely preposterous. Gray Kincaid deserved everything he got. She hated him! She had nothing to feel bad about!

When she was almost to the top step, she stopped, looking at the snowscene in her hands. She shook it hard, watching the flakes stir to the top, then fall softly around the miniature sleigh. Pain touched her again, and she decided then and there that every time she felt a twinge of conscience about what she was doing to the Yankee, she would shake the crystal globe and remember that long-ago Christmas and everything Gray Kincaid had taken away from her.

6

Tyler came downstairs a short time later, after repairing her coiffure and touching her lips with coralline salve to make them more tempting. Gray was sitting in a chair by the parlor fire, absorbed in his own reflections as he contemplated the blazing coals. She took her usual deep breath to calm herself. This was an important evening. He didn't distrust her any longer, and tonight, if she could rely on her instincts, he would buy the stocks. She would have to be extremely careful, because if she made one wrong move, he might back out of the deal.

Gray turned at the rustling murmur of her silk skirts and came quickly to his feet. He was such a handsome man, she thought begrudgingly, so big and tall and dark. No wonder poor little Betsy had been foolish enough to lose her head over him. No doubt many women had made complete fools of themselves for him. This time, however, it would be the other way around. His jilted paramours from all over the city would applaud her for what she was going to do to him, she decided as his azure gaze swept over her with a glow of admiration.

"I've got a bouquet for you," he said, holding out a delicate nosegay of hothouse flowers in an expensive bracelet holder.

His thoughtfulness brought a wave of pleasure which appalled Tyler. As she looked down at the lovely mixture of tea roses, smilax, and heliotrope, she gave a vigorous mental shake to the snowscene she had left on her dressing table, just to help her remember who he was and what he had done.

"They're beautiful. Thank you so much," she murmured, snapping the silver band upon her gloved wrist.

"I trust you're feeling better now?" he asked.

"Oh, yes. Now that you know the truth, I can live with myself again."

Gray's mouth quirked. "It really isn't worth so much remorse, Tyler. It isn't as if you were scheming to rob me."

Tyler froze, went pale, swallowed hard, then gave a short, brittle laugh. "No, it isn't like I'm doing that," she replied.

"Let me help you with your wrap. It's very cold outside."

"Thank you," Tyler said, handing him the dark green cloak with soft rabbit lining.

She stood still as he draped it carefully around her shoulders, intent on fastening the black silk frogs at her throat. Once they were secured, he lifted her hood carefully, arranging it over her hair before gently tucking a wayward auburn strand beneath the white fur. His smile was tender.

"There, I want you to be warm enough. I intend to make certain you don't get sick again."

Something stirred in Tyler's heart. It had been a long time since anyone other than Harriet had shown such concern for her. Not since she was little and her father buttoned her little velvet jackets and tied her bonnets under her chin. She shook off the second benevolent feeling of the night toward Gray Kincaid, angry that she had been affected by his gentleness.

"Please don't concern yourself so," she murmured, forcing a smile. "I am well now, truly I am."

His attention wandered to her rouged mouth and lingered there long enough for Tyler to wonder if he was going to kiss her. But his hands fell from her cloak and he stepped back.

"Then come. I have a surprise for you," he said.

He slung his sable-lined evening cape over his broad shoulders as he led her down the hall to the side door. Outside, a small red-and-white conveyance waited in the driveway. The bells on the harnesses jingled merrily as the black horse stamped his hooves and snorted in the cold night air.

"A sleigh!" Tyler cried, unable to hide her delight.

Gray laughed, warm and low. "I had Jonah bring it around while you were upstairs. I thought you might enjoy taking it to the hotel. There are plenty of furs to keep you warm and heated bricks to put under your feet, but we can take the carriage, if you'd rather."

"Oh, no. I've always wanted to ride in a sleigh!"

Tyler quickly stepped up on the curved runner, then inside, and Gray followed, sitting close beside her. As the driver slapped the reins and the sled moved forward, he tucked several furry wraps around their laps.

It was a sparkling, frosty, starlit night, and Tyler smiled at the silvery tinkling of the bells and the muffled thumps of hooves against packed snow.

"This is wonderful," she said truthfully, leaning back against the seat and looking at Gray.

"Hold the fur against your face, and you'll warm the air before you breathe it."

"You mustn't fuss over me. I'm perfectly all right now. The fresh air feels good!"

"Well, if you do get cold, tell me."

Tyler nodded, watching a similar cutter with a bundled-up driver jangle past them.

"Do you use your sleigh often?"

"Yes. You see many on the streets during the winter months."

Tyler gave a contented sigh. "I've always wanted

to ride through the snow like this. That's why Papa gave—''

Tyler caught herself before she said anything incriminating, astonished by her careless blunder. Never before in her life had she let slip to a target anything personal about herself.

Gray looked curiously at her. ''Your papa what?''

''Oh, nothing. It is rather cold, though, with the wind blowing on your face.''

She shivered noticeably to give credence to her observation, wanting to maneuver him away from any discussion of her father.

''Lean against me, then,'' he whispered, draping an arm around her shoulders and pulling the furs closer under her chin.

Tyler did, glad her ruse to get him off the subject had succeeded. She did feel warm in Gray Kincaid's arms, more than she should. She had not been held often, not since her father's death. Uncle Burl had not been affectionate in that way, and he had made sure none of their gentleman marks got close enough to take such liberties. She really should object in a ladylike fashion, she decided, but she was trying to get him to sign tonight. After all, there was no way he could take advantage of her, not with the driver less than a yard away.

''Better?'' Gray murmured, his lips nearly touching her ear.

''Yes. I'm quite comfortable now. Are you cold?''

''Hardly,'' he returned wryly, causing Tyler to lean her head against his shoulder so she could see him better.

His face was very near hers, and he was smiling down at her. His features were shadowed by the dim lights of the lampposts they passed at intervals, and she concluded it was time to let him kiss her. She drew her hand from beneath the furry coverings, placing her palm against his dark, lean cheek.

''I cannot thank you enough, Mr. Kincaid, for all your kindnesses,'' she murmured shyly.

That should do it, she thought, filling her eyes to the brim with gratefulness and keeping her face tilted up at just the right angle. She waited for him to lower his face toward hers, then closed her eyes, prepared for the hesitant, tentative brush of lips she usually endured from young men when she encouraged a chaste first kiss.

His skin felt warm as it touched her cold cheek. But once his lips came down upon her mouth, she realized belatedly that he was not a man who behaved in polite, expected ways.

Gray Kincaid knew how to kiss a woman and do a thorough job of it, and Uncle Burl wasn't around to stop his aggressive, ungentlemanly behavior. A streak of fear shot through Tyler as his gloved hand held the side of her face, his thumb forcing her chin toward him. For a moment all she could think was that his lips felt hot, as if they were burning into her mouth. And he didn't stop at once as others had, but kept molding her mouth and tasting her, over and over, as if she were some new and delectable dessert he couldn't get enough of! Her mind whirled, and she felt breathless and weak, as if all her bones had turned to mush.

Panic tore a moan from her. Or was it provoked by pleasure, she wondered in dismay—a thought that gave her the presence of mind to pull away. He didn't try to stop her, and didn't apologize for kissing her. Tyler couldn't look at him.

Though her sudden shyness probably seemed a genuine response from his standpoint, inside she was in a terrible turmoil. He had been her enemy her entire adult life, she thought wildly. But as hard as it was to admit it, she liked the way he had kissed her. She was still trembling from what his mouth had done, and it was enough to frighten the wits out of her! He must never, ever kiss her like that again! She couldn't allow it!

"You must think me very brazen to permit you to do that." To her mortification, her voice quivered.

"No," he said with a smile. "I don't think you're brazen."

"I'm afraid it really can't happen again," she went on, her nervousness genuine. "My brother, Chase, would no doubt call you out and put me in a convent if he knew about it."

Gray only laughed. "I assure you I wouldn't want to be responsible for that."

Relieved, and also a little miffed that he apparently didn't care if he kissed her or not, Tyler sat back and was glad when they arrived at the crowded corner of Michigan Avenue and South Water Street, where lights from the Richmond Hotel glowed brightly. She was already thinking about riding home in the same intimate confines with Gray Kincaid—a prospect that filled her with dread.

Gray held tightly to Tyler's elbow as they entered the elaborate lobby of the Richmond Hotel. He could tell by the rosy flush on her high cheekbones that she was still feeling the effects of their first kiss. And he hadn't been left untouched himself, he thought wryly. He wanted her, more than he liked to admit. He hungered to undress her, slowly and lingeringly, until the soft body beneath all the bows, flounces, and ribbons was revealed. He longed to hear what she'd say when he stripped away the last thin silk barrier between them. Perhaps she would utter more of the breathless moans his lips had coerced from her in the cutter. He swallowed hard. If he didn't curb his lascivious thoughts, he would not last through the lengthy courtship Chase Lancaster would undoubtedly demand for his sister.

"Do you see Harriet and Charles?" Tyler asked as they stopped at the gaily festooned entrance to the ballroom, bringing Gray's attention back to her face. He was amused at the way she shifted her gaze away from him, as if she was still embarrassed. She was innocent in the ways of love, and her husband would have the enviable duty of introducing her to the delights of the marriage bed. Because of the way her lips had parted slightly in shy offering just before she had pulled away from him, he felt sure she had an innate sensuality which would blossom under the right tutelage. His own.

"There they are, by the buffet table," he said a moment later, leading Tyler along the perimeter of the glossy dance floor where gentlemen twirled ladies bedecked in lace, plumes, and satin.

He ignored the stir they created among his friends and acquaintances, squiring Tyler toward the table where Harriet sat with Charles, looking quite conspicuous in her mourning black.

"So here you are at last," Charles said cheerily. "Etty and I were feeling abandoned since Betsy's becoming so popular with the young gentlemen. She's danced nearly every dance. I'm proud to say."

"Sorry we're late," Gray said, noticing that Tyler had grown extremely uneasy since they had entered the ballroom. He pondered that as he politely seated her beside Harriet, admiring the graceful way Tyler arranged her dress around the velvet chair.

"Is anything the matter, dear?" Harriet asked Tyler, her face wearing its usual worried lines.

Tyler shook her head while Gray sat down beside her. "It's certainly crowded here tonight," she remarked, glancing around.

Gray observed the way she fidgeted nervously with her closed fan. He hoped she wasn't developing Harriet's jittery disposition.

Charles was nodding. "Yes, this ball's one of the most popular of the year, since so many young ladies select it for their debuts. Not a few people here tonight have already asked to be presented to you, my dear," he said to Tyler.

"To me?" Tyler repeated, obviously dismayed.

"Yes indeed, and I'm afraid I'm the culprit who's been telling everyone what charming ladies you and Harriet are. You're quite the talk of the town."

"Are people really talking about me, Dr. Bond?"

Tyler asked quickly. Gray frowned slightly at Tyler's agitation. She tended to be shy—he had noticed that before. But her fears seemed unwarranted now.

"Any young lady whom Gray shows an interest in is fodder for the gossip mill, especially if she's a young, beautiful stranger he pulled out of the Chicago River. Etty and I were just discussing some of the incredible stories I've heard bandied about concerning you, my dear. Why, when Betsy described you to her good friend John Mooney, he actually said you sounded like an awful woman who robbed him aboard a steamboat last year. Can you imagine our amusement at such a ridiculous notion?"

Tyler's answering laugh was half strangled. Oh, Lord, she thought, nerves as tight as wet leather. John Mooney, here in Chicago? She remembered him only too well! Filled with dread, she studiously avoided Gray's piercing eyes, which seemed to be on her all the time now. A glance told her Harriet looked ready to throw up her hands and confess every sin she'd committed since birth. Suddenly frightened of what the evening might bring, Tyler furtively scanned the room for John Mooney.

"Would you care for an ice, or a glass of champagne?" Gray asked her.

"An ice would be lovely," Tyler replied, certainly not wanting to muddle her mind with spirits. She had already made a dreadful mistake by coming at all! She would have to think up a reason to leave early. Perhaps a relapse was in order.

Gray returned soon with her refreshment, but Tyler hardly touched it, counting the minutes until she could properly suggest they leave. When a lilting redowa began at the far end of the room, Gray turned to her.

"May I have the honor of a dance?"

Making herself even more conspicuous by waltzing around with Gray, whom everyone in the room was already watching, was the last thing Tyler wanted to do.

"I'm not sure I should. I'm still a little weak."

To her chagrin, Gray looked at the doctor. "She's well enough for just one turn around the floor, don't you think, Charles?"

"I should say so, if you hold her good and tight," Charles answered, winking at Gray.

"You can rest assured of that," Gray said, rising.

Gray Kincaid certainly had a knack for making refusal impossible, Tyler decided as he helped her out of her chair. But once in his arms, she enjoyed herself and found that her tall partner was a good dancer.

"You seem upset," Gray noted on the second circuit of the dance floor. "Is it what Charles said about the gossips, or is it the kiss I gave you on the way here?"

Tyler felt color rising in a hot tide and was embarrassed about it, though, no doubt, it made her look maidenly. It certainly made her *feel* maidenly. Thank goodness, he didn't have an inkling why she really was upset. The kiss was the least of her problems.

"I'm not upset. I'm just nervous, I think."

Uncle Burl was so right about telling the truth as much as possible, she thought. It was amazing how often a smidgen of veracity helped make her lies convincing.

"Don't be nervous. Few people here will have the rudeness to confront us with their nosy tattle. They prefer to whisper about us so they can invent their own romantic tales."

"Have you heard stories about me, too?" Tyler asked.

"Of course. You're a Venetian princess in one, and a harlot from the docks of San Francisco in another."

Tyler had to laugh. "I like the first one better."

"Don't worry about it. I suppose everyone will be disappointed when they learn the truth about you."

Tyler smiled, feeling another unwanted flash of

guilt. They would not be disappointed at all. If her plan was successful, they would clap with malicious glee and Gray Kincaid would be the laughingstock of Chicago. She was suddenly angry at herself for giving in to such sympathy for him. It wasn't her fault he had stolen Rose Point!

She was glad when the orchestra finished the song, but her relief was fated to be short-lived. A tall man was now conversing with Harriet and Charles at their table. She felt distinctly better when he turned and she realized it wasn't John Mooney. She didn't recognize the stranger, but Gray apparently did.

"Well, I'll be damned, there's Stone. He wasn't supposed to be back from New Orleans this soon. Come, Tyler, I'll introduce you to my younger brother."

Stone Kincaid was tall, like Gray, with the same black wavy hair, but he wore a close-cropped beard and mustache that made him appear more forbidding. Tyler hung back a step or two as the two men shook hands, greeting each other like close friends.

"I wasn't expecting to see you so soon, especially here at the Richmond. You're not much for this kind of thing. Carly never could drag you along with us to these affairs."

"I got home just after you left, and Hildie told me where you were. I have some important business to discuss with you. It can't wait."

Tyler became immediately wary. Stone's eyes were blue, not the vivid azure of his older brother's, but more like the blue-gray of steel. And there was something in their depths—a strange, angry emotion hidden deep inside them—that made Tyler uncomfortable. He seemed very reserved and aloof.

"This is Tyler Lancaster, Stone," Gray said, bringing her forward. "Tyler, this is my brother, Stone."

"How do you do, Miss Lancaster," Stone Kincaid said with a courteous bow, his smile as pleasant as

Gray's, but lacking any real warmth. She sensed that Stone Kincaid was a man who distrusted people.

"How do you do," she answered as Gray seated her.

"You'll join us, won't you?" Gray asked.

Stone shook his head. "I don't have time. I've decided to take one of our expresses to Colorado later tonight. I've been away much too long already." He lowered his voice. "I do need to talk to you in private for a moment, Gray. It's very important."

"Is Carly all right?" Gray asked at once.

"She's fine, and she sends her love to everyone. She especially told me to tell Charles how much she misses him," he said, smiling at the doctor. "She said when she gets home she expects you to tell her all the gossip she's missed."

"There isn't as much since she's been gone, the little minx," Charles said, laughing. "But we do miss that child at the hospital. The patients loved having her around. Carlisle's a born nurse."

"You will excuse me, won't you, Tyler? Harriet and Charles will keep you company while I smoke a cigar upstairs with Stone."

"Of course," Tyler answered automatically, her worried eyes still scanning the crowded room for John Mooney as the Kincaid brothers departed.

Smoking rooms for the gentlemen were situated on a high mezzanine overlooking the restaurant and ballroom. The smell of good cheroots greeted Gray as he walked with Stone to an isolated marble pillar along the gleaming oak balustrade. He lit the long, narrow cigar he had chosen from a gold tray on the marble bar top, then perched a hip against the banister.

"All right, what's so important that it can't wait?"

"You'll be glad I came when you hear."

Gray cocked a brow, holding the cheroot idly between his fingers. "I'm listening. What is it?"

"I'm not particularly looking forward to telling you."

"What has Carlisle done now? In her last report, Mother Andrea Mary said she was doing exceptionally well."

"It's not about Carly. It's about your friend downstairs."

Gray had been admiring Tyler at the table below as she took some tidbit offered to her by a black-coated waiter. He had also been wondering how it would feel to comb his fingers through her soft auburn hair. At Stone's words, he swung around in surprise and looked at his brother. Then it dawned on him what Stone meant.

"Oh, you received my telegraph message about checking out Tyler's stock deal? I was beginning to think you hadn't had time to bother with it."

"I got it last week, and I checked out her background, Chase Lancaster's as well."

"You got in touch with her brother, then?" Gray prompted when Stone hesitated. "Is the railroad to Mexico feasible or not?"

"He's not her brother. He's her cousin."

"What?"

"And her name's not Lancaster."

"What?" Gray repeated, standing straighter.

"It took me a while, but I finally found out the whole story, and a sordid one it is. She came here to rob you, I suspect, and that's not even the worst of it."

"What the deuce are you talking about?"

"I told you you wouldn't like it, but it's the truth."

Gray's face went tight, a muscle twitching in his cheek as his teeth came together. "Go on, then. Tell me all of it."

"Her real name is MacKenzie, Tyler MacKenzie." He paused, as if letting the shock sink in. "She's Colin MacKenzie's daughter."

"My God," Gray said, his gaze returning in disbelief to the girl below. "I didn't even know he had a daughter."

"Apparently she's his only child, but that's really all I could find out about her younger days."

"She can't be. Are you absolutely certain?"

"Yes. I never could get in touch with Chase Lancaster himself about the railway deal. He was in Mexico somewhere, but I did find out he owns a Mexican ranch around Monterrey, like the girl said. Bob Winston, you know, our liaison at the American Bank in New Orleans, handles Lancaster's accounts. Apparently Mr. Lancaster is an important man in Mexico City, one of President Juarez's ministers."

Gray didn't answer. He stared down at Tyler, trying to digest everything Stone had told him. Tyler, MacKenzie's daughter—it was impossible! He felt stiff and tense with the old hatred. Colin MacKenzie. The very name brought it all back so clearly. Gray could almost feel the rain on his face, hear the thunder of horses' hooves, see his father's body covered with mud and blood after it had been dragged for miles along rock-strewn country roads. Gray shut his eyes. He thought he had buried those poisonous feelings when he had ruined the bastard MacKenzie and taken his plantation. But now it was all welling up again.

"Gray? Are you hearing any of this?"

"What did Bob know about Tyler?"

"Not much. He said Chase has been looking for her since his father died about six months ago. Burl Lancaster was the brother of Colin MacKenzie's late wife, and the girl's guardian. Apparently there'd been bad blood between Burl and his Mexican wife, and she took Chase back to Mexico City with her years ago, which explains why Chase had so little contact with the pair."

"And now she's after me because she thinks I drove him to suicide," Gray muttered, realization dawning.

"That's my guess," Stone answered quietly.

Both men were silent for a moment, but Gray's eyes never left the girl in the green-and-white dress at the table below. It was hard to believe she was really MacKenzie's daughter, harder still to believe she had taken him in so easily.

"Are you going to notify the police?" Stone asked.

"And tell them what? That I ruined her father because I loathed him, and now she's come here to destroy me the same way? She hasn't done anything illegal yet."

"Do you know what she has in mind?"

Gray flashed a bitter smile. "Yes, I do, and I was going to buy her phony stocks tonight, as a matter of fact. You made it back in the nick of time."

"That sounds like one of their games, all right."

Gray turned to face him. "What do you mean? Has she done this sort of thing before?"

Stone laughed, shaking his head. "You could say that. Bob Winston knew that Tyler and her uncle lived in Natchez for a time during the war, so I stopped there on the way home. I learned quite a bit about the pair of them. It seems they were known far and wide for their confidence games. I talked to one tavern keeper on the river who knew Burl well." He leaned a shoulder against the pillar, glancing down at the milling crowd. "They worked the steamboats during the war, preying on Union soldiers and Northern businessmen exclusively. Anybody with Southern sympathies considered them regular folk heroes. And I'm not talking penny-ante schemes like you and I used to do now and then on the streets to support Mother and Carly when we first got to Chicago. I'm talking elaborate hoaxes and big money. You wouldn't believe some of the outrageous stories I heard about the two of them. I keep thinking some of it's got to be exaggerated."

"Like what?"

"Like, one time your pretty little Tyler down there," Stone answered, jerking his head in her direction, "faked her own death after enticing some

poor man named Henry Hardcastle into offering her
marriage.''

"She's married?" Gray asked quickly.

"No, but the wedding was all planned when Burl
had her taken off the steamboat in a draped casket.
It was only afterward that the grief-stricken fiancé
realized his entire bankroll had been lifted. Of
course, he never suspected her since she was supposed to be dead. Even when the poor bloke finally
found out the truth, he was so obsessed with her
that he was ready to forgive her if she'd only come
back to him.''

"Good God," Gray muttered blackly. "If they
were that blatant, why didn't they get caught?''

"It seems that since they gave most of their loot
to the Rebels, the Southern authorities considered
their schemes patriotic and looked the other way.
And it appears they never stayed in one place long
enough to be apprehended. They were regular leg-
ends along the river until Burl was shot dead in a
poker game.''

"Has Tyler been robbing people since then?''

"No. Apparently she laid low for a time, because
Chase Lancaster couldn't find her, and he had a
whole team of private investigators on her trail.''

"Why does Chase want to find her?''

"He wants to take her to Mexico with him, to keep
her out of trouble, I guess. According to Bob, he
feels responsible for her because it was his father
who led her into this line of work.''

Gray frowned. "She couldn't have been more
than twelve or thirteen during the war, about Carly's age. How could a grown man use a child like
that?''

"Burl Lancaster was a crook. Apparently he didn't
have many scruples.''

"So that means she has no other relatives, besides
Chase Lancaster in Mexico?''

"Chase's mother's still alive. She's Tyler's aunt
and from what I hear, the family is an upstanding

aristocratic family in Mexico City. I'm sure they don't know anything about what she's trying to do to you."

"Chase is as honest a man as I've ever met."

"You know him?" Stone asked in surprise.

"I was in Mexico about a year ago when Juarez was trying to attract foreign investors. We became good friends then," Gray explained, his mind still on Tyler. "I'd better telegraph him and let him know where she is. In the meantime, I suppose I should play along with her nasty little trick until I hear back from him. She sure as hell needs someone to take her in hand."

Stone exhaled a cloud of blue smoke, eyeing his older brother speculatively. "You're certainly accepting all this better than I expected."

Gray smiled for the first time, but his eyes remained cold. "I'm not an easy man to dupe, you know that, yet she had me ready to hand over ten thousand dollars in cash. I can't decide whether to wring her neck or admire her style."

"Didn't you suspect her at all?"

"Whenever I began to, she was smart enough to throw me off with what I suspect now were a bunch of half-truths. She's very good at her little games, I'll give her that much."

"And she's very beautiful," Stone remarked casually. "I guess you noticed that, too."

"Yes, I noticed," Gray answered, stubbing out his cigar, a flush of anger overtaking him as he remembered how he had even toyed with the idea of marrying the deceiving little Jezebel.

"Come on, Stone, it's time to rejoin my little guest. Now I'm the one holding the aces, which is the way I like it. And something tells me the next few weeks will be most interesting for all of us. Too bad you won't be around to see the finish."

Gray remained acutely aware of Tyler MacKenzie as he bade Stone good-bye at the lobby entrance, then made his way back to the table. He still didn't want to believe Stone's story, but he had to. It made sense now that he had all the pieces of the puzzle— Tyler's calling out for her father during her delirium, Harriet's constant nervousness, and Tyler's strange reaction to the snow globe. Good God, he realized with a start, it had been hers. He could remember taking it from one of the bedrooms of the MacKenzie plantation after he had commandeered the house as headquarters for his troops. That had been after Colin MacKenzie's death, and there had been no daughter there at that time. He was sure of it. Tyler must have already gone to her uncle by then.

Tyler looked up and smiled as Gray took his place beside her. He smiled back, amazed at how easily she played the innocent. His teeth clamped down when he remembered the way she had offered her lips to him earlier, then blushed so prettily and called herself brazen. He had been amused then, but now, after the initial shock of learning her real identity, anger was beginning to consume him.

"I hope nothing is wrong in your family," Tyler said softly.

Gray met her wide eyes with a cool stare. "Nothing I can't handle. I'm sorry to have left you here alone for so long."

"Is your brother going to join us?"

"No, he's tired from his trip. He's leaving in a few hours for our Colorado offices. They've had some trouble with the Sioux out there since he's been gone."

Gray watched her lift her glass, barely listening to Charles's story about the near miraculous recovery of one of his patients. Just how far had she been willing to go? he wondered. How far had she gone in the past with Henry Hardcastle and all the other men she and her uncle had plotted to rob? How many men had she smiled for and charmed and lied to? Had she teased them with her soft looks and chaste kisses until they were foolish enough to want to marry her?

Unaccustomed rage, surprisingly violent, rose in him. He quickly tamped down the boiling emotion. A show of anger might scare off Tyler MacKenzie, and he wasn't through with her yet.

"Why, here comes John Mooney, Gray," the doctor was saying. "I have a mind to dress him down sharply right now for comparing Tyler to some low-down thieving harlot."

Gray turned his eyes on Tyler and watched with grim satisfaction as all the color drained from her lovely lying face. The man in question strolled toward them with a wobbly gait. If she was the one who had robbed John Mooney, she was in deep trouble, and she knew it.

"Good evening, Doc, Gray," the newcomer said, his speech slurred. "I came over to meet your lady there." He gave a tipsy laugh. "I say, she does look like that girl who took me on the *Lady Jane*." He peered down at Tyler, who was trying to hide her face by leaning close to speak to Harriet. Harriet was clutching her heart with one hand and fanning her face with the other. For the first time Gray wondered just what part Tyler's "aunt Harriet" played.

"You *are* the one!" John Mooney exclaimed, his mouth dropping slack. "I'll never forget those blasted red-brown eyes of yours! You're the little tart who took my wallet! You and that damnable smooth-as-oil uncle of yours!"

To Gray's enjoyment, Tyler MacKenzie looked as if she had swallowed a large, sharp object. "Why, sir, I don't know what you mean—" she choked out hoarsely, eyes huge and hands trembling. She began to pump her fan furiously before darting an appeal for help toward Gray.

Gray, relishing Tyler's agony, didn't move a muscle. She certainly deserved to squirm. But Dr. Bond was incensed by Mooney's accusation. He jumped to his feet, his face livid with outrage.

"How dare you insult Miss Lancaster, Mooney!" he blustered.

Gray rose more slowly and put a restraining hand on the older man's arm. He wasn't about to let his friend enter into a potentially dangerous altercation by defending a thief like Tyler MacKenzie.

"You've had too much to drink, John."

Gray's admonition to the angry young man was uttered in a low, quiet voice, but John Mooney wasn't so drunk as to miss the underlying threat. Gray Kincaid was a powerful man, and a deadly shot. Everyone in Chicago knew it.

"But I'm just trying to warn you, Gray. She'll make up to you like you're really special, then she'll steal you blind like she did me! That's how I lost Father's money!"

"You're mistaken, John," Gray said evenly, cutting him off. "Go home and sober up."

The young man flushed with humiliation, and Tyler looked down at her lap when his bleary eyes focused on her.

"Someday you're going to get what you deserve," he muttered hoarsely. "You took everything I had. You made me nothing in my father's eyes, and you'll pay for it. Someday you will."

When he moved away, Gray turned his attention back to Tyler's ashen face.

"Are you all right?" he asked, noting with satisfaction that her hands were still shaking. John Mooney had given her a good scare, and she would no doubt be eager to get out of the hotel before another of her poor victims spotted her. Her next words proved him right.

"Oh, my, I just don't know what to say," she murmured pitiably. "I'm feeling quite ill."

I just bet you are, Gray thought. But it was Harriet who really looked sick. She was holding her chest again, much to Charles's alarm. It was hard for Gray to believe she was part of such a nasty scheme. She seemed a nice, genteel lady, and she had certainly

charmed Charles. But Gray supposed those were the
qualities required for their line of work.

"Perhaps I should take you home, then," he suggested to Tyler, eager to get her alone. "Charles,
you'll bring Harriet home later, won't you?"

With that he quickly took Tyler's arm and guided
her toward the lobby before Harriet had a chance to
object.

7

Snow was spiraling softly to the ground as they left the hotel, but Tyler breathed a sigh of relief when she attained the sanctuary of the sleigh. This time, to her surprise, Gray sat across from her, though he did lean forward to carefully arrange the furs around her legs. Perhaps it was best that he kept his distance. She was still quaking inside from John Mooney's accusation. She remembered him all too well, mainly because he had been so young and sweet. He was one of the few men she had felt guilty about helping her uncle rob.

It had been so close this time. What if Gray was suspicious again? He had defended her, but she could sense a difference in him.

"Don't be upset with John. He'd had too much to drink. Nobody's going to believe him," Gray told her from across the sleigh. "You have to pity the poor fellow. Some girl stole all his money when he was coming upriver from New Orleans a year or so ago. His family owns a weapons factory here in Chicago, and that was the first time his father had allowed him to go south with rifles to be shipped to England. It was a kind of test to prove the boy worthy of a responsible job with the firm." Gray shifted position, rearranging his long legs in the small space between them before he went on. "When John came back empty-handed, his father refused to let him work with the rest of his brothers. The poor boy was disgraced, so he's turned to carousing lately. Of course, it was his own fault, being taken in by some phony little thief like he was."

Tyler felt sick, and she had a terrible suspicion her face showed it. Never before had she known for sure what had happened to one of her marks after she and her uncle had escaped with their money. And she had liked John Mooney better than any of the others. Guilt settled over her, heavy and dispiriting. Desperately she sought a different subject.

"I was glad to meet your brother," she ventured.

"Yes, it was good to have him back. I'm just sorry he had to take off for Denver so soon."

"He has angry eyes," Tyler blurted out in a way that was totally unlike herself.

"My brother's not a sociable man, especially since the war. He spent a long time in a Confederate prison. Andersonville, down in Georgia. One of his friends betrayed him, a man named Emerson Clan. Stone's been looking for him for five years."

"Oh, how awful," she murmured with genuine sympathy.

"Where were you during the war, Tyler?"

Burying my father, she thought bitterly, but she didn't let her feelings show. "I was in Montgomery most of the time with Aunt Harriet and my other relatives."

Gray watched her, amazed at her ability to lie while keeping a perfectly seraphic look on her face. He found his feelings toward her changing from moment to moment, like quicksilver. Gone was the amused indulgence of the past week. He was furious all of a sudden, so angry he could barely contain it. He hadn't been so enraged in years, not since before the war when Colin MacKenzie had murdered his father. Like father, like daughter, he thought, grinding his teeth. He knew he had to keep

Tyler from seeing his true feelings. But it was more
difficult than he would have believed, and he was
glad when the sleigh stopped at the side portal to
his house.

Tyler watched Gray alight and then reach up to
assist her. There was definitely a difference in him;
she could sense it. Had it been caused by whatever
he had discussed with his brother, or by John Mooney's accusation? Perhaps his business had suffered
some kind of setback. She hoped not, then wondered why she should care. He was her enemy. She
put her gloved hand into his proffered one, hoping
that whatever his problem, it wouldn't interfere with
the stock deal.

"Do you feel up to discussing your brother's
railroad now?" he asked as he led her up the icy
sidewalk.

Relieved, Tyler peered up at him through the
falling snow. "Yes, if you do. You seem a bit distracted."

"Not distracted," he answered laconically, without further explanation, leaving Tyler to puzzle over
that remark as he ushered her into the side hall.

A dim lamp burned on a candlestand near the
staircase, but the rest of the house was dark and
quiet.

"It's cold down here. We'll talk upstairs," he told
her, helping her off with her cloak, then standing
back to allow her to precede him.

Tyler hesitated, wondering where he had in mind,
but she lifted her skirts and climbed the steps. Once
upstairs, however, he led her toward his own bedchamber at the end of the hall. Tyler stopped halfway there.

"You don't mean you want to discuss it in your
bedroom," she said, scandalized.

"You wouldn't want me in yours, would you?"

She definitely would not. No unmarried lady
would think of allowing a man in her bedchamber.

"There's an adjoining sitting room in mine," he

went on, and though Tyler remembered the chairs congregated around his fireplace from the night she had searched his room, she still hesitated.

"It really isn't proper, Mr. Kincaid."

Gray lifted a mocking eyebrow. "Just what do you think I have in mind, Miss Lancaster? A seduction, perhaps?"

Something in the way he said it made Tyler feel silly and childish, but she laughed.

"Of course not, Mr. Kincaid. You've shown yourself to be a perfect gentleman."

In his private quarters a lamp had been left turned low on the round table in front of the fire. Tyler quickly made her way into the sitting room without even glancing at the big maroon-draped four-poster, the bedclothes already turned back invitingly for the night. She felt uncomfortable, though she didn't think Gray Kincaid would be forward with her. It was true that, except for the kiss she had encouraged earlier in the sleigh, and despite his well-documented reputation as a ladies' man, he had been most gallant. She sat down, watching him lounge carelessly in the chair directly across from her.

"Please, Miss Lancaster, tell me all about your stocks."

"Well, I have them in my room if you would like to read them yourself," she offered, wanting him to see the legal-looking documents. She had paid a St. Louis forgery expert a handsome sum for them.

"I think I'd rather hear you tell me about them," he replied.

His penetrating gaze never left her, and Tyler grew increasingly nervous. The firelight played over the lean, handsome contours of his face, making his eyes look brilliant and beautiful. What was it about him that always left her wary and nervous, with strange sensations in her stomach? She hated him for that, she really did.

"All right. I've already told you most of it, but

Chase would like each investor to buy stocks in the amount of one hundred thousand dollars. He would require a ten percent initial payment, which Harriet and I would take to him. The railway to that part of Mexico is needed badly, and he is confident that you will earn your investment back the first year it goes into operation." She stopped, but he remained silent, still staring at her. "Do you have any questions you'd like to ask me?"

"No, please go on," Gray answered, but when she did, he barely listened. Deep inside, he was becoming more and more angry with each of her dirty little lies. He wondered again how far she was willing to go to convince him to invest. Was she a whore as well as a thief and a liar?

A muscle moved spasmodically in his lean cheek, and he was appalled at how that thought ate at him. He felt betrayed, of all things, and furious enough to take her by her slender shoulders and shake her senseless.

Tyler stopped in midsentence as Gray suddenly lunged to his feet. His furious expression forced a gasp from her. Before she could move, he was in front of her chair, and she cried out in pain as his fingers closed brutally over her upper arms, jerking her sharply to her feet.

His eyes looked like blazing turquoise now, but she hardly had time to consider that as he shifted his arm, sliding it around her back until she felt his fingers at her nape, holding her head in a vise. She attempted to struggle, but his mouth came down on hers, hard and punishing.

She didn't like his kiss at all this time. It was an angry, savage kiss that hurt her and filled her with terror. She tried to push against his chest, but his hold only tightened. He half lifted and slightly turned her until her back was forced up against the wall, his mouth prying her lips open so that his tongue could launch a cruel attack.

Tyler couldn't move in his grip, couldn't even

push him away. Her knees went weak, but it hardly
mattered since he was holding her bodily off the
ground, the long, hard length of his chest and hips
pressing her to the wall. His tongue was insistent
now, warm, probing, gentler than before, and Tyler
moaned, clutching his wide shoulders for support,
feeling as if she were in a strange, erotic dream.

Unknowingly, she wet her lips when his mouth
finally left hers, his face pressing against the open
throat of her gown as his hands slid down over her
waist to cup her hips. He pulled her up against him
with a sudden movement, his lips tracing the line of
her throat and forcing her head back until he found
her lips again with hot, eager urgency.

Tyler made another muffled sound, a feeble,
pleasured whimper, as her body flooded with desire
and confusion.

"Please, please . . ." she managed breathlessly.
Then her whole body went rigid as his hand opened
the front of her gown, his fingers intruding boldly
and possessively inside her neckline. A sharp jerk
sent the pearl buttons flying; a second one tore loose
her silk corselette. Then his palm was pressing hard
upon her naked breast.

Outraged, humiliated, betrayed, confused, Tyler
jerked hard to free herself from his grip, trembling
all over. To her surprise, he released her at once.
The moment he did, she brought her hand up
against his dark cheek in a stinging slap. To her own
shock and further humiliation, she then burst into
frightened tears.

Gray put his hand to his face as she scrambled
away and fled the room, leaving the door open behind her. He walked slowly to the threshold to see
where she would go, looking down the dim corridor
in time to see her rush into her own bedchamber.
Even from where he stood, he could hear the bolt
being thrown. He didn't think she would come out
again, at least not until morning. Actually, she was

probably barricading the door with heavy furniture to prevent his entrance.

Leaving his own door open in case she did try to leave the house, he went back to stand before the fire. Perhaps it had been a cruel thing to do, but by kissing her he had rid himself of the anger eating at his insides. At the same time, he had found out what he wanted to know. She was no whore. Perhaps a well-practiced flirt, perhaps even a cold-blooded temptress. But not even the most consummate actress could have faked the fear in her eyes, and her tears had been real as well. She had been terrified. That would soon turn to anger. She would hate him in the morning even more than she already did.

He smiled then. His own fury had dissipated, but he still wrestled with the reasons for his intense rage and his staggering relief to find she was not some easy slut ripe for the taking. She had a way of getting under his skin and burrowing in deep, and no matter how much he sought to deny it, he still wanted her. He wanted her more than he had ever wanted any other woman. Probably a lot of other people wanted her at the moment, too, he thought with a wry twist of his lips—the law and a platoon of angry men she had swindled up and down the Mississippi River.

But right now his first priority must be to contact Chase Lancaster so they could decide what to do with her. No doubt, together, the two of them could straighten out thieving little Tyler.

Actually, he'd like to have that job all to himself. He would derive a great deal of pleasure from setting her on the straight and narrow.

For now, his most pressing concern was getting her to stay in his house until he could notify her cousin. Something told him Tyler was packing her bags at this very minute.

An insistent tapping finally roused Tyler. She sat up sleepily on the satin chaise longue near the fireplace, where she had finally succumbed to exhaustion. Her hair tumbled in disarray over her shoulders, and her lovely green-striped taffeta dress was rumpled. It's him, she thought dully, eyes heavy with sleep. What would she do now?

Looking around the dim room, misted with morning sunlight peeping from the edges of the drawn draperies, she was afraid to move. She wouldn't let him in—she couldn't face him! Not after what had happened in his bedchamber the night before.

"Tyler, dear? Are you awake?"

"Etty!"

Tyler was greatly relieved to hear her friend's soft voice just outside the door. She hastened to push aside the heavy table that she had dragged into place, and threw back the bolt. Harriet gasped as she was unceremoniously yanked inside the room, and the door slammed resoundingly behind her. The bolt went back into place, and Harriet stared at Tyler, her wide eyes magnified behind her spectacles.

"Tyler, you look awful! Why, you're still dressed in your party gown." Her gaze took in Tyler's dishabille with amazement until Tyler suddenly threw her arms around Harriet's neck and leaned her head wearily on the older woman's matronly shoulder.

"Oh, Etty, it was so awful! I didn't know what to do. I was so scared."

"What happened, child?" Harriet cried, alarmed. "Tell me, please!"

Tyler pulled away, not sure she could tell anyone about her humiliating ordeal. The memory of Gray Kincaid's strong hands touching her with such intimacy flooded her cheeks with hot embarrassment. She fought the recollection of being held so forcefully and kissed so brutally, ashamed that for a few moments she had actually taken pleasure from such horrible treatment. What kind of person was she? No, she amended angrily, what kind of man was *he* to take advantage of her, a guest in his house!

"Gray took me to his bedchamber last night and attacked me," she said without preamble.

Harriet's hands went up to her mouth; then her legs gave way and she sank heavily into the nearest chair, her hoop rising precariously.

"Oh, Lordy, Lordy," she moaned. She looked so horrified that Tyler hastened to reassure her that nothing too irrevocable had occurred.

"Well, maybe it wasn't that bad. But he did kiss me, hard and long, and then he slid his hand down inside my bodice and tore it, and . . ." Tyler wet her lips, involuntary shivers invading her heated flesh as she thought of how those hard brown fingers had felt.

"Oh, Lordy, Lordy," Harriet groaned again, louder this time. "This is all my fault. I knew I should have come home with you last night. Oh, Tyler, how can you ever forgive me for failing to protect you?"

"Forgive *you*? You didn't do anything! It's that wretch of a Yankee snake I'll never forgive! You should have seen his eyes. Why, they were just so— so diabolical."

Harriet stared at her, lips pressed together in dismay. "I can't believe Mr. Kincaid would behave in such a dishonorable way. He has always been so kind and respectful to both of us. Why, I breakfasted with him not an hour ago, and he acted as if nothing was amiss. He told me you still weren't feeling well. Look, he even gave me this note for you before he left."

Tyler's attention went to the letter Harriet had withdrawn from her skirt pocket, but she was relieved to hear that Gray Kincaid was no longer in the house. She didn't ever want to see him again.

"Did he say where he was going?"

"He just said he would be leaving town on a business trip—something unexpected came up. I forget exactly what. Hildie was pouring my coffee then, and she was asking about the creamer, you know, if I wanted any—"

"How long will he be gone?" Tyler interrupted impatiently.

"A few days, I believe he said. The servants had already taken his baggage by the time I came downstairs this morning."

The news of the Yankee's departure was welcome, indeed, and Tyler looked at the letter Harriet held, loath to touch it. Another unwanted shiver coursed through her.

"Etty, you read it to me."

"Me? But what if it's of a private nature? What if it's about what happened last night?"

"I don't give a fig if it is. You read it to me. I don't want to."

Harriet reluctantly unfolded the stiff white vellum and adjusted her bifocals before she began to read Gray Kincaid's neat script.

" 'My dear Miss Lancaster, I realize you must despise me for what happened between us last night. I can only say I am stricken with the deepest remorse for my unconscionable conduct. I beg your forgiveness, and I sincerely hope you will find the kindness in your heart to accept my profound apology. Due to an unforeseen emergency, I must go away on business for several days. But I implore you to stay on as my guest until I return, so that I may complete my investment in your brother's railway line. Until then, my fondest regards, G.' "

"Oh, that cad! To do that to me, then think that dangling his investment in front of me will make me stay here and wait for him like some moonstruck maid!"

"But he says he's sorry and that he's going to buy the stock. Isn't that what you wanted?"

"No, I want to get away from here! Away from him! I don't ever want to lay eyes on him again!"

Harriet watched Tyler pace across the room, snatching loose the ribbon fastenings of her rumpled

gown as she went. Oh, dear Lord, Harriet thought,
my nerves just aren't going to survive much more
of Tyler's dangerous plot. It had gone on too long,
gotten far too complicated and out of hand. Thank
goodness, Tyler was ready to give up at last and
leave Chicago.

Harriet sighed. Soon she wouldn't have to deceive
poor dear Charles anymore. More than anything,
she had hated lying to that kind, magnanimous
man. He had treated her like a queen from the moment they had met. She nibbled at her bottom lip,
imagining his face when he found out what she and
Tyler had been up to. Even Gray Kincaid had been
generous and hospitable to them, at least until his
deplorable conduct with Tyler last night. Suddenly,
Harriet wanted to flee Chicago this very moment,
without a word to anyone.

"I'll pack our things, Tyler, and we can leave quietly without telling a soul. The trains go south on
the hour. We'll have just enough time to catch the
next one."

Tyler had disappeared behind her dressing screen,
but at Harriet's words, she reappeared, tying the
sash of her black satin robe with an angry twist.

"Oh, no, we won't, not just yet. If our dear host
is going to be gone for a few days, we'll stay on long
enough to get what we came for."

"What do you mean?" Harriet asked fearfully,
recognizing the look in Tyler's eyes as the one which
usually got both of them into deep trouble.

"I've got a new plan now, one Uncle Burl and I
used successfully a couple of times. To thunder with
the stocks. I found money in his safe downstairs,
lots of it, and I'm going to take enough to buy Rose
Point back."

"Tyler! You don't mean you're going to steal it!"

"I'm just going to take what is rightfully mine. I
didn't tell you before because it hurt too much, but
you know what else he has in his safe? Mother's
jewels, all of them." Her voice cracked with pain.

"He stole everything Father and I had, and I'm going to get every bit of it back."

Harriet was so upset by Tyler's emotional outburst that she was left speechless. Then reason returned, and she tried to use some of it on her young friend.

"Tyler, Tyler, dear child, we cannot do such a thing. Mr. Kincaid will know we stole the money if we're gone when he returns. He'll have the law after us, and he's rich and powerful enough to hunt us down. You know that."

Tyler paused, sinking to her knees and taking both of Harriet's soft, plump hands in her own.

"Please don't fret, Etty, because none of that can possibly happen—not with the plan I have in mind."

"But your plans never succeed, Tyler. That's why we're in this terrible mess!"

Tyler shushed Harriet's protests. "This one's different. It works like magic every time. How can Gray Kincaid suspect me of robbing his safe if I'm dead?"

"Dead!"

"Oh, not really dead. But he'll think I am. You see, I'll just fake my death from some kind of dread disease," she went on blithely, disregarding the rather frightening way Harriet's eyeballs were bulging out. "One that's highly contagious, of course, so no one will want to get too close to the remains or fiddle with the coffin."

"Coffin? Oh, mercy, oh, Lordy me—"

"Oh, Etty, don't look like that. You'll hurt your eyes." She patted the older woman consolingly. "I'm telling you it has worked before, twice. We can pull off the whole thing while Gray's gone, and if he ever does figure it out, which I doubt, we'll already have the money to buy Rose Point."

"No, no, I will *not* have a part in this," Harriet said resolutely, shaking her crown of braids. "It's just too much."

"But, Etty, it'll be so easy. All you have to do is

act bereaved and keep an eye on the coffin so I don't get buried by mistake.''

"Buried by mistake!" Harriet shook her head violently. "Tyler, I absolutely refuse. I will not allow you to do it, do you understand?''

Tyler hardly heard Harriet's protestations as she paced excitedly across the floor. She was going to get her revenge against Gray Kincaid after all, and she was going home to Rose Point at long last.

"I suppose I'll have to become ill somewhere other than the house. You and I will have to plan an outing. The disease will hit me fast and, in my weakened condition, I'll be taken swiftly with very little suffering. See, Etty, how everything fits so well?''

"No, no, I won't listen to this insane plan," Harriet cried, pressing her hands over her ears. Then a thought occurred to her. "Your idea will never work anyway. Charles is a physician. You can't hoodwink him, and he's fond of you. He would insist on taking care of you.''

Harriet took encouragement when her words did seem to give Tyler pause. She held her breath as Tyler frowned, considering the problem.

"You're right, of course. Well, then, we'll have to make sure he's not around," Tyler declared. She looked searchingly at Harriet. "Didn't you tell me once he travels on Thursdays to some of the outlying towns and farms?''

Harriet nodded glumly.

"Then that's it. We'll do it on Thursday. Gray probably won't be back by then. We'll load the coffin on the train and be halfway to Memphis before Gray even gets home.''

"Oh, Tyler, please," Harriet said in earnest supplication, "let's just forget all this. We were happy together in St. Louis for six months after Burl died. We can go back there. If we leave now, we'll be safe.''

"Etty, you know that the money Burl left us is gone. How would we get on? And don't you see?

That boardinghouse isn't where I want to live for the rest of my life. Rose Point is my home, and Gray took it from me,'' Tyler said, her soft words so full of haunting, forlorn sadness that Harriet felt the familiar weakening of her resolve. She knew Tyler was wrong, terribly wrong to even contemplate this scheme, yet she couldn't bear to see that awful pain in the young woman's eyes. And deep in her heart, Harriet knew Tyler would never be happy until she was back on her beloved Rose Point.

Although Tyler's plan went against all decency, Harriet knew she would help her, just as she always did.

"Don't you think you'll feel dreadful about hurting these people who have been so charitable to us since we've been here, Tyler? Charles, and Gray, and the servants—especially Hildie—they've all been kind and accommodating to us. They've grown fond of you. They'll be terribly grieved to think you're dead.''

"I don't like to hurt them, but this is the only way to get Rose Point back, and I swore on Papa's grave that I would,'' Tyler answered quietly, staring out the frosted panes at the snow sparkling in the morning sun.

Harriet looked at her slender back, wondering if Tyler would really be happy at Rose Point after all the dishonest things she was doing to get there.

"What if people don't believe me?'' Harriet asked in resignation.

Tyler turned from the window and flashed her irresistible sunny smile as she came back across the room to give Harriet's shoulders an affectionate squeeze. "Oh, of course everyone will believe you, Etty! You're the most honest person in the world!''

8

The newest, most powerful of the locomotives built by the Kincaid Railway Company roared up the tracks, billowing a cloud of crusty soot, black smoke, and glowing sparks into the late afternoon sky. Inside his personally designed, private luxury car at the end of the train, Gray leaned back in his chair, struck a match, then puffed on his favorite pipe until the tobacco caught.

In minutes, he would disembark at the platform of the LaSalle Street Station. He was glad the trip to St. Louis was behind him. He glanced at his surroundings, barely noticing the cream wallpaper and gilt panels, then gazed out one of the gleaming plate-glass windows hung with rich dark brown draperies trimmed in gold satin. The car's large office, sitting room, and spacious adjoining bedrooms constituted his home away from home, and even the click-clack of metal wheels against the tracks no longer fazed his concentration—especially in the past few days when his mind had been totally absorbed with Tyler MacKenzie.

Gray was ready now to deal with her. His inquiries in St. Louis had given him more than enough evidence to both try and convict her. Although he had unearthed eyewitnesses to her crimes, he still found it hard to believe she and her uncle had actually committed all those foul deeds.

Apparently, she had served as pawn in her uncle's illegal games. Burl Lancaster had been the brains, and Tyler had been the beautiful distraction—a job for which she had been born, with her big, artless, cinnamon-hued eyes.

He shook his head, amazed that the two of them had never been caught and imprisoned, if not outright lynched by some enraged victim. He supposed they owed that miracle to luck, and to the fact that they were good at what they did.

In fact, according to a constable in St. Louis, Burl Lancaster must have had the mind of a criminal genius to successfully pull off some of his nefarious stunts. Especially the one Stone had mentioned, in which Tyler had faked her death. It was preposterous to think they had gotten away with such a ploy, but as Stone had said, poor, duped Henry Hardcastle still wanted Tyler back.

Frowning, Gray set his pipe on the marble ashtray atop his desk. He shouldn't be surprised. Lovely little Tyler, so shy and sweet and soft-looking, had that effect on men. However, he told himself grimly, her days of crime were over, finished for good. Her most recent conspiracy had been a bad idea. She just didn't know it yet.

Gray continued to stare out the window as the train finally began to slow just before reaching the Chicago depot. He watched the long, covered platform pass by until they rolled to a halt alongside a steaming, hissing southbound train, fired up and ready to depart. Oh, yes, Tyler was in for a big surprise. He had already communicated with her cousin in Mexico City about all the gory details of her latest attempt at thievery, and Chase Lancaster had immediately telegraphed back his apologies and clear instructions for Gray to keep Tyler with him until Chase could take her off his hands. With Burl Lancaster in his grave, the poor man had vowed to take

Tyler in. He'd been trying to catch up with his wayward cousin for six months, just as Stone had said.

As the coach shuddered to a standstill beneath his
feet, Gray stood, languidly stretching tired muscles.
He put on his coat and glanced around his private
quarters one last time. A porter was clearing his
supper dishes from a round, marble-topped table by
the wide windows, and Gray bade him good-bye as
he picked up his hat and stepped onto the front observation platform. He surveyed the buzzing mass
of humanity swarming over the depot as he swung
lightly down from the train, suddenly eager to see
Tyler again. As much as it annoyed him to admit it,
he had missed the treacherous little beauty.

He strode briskly toward the Van Buren Street entrance, where the hired conveyances usually congregated to await fares. He was just about to summon
a hack when he stopped in surprise. Several yards
beyond him stood his own rig. His gaze settled as if
glued upon the tall black plumes rising from the
headgear of the pair of matched grays he had recently purchased in Denver.

"My God, funeral trappings?" he muttered, hurrying forward when he caught sight of Charles Bond
standing near the tall rear wheel.

"Charles!" he called before he was halfway to the
older man. Dr. Bond turned quickly, his face set in
tired, haggard lines.

"Gray, thank God, you're here. Something terrible's happened. It's so dreadful, I can't accept it myself." The old man removed his thick-lensed
spectacles to wipe his teary eyes. "It came upon her
so swiftly. She was so young and beautiful, just a
child really, with all her life before her—"

"For God's sake, Charles, what's happened?"

"Tyler fell ill again while you were gone." Trying
to steady his trembling lips, he choked on his next
words. "The Lord took her yesterday, before I could
do anything to save her."

Gray's whole body tensed, and the most horrible,

unbearable weight pressed down upon his soul like a heavy slab of lead. Tyler, dead? He fought the emotion running rampant through him, freezing the blood in his heart. But he knew it for what it was— wrenching, numbing loss.

"You couldn't help her?" he managed in a shaky voice.

"That's what broke my heart, Gray. If only I'd been in town, maybe I could have done something for her." A tear escaped the old man's eye and ran down his weathered cheek.

"You weren't here when she succumbed?" Gray asked quickly, hope beginning to rise.

"No, and I'll regret that until the day I die. I was out at Wilford Jones's farm when it happened."

"Who *did* tend to her?"

"Some doctor by the name of Rounsaville. I've never even heard of the man, and when Harriet told me about the contagious disease that took the poor child, she was so distraught she couldn't even remember the doctor's address."

Relief rolled over Gray as he realized what was really going on. Anger came then, fast and lethal. "Yeah, I'll bet she was too distraught to remember much else about the doctor either, wasn't she?"

"Well, you can't blame her," Dr. Bond said quickly, coming to the dear lady's defense. "They were like mother and daughter." His voice was wavery with emotion, and a moment passed before he could continue. "It's such a terrible tragedy! Tyler was so young and pretty, so sweet and kind-natured—"

"Yeah, and so crooked."

Dr. Bond looked utterly astounded at Gray's crude remark. "Crooked? What do you mean?"

"I'll let Harriet explain it to you, if she's got the guts to. Where is she anyway? I suspect she's hanging over the casket, too grief-stricken to speak to anyone."

"Why, of course she is. She hasn't left Tyler's coffin for a moment, poor thing."

"Somehow that doesn't surprise me." Sarcasm dripped from Gray's response.

Dr. Bond's expression turned angry, and high spots of color suffused his face. "I must say, Gray, you're taking a callous attitude about that poor girl's death. I thought you liked her."

"Tyler's not dead," Gray told him bluntly.

"What?"

Gray ignored the doctor's look of astonishment. "Which train are they on, Charles?"

"The southbound one. They're in the next-to-the-last coach. Harriet insisted on a private storage compartment for the coffin."

"Yes, I'm sure she did. Now listen, Charles, that's a Kincaid express, and I want you to do something for me. Go up to the front and tell the engineer not to move an inch down this track until he gets a direct order from me. And make it quick. They're due to pull out at any minute. I'll send Harriet to the carriage, and she can explain everything to you."

"Wait, Gray. Confound it, what in the deuce is going on?" Dr. Bond demanded, but Gray was already taking long, purposeful strides toward the funeral car. Thoroughly confused by Gray's bizarre behavior, Charles finally shook his head and hurried toward the smoking locomotive.

"Oh, please, please, Tyler, get back in the coffin. Someone will come!" Harriet moaned, anxiously wringing her hands.

"I will in a minute. I've just got to stretch my legs," Tyler answered, holding up the skirts of her black silk dress and striding energetically around the small compartment, her long black mourning veil floating out behind her. "Thunder, I've been in that thing over three hours, and they nearly froze me to ice when they left me out on the platform so long."

"I'm sorry, dear, but the porters couldn't decide where to put you."

"That's all right," Tyler replied, plopping down on a padded bench to rub her cold feet.

"Don't you think you ought to lie down, Tyler?" Harriet glanced fearfully at the door.

"Oh, quit worrying, Etty. The hard part's over now. Anyway, the door's locked, and there aren't any windows. I'm starving! Aren't you?"

"However can you think of food?" Harriet cried, stepping forward to make sure the door was locked. "I don't see how you could eat a bite after all we've put poor Charles through." She looked woefully back at Tyler and shook her head. "You look absolutely ghastly with that white powder all over your face."

"Well, for pity's sake, Etty, I'm not supposed to look good," Tyler reminded her with an impish smile.

Harriet shivered at her words, afraid the chill she felt might be a precursor of doom. "I shudder to think what would have happened if Charles or someone else had insisted on viewing you."

"Oh, I told you no one ever wants to get anywhere close to an infectious disease, especially if it killed somebody. Now really, Etty, there's nothing to worry about. The train's gathering steam, so we'll be on our way any time now. Come, look what I've brought for us."

Harriet sank down onto the bench, looking quite desolate as Tyler unwrapped a scarf packed with cake, sandwiches, and several large red apples.

"If only I hadn't had to hurt Charles the way I did. He was so upset and tearful, and so very considerate, that I truly feel dreadful letting him think you were dead. He's such a good man."

"I know you did, and I'm sorry you had to do it, but don't you see, it was the only way." Tyler meant to comfort her friend, but inwardly she relived the sound of the tender-hearted man's stifled sobs, his genuine shocked grief, upon learning of her death. She couldn't let herself think about that right now. She had succeeded in what she had set out to do, and they were going home at last. It was all over and done with, and like Uncle Burl had said, it didn't help to worry about the past.

She took a bite of her apple. "Come on, eat something, Etty. You'll need your strength."

Harriet shook her head, watching as Tyler uncorked a small tin and set it on the scarf with the rest of the food. Only a moment had passed when the most disagreeable odor wafted up between them. Harriet immediately put her black hankie against her nose.

"Oh, Lordy, what is that horrid smell?" she asked, her words muffled under the silk.

Tyler popped a piece of cake into her mouth. "Two pounds of Limburger cheese."

"Mercy me, is it spoiled or what?" Harriet cried, vigorously waving the air in front of her.

"Well, it's three days old. I got it to hide under the casket drapings. People will think it's the body and stay away from us. We'll close the tin once the train gets started, then it won't bother us so much."

"Oh, for shame, Tyler! What an awful thought! How in heavens do you come up with such frightful ideas?"

"Uncle Burl thought of it. It never fails to work. Oh, my, it does stink, though," Tyler said, pinching her nose.

A knock on the door ended their conversation. Startled, their eyes met in alarm; then Tyler jumped to her feet, snatching up all the food in the scarf and sprinting toward the casket. She tossed the bundle inside, then scrambled in so wildly that the coffin nearly overturned.

"Oh, Lord, have mercy on us," Harriet squeaked out.

"Get rid of them," Tyler hissed, lying down as Harriet closed the lid and the knock sounded again.

A muffled prompting came from inside the casket, and Harriet readjusted her heavy black veil with trembling fingers. Forcing herself to swallow, she moved reluctantly to the door. Whenever would this nightmare be over? she asked herself dolefully.

A short, stocky Negro dressed in a white porter's coat stood in the narrow hallway with two freight handlers behind him. He tipped his green visored cap courteously.

"Sorry fo' disturbin' you, ma'am, but they be a problem with dis heah compartment. De train captin has to talk to you. He be waitin' in de next car."

"I really can't leave here," Harriet began, letting her vague gesture at the coffin suffice as an explanation.

"Only gonna take a minute, ma'am. You gonna haf to see him afore dis heah train can go anywheres."

Harriet hesitated another moment, but she really didn't expect that too many people would take it upon themselves to tamper with a casket hung with black crepe, especially when it smelled so atrociously. The three men were already wrinkling their noses and casting significant glances toward the funeral bier. Lord help Tyler, closed up with the foul-smelling cheese!

She followed the friendly man outside, gladly inhaling the fresh air, then through the connecting platform to the next car, where he opened a door. He stood back to let her precede him. But she drew up in horror as her eyes found Gray Kincaid standing motionless, his back to the windows of the tiny compartment. She stared into his keen blue eyes, hardly aware of the porter closing the door softly behind her.

"I know everything, Mrs. Stowe," Gray said quietly. "I know Tyler's not really dead, and I know about her past thievery with her uncle Burl."

Harriet stared at him, dumbfounded, so stunned and dismayed that she couldn't move. As the full impact of his pronouncement hit her, she reached to grasp the handrail beside the door.

"Is it your heart?" he asked in concern. "Here, maybe you'd better sit down."

Harriet let him assist her to a cushioned chair near the door and lifted her veil to fan her hot cheeks as Gray stood in front of her. The hoax was finished at last, she thought in joy; all the lies and deceptions were at an end! Pure, grateful relief rushed through her like a cleansing breeze.

"I'm glad it's over," she said, meeting his steady gaze. "I tried to talk Tyler out of it from the beginning."

"More than anything else, I've wondered why you were involved in such a fraud, Mrs. Stowe. With all due respect, I would expect you to have better sense."

Harriet flushed at his mildly uttered rebuke, but she didn't try to defend herself. She had no case.

"Please, first of all, I want to tell you that my name isn't Stowe. It's Stokely, and I only told you that because I got all mixed up when Tyler fell into the river. She wasn't supposed to do that, and it frightened the life out of me. And"—her face darkened even more as she continued with her confession—"I don't really have a heart condition, though I might have one now after all I've been through these past weeks."

Gray surprised her by giving a short laugh. "I sincerely hope not."

Encouraged by his lack of visible anger, she went on. "Please don't be too hard on Tyler, Mr. Kincaid. I know she's done some truly disgraceful things, but it's all she's known since she was a child. Down deep, she's got a good heart."

"It must be very deep," Gray responded dryly.

Harriet stared up at the tall, handsome man before her, his face set and inscrutable. Suddenly afraid for Tyler, she spoke again, wanting desperately for Gray Kincaid to understand Tyler.

"I lost my husband during the war, Mr. Kincaid. My husband and all four of our sons." She stopped, remembered heartache possessing her. "Michael and the boys never came home, not even in death. They were buried where they fell, scattered like leaves. All I had left was our truck farm and little Cole. He was my grandbaby, barely a year old and sickly from birth. His mother died giving him life." Her forehead creased with pain.

"I managed to keep the farm for three years before the bank took it. I went to St. Louis then, looking for work. It was hard to come by, especially with a little one along, fighting consumption like Cole was. Anyway," she said with a heavy sigh, "Tyler was the only one who was willing to help us. She hired me as her maid, even though Burl Lancaster said that they couldn't afford it. And she took care of my grandson, Mr. Kincaid, when I succumbed to fever and was too tired to even lift my head. When Cole died almost two years ago, she sold a pair of earbobs to pay for his funeral—earbobs that had been made for her when she was born, solid gold with her own initials . . ."

Her flood of words died. She was quiet, her eyes swimming with tears. It was strange to want to cry now, from telling Gray Kincaid about it, but teardrops began to fall. She dabbed at them with her handkerchief.

"I think I understand your loyalty to Tyler, Mrs. Stokely, and you don't have to worry. No harm will come to her. I'm only taking her to New Orleans with me, where I intend to turn her over to her cousin, Chase Lancaster. He's been trying to track her down for a long time. Did you know that?"

Harriet sniffled as she wiped her tears away. "No, but Tyler has always spoken well of him, even though Chase rarely saw his father. I believe he'll be good to her. She needs someone to look out for her interests. She was devastated when Burl was shot. She adored him."

"He didn't do a very good job of raising her, if you ask me," Gray said, cold dislike rising up to brand the man he had never met.

Harriet couldn't disagree. "Despite all that, they did love each other. He told her that there was nothing wrong with what they did as long as their victims deserved it. He taught her all these shams and tricks. Can you understand her behavior better now?"

"No," was Gray's blunt reply, "but in any case, she'll be well taken care of. At least I won't allow her to steal or cheat anymore." He stopped, his eyes searching her face. "Charles is awaiting you at the carriage. I believe you owe him an explanation. Then I think he'll probably end up asking you to marry him."

Harriet's jaw dropped, but her expression betrayed the happiness such a proposal would bring to her. "But I can't just go off and leave Tyler here all alone—"

"I'll be with her, and I'll look after her until I deliver her to Chase. I was going to New Orleans, anyway, for my sister's graduation from convent school, so I'll just take Tyler with me. While I'm gone, you're welcome to remain my guest." At Harriet's continued reluctance, he added, "I'll have Tyler write you a long letter as soon as we reach the city."

Harriet was loath to leave Tyler to Gray Kincaid's mercy, but she knew in her heart that he wouldn't hurt her. Besides that, she felt he was doing for Tyler what someone should have done a long time ago. Her eyes met Gray's again. Her voice was almost apologetic.

"She told me that you, well . . . that you were forward with her—"

"I give you my word of honor, Mrs. Stokely, that I will not compromise Tyler in any way."

Harriet was relieved. "Then I'm glad she'll be with you, sir. I believe you're just the kind of man she needs."

Gray considered her words as she took her leave; then he stepped into the hallway and looked toward the car where Tyler waited so unsuspectingly. It was time to greet his treacherous little corpse face-to-face.

9

Tyler covered her nose, thinking the Limburger fumes were surely going to kill her. Wouldn't that be a fine epithet on her tombstone, she thought furiously: HERE LIES TYLER MACKENZIE, MURDERED IN HER CASKET BY SOME OLD CHEESE.

Grimacing, she shifted uncomfortably in the stifling, malodorous confines of the narrow, white satin-lined box, wishing the men outside would leave so she could fling open the lid and suck some clean-smelling air into her lungs. How stupid to have become so disconcerted that she had thrown the cheese tin inside the coffin with her! She tried with her foot to poke the offending substance as far away from her nose as she could. Harriet, please come back, she prayed.

She lay still, listening for her friend's voice, but only the conversation of the waiting freight handlers filtered through to her.

"How long yo thinks dat body been in dere?" asked one, obviously pinching his nose as he spoke.

"Arrgh. He be a ripe one for shore. I ain't neber smelt no smell anywheres close to de badness of dat 'un afore."

Tyler quit listening. If they thought it was bad out there, they ought to be inside with her. She pulled

her black net veil over her nose and held her breath
until she heard the outside door open a few seconds
later. Heart lifting, she waited expectantly for Harriet to liberate her. Instead, the sound of the men's
voices and their shuffling footsteps came closer. She
gasped in surprise as the coffin was suddenly lifted
from its supports.

Thoroughly alarmed now, she strained to hear
what was being said, but she could only ascertain
that they were moving her to a different car. Some-
what relieved, she braced her hands on either side
of the casket as the train gave a threatening lurch,
then began to move out of the depot. At least they
were safely on their way south, she thought.

The transfer took only a moment or two, and Tyler waited impatiently, breathing out of her mouth
as the porters left the new compartment, still arguing loudly over how long she'd been dead. Now
only the distant clacking of metal wheels was audible. Good grief, where was Harriet? What if she had
been forced off the train for some reason, and Tyler
was left with the cheese? But she quickly dismissed
that horrible notion. It was ridiculous. Harriet would
never leave her, and who would dare interfere when
she was in mourning and accompanying a smelly,
dead relative home for burial?

Tyler chided herself for being silly and jumpy. No
doubt Harriet had to sign a paper granting permission to travel with a cadaver, or something like that.
She would be back in a minute, and even if she
wasn't, if something had gone wrong, all Tyler had
to do was climb out and hide until she could leave
the train. There was no real danger.

Feeling better, she decided she had no choice but
to wait, and she stared at the white satin lid, just
barely visible in the dim light filtering from the hidden ventilation holes behind her head.

Oh, Etty, hurry, please, she thought, hoping that
Harriet was all right. The poor woman had been so
fidgety and distraught for the past few days that Ty-

ler had begun to worry about her. Actually, Harriet's emotional state had worked well to convince everyone she was truly suffering grief and shock. Even so, Tyler was glad they had made their getaway before Gray returned. She had a feeling he was a little too smart not to have suspected something. He probably would have insisted on seeing the body himself, stink, contagion, and all. But he had not appeared in time to stop them, and soon she would arrive in Natchez and purchase Rose Point with the ten thousand dollars she had taken from his safe. She and Harriet would live there together for the rest of their lives.

She smiled, endeavoring to let those welcome thoughts alleviate her olfactory distress. Think of Rose Point, she told herself desperately. Think of the hilltop house of white brick and double pillars and curved front portico. She would walk down the cool corridors with Harriet and breathe clean country air.

Only moments had passed when intense dread assailed her. She couldn't breathe! An overwhelming, crashing fear followed. She had to have some fresh air! She couldn't stand the cheese for another moment! It was so quiet outside; surely no one was there! Feeling faint, she pulled down the inside lock, pushed open the lid, and sat up, heaving in great gulps of air.

"I wondered how long you'd last in there," came a familiar, deeply timbral voice from behind her.

She jumped so violently that she nearly fell out of the coffin. Her eyes were wide and disbelieving as she saw Gray Kincaid lounging in a comfortable armchair beside her, his large white pocket handkerchief held to his nostrils.

"You nearly scared me to death!" she cried.

"Since you're the one rising from the dead, I find that remark ironic," he stated, then wrinkled his nose. "Good God, what a stench! You must have

the fortitude of a camel to stay cooped up in that
box so long.''

Tyler sat staring at him. She'd never felt so stupid
and humiliated in her life, but she was caught red-
handed. He knew it, and she knew he knew it. Trying to retain at least a particle of dignity, Tyler sat
erect in the open casket, determined not to meet his
mocking gaze again.

''How did you know?'' she finally asked sullenly,
crossing her arms around her waist for lack of anything else to do with them. She certainly didn't intend to make herself look any more foolish by trying
to scramble awkwardly out of the coffin.

''You would be surprised what all I know about
you, love—and not one bit of it good.''

Tyler was almost sure she heard the barest trace
of a threat beneath his quiet words. Suddenly afraid,
she caught her teeth on her bottom lip, which had
begun to tremble.

''What are you going to do with me?'' she asked.
''And what have you done with Harriet?''

Gray was silent for a long moment, and Tyler bridled, aware that he was purposely making her
squirm—and no doubt enjoying every minute of it.
Acutely wary now, Tyler watched Gray rise until he
seemed to tower over her like some dark, wrathful
god.

''I ought to keep you in that stinking coffin until
we get to New Orleans, just to teach you a lesson.''

His calm threat threw terror into Tyler. ''You
wouldn't!'' she cried, already poised to claw and
scratch if he took even one step toward her.

For the first time, a frown darkened Gray's brow.
He placed his pipe in an ashtray on the table.

''No, I'm not that uncivilized, lucky for you,'' he
muttered furiously. ''Now get out of there before I
damn well change my mind.''

Tyler was helped in that endeavor by a particularly ungentle hand on her arm. Once on her feet
again, she tried to twist haughtily away from his

grasp. His fingers dug tighter around her upper arm as he thrust her backward into the chair he had just vacated. She stayed put, seething as he leaned over to inspect the interior of the pine box.

"Limburger? How inventive. To make you smell as bad as you look, I take it," he said, surveying the thick white substance caked over her face.

He picked up the open tin of cheese with his handkerchief and held it out at arm's length as he moved to the window. Tyler watched him toss the offending foodstuff into the passing night. He left the glass down to rid the compartment of the lingering smell, then retrieved another small sack from the casket.

"Your bag of loot, I presume?" he asked sarcastically.

Tyler rubbed her arm where he had gripped her, not willing to answer. "Where's Harriet?" she repeated.

Gray ignored her again as he dumped the contents of the bag onto the tabletop. Tyler began to look for a means of escape, but she couldn't work up enough courage to make a run for the door. Gray turned glittering eyes on her. His dark face looked cruel and frightening with the lamp reflecting upon his well-defined cheekbones and chin.

"You helped yourself to my safe, I see," he murmured almost conversationally. "Like any self-respecting thief."

Tyler's mouth clamped shut as he picked up a half-eaten apple and raised a questioning brow.

"So I was hungry," she muttered, feeling silly again.

"It would seem you planned a banquet." He looked distastefully at the cake and sandwiches smashed against the foot of the box. "And my money and jewels appealed to your appetite as well, I see."

"*Your* jewels!" Tyler exploded, no longer able to withstand his derision. "They're mine! My mother's! You're the one who stole them from us! And you know it! I only took enough of your stupid Yankee money to buy back Rose Point! I wouldn't touch the rest of it any more than I'd touch you," she added viciously.

Gray's smile was cold and cynical. "If I remember right, the last time we were together you obviously weren't so fastidious about touching me."

Tyler felt heat gush into her face, and she hated herself for that betraying reaction.

"You're the one who enticed me into your bedchamber and mauled me like the animal you are!"

"Yes, I find mauling rather enjoyable when the one being mauled is moaning and pressing her fickle body as close to me as she can."

Tyler was forced to lower her eyes. "You caught me by surprise, that's all. I didn't know what was going to happen. How could I?"

His answering laugh was so contemptuous that it made Tyler shiver. "I think you knew exactly what I was going to do," he returned, "but your deliberate flirtation intended to convince me to buy your stocks got way out of hand. Then you panicked. Isn't that what really happened?"

Tyler refused to answer, knowing full well that he was baiting her. Abruptly, she decided that mute, defiant silence would be her best bet, especially since she was guilty of just about everything of which he accused her. He had caught her tight in his trap, and she was at his mercy.

According to Uncle Burl's strictures, it was time to weep and beg for forgiveness, but somehow she couldn't bring herself to do it, not with Gray Kincaid waiting for that exact reaction. She would never beg him for anything—never, ever.

"I guess you can have this back, since I gave it to you," he said. When Tyler looked up, he tossed her the glass snowscene, which had also been in her bag with the money and jewelry.

She shook it at once, vigorously, to remind herself

just how much she hated him, and held the ball between her fingers, pretending they were really
squeezing Gray Kincaid's neck.

After that, she assumed an injured air and stared
into the night, though she did shoot him a furtive
glance as he gathered up the bag of money and her
mother's jewels and knelt before the ornate desk in
the corner. He opened twin doors to reveal a small
safe. She shifted her gaze back to the windows as
he placed the valuables inside and gave the dial a
swift spin.

Maybe she could steal the money and jewels
again, she thought. That would show him—

"Don't even think it, Tyler," he warned, and her
shocked expression no doubt told him he had, indeed, guessed her intent. He shook his head, giving
her a black frown until she turned to window-gazing
and snowscene-shaking once more. She listened,
however, as he opened the compartment door.

"You can take the casket back to the freight car
now, boys. As you can see, the young lady has mi-
raculously risen from the dead, just as I predicted
she would."

Tyler stifled more waves of humiliation at the low
guffaws of the porters entering the room.

"She smelt bad nuf to be a dead 'un," said one.

"You shore she ain't no haint, Mr. Kincaid, sir?"
said the other. "She shore looks pale and poorly."

"No, Homer, she just has an aversion to Limburger cheese," Gray Kincaid replied, laughing.

Tyler kept her eyes riveted on the darkness outside, far more concerned with her own fate now that
Gray knew she had robbed him.

"Are you sure you won't join me for supper?"
Gray asked later from the round marble table at the
other end of his private car.

Tyler made the snowflakes in the crystal globe
dance without looking up at him. He still refused to
tell her his plans for her or what he had done with

Harriet. Anger boiled inside her. He was purposely tormenting her!

"You're about to shake that thing to pieces," he commented dryly.

"I like to pretend it's you," she snapped back. His answering laugh infuriated her.

"If you really don't like this roast turkey and chestnut dressing, maybe I could scrounge up an apple or some smashed cake for you," Gray offered as he poured more wine from the magnum chilling in a silver bucket beside him.

"Tell me if Harriet's all right," she said softly. "Please," she added at length in a stiff, reluctant tone.

"Harriet is back in Chicago with Charles. She's staying at my house as my guest, so you don't have to worry about her."

"She isn't on the train? But I need her!" Tyler blurted out, distressed to find herself unexpectedly abandoned by her only friend.

"That's selfish of you," Gray observed casually, "but I suppose I shouldn't expect anything else. As for Harriet, in Chicago she'll have a chance for happiness with Charles. Don't you want her to be happy?"

"Yes, of course I do, but—"

"But what?"

"But nothing. Just leave me alone."

"I wouldn't leave you alone here with my safe any more than I'd leave a cat in a birdcage."

Tyler's gaze went to the windows. Silence prevailed for a while, until her stomach growled loud enough for Gray to hear it. He laughed, and Tyler flushed.

"Aren't you curious as to where we're going?" he asked, "and what I intend to do with you once we're there?"

"You know good and well that I am, but not enough to beg you to tell me."

"Suit yourself."

Tyler frowned. Why hadn't she kept her mouth shut? She did want to know, and now he would make her ask him again, the wretch. He was enjoying himself, and she was making it easy for him.

"All right. Where are you taking me?"

"Well, Tyler, I'll tell you what. We'll play a little game. That idea ought to appeal to you since you seem to enjoy games so much. It's really very simple. You answer a question of mine, then I'll answer one of yours. That's easy enough, wouldn't you say?"

Tyler gritted her teeth until she thought they would splinter. Her eyes glittered with suppressed ire.

"All right," she agreed tightly.

"Why did you go to all this trouble? Surely you knew you couldn't get away with it."

"I almost did, didn't I? If you hadn't come back early, we would have been gone forever."

"Ah, but 'almost' doesn't count for much, does it, Tyler?" he reminded her with yet another scornful smile.

She was silent.

"Tell me about your life with your uncle Burl," he said then, as if they were having a polite conversation over afternoon tea. "When did you go to live with him?"

"After you killed my father and stole Rose Point!" she cried, turning on him, eyes ablaze.

Gray set down his glass very carefully and leaned indolently back in his chair to watch her.

"Neither of those things is true, and you know it," he replied calmly, though inwardly he was aghast at the hatred on her face.

"Yes, it is true! You burned Father's cotton and took Rose Point! You stole everything from him! He'd still be alive today if it hadn't been for you!"

"Your father shot himself at Rose Point. I had nothing to do with it. He lost the plantation because he mortgaged it to the hilt to subsidize one of the

Mississippi Confederate regiments. Then he didn't have the guts to face bankruptcy, so he killed himself.''

Tyler shook so hard she could hardly speak. ''Liar, you're a damnable liar! Uncle Burl told me everything. You chose my father to ruin. You chose Rose Point from all the surrounding plantations.''

''It was wartime, Tyler. Unpleasant things happen in wartime.''

''I don't care. I hate you! I'll always hate you! I'll hate you until the day I die!'' She stifled a sob and turned away, covering her face with her hands.

Gray watched as she began to cry, determined not to be affected. He wanted to think she was faking, playing another trick to work on his sympathy, but he knew instinctively that she wasn't. She was miserable and confused, exhausted and defeated. And he knew how that felt. He had seethed, boiled, and then wept in the exact same way one long-ago, stormy night in Mississippi.

Rising, he went to her and pulled her into his arms as he sat down beside her. She immediately put up a fight, but it was a feeble one, and she eventually lay weakly against him, weeping. Silent, he held her for a long time, letting her cry until the sobs dwindled into embarrassed-sounding sniffles. He held out his handkerchief. She took it, then sat back, looking at him out of red, swollen eyes, the white powder streaked and smeared across her young face.

''Why are you being so nice to me now, after what I did?'' she demanded, wiping her eyes.

Indeed, why was he? Gray wondered. But deep inside, he knew the reason, and it scared the hell out of him.

''You remind me of me, I guess. Once a long time ago I went after revenge, and now I regret it. I guess I don't want that to happen to you.''

''Did you get your revenge?''

''Yes, for a while.''

Tyler waited for him to elaborate, but he didn't, and she was too weary to pursue the subject.

"How did you know who I was?"

"Stone told me that night at the Richmond Hotel."

"That's the night you tried to—" Her words faltered, her dark lashes sweeping down.

"Yes," Gray said. "I wanted to see how far you'd go to make your sham succeed." A slow, dark color stained Tyler's cheeks as he finished. "And I learned that some of the stories Stone had heard about your dalliances with men were probably exaggerated. That's when"—he paused, his lips curving into a grin—"I decided there might be some hope for you."

"How dare you think I did such things with men!" Tyler cried, her anger rising again. "Uncle Burl would never let anyone touch me! He loved me and watched over me."

"Don't praise that man to me," Gray said sharply. "From where I stand, he was nothing but a cold and calculating corrupter of children. You're lucky he didn't get you hanged for your thievery."

"Don't you talk about him that way. Don't you ever! He took me in when I didn't have anybody, thanks to you! He raised me and loved me and took care of me!"

Gray didn't answer, and their gazes held for a moment, long enough for Tyler to recognize the sympathy lurking in the depths of his eyes. She looked away, not liking the way it felt to be the object of his pity.

"What are you going to do with me?"

"I've already telegraphed Chase, and he's going to meet us in New Orleans and take you to his hacienda. He's been searching for you for a long time. Did you know that?"

Tyler shook her head. She was vastly relieved that Gray Kincaid did not want to press charges against her for breaking into his safe, and she couldn't have been more pleased to learn that she was going home with Chase. She had always liked her cousin, even though she hadn't seen him since the war and knew he was very much against her involvement in his father's schemes. Uncle Burl hardly ever spoke of his handsome, blond-haired son; they hadn't gotten along well.

When she remained quiet, Gray smiled as he noted again the havoc her hot tears had played with her death mask.

"Why don't you wash your face? You'll feel better. There's a water closet and bedroom just beyond those drapes."

He watched her move away as bidden, but remained where he was, feeling as drained emotionally as she no doubt did. He wondered just how much she really knew about her father.

Even the thought of Colin MacKenzie made his stomach twist into strangling knots. If she knew what her father had done to Gray, Stone, and Carly—to everyone in his family—would she understand his motives? Or would she still blame him for causing her father's death? Worse, would she hate him more for telling her the truth, and thereby tarnishing the sterling, cherished memory of her father? He wondered if Tyler knew him for what he really was—a vicious, cruel tyrant. Or did she close her eyes to his faults and remember only what she wanted?

Gray leaned back against the upholstered sofa, resting his head on the cushions. He sighed, staring at the curtains draping the entrance to the bedroom where Tyler had disappeared.

What a strange, ironic twist of fate, he thought, that in a way he himself was responsible for all the terrible misdeeds Tyler had perpetrated. Just as he had told her, he had managed to wreak the vengeance he had thirsted for so single-mindedly during his youth in the streets of Chicago. To others, he had called it necessary, an act of war.

But it had been more than that. It had been premeditated, cold-blooded revenge, his long-nurtured, well-thought-out plan to repay Colin MacKenzie for his crimes against the Kincaid family. When the Confederacy had seceded, he had immediately put together his own unit of volunteers, all friends or employees of his companies, to fight against the South. The Union Army had received him gladly, giving him the rank of captain and honoring his request to serve in Mississippi.

Once there, he'd methodically forged his way to Natchez, with Rose Point as his eventual destination. When the opportunity had arisen, he'd sent an entire unit to the MacKenzie plantation to burn its cotton. Without even setting foot in the house he hated so intensely, he had made Colin MacKenzie a pauper. He'd never expected the man to commit suicide, but when he had, Gray had only felt satisfaction.

After the war when Rose Point had come up for sale, Gray had bought it with a feeling of grim gratification. But one walk through the luxurious rooms had been all he could stomach of the place. The damned house was too full of painful memories, and he had ordered it boarded up and left to rot, along with every stick of furniture inside. Vengeance complete, he had rarely even thought about the place until nearly eight months ago, when he had decided to put it up for sale.

Now, years later, he was faced with the end result of his unscrupulous acts against Colin MacKenzie: MacKenzie's daughter, innocent, appealing, thieving, lying, homeless, and orphaned, thrust into the corruptive company of Burl Lancaster. Gray knew he was as much to blame as her cheating uncle and cowardly father.

He leaned forward, his elbows on his knees, his head in his palms. Poetic justice? Was that what this was all about?

For better or worse, Tyler had ended up in his hands. He could try to make amends for his past actions, or he could shrug off his responsibility and send her packing with her cousin. That was what she wanted. He had detected the relief in her eyes when he had told her his plans for her. But, God help him, was that what *he* wanted?

He stood, bracing his arms on the narrow windowsill of the open window, letting the brisk night air ruffle his hair as the shrouded landscape of Illinois rushed by in the darkness. He visualized stepping off the train in New Orleans, imagined Chase Lancaster taking Tyler's arm and leading her away. His heart twisted at the mere idea of losing her. My God, surely he wasn't in love with her!

He straightened up, running his fingers through his thick hair, then shook his head. Lord, if he was, he was doomed, because he was the one man on earth with whom Tyler would never share her life. *I hate you. I'll always hate you. I'll hate you until the day I die*, she had cried. But she was young and obviously didn't know what was best for her. Her cousin, Chase, was a sensible man and a good friend of Gray's. Perhaps they could arrange a suitable solution to the problem.

But what solution was there, other than marriage?

He had already considered taking her as his wife, before he knew the truth about her. Now it made even more sense to him. Why shouldn't he marry Tyler?

Smiling, he crossed the room, thinking Tyler had been too quiet for too long. He parted the portiere and found her on the bed, lying on her side with her knees drawn up and one hand beneath her cheek, sleeping like a child. Her face was scrubbed clean of the pale powder, but dark circles lay like shadows beneath her long, thick eyelashes.

Never had he seen her look quite so young and soft and desirable as she did just then, and he strained to curb his desire to reach out and stroke her cheek, to lie down beside her and pull her into his arms. He contented himself by gently lifting a long, shiny lock of her hair and caressing the silky texture between his thumb and forefinger. God, how he wanted her, he realized, half appalled by the force of his feelings.

Suddenly eager to reach New Orleans and meet Chase Lancaster, he pulled the heavy blue bedspread up over her shoulders, then doused the oil lamp affixed to the nightstand. He was a patient man. He had won his fortune, his reputation, and his revenge on Colin MacKenzie with such patience—and now he would win the heart of MacKenzie's daughter in the same way. Sooner or later, he always got what he wanted.

10

Tyler stared glumly out the drape-lined window. The long gold fringe attached to the curtain's bottom edge swayed desultorily in cadence with the train's motion. She was completely and totally bored. For nearly five days and endless miles, she had watched never-ceasing stretches of forest, interspersed with fields being tilled for planting. They had chugged southward toward Louisiana through one small rural town after another, all looking alike with their long wood-planked platforms and depots covered with sloping tin roofs rusted by rain and winter weather. Only the names painted on the swinging wooden signs varied—Jamesville, Willow Roe, Rolling Fork, nondescript little hamlets whose inhabitants always stopped to gawk at Gray Kincaid's palatial black-and-gold car.

She sighed, glancing toward the fringed portiere that separated the spacious bedroom where she sat from the equally large parlor. She listened, trying to figure out what Gray was doing, but couldn't detect a sound over the rhythmic clacking of the train. He was probably working; that was all he had done since the night he had dragged her unceremoniously out of the coffin.

For the first two days, she had been too angry and

135

embarrassed to seek out his company, and he had
made no attempt to talk to her. He hadn't even
looked at her. In the beginning, that had suited her
fine. She had felt too vulnerable to be close to him.
His touch was dangerous.

Thoughts of the tall, dark Yankee's burning lips
and roaming hands initiated waves of response inside her body. She remembered vividly that night
in his bedchamber when her bodice had come free
with a deft twist of his fingers. Even more unforgettable was the feel of his mouth wandering over her
bare flesh. She swallowed hard, then frowned, furious with herself. She had melted under his touch,
like the fastest of low women. How could she have
let him go so far? What would have happened if she
hadn't found the strength to resist?

In her heart, she knew what would have happened, and it appalled her. She would have relin-
quished any vestige of her virtue, the honor that
Uncle Burl had protected so vigilantly for so long.
Vague notions of what it was like to lie with a man
flickered in her mind. Her uncle had told her count-
less times that it was not a happy experience for a
lady, that the act was by nature designed for the
enjoyment of men. She knew only that for her it
would be painful, humiliating, and frightening. In
fact, that was her uncle's exact description of the
marital act. And after that intimate talk, which
they'd had when she was just thirteen, Tyler had
decided that there was not a man alive she would
ever want to marry enough to go through such tor-
tures.

She couldn't help but wonder, though, how the
first part—the kissing and holding, like Gray had
done to her in the sleigh—could feel so good when
the rest of it must be a trip straight down to hell.
None of it mattered anyway, she decided. She didn't
want a man. They weren't worth the fuss, and with
the exception of Gray Kincaid, they were entirely
too easy to manipulate. Why, all they ever thought

about was catching a glimpse of her ankle or bosom. No, she didn't need them. Even so, she could not forget the gentleness and kindness Gray had displayed toward her that first night on the train, even after all she had done to him.

Her feelings were so ambivalent, in fact, that she had spent a great many hours at the window, trying desperately to sort through the confused emotions bumping around inside her head. Meanwhile, *he* sat blithely at his desk in the parlor, writing or reading the endless stacks of newspapers and telegraph dispatches brought to him from nearly every depot at which they stopped. His business enterprises were apparently more widespread than she had first imagined.

Out of boredom, she had begun to speculate about his background. Other than his wartime crimes against her family, she knew nothing about him. It was strange that more concerning him hadn't surfaced when she and Harriet were living in his house. To Tyler's knowledge, Charles had never mentioned Gray's past.

Thoughts of Harriet made Tyler's spirits dip to a new low. She missed her dear, loyal friend and wondered if Charles Bond really would propose to her—and if Harriet would accept. They certainly did make an agreeable couple, and Harriet had often recounted to Tyler how much she admired the kindhearted doctor. As soon as she was safely with Chase again, Tyler would send a long letter to Harriet, asking her about everything and inviting her to come to Chase's hacienda, if he had no objection.

Standing, Tyler paced restlessly along the expensive carpet, woven in the design of rich, golden leaves on a dark brown background. The porter should be arriving soon with breakfast. Homer was a friendly sort, who always gave her a big smile and cheerfully wished her good-day—which was more than her traveling companion did. For the most part, Gray Kincaid acted as if she didn't exist.

"I should thank my lucky stars for that," Tyler whispered to herself.

Nevertheless, she was lonely and tired of being cooped up with nothing to do and no one to talk to. And she was hungry. Breakfast was late, but now and again she could hear the rattle of pans from the private kitchen at the far end of the car, where the guest compartments were located. Perhaps if she went into the parlor before Homer entered with their meal, Gray would ask her to have breakfast with him. Then she could find out when they would reach New Orleans, and if he had heard any more news from Harriet or Chase.

Her course decided in her usual impulsive way, she stepped through the heavy brown velvet drapes. She didn't see Gray at first, then colored when she found him standing before a wall-hung mirror in the adjoining water closet. He was shaving and had apparently forgotten to draw the curtains together. Unaware of her presence, he continued to wield the straight razor across the finely molded planes of his square jaw. He had not yet donned his shirt, and Tyler's gaze fell unwillingly on the muscled ridges of his broad, bare back as they rippled fluidly beneath the skin. When he caught sight of her in the looking glass, he turned around quickly.

Tyler tried not to notice the thick furring of black hair across his muscular chest and the way his powerful biceps bulged as he reached for a towel. To her chagrin, the first words she spoke came out in the most idiotic, stammering way imaginable.

"Oh, pardon me, please. I—I didn't know you weren't dressed—"

"That's quite all right. I'm just finishing," he told her, the side of his mouth lifting in a slight smile. No doubt he was amused by her nervous apology. She watched in fascination as he toweled off the last of the shaving soap whitening his dark face, then reached for a starched white shirt hanging from the wooden clothes valet beside the washstand. Tyler, by now thoroughly embarrassed, turned away as he slid one muscular arm through the sleeve. She had never seen a man at his toilette, not even her uncle. At the moment, she felt self-conscious and forward to have interrupted Gray while his chest was bare and all his muscles showed so disturbingly.

"Is anything wrong?" he asked as he stepped toward her, his fingers at work at the front of his shirt. He left the top buttons open, and Tyler watched him pull up wide white suspenders to rest on his broad shoulders. Somehow that simple gesture seemed remarkably manly, and unsettling.

"No, it was just stuffy back in the bedroom this morning, so I thought I'd come out here for a while. I didn't mean to disturb you."

"You didn't," he answered. "As a matter of fact, I'd be pleased if you'd join me for breakfast. I hear Homer coming with the serving cart now."

"If you're sure you don't mind," she replied, thinking their conversation was absurdly polite after all the cruel things they had said to each other only a few nights ago.

Gray smiled then, slowly and rather irresistibly, and against her will, Tyler admitted to herself that he looked even better in his casual attire than in the expensive, well-tailored coats he favored. She liked the way the freshly laundered white linen shirt lay open without the stiff white collar he usually wore.

She sat down in the chair he was courteously holding for her, just as Homer entered, smiling from ear to ear. The servant placed a platter of fresh, warm turnovers and a silver pot of steaming coffee before them. Tyler watched him fill her cup, acutely aware that Gray, sitting across from her, was observing her every movement with those azure eyes of his. She studiously sipped the savory brew, pretending not to notice.

"We'll be arriving in New Orleans later this afternoon, Tyler," he remarked, lifting his coffee cup to drink. His casual revelation thoroughly captured her interest.

"Really? Will Chase be there?"

"I'm afraid not. But you shouldn't have long to wait. He'll probably arrive in the next few days."

"I see," she said, wondering where she would stay in the meantime. Gray seemed to know what she was thinking, which disconcerted her.

"I've assured him that you're welcome to be my guest until he arrives. Stone acquired a house for us when he was in New Orleans to see Carlisle earlier this month." His smile came again, easy and relaxed, as if their bizarre past had never occurred. "My sister will be our chaperone, which would probably amuse most of our acquaintances back home." He looked down to dribble cream into his cup. "I think you'll like her, though. She's almost eighteen, and now and again something about you reminds me of her."

Tyler was curious about how she might resemble his younger sister, but feeling silly about asking that question, she casually remarked, "Carlisle is such an unusual name. And your name, too, really, and Stone's are all quite out of the ordinary."

Gray looked down at his plate, and at first Tyler thought he considered her observation rude. But when he raised his gaze to her, his smile was pleasant.

"Mother was a romantic, I guess. Before we were born, a party of English lords visited a family near where we lived. Lord Charles Carlisle, Lord Reginald Gray, and Lord Wilbur Stone. She thought the three of them were grand and elegant, so she decided to name us after them."

"I see," Tyler said. "I was named after my mother's aunt."

"Tyler is a very pretty name. It fits you."

Tyler couldn't repress her pleased smile, but their conversation had given her an opening for discussing his past. She took it. "Were all three of you born in Chicago?"

"No, we came to Chicago when I was eleven. Would you like to meet Carlisle today? She will graduate from her convent school this afternoon, and I would be delighted to have you accompany me."

Tyler was quick to note how he had maneuvered the conversation away from his family's past. She wondered why, but she was more than interested in meeting Carlisle Kincaid, especially if the girl reminded Gray of herself.

"Thank you, I'd like that," Tyler murmured, thinking how horrible it must be to live in a nunnery and move in long, silent lines behind black-habited sisters, as she had seen the young convent girls do in St Louis. *She* would surely die in such a place. Thank goodness Uncle Burl hadn't been a believer and had chosen to teach her himself. If Tyler were Carlisle Kincaid, and Gray had sent her to a convent, she would certainly hate him forever. She wondered how Carlisle felt about her brother.

At half past two o'clock that afternoon, the train finally chugged into New Orleans. Tyler was beside herself with excitement. Just to get off the rocking, clacking metal beast was a wonderful prospect, not to mention leaving the intimate confines of Gray's private coach.

The more time she spent alone with Gray Kincaid, the more he affected her in perverse, alarming ways. It was simply astounding, since she had hated him for years. Her fervent hope was that Chase would soon take her away from the churning, internal turmoil she experienced every time Gray's clear blue gaze settled on her face.

She watched him as he picked up his tall beaver hat and gloves. For the graduation, he had donned a charcoal-colored jacket with waistcoat and trousers of pearl gray. He looked most handsome with his gray striped cravat folded neatly at his throat, and she eagerly followed him outside. He stepped to the ground, smiling as he assisted her from the railed platform.

Once Tyler was able to draw her attention from his bronzed face, the first thing she noticed about the city was the wonderfully warm air. The lovely smells and sights of awakening spring were everywhere. Her eyes roamed delightedly over the lush green banana tree leaning against a nearby brick wall where spidery ferns and bright red bougainvilleas filled rectangular flower boxes. It was hard to believe that snow had covered the ground in Illinois the day she had been carried aboard the train in her casket.

"Come on, Tyler, we're running late, but we can make it if we hurry."

Tyler had to run to keep pace with him, but she didn't mind. Her pleasure at being in the South again was intoxicating, bringing a happy smile to her lips. Louisiana was said to be very much like southern Mississippi, at least in climate and weather, and the bright sun felt absolutely wonderful when she tilted her wide-brimmed white hat to let the warmth kiss her face. Moments later, Gray assisted her into a large, open carriage that stood for hire at a busy intersection near the depot. As Tyler arranged her cumbersome pannier and skirt of pink-sprigged white silk around her on the well-worn black leather seat, Gray settled opposite her.

"Tell me, Tyler, have you ever robbed anyone from New Orleans?" he asked a moment later as the hired hack rattled briskly along the narrow, shaded avenue. Tyler started guiltily at his words, her gaze moving from the quaint stucco houses with their lovely iron galleries to fasten warily on his face. But she relaxed when she found his eyes warm with humor.

"Not lately, but I've only just arrived," she replied flippantly, presenting Gray with a dimpled smile that earned a low laugh from him.

In truth, Tyler had never been to the old French-settled city at the mouth of the Mississippi River, and she found the narrow, cobbled streets and galleried pastel houses as unique as her father had once described them to her, upon his return from a slave-buying trip before the war.

Thoughts of her father sobered her, making her remember that she was laughing and joking with the very man who had caused his death. Guilt flooded over her, numbing her to Gray's efforts to be friendly. She reached into her drawstring reticule and retrieved the globe. She shook it, watching the flakes swirl, and hardened her heart against him. Soon she felt strong enough to resist the easy charm he was exhibiting. The remainder of the ride to Carlisle Kincaid's convent school passed in heavy silence.

Located just off Bourbon Street, the Sacred Heart Convent of the Creoles had been erected in the old square of the city, which Gray told Tyler was called the Vieux Carré. A tall white stone wall, pockmarked with age and decorated with unusual bow-and-arrow ironwork and a barred portcullis, now raised, guarded the entrance. Tyler felt a shudder of distaste as their carriage rolled to a stop. The place looked just like a jail, she thought. She couldn't imagine young girls actually living inside such cold, austere walls.

She looked at the other fine conveyances lining the narrow thoroughfare of Dumaine Street. Knots of elegantly dressed men and silk-skirted ladies with feather-decked bonnets were moving along the curbstones, the men no doubt intent upon viewing their darling daughters emerge from their final day of finishing school, ready now, Tyler surmised, to set about the more important task of attaining suitable husbands. It was a wealthy crowd, and Tyler realized the young graduates must be the crème de la crème of New Orleans society. She smiled to herself. If he were still alive, her uncle Burl would no doubt be casing the strolling couples, looking for the one with the fattest wallet and finest frock coat and cane.

"You've become very quiet," Gray observed as he lifted Tyler to the ground. "Do convents make you nervous?"

"I'd be nervous only if I had a brother who made me live in one," she answered breezily, detecting the sarcasm in his question. She was definitely more comfortable with his anger than she had been with his levity. He didn't answer, and nothing else passed between them as they entered the gates of the nunnery.

To Tyler's relief, the interior courtyard was not nearly as stern and forbidding as the outer walls. Instead, neat flower beds of yellow-and-white jonquils were set out in orderly precision, while purple wisteria climbed the white walls. Tyler wondered if the Sisters were members of some gardening order, then looked up as a shrill squeal rang out, followed by peals of high-pitched giggles. She soon realized the young graduates were being lined up beneath the lofty arches of the cloister colonnade for their procession. Perhaps it wasn't such a strict, constrained place after all, Tyler decided, though she still wouldn't want to live there.

As Gray seated Tyler on one of he white chairs set in rows upon the grass, then took the seat next to hers, the first tinkling chords of a piano hushed the buzzing conversation of the onlookers. Smiling girls began their graceful walk toward the dais, which was built several feet off the ground. They all moved with suitable decorum and were dressed identically, in plain white graduation robes and shoulder-length headdresses similar to the staid wimples of novice nuns. Tyler scanned the line of young women, trying to pick out one who resembled Gray or Stone Kincaid.

"There's Carlisle," Gray whispered, leaning close. "The last one there, nearest to us."

Tyler couldn't see Gray's sister well, but she could tell Carlisle Kincaid was slightly taller than most of her friends. She looked prim and sweet with her hands folded prayerfully in front of her, and Tyler watched with interest until she sat down in the back row.

Fortunately, the ceremony was brief, the longest part a lengthy prayer from the Mother Superior, an elderly, flushed-faced nun named Andrea Mary. Next came the presentation of the red-ribboned diplomas to each deserving young lady, every one of whom received enthusiastic applause from family and friends.

While the program progressed, Tyler sat wondering what it would have been like to receive a formal education alongside young women like Carlisle Kincaid. She had never known another girl near her age, except for fleeting encounters aboard steamboats or trains. Rose Point had been much too isolated for close friendships, and her uncle had always discouraged alliances with fellow travelers, unless they were marks. It was too dangerous, he said; she might be remembered by witnesses who could identify her.

In any case, she would never have traded her free and easy years with her uncle for a boring bunch of nuns and giggling girls. So engrossed was she in her own thoughts that she hardly realized the program had ended until Gray pulled her to her feet and led her toward his sister.

"Carly!" he called when they had almost reached her. As the young girl turned, he laughed. "God, let me look at you!"

Tyler watched him hold his sister out at arm's length, beaming down at her. Carlisle smiled up at him, then hugged him.

"Oh, Gray, I'm so glad you made it!" she cried. "I didn't think you were going to get here in time to see me graduate!"

"I promised, didn't I? I wouldn't have missed it for anything."

Tyler watched them, thinking that, up close, Carlisle Kincaid had the most celestial-looking face she had ever laid eyes on. Her hair was completely hidden by her head scarf, so Tyler had no idea of its color, but the stark white cloth drew attention to her small, heart-shaped face. Carlisle's eyes were large and pale sea green, with long black eyelashes. Her skin was flawlessly clear and had a natural flush beneath high cheekbones. She was so pretty that Tyler felt she could have posed for an angel in one of the paintings by Rubens Tyler had once seen in the City Museum in New York.

"I'm so proud of you, Carly," Gray was saying now. "Mother Andrea Mary told us you've been a model of decorum. I was afraid I'd made a mistake by sending you so far away, but I guess it was the right thing to do, after all. Have you forgiven me yet?"

"Oh, of course I have. It wasn't so bad here once I got used to it," Carlisle admitted shyly. "And I've made lots of new friends. But I did miss you and Stone terribly."

"We missed you, too, and I can't tell you how much we're looking forward to having you home with us again. Charles sends his love, of course."

"Is he well? And Betsy, too?" Then Carlisle's green gaze found Tyler.

"Yes, he's fine, and Betsy's about to acquire a stepmother, if my guess is right. But let me introduce you to our guest. This is Tyler MacKenzie. She'll be staying with us here in New Orleans until her cousin arrives to meet her. Tyler, this is my sister, Carlisle."

"How do you do," Carlisle murmured politely, stretching out her hand toward Tyler. "I am very pleased to make your acquaintance."

"How do you do," Tyler returned, surprised to be offered a handshake by another woman. Even more surprising, Carlisle Kincaid had a very firm grip.

"Well, come along, I've got a hired buggy waiting for us. I have to stop by the bank to meet with Bob Winston for a little while, but then I want us all to have supper together so we can catch up. I'm very proud of you, Carly."

"Thank you, Gray. That sounds wonderful," Carlisle answered in her low, calm voice.

Once inside the carriage, Tyler sat back silently as brother and sister chatted about Stone and their other friends in Chicago, most of whom Tyler had never met. She was already beginning to feel uncomfortable in the other girl's presence. Carlisle was so cloyingly sweet that Tyler was surprised honey wasn't dripping off her. Once the perfect Miss Carly learned about Tyler's unsavory past, she would probably swoon dead away. Somehow that image amused Tyler, and she secretly vowed to tell Carly all about herself, just to see the scandalized expression on the girl's seraphic face.

When the driver stopped before a three-story yellow brick structure on Canal Street, Gray swung easily down to the pavement and regarded each girl in turn.

"This appointment won't take long, but there's no need to bore you ladies with it. I'll tell the driver to take you to the house. It's at the corner of Third and Prytania, and I telegraphed the staff yesterday to have it ready for us. You can take the afternoon to rest or get ready for tonight."

"Yes, Gray," Carlisle said obediently.

Yes, Gray, Tyler mocked her inwardly, annoyed at the way Carlisle kowtowed to her big brother. Just to show him that she didn't intend to be as pliable as his sister, she said nothing.

"Until later," he said, contemplating her for an extra moment before he handed the driver a coin and gave him their destination.

As the old Negro driver in his black-satin top hat

slapped the reins across the horse's broad brown back, the two young women looked at each other. Carlisle smiled sweetly but didn't speak, so Tyler felt obligated to break the silence. How tiresome to be saddled with such a namby-pamby girl until Chase came.

"You don't look much like your brothers," she ventured, unable to think of anything else to say to a girl with whom she clearly had nothing in common.

"No, I look like my mother," Carlisle told her, presenting her with another sugar-coated smile. "I guess you think Gray's the most wonderful man in the world, don't you?"

Tyler stared at her, wanting to laugh at the absurdity of that question. Carlisle would find out the truth about Tyler's hostile relationship with Gray soon enough. Why shouldn't Tyler be the one to set her straight?

"He's about as wonderful as swallowing pepper," she answered casually, watching for astonishment to overtake Carlisle Kincaid's face. To her surprise, however, Carlisle laughed, and loudly at that.

"So you don't like him? Indeed? What luck! Most of his women trip over their tongues if he barely gives them a glance."

Tyler's jaw dropped, and she stared at Carlisle with the exact look of astonishment that she had striven to engender upon the other girl's face. She was even more shocked as Carlisle suddenly pulled off the white scarf, releasing a tumbling cascade of golden-red hair, and sent the headgear unceremoniously flying over the side of the buggy, to flutter to the street like a large, wounded albatross.

"Lord, it's good to get rid of that silly old thing! I hate it with a red passion! It's hot as Hades and it hides my hair. My hair's my best feature, don't you think?"

Tyler stared incredulously at the girl across from

her, then began to laugh as Carlisle pulled open the buttons of her saintly robe and squirmed out of it. Underneath, she wore a stylish, scoop-necked gown of apricot watered silk.

"You won't tell Gray, will you, Tyler?" Carlisle asked, pinching her cheeks to give them more color. "If you do, he'll probably send me back to that horrid place for another year of droning prayers and rosary beads."

Tyler laughed again. Suddenly she liked Carlisle Kincaid very much. "No, I won't tell him. I was thinking all along that he was cruel to make you go there. I thought you'd probably hate him for it."

"Hate Gray? Oh, no, he always means well and loves me dearly. But sometimes he thinks he's my father instead of my brother. Actually, he didn't have much choice after I almost got arrested in Chicago."

"Arrested? Whatever for?"

"Nothing. That's what's so provoking. I was merely parading in front of City Hall with Mrs. Stanton and some other women from the National Suffrage Association. Have you heard of them? We were trying to make President Grant give the women of this country their suffrage. For pity's sake, where would all these men be without their mothers and wives and sisters? Don't you agree?"

"Yes! I surely do!"

"Oh, you and I are going to have a jolly time together!" Carlisle proclaimed delightedly. "And to think I took you for one of Gray's silly, addlepated conquests. I mean the ones who lie down and let him walk roughshod over them, then thank him for it. I just don't understand women like that, do you?"

"No!" Tyler agreed heartily, then had to ask, "Does Gray have a lot of women?"

It was Carlisle's turn to laugh. "Does a tomcat prowl?" she replied with a sly grin, then grew serious as she leaned back to contemplate Tyler.

"You're the one who fell through the ice, aren't you?"

Tyler stiffened. "You know about that?"

"Yes. Stone told me. He said you were out to swindle our family, so I must tell you I was amazed when Gray introduced you back at the convent. Is that true?"

Tyler felt a prickle of conscience, but tried to ignore it. Why should she care what Carlisle Kincaid thought?

"Yes, I did try to swindle your family, but all I wanted was what your brother stole from me during the war. He took my plantation and everything else my family owned. I'll hate him as long as I live." She started to add her father's death to Gray's crimes, but couldn't seem to say it aloud.

"Gray did all that? Goodness, no wonder you detest him. I certainly don't blame you. I'd hate anybody who hurt Gray or Stone. Actually, I was fairly young when my brothers were in the army. I stayed with Dr. Bond and his daughter, Betsy, but I know terrible things happened. Neither one of my brothers acted the same when he came home—especially Stone. He has the most dreadful nightmares sometimes and shouts out loud enough to awaken everyone in the house. He was in some dreadful prison for months and months, you know, and now he can't stand to be cooped up anywhere, not even in a carriage like this one." Carlisle's high spirits seemed to plunge considerably at the thought of her brother's suffering. "I'm frightfully sorry about your plantation and all, and I bet Gray is, too, now that the war's over. Did your swindle work?" she asked abruptly.

"No. Stone told Gray about me before I could get away with it."

"Well, I guess I should be glad about that, because he *is* my brother. But I'm not going to hold it against you. I'd probably do the very same if I were you."

Tyler could barely believe her ears, but Carlisle gave her no time to respond. She suddenly stood up to tug at the back of the driver's coattail.

"Driver, please stop at the St. Charles Hotel on the way home," she ordered crisply, as if she was quite accustomed to handling servants.

Sitting down again, Carlisle turned her full attention back to Tyler. "I have some friends staying there. Actually, it's my best friend from the convent and her brother, Javier. He is so dreadfully handsome that I get gooseflesh just thinking about him. They're from Mexico, and they've asked me to come visit them for the summer. That's why I've been so sweet to Gray. He'll never let me go if he thinks I haven't changed my ways. You did say you wouldn't tell on me, didn't you?" she asked, suddenly worried.

"Oh, no, not a word. I promise."

"Oh, look, there's Javier and Arantxa now. Driver, pull over, quick!"

Tyler had to giggle at Carlisle's startling transformation in the mere ten minutes since Gray had left the coach. It was funny now to think that she had likened Carlisle to an angel.

"Arantxa!" Carlisle called, grabbing the top of the door for support as the coach lurched to a sudden stop at the curb. The couple strolling along the board sidewalk toward the big hotel turned and smiled upon sight of Carlisle. "How does it feel to finally escape from the Mother Dragon?" she cried out excitedly, causing a few matronly passersby to turn and look at her with disapproval.

"Wonderful, *querida*!" the raven-haired Mexican girl answered, her dark eyes shining. "Did you ask your brother for permission to come home with us?"

"No, he's not buttered up enough yet. But Tyler here is going to help me, isn't that lucky? Come, Javier, and meet my new friend, Tyler MacKenzie."

The man with Arantxa stepped forward. Tyler

thought him very handsome with his swarthy dark skin and piratical good looks.

"Tyler, these are my best friends in New Orleans, Javier and Arantxa Perez. They're twins, can you tell?" Carlisle went on. "And they have led the most exciting life you could ever imagine. Their family even fought the Juaristas during their revolution."

Tyler immediately grew wary, remembering she'd heard that Chase was a friend of Benito Juarez, the current President of Mexico.

"I'll send you a message as soon as I've got Gray softened up enough for your visit. But we really can't linger here, or he might beat us back to the house."

"All right, Carlita. But remember, our ship to Matamoros sails next Saturday. You must be ready by then."

"That'll give me plenty of time," Carlisle replied without the least concern. "Gray already thinks I'm ready to take the veil, I've been so goody-goody around him."

Tyler laughed with the other young people, thinking it was going to be wonderful fun to associate with Carlisle and her friends until Chase arrived. Perhaps she could even see them after her cousin took her back to Mexico with him! Her future began to look bright after all. And to think that she had dreaded her stay in New Orleans!

11

Gray strolled through the airy, whitewashed chambers of his latest real estate acquisition in the American district, admiring the fine furnishings which Stone had purchased when he had last been in town. Gray was more than pleased with their new investment. Something about the big, rambling house reminded him of the one they owned in Chicago, and made him feel more at home than he usually did in other cities. Only the French-inspired black wrought-iron galleries across the front and back were different. In any case, the dwelling would do nicely whenever any of them visited New Orleans.

He paused in the front parlor, his hand resting on the banister of the steep, narrow staircase that rose to the second story. He could hear Carlisle and Tyler laughing in the dining room, and he moved toward the sliding doors, thinking they had certainly become fast friends in a short time. Knowing both of them as well as he did, he wasn't sure if their quick camaraderie was good news or bad. His misgivings about the twosome increased a degree when their giggling and whispering stopped the moment he appeared before them.

"Good evening, ladies."

153

Carlisle flashed him her usual bright smile. Tyler regarded him expressionlessly, informing him mutely that her ill feelings toward him had not changed a whit.

"I'm so pleased you brought Tyler along with you," Carlisle told him. "You'll never imagine what we've discovered."

"What would that be?"

"That we'll both be in Mexico at the same time! Isn't that splendid? Tyler said her cousin's on his way to fetch her, and Arantxa's family has invited me to come for a visit in Mexico City. You will let me go, won't you, Gray?"

Gray beheld her shining green eyes and was glad to see her a trifle more animated than she had been at her graduation ceremony. She had acted so subdued and docile that he had feared the nuns had broken her spirit. He had enrolled her in the convent school to calm her down a bit, at least to the point where she would observe propriety. But without her sparkling eyes and lively manner, Carlisle would not be Carlisle.

"I was expecting you to come home to Chicago with me," he said. "You've been sorely missed, you know. Stone's in Denver right now, but he's planning to return when you get there."

"Oh, then perhaps I should go home with you," Carlisle agreed quickly. "I shouldn't put off my decision anyway, not just to please Arantxa."

Gray sat down on a red satin settee opposite the girls, who'd installed themselves on a long, tapestry-stitched bench in front of the fireplace. "What are you talking about? What decision?"

"Why, to take the veil, of course," Carlisle replied innocently. Tyler immediately looked down, hiding her amusement.

Gray, however, made no such attempt. He laughed out loud. "Don't be absurd, Carly."

Carlisle's face quickly assumed an injured expression. "How can you laugh at such a serious commitment, Gray? It took many hours of prayer and meditation to arrive at this decision, but the good Sisters helped persuade me that their simple life would give me an inner peace I'd find nowhere else.''

Tyler stole a quick peek at the incredulous look on Gray's face. Carlisle had been right. Her brother didn't like the idea of his sister becoming a nun— not in the least.

"Over my dead body," he informed Carlisle in the implacable tones he had used on occasion with Tyler.

Tyler waited for Carlisle's reaction, deciding that she was extremely skilled in manipulating her bossy older brother. Perhaps Tyler herself would be wise to listen and learn.

"But, Gray, I was sure you'd be pleased. You're the one who insisted I go to the Sisters for instruction.''

"To be trained as a dutiful wife and mother, for God's sake, not a nun! I won't allow it, Carly. You'll thank me in time, I promise you.''

Carlisle looked as if she were about to burst into tears, and Tyler watched Gray reach out to console her, just as Carlisle had predicted he would moments before he had joined them.

"Perhaps you should visit your friends in Mexico after all. The journey would give you time to think this through. I know you'll come to realize what a mistake you'd be making.''

"Perhaps you're right," Carlisle replied with a hard sigh, her face a study of dejection. "Arantxa's brother, Javier, would like to come by in the next few days to extend the invitation from his parents. Would you see him?''

"Of course. I'll be working here at the house all week. If I deem him a suitable escort, I don't see why you can't go visit them, at least for a little while.''

"Thank you, Gray," Carlisle murmured, her eyes

brimming with gratitude. "You're always so good to me."

Tyler was impressed. She suddenly wondered if the nuns had instructed Carlisle in the Thespian arts. She looked up as Gray turned to her.

"And how do you like New Orleans thus far?"

"I hardly know yet. Have you any idea when Chase might arrive?" Escape sounded wonderful after so long in Gray Kincaid's disquieting presence. Once she was safely away, she would never have to think about him again.

"Actually, there was a message from him waiting for me this afternoon at the bank. Apparently Chase left Mexico City nearly a week ago, so he should arrive any day now."

"I'll be very glad to see him."

"As will I. We have a good deal to talk about," Gray answered in his unperturbed way—which never failed to ruffle Tyler's own composure.

During supper, Tyler left the table chatter to Carlisle and Gray, reverting to silence once again. A wonderful flaming cherry pudding was served last, but instead of joining the two young women for the dessert, Gray pulled out his heavy gold pocket watch and snapped it open to check the time. He stood.

"If the two of you will excuse me, I have an engagement this evening. I'll be home very late, so I'll bid you good night now."

Tyler and Carlisle watched him take his leave, then gazed across the table at each other.

"You did that very well. Uncle Burl would have welcomed you as a pupil."

"And I would have liked him, I know, after hearing about all the adventures you had with him. He must have been the most daring man imaginable. I always did think stories about Robin Hood were romantic."

"Yes," Tyler agreed. But she hadn't told Carlisle about John Mooney. Guilt sent a tingle up her spine again, and she recalled Gray's words on the train when he had called Burl Lancaster a cold and calculating corrupter of children. Had her uncle really been as bad as Gray had said? Were their activities plain theft and robbery instead of good works for the Southern cause?

Angry at herself for doubting her beloved uncle, Tyler gave herself a mental shake. Why did Gray have to get her so confused about everything? What did he know about it anyway? He had never even met her uncle. Besides, Gray was a Yankee. Of course he wouldn't understand their Southern sympathies.

"I hope Javier makes a good impression when he comes," said Carlisle. "That's all it'll take now for Gray to let me go. And I'm determined to hear exactly what they say."

"But won't they want to talk privately?" Tyler asked.

"Yes, but Gray will take him to his office. He receives everyone in there, and I already discovered a trellis on the side of the house that's sturdy enough to hold my weight. If I raise the window before Javier arrives, I'll be able to listen to every word. Arantxa says Javier's taken with me already."

"But Gray's chosen a room on the second floor for his office."

Carlisle shrugged off Tyler's protest. "No need to worry. I'm not in the least fearful of heights. Will you help me convince Gray if he isn't impressed with Javier?"

"Gray doesn't listen to me. He thinks I'm stupid and a thief. A liar, too."

"He also thinks you're beautiful. I can tell by the way he stares at you when you aren't looking. Surely you've sensed it?"

"He's just afraid I'm going to steal something."

Carlisle laughed. "Oh, no, it's not that. I've seen the way he looks at women he finds attractive. Actually, I'm surprised he's taking some other woman out tonight, with you right here to ogle all evening."

"Does he have a woman here in New Orleans, then? A special one, I mean?" Tyler asked quickly, then felt angry at herself for caring.

"Sure he does. Gray has women nearly everywhere he goes, and they all behave as if he's the emperor of Rome. It's really amusing to watch the way they carry on around him."

For some reason, Tyler didn't think it was amusing. She was wondering where he was going and with whom, and that made her furious all over again. What was the matter with her anyway? Hadn't he called her every terrible name in the book, dressed her down like some naughty child? He hated her, and she hated him. She hoped Chase came that very night so she would never have to lay eyes on Gray Kincaid again.

"Did you see much of Stone before he left for Colorado?" Carlisle asked.

Tyler shook her head. "No, he just acted the telltale on me and left."

She smiled, but Carlisle's face took on the most somber expression she had yet seen.

"I'm very worried about Stone, Tyler."

Tyler was surprised. "Oh?"

"It's just that he's changed so much since the war." She frowned. "When he was here to see me, he was even worse than I remembered—so quiet, but with that horrid, faraway expression on his face. Sometimes I fear I'll never have my old laughing, teasing Stone back."

Carlisle's face grew more melancholy, and Tyler reached over to lay a consoling hand on her sleeve.

"Whatever happened to make him change so?"

Carlisle sighed. "The Rebels put him in some awful prison called Andersonville. He must have suffered dreadfully there." A long shiver shook her. "You should have seen him when he came back from down south. He'd lost so much weight that he looked like a skeleton. That's when he got that terrible lost look in his eyes, too. Did you notice it?"

Tyler nodded. "Yes, I thought he seemed angry. Gray said he was betrayed."

"Yes, by a friend, too. I never met the man, but I know his name is Emerson Clan and that he's from Alabama. He and Stone graduated from West Point together. I can remember Stone mentioning him often in his letters from the academy. They shared the same dormitory room."

"How did he betray him?"

"Gray didn't think I was old enough to hear all the details. But I do know they were both lieutenants in the same unit when the war broke out."

"I thought you said Clan was from Alabama."

"He was, but he claimed allegiance to the North— at least that's what he made everyone believe. He was really selling information to the Confederates."

"Selling it! What a scoundrel!"

"Anyway, Stone figured it out after the Rebels had intercepted his unit's movements on several different occasions, and he turned Clan over to their commanding officer. He was to be hanged, but he managed to escape during a skirmish." Carlisle shook her head. "That's when Stone and most of his men were captured and sent to that frightful place. I'm not sure, but from what I've overheard, I think that once the prison officials found out Clan had been working for the South, they made him a guard. He treated the prisoners abominably, especially Stone. That's why Stone wants him so much."

"I'm sorry, Carlisle. I had no idea. Perhaps Stone will find him soon. Then he'll be himself again."

"He's been searching for him ever since he returned home from prison. That's the real reason he was visiting down here last month. He said he came to see me, but he also told me he's got Pinkerton men looking for Clan, too. Have you ever heard of them? Mr. Pinkerton is from Chicago."

Just the name gave Tyler a chill. The Pinkerton

detectives had been Burl Lancaster's most feared adversaries.

"Have they found out anything for him?"

"Only that Clan has a cousin on a farm near Mobile. His name is Dillard Weeks. They've been watching him, but no one thinks Clan will show up. He's very cunning, they say. Every time Stone gets a lead, Clan disappears before he can get there. I just wish there were something I could do."

The well-oiled gears inside Tyler's head began to turn, searching for a solution, and she sat thoughtfully for a few minutes.

"Is Clan very dangerous?"

Carlisle brightened. "You've come up with an idea, haven't you, Tyler? I can see it on your face. Tell me, please. I'd do anything to help Stone. I can't bear the way he's become. When I lived at home he awoke from nightmares nearly every night. I can still hear those horrendous yells."

"Well, once Uncle Burl did entice a man into a clever trap. It might work for Stone. Is Clan dangerous?" she repeated.

"Not too dangerous, I shouldn't think. Just dishonest and greedy. Everyone thought him quite the Southern gentleman until he was found out. Tell me what your uncle did."

"Well, one of Uncle Burl's friends, a man named Smith who'd once been his partner, managed to steal his wallet one night during a poker game. In order to get it back, Uncle Burl figured out a way for Mr. Smith to come to us without knowing it was a plot to recover our money."

"Did it work?" Carlisle asked in excitement.

"Oh, yes. Most of my uncle's ideas were good ones."

"Tell me how you did it!"

"We sent this official-looking letter to him, telling him my grandfather had died and left his uncle five thousand dollars. Then we informed him that his uncle had recently passed away, too, making Mr.

Smith the beneficiary. You wouldn't believe how fast he came running. He'd never seen me before, and since I used an assumed name, he didn't realize my connection to Uncle Burl. I got his wallet, as well as my uncle's.'' Tyler smiled. ''They had a good laugh about it later. They were really very good friends. They just liked to outdo each other.''

''But, Tyler, that's a perfect plan! I could write to Clan's cousin and tell him about a bequeathment. My goodness, I could even make him go straight to Chicago to collect it. Then all Stone would have to do is take Clan to jail.''

''Now wait, Carly. You have to be very careful with this kind of thing. It's more difficult than it sounds. Where would you have him report to collect his inheritance?''

Carlisle paused, thinking. ''Well, why not send him to our house on Lincoln Avenue? No one's ever there but Gray or Stone, and either of them could apprehend Clan with no trouble. You've seen how big and strong they both are.''

''No, that wouldn't work. You'd need him to come to a lawyer's office or somewhere like that, or he might realize Stone's involved. You said yourself that Clan was clever.''

''I still believe it would work. Anyway, why don't we tell Gray about it and see what he thinks?''

''Oh, no,'' Tyler objected at once. ''He's already angry with me for robbing him. He might press charges against me if he found out I was putting such ideas in your head.''

''Oh, pooh, he wouldn't dare. He wants to help Stone even more than I do. That's the very worst part, you know, that neither of us can help our brother.''

''But these kind of schemes take a lot of thought and careful planning. Believe me, Carly, I know what I'm talking about.''

Carlisle's enthusiasm faded into disappointment. ''Oh, all right. I won't do it. But I am going to tell

Stone about it the very next time I see him. I'm sure he'd be willing to try anything to catch up with that old Clan." She sighed deeply. "Do you have any tricks that would make Gray like Javier?"

"No," Tyler answered, glad Carlisle was off the subject of the plot to capture her brother's enemy. Emerson Clan sounded like a sly man. She was not even sure her uncle would have tangled with him. He'd always taught her to choose her victims carefully.

"Let's go upstairs, and I'll help you unpack," suggested Carlisle. "Perhaps we can think of a way to sneak down to the St. Charles tomorrow without Gray knowing so we can meet Arantxa and Javier."

Tyler followed her, thinking that sounded like a wonderful idea.

Chase Lancaster stopped on Third Street and peered down the cool, tree-lined road in the Garden District. The sun-dappled thoroughfare led between mansions set like jewels in well-tended emerald lawns. His destination lay three houses down on the adjacent corner—a rambling white stucco house with graceful black iron porches. A sudden breeze caught his dark blond hair, feathering it back before catching hold of some wispy Spanish moss on a gigantic limb above his head, making the long, ghoulish shrouds sway.

As Chase stepped off the wide wooden sidewalk, called a banquette by the inhabitants of the city, he felt certain he would soon be delivered of the worry which had burdened him for so long.

The team of detectives he had hired had combed the country for months looking for his cousin, with no success. Chase knew he owed Gray Kincaid a heavy debt of gratitude for contacting him instead of relinquishing Tyler to the authorities. From the sound of things, she had given his poor friend enough cause to throw her into a cell himself.

Although Tyler had been nothing but trouble of

late, Chase was eager to see her again. He'd been
fond of his younger cousin since the days when they
had played together as children on the vast verdant
lawns of Rose Point, before his mother had left his
father.

As he crossed the quiet residential street, he came
upon the low, flat-topped stucco wall which separated the shade-splashed yard of Gray Kincaid's big
white house from the thoroughfare. He strode along,
admiring the setting, impressed with the lush fo-
liage of the Louisiana delta, especially after a long,
hot journey across the dusty ocher plains of Mexico.

Suddenly, a glimpse of bright blue caught his attention. Stopping, he leaned his palms on the
smooth top of the wall and peered through the long
streamers of wind-stirred gray moss adorning the
trees. His eyes widened in disbelief as he realized a
young woman was clinging precariously to a trellis
near the second-floor windows.

His first thought was that she was in trouble. He
wasted no time in vaulting the wall and moving
swiftly beneath the ancient live oaks. Keeping his
eyes locked on the damsel in distress, he had a sudden, sneaking suspicion that it was his cousin, Tyler, up to no good. She was certainly known far and
wide for her misdeeds.

As he rounded a high hedge of azaleas, however,
he saw a luxurious mass of wavy golden-red hair
caught up in a chignon, and realized it was not his
long-lost cousin.

From his vantage Chase's eyes were drawn inexorably to a pair of long, shapely legs, visible to mid-
thigh and clad only in thin white silk stockings. He
grinned at the scandalous manner in which the girl
had tucked her bulky skirts into her wide sash to
facilitate her climb.

Several steps brought Chase to where she had dis-
carded her petticoats, small padded pannier, and
dainty white satin pumps with perky blue bows on

the toes. The intimate apparel lay in a carelessly scattered heap at the tip of his leather boots.

As he watched her maneuver with some difficulty closer to an open casement window, apparently oblivious to his presence below, Chase realized with some amusement what she was up to. The little lady was eavesdropping on someone inside.

"Ahem," he said, loudly clearing his throat, then grinned when she jumped and almost lost her balance. A pair of shocked green eyes fastened on him, and to his further enjoyment, she vigorously shook one hand in an attempt to shoo him away.

"Do you need assistance up there, miss?" he called politely.

"Will you hush?" she hissed.

"I'm only concerned that you might fall and hurt yourself," he told her, obediently lowering his voice, thinking the high flush on the young woman's face certainly enhanced her angelic beauty. "It would be a pity to break such a lovely pair of legs."

The lady bristled, then glanced again at the open window before descending a few feet toward the ground. Chase watched in silent amusement as she glowered down at him.

"Would you stop looking up my dress?" she snapped. "What kind of man are you?"

"Red-blooded, I suppose," Chase replied, not about to take his eyes off such a splendid display.

"Who are you anyway?" she demanded in a shrill whisper. "If you were a gentleman, you'd stand back and let a lady climb down with a little modesty."

"You are referring to yourself when you say lady, I presume?" Chase asked, then gave a low laugh at the way she curled her slim nose. "Not many ladies I've met," he continued blithely, "would bare their legs and cling like a monkey to the side of their house."

"Monkey! Why, you big, rude—" she began, but in her anger her foot slipped, and she slid down a few slats before she could stop herself, alarming Chase enough to reach out and grab her around the knees.

"Let go of me, you idiot!" she cried furiously, but Chase only laughed. Her dark-lashed eyes were full of emerald fire as he lowered her to the ground, not exactly unaffected by the way her curvaceous body slid slowly over his loins.

Red-faced with rage, the girl shoved violently against his chest as soon as her feet touched the grass.

"How dare you?" she cried, jerking her skirts out of her sash. "What are you doing here anyway? This is private property! You're trespassing, and I can have you thrown in jail for being in my yard!"

"Carlisle! Carlisle!" rang an excited call from somewhere within the house, and both Chase and the girl turned as Tyler MacKenzie came racing around the corner, pink skirts flying.

"Quick! They're coming downstairs to look for you—" Tyler's frantic warning promptly died on her lips when she spied her cousin standing beside Carlisle. Her shock quickly turned to joy. "Chase! You've come!"

She flew into his arms with a great flurry of silk and fluttering ruffles, and Carlisle took a step back as Chase Lancaster swung Tyler off her feet. Carlisle frowned, not at all pleased to learn who he was. A boorish, obnoxious passerby was one thing, but now she would have to suffer his presence for the length of his stay as their guest.

A terrible thought hit her. What if he tattled to Gray about catching her eavesdropping? Gray would be furious with her and wouldn't let her go to Mexico! The uncouth blond-haired man was just loutish enough to tell on her!

"Oh, Carly, come, let me introduce you. This is my cousin, Chase Lancaster. Or have you already met him?"

"You might say that," Chase answered, grinning impertinently.

Carlisle's temper flared hotter as a pair of mocking dark blue eyes roamed up and down her figure, studying her as if she stood naked before him. Thinking he was the most arrogant, annoying man she had ever met, she nodded curtly and looked away from his handsome, sun-bronzed face, concentrating instead on slipping her stockinged feet into her pumps. As Chase and Tyler embraced again, Carlisle kicked her petticoats and pannier behind a bush. She certainly couldn't put them on now.

"Oh, Chase, I'm so glad you're here, I mean it. It's been so long. Carly's been wonderful, of course, but I can't wait to get away from Gray Kincaid."

Chase held her so he could look into her small, happy face. "I would think you'd be indebted to him for being so magnanimous with you. I understand you tried to rob him."

He noticed Tyler didn't deny it, and neither did she look willing to admit any gratitude. The sound of masculine voices from the front porch floated to where they stood, and Chase looked up as Gray Kincaid appeared on the side steps in the company of another man.

"Thank you for coming, Senor Perez," he was saying. He smiled when he caught sight of Chase. "Chase! It's good to see you again," he said, striding forward to pump Chase's hand.

"*Gracias*. It's been a long journey," Chase replied, noting how the coppery-haired beauty moved immediately toward the man named Perez and gave him a warm, melting smile.

Gray noticed Chase's interest, then seemed to remember his manners. "Please pardon my rudeness, Senor Perez. It just surprised me to see Chase here. Chase Lancaster, this is a countryman of yours, I believe, Senor Javier Perez. He and his sister are good friends of my sister, Carlisle."

Chase recognized the Perez name at once, though

he had not met the young man. He showed none of his dislike as he reached out to shake hands with the black-mustachioed Mexican youth.

"I've heard of your family, of course," he said.

Javier Perez met his gaze. "And your name is well known to me as well, Senor Lancaster. You are still the foreign advisor to El Presidente, no?"

"I am," Chase responded, glancing at Carlisle Kincaid in time to see her look of surprise. He wondered about her reaction as Gray spoke again.

"Let's go inside where we can talk," he suggested, noticing how Tyler was clinging to Chase's arm as if her long-awaited savior had finally come and she wasn't about to let him out of her sight. Gray, however, had different ideas.

"Perhaps you ladies will escort Senor Perez to the gate." He turned to Javier. "And again, sir, I assure you I will take your kind invitation under consideration. In any case, we certainly appreciate the generosity of your parents for extending their hospitality to Carly."

"You will let me go, won't you, Gray?" Carlisle asked anxiously, unable to bear not knowing.

"As I said, I will consider it," her brother answered. "Now, I'm sure Chase would like a spot of brandy after such a long trip."

"Indeed, I would," Chase agreed, glancing at Gray's sister again, his eyes still full of amusement. Her glare told him unequivocally that Miss Carlisle Kincaid didn't like him one bit.

Chase watched the flame-haired girl move gracefully down the path with Tyler and Javier Perez. He then followed Gray into the cool interior hall, wondering if the fair Carlisle's desire to visit Mexico was what had prompted her to hang on a trellis thirty feet in the air. Something in the way she had looked at the young Mexican made him think it was.

12

Not long after his unorthodox meeting with Carlisle Kincaid, Chase sat in the very room outside which she had eavesdropped so shamelessly. As Gray poured them both a snifter of brandy, Chase rose, moving across to the tall window casement. He leaned over the sash to make sure no beautiful young woman clung outside on the trellis now. All he saw below was a filmy white undergarment peeping from beneath an azalea shrub.

"Is something wrong?" Gray asked from behind him.

Chase turned and accepted the proffered glass.

"No. I'm just glad I'm here and Tyler is safe."

"I'd like to talk to you about Tyler, if you don't mind," Gray said as he sank into one of the elegant Chippendale chairs beside the white brick fireplace.

Chase selected a matching seat across from him. "Don't tell me she's concocted another plot," he said, fearful of what new, audacious scheme Gray would relate to him.

"No, not yet," Gray said with a grin that allowed Chase to relax. "But I keep my guard up."

Chase laughed. Gray didn't.

"I guess it's difficult for you to understand why

Tyler behaves as she does," Chase remarked, sipping his brandy and finding it of excellent quality.

"I understand her motives well enough. I've been driven by revenge a time or two in my life. What disturbs me more is that she doesn't seem to realize that what she's done is wrong."

"You would understand if you knew my father and the way he raised her."

"Tell me about him."

"My father was like two different men rolled into one. On the one hand, he was a rogue, a swindler, and a gambler, as crooked as the devil on Sunday. On the other hand, he was one of the most charming gentlemen you'd ever want to meet. I don't think there's a man or woman alive who ever met him and didn't like him—until he robbed them blind."

Gray smiled, thinking Chase could have been describing Tyler.

"Mother left him when I was just a boy, around eight years old, and it's a good thing she did, or I might have been his accomplice along with Tyler."

"When did Tyler go to live with him?"

"Her father committed suicide. Did you know that?"

"Yes," Gray answered. "Did she witness it?"

"No one knows for sure. Her mammy discovered his body at his desk in the library, but they didn't find Tyler until later that evening. She was hiding in a boot closet under the stairs, so they thought she probably either saw him do it or found his body. Either way, it was a terrible trauma for a twelve-year-old. She adored Colin."

Gray set down his glass and heaved a deep, frustrated sigh. "She blames me for his death, among other things."

"I know she does, and I can tell you why. From the moment she went to live with my father, he told her you were responsible. He encouraged her hatred. It gave him a way to control her. I think." He shook his head. "Once, during the war when I came

here to engender support for the Juaristas, I sought
Burl and Tyler out. They were living in Natchez
then, and I can remember hearing him promise Tyler that if she was good and learned all the things
he taught her, he would help her get even with the
man who was responsible for her father's death and
for taking Rose Point away from her. It was a reward
he held out to her, a goal in life.''

''My God, what kind of man would do that to a
girl like Tyler?''

''I don't know. I was so appalled at the way he
was raising her that I begged her to come live with
my mother and me in Mexico. Burl wouldn't hear of
her leaving him, and Tyler loved him too much to
go against his wishes. Now, I wish I'd found a way
to get her away from him.''

''I don't see how she could be devoted to him,''
Gray said.

''It's hard to say. He was complex and charis-
matic, and as unscrupulous as hell. He always told
Tyler that stealing and lying were all right if you
were doing them for a good reason, or to evil people
who deserved them. She told me that herself. I remember him asking her to memorize illegal acts as
if she were in a classroom learning sums.''

''What do you mean?''

''He taught her to break into safes, for one thing.''

''He must have been a good teacher. I ordered
mine from the best ironmonger in Philadelphia, and
it didn't faze her in the least,'' Gray remarked dryly.

''I know it's hard for you to believe, but my father
did love her, too. He protected her virtue like a true
Southern gentleman, I can vouch for that.'' Chase
hesitated, giving a slight shake of his head. ''Actually, Tyler is just another one of his victims. Inside,
she's as sweet and compassionate as other women
with proper upbringings. But she went to him when
she was vulnerable and unstable, and he used her.''

''You're the second person to tell me she's basically good. The woman she was traveling with, Harriet Stokely, said the same thing."

"I don't know the lady," Chase replied, swirling the rich-colored liquor in his glass, "but I'm glad I'm here and finally able to take Tyler home with me. I intend to undo all the things my father taught her. She's still young, and I've already decided to arrange a marriage for her as soon as possible. Probably to an older man, one who's understanding and kind, and who'll be patient with her. Once she has a husband who'll give her children and a home, I think she'll come around."

Chase watched as Gray suddenly stood and paced restlessly across the room to his desk. Neither spoke while Gray took several moments to select a pipe.

"Would you like a cigar?" he offered Chase, gesturing to an inlaid silver box on the mantelpiece.

"No, but I'll have another drink. This is excellent brandy. We don't get much French wine since we rid Mexico of Maximilian."

Gray nodded absently as he packed the bowl with fragrant tobacco. "I have a proposition for you, Chase—one I'm sure you'll find strange under the circumstances."

Chase waited expectantly.

"I want your permission to marry Tyler. Now, before you return to Mexico."

At first Chase could only stare at the man across the room. "Are you serious?"

"Yes."

"Why?"

Gray paused. "I guess I feel responsible for her. I did ruin her father and take her plantation."

Chase's brows drew down. "That was war, and regardless, feeling responsible is not a good reason for marriage. Do you love her?"

Gray stared out the windows into the high branches of the live oak trees and was quiet for long moments. "Perhaps I do, I don't know. I do know I want her and that I have ever since I first saw her, despite all she's done. I'd like to try to make up to her everything she's suffered since I bought Rose Point.''

"You own Rose Point?" Chase's surprise was evident.

"Yes, I acquired it when it was put up for auction during the war."

"Does Tyler know that?"

"Yes." Gray almost smiled. "She robbed my safe to buy it back from me. Ingenious scheme, was it not?"

Chase frowned. "Does Tyler want to marry you?"

Gray ran a restless hand through his hair. "Good God, no. She tells me every chance she gets that she hates me and will do so as long as she lives. I suppose that's one of the rote speeches Burl taught her?" he asked angrily.

Chase nodded. "Unfortunately, one of his most frequent, I'd say."

"Still, I think she'll accept the marriage in time. I can be patient when I want something badly enough. And I do want her, Chase."

The two men exchanged a serious look.

"I think you're asking for trouble," Chase felt obligated to warn him.

"Do you think I haven't thought of that?" Gray paced back and forth a few times, then stopped, tossing back the remainder of his brandy.

"I don't know, Gray. This is all so sudden. Why the hurry? Why not take some time to get to know each other?"

"Oh, come now, Chase, if we give Tyler time to think about it, she'll probably disappear forever. We both know she's not been exhibiting mature judgment up to this point. It's your decision, not hers."

"I know, but I don't want to see her unhappy. She's gone through enough suffering. I love my cousin, Gray."

"I give you my word of honor that I'll do my best to make her happy. And you know that I'm able to support her in luxury." He grinned. "Especially since all my finances were laid out for you in the secret report you had done on me when I was in Mexico last year."

"So you know? Sorry, Gray, but Juarez no longer takes chances. Mexico's been raped too many times by foreigners. We're very careful now about choosing allies. But Tyler's situation has nothing to do with your finances. She's going to throw a tantrum if we even suggest a betrothal to you." As Chase spoke, however, some instinct deep in his gut told him that Gray Kincaid was exactly the kind of husband Tyler needed. He was strong, honest, and honorable, and he looked more than anxious to have Chase's permission. If nothing else, he would take care of Tyler and keep her on the right side of the law.

"Then it's done, *amigo*," he said after a lengthy pause. "But I must say I dread like hell telling her."

Gray looked relieved and very pleased, which made Chase more confident that he was doing the right thing for Tyler.

"There's something else I need to know, Chase," Gray said, refilling his drink.

"What's that?"

"It's about Carlisle."

"Your sister?" Chase waited, ready and willing to discuss that fair subject.

"As you heard outside earlier, she's desperately eager to visit the Perez family in Mexico. Arantxa Perez was her roommate for the past year in Sacred Heart. But I know little about her, except that she comes from a wealthy family living in Mexico City. Do you know if they can be trusted to chaperone Carlisle properly? Javier, the man you met in the yard, is to escort the two girls to his parents' home."

"I wouldn't trust him with any sister of mine," Chase answered without hesitation. "Javier's known to be wild. There are even rumors he runs with a revolutionary faction, though I can't say for sure."

"Then I will have to forbid the trip. Carly will be disappointed, but she'll get over it," Gray decided, downing the last swallow of his brandy as the dinner bell rang downstairs. "Now we had better go down and join the ladies. We can tell them our decisions while we dine."

"I think, *amigo*, that I will give you the honor of informing them."

"Are you sure they're still in the study?" Tyler asked Carlisle, alarmed at how long Chase had been closeted with Gray Kincaid.

"Yes. I listened at the keyhole for a little while just before I came to your room," Carlisle replied. "Unfortunately, I couldn't hear much."

"Oh," Tyler said, arranging her skirts carefully before she sat down on a small sofa. "What do you suppose they're talking about?"

"That nasty cousin of yours is probably blurting out every detail about my eavesdropping, the wretch. He is certainly the rudest man I ever met."

Tyler noted how the angry flush on Carlisle's face made her light green eyes sparkle.

"Chase isn't so disagreeable once you get to know him. Truly, he isn't. You just got off on the wrong foot with him. He's always been special to me, even when we were little. He's a lot older, of course, but I remember Chase letting me ride in front of him on his pony when he came to visit at Rose Point. And he tried to teach me Spanish, like he and his mother spoke, but I wasn't very good at it." She smiled, recalling some of the most pleasant memories of her childhood.

Carlisle sniffed disdainfully, not the least bit impressed. If Chase Lancaster was once a nice boy, he'd certainly outgrown it.

"All I can say is I pity you for having to go home with him. I'd die if I had to be around him for more than a minute at a time."

Tyler couldn't defend her cousin further, because

Gray opened the sliding doors. She immediately lowered her gaze from the pair of pure blue eyes that sought her out, but not before she had seen some emotion in them. What was it? Triumph, perhaps? Or satisfaction? Or was she just imagining it? It definitely was not the mockery she had seen on and off during the train ride south.

"Well, it's about time. We've been waiting half an hour or more," Carlisle complained, promptly earning a disapproving glance from her brother.

"Don't be uncivil, Carly. We have guests."

Chase flashed his lazy grin, and Carlisle gritted her teeth, then marched to the table to take her seat before he could offer to escort her.

Gray politely held Tyler's chair for her, then sat beside her at the head of the table. She was glad when Chase took the seat next to her, and turned to give him a happy smile. His arrival had ended all the worry, humiliation, and confusion she had suffered during the past few weeks. She felt much safer with her tall, tawny-haired cousin at her side.

Chase patted the hand she laid on his coat sleeve, but his eyes were soon drawn across the table to linger on Carlisle. She rudely wrinkled her nose at him when Gray looked away to wave the servants forward with the meal. Tyler was surprised to hear Chase's low chuckle.

All four diners remained silent as the maids served the first course. Tyler watched Gray out of the corner of her eye. He looked as handsome as usual in the dark blue frock coat and gray satin vest. When he saw her watching him, he smiled so warmly that a flurry of goose bumps went scurrying up her bare arms. She hated herself when that happened!

"How did you like Javier, Gray?" Carlisle asked, unable to contain her curiosity a minute longer.

"He seemed a personable enough young man."

Carlisle waited for him to elaborate and when he didn't, she pursued the subject herself. A glance told her Chase Lancaster still had the same asinine, knowing smirk on his tanned, handsome face. He knew she was afraid he would carry tales to Gray about the trellis, the worm.

"Have you made a decision yet about my visit?" she prompted, deciding to pretend Tyler's cousin didn't exist.

"We can discuss that later, Carly. I'm sure our guests aren't interested."

"But the *Mayan* sails the day after tomorrow, and I promised Arantxa I'd let her know."

Gray looked annoyed. He set down his water goblet. "All right, then, you can send her your regrets. I've decided Javier Perez is too young to chaperone you on an ocean voyage."

"But Arantxa's going as well, and she and I would share a cabin."

"It's out of the question. I don't know his parents, or if they'd be suitable hosts for you."

"But, Gray—"

His stern expression silenced her. "I don't think we should burden Chase and Tyler with any more of this conversation, Carly. My decision is final."

Tyler watched Carlisle's jaw clamp tight, feeling sorry for the girl and angry with Gray for refusing to let her visit her friends. He was a despot! Thank goodness, Chase wasn't like that.

"May I make a suggestion?" Chase said, drawing all eyes to him.

Gray nodded, and Chase smiled at Carlisle. In return, he received a sour stare.

"I would be honored to escort your little sister to my country," he said smoothly. "I have booked passage on the *Mayan* myself two days hence. I have many fellow countrymen living here in the city. I'm sure I could find a suitable duenna for the journey. Once we reach Mexico, there are many guest rooms at my hacienda."

"At *your* hacienda," Carlisle sputtered angrily, then gave a scornful laugh.

Gray turned to her. "I think that's a very generous offer on Chase's part, Carly, but if you object, you'll simply have to forgo a journey to Mexico.''

Carlisle controlled her annoyance, realizing at once that Chase Lancaster's suggestion might be her only chance to visit the Perezes. Her voice was much more polite when she spoke again.

"It's not that I don't appreciate Mr. Lancaster's kindness, of course, but I was so looking forward to visiting Arantxa's home. We have made so many plans.''

"I would be happy to escort you to Mexico City, if Gray approves of such a visit,'' Chase volunteered, again his dark blue eyes glinting as they roamed Carlisle's flushed face. "In fact, I have business there with El Presidente later this month.''

Carlisle fumed inwardly, well aware that Chase Lancaster knew she was nearly choking on her anger. He was probably enjoying it.

"If you want to go, I think Chase's idea is the only one I can agree to,'' Gray said. "So I guess it's your decision, Carly.''

Carlisle stared helplessly at her brother, then turned glittering green eyes on the blond-haired man smiling indolently at her from across the table.

"Thank you very much, Senor Lancaster. I appreciate your kindness.'' You rotten dog, she added to herself.

"The pleasure is mine, senorita,'' Chase replied equably. You fiery little beauty, he added to himself.

Tyler spoke up then, hoping to dispel the almost tangible tension. "But it will be wonderful, Carlisle! We will be living at the hacienda together, and I can get to know your friends better. The four of us will have a splendid time!''

At Tyler's words, Carlisle brightened with genuine pleasure, not having thought of that part of it. But she was immediately wary when she saw her brother exchange a significant glance with Chase Lancaster. Tyler noticed it, too.

"What is it, Chase?'' she asked innocently, afraid

he had remembered a reason why Carlisle couldn't visit them after all.

"There's been a change of plans," Chase began, obviously uncomfortable.

Tyler's smooth brow furrowed. "A change? What is it? Carlisle can still visit us, can't she?"

"Perhaps I should talk to you about it in private," Chase suggested.

Something in his regretful tone frightened Tyler. "Please tell me, Chase. What's the matter?"

At Chase's silence, Gray spoke, his eyes never leaving Tyler's concerned face. "There's no reason to delay telling you. You'll have to know sooner or later. I have asked Chase for your hand in marriage, and he has kindly agreed."

The heavy silver fork Tyler had been holding dropped from her numb fingers and clattered against the edge of her fragile china plate. Her mouth fell open.

"What?" she managed in a strangled voice.

"We discussed it at length, Tyler, and I truly believe it's in your best interest to marry Gray," Chase began hurriedly, putting his hand on her arm.

White-faced, all Tyler could do was stare at him. The pronouncement was so unexpected, so shocking and absurd, that her tongue had completely ceased functioning. My God, they couldn't have decided such a thing without consulting her!

"Of all the dirty, low-down, double-dealing tricks I've ever heard, this is the lowest," Carlisle said from across the table. "Just who do you two think you are?"

Glad for the opportunity to think what to do, Tyler sat silent as Gray turned warning eyes on his sister's face. "This is none of your business, Carlisle."

"Just like it isn't any of Tyler's business who she marries? It's absolutely medieval for you two to force her to marry you against her will. I can see why you want her for your wife—she's so beautiful and clever, and all—but she doesn't love you. Why, she doesn't even *like* you. She can't stand the sight of you!''

Both men looked disturbed by her blunt words, but Tyler's mind still whirled like a windmill. She had to think of something, anything, to call the ridiculous proposal to a dead halt!

''Are you finished, Carlisle?'' Gray asked in a dangerous voice, which Carlisle promptly chose to ignore.

''No, I am not finished! I think it's a nasty, mean shame. Why, the next thing you'll do is marry me off to some ignorant lout like Chase Lancaster over there!'' She flourished her hand in Chase's direction, making him grin.

''Carlisle—'' Gray warned through set teeth.

''You can't make Tyler marry you any more than you can make me marry somebody I don't want to!'' Carlisle went on. ''Marriage is sacred, to be entered into only one time in your entire life, with someone you love more than anyone on earth. It should be beautiful and splendid, and last forever and ever.''

Tyler jerked up her head, inwardly blessing every hair on Carlisle's head for giving her a wonderful idea to escape her predicament. But Carlisle was not ready to end her tirade.

''I'd like to see you make her marry you. You'll have to drag her kicking and screaming down the church aisle, and won't that look good on the society page!''

Gray could barely constrain his anger. ''Dammit, Carly, I don't want to hear another word out of you!''

''I am honored by your proposal, Mr. Kincaid, but I'm afraid I can't marry you,'' Tyler said softly. ''I'm sorry.''

Dead silence ensued.

Both men seemed nonplussed by the graciousness of her answer, obviously more at a loss about how to handle Tyler's gentle refusal than Carlisle's furious one.

"I expected you to be adverse to the wedding owing to our past history," Gray began in so patronizing a tone that Tyler stiffened, "but I don't think you understand the situation. The decision has already been made."

"I don't think *you* understand," she returned evenly. "I cannot marry you, or anyone else, even if I wanted to. Because, you see"—she paused, letting all three veritably hang on her words—"I am already married."

A cannonball could have landed between the potatoes and the roast beef and no one would have noticed. Gray stared, Carlisle sank back in her chair in shock, and Chase looked aghast.

"I don't believe it," Gray said.

"I don't either," agreed Chase.

"Well, I do!" cried Carlisle, clapping her hands. "Whoever is he?"

"He is obviously a figment of her fertile imagination," Chase answered tightly. "Surely you don't think any of us will be taken in by such a ruse, Tyler."

"I believe her!" chimed in Carlisle again.

"It's true," Tyler said calmly, her eyes as earnest as she could make them.

Gray and Chase exchanged dubious glances.

"Anyone I know?" asked Gray sarcastically.

"No."

"Enlighten me, then. Where have you been hiding this husband of yours?"

"I don't know where he is."

"Oh, for God's sake, this is absurd. You are *not* married," he ground out furiously.

"Yes, I am," she insisted, as composed as Gray was ruffled.

"Any reason why no one knows about it but you?"

"It happened when I was only sixteen." She

paused, trying to appear embarrassed. "I met a boy aboard the steamboat we were traveling on, and we eloped. Uncle Burl found us just after the ceremony. He took me away and intended to have the marriage annulled, but he never got around to it."

"And you never told anyone?" Chase demanded.

"Only Harriet. You see," she went on, lowering her lashes, "I was ashamed."

She glanced sidelong at Gray, who had remained quiet during the last exchange.

"What's the boy's name?" he asked suddenly.

Tyler's mind spun, striving for a name he couldn't trace. "I'd rather not involve him."

"I'd say he's already involved," Gray answered dryly.

"His name is Henry Hardcastle," she told him. If Gray should send out inquiries, she thought, he would find records of such a marriage license somewhere in St. Louis. And that should convince him.

Gray rose and moved away from the table, and his somber expression made Tyler feel like laughing. How dared they try to force her into marriage with him, of all people! What did they think she was—a rug to tromp upon?

"Where in blazes is this boy now?" Chase suddenly demanded. "You must have some idea!"

"No, I really don't. It was a whirlwind affair, and Uncle Burl had him arrested. I never heard from him again." She waited tensely, and as the silence stretched out again, she knew she had won—at least until she came up with a better idea.

"It must have been terrible for you," Carlisle murmured comfortingly "To be dragged away from the altar by your uncle like that."

Chase didn't look particularly sympathetic, nor did he look convinced. "Gray, what do you make of this?"

Gray turned, his face unfathomable. "This changes things considerably, of course, but there's little that can be done about what's past."

Tyler went limp with relief. Oh, thank goodness, she thought wildly. She was already planning to escape before they could search out the truth about Henry Hardcastle.

"Chase and I will have to discuss this further," Gray continued. "Would you ladies please excuse us?"

Chase stood as the two girls left the room, Carlisle's arm consolingly around Tyler's shoulders.

"I'm sorry, Gray, I had no idea about this elopement. I suspect we can track down the fellow and arrange an annulment eventually, but not before I have to sail," Chase said as Gray crossed the room to slide the doors together after the departing women. "Perhaps we could have the wedding at my hacienda a few months from now."

"That won't be necessary, Chase."

"You're withdrawing your offer?"

"Hardly. In fact, I've decided to move the ceremony up. Tyler and I will be wed tomorrow if I can get the license by then."

"What?"

"Tyler's not married to anyone. She's lying again, probably stalling for time. But she's in for a surprise."

"How can you be sure her story isn't true?"

"Because my brother told me about her attempt to bamboozle Henry Hardcastle. The vows were never read. I interviewed the minister himself when I was in St. Louis investigating Tyler's past. Of course, she has no idea that I know anything about it."

"Why, that little minx," Chase said. "Are you sure you want to marry her, after this trick?"

"Oh, yes, quite sure. That's why the wedding's going to be tomorrow, before she can come up with another plan to put me off. I'll be busy arranging the details, but I trust you can keep an eye on her for me. I have a feeling she'll run away if given half a chance."

"Gladly. I'm beginning to think I made a good decision when I agreed to let you marry her. It appears you've become adept at handling her schemes."

"I'm learning, my friend. I'm learning."

13

Tyler woke up with a jolt, sitting up in bed and trying to discern what had roused her so abruptly. There was no one in her dim, quiet bedchamber, but she immediately knew that something was dreadfully amiss. What had worried her so when she went to sleep last night? Jumbled thoughts pushed around in her drowsy mind until she remembered. Chase was making her marry Gray Kincaid, her worst enemy.

She rubbed her eyes, red-rimmed from the long hours she had lain awake plotting her course of action. Her lie about Henry Hardcastle would distract Gray for a time, until she could board the ship with Chase and Carlisle. Thank goodness the *Mayan* was sailing so soon. Once in Mexico, she would have time to convince Chase to oppose the absurd, ridiculous wedding. If something went wrong, there was always Plan B to fall back on. She had worked out a Plan C as well. As Uncle Burl had always said: two ideas are better than one; three, better than two.

Right now, she needed to get up and feed Gray and Chase a few more juicy, untraceable details about her nonexistent groom. She hadn't decided whether to tell Carlisle the truth yet. She liked Carlisle, but involving her in such a hoax would only get her in a scrape with her brother. Then he would never allow her to visit the Perez family.

When she heard the click of the door latch, she turned quickly toward it, pulling the coverlet to her chin. As if conjured into existence by Tyler's thoughts, Carlisle appeared in the doorway, carrying several white dressmaker's boxes tied with bright satin ribbons.

"Are you awake?" she asked, peering into the heavy gloom. "Oh, yes, I see you now. Good. I've been waiting hours to show you these!"

"What time is it?" Tyler asked, hoping she hadn't missed breakfast.

"Nearly two in the afternoon," Carlisle answered, going back to the hall to retrieve the pot of hot coffee the maid had left outside Tyler's door.

"Two!" exclaimed Tyler, shocked.

Carlisle set the tray on the bedside table, glancing at Tyler as she carefully poured the hot brew into a black china cup patterned with red Chinese emblems.

"Yes. I was going to wake you so you could go to Madame Broussard's with me, but Gray said to let you sleep as long as you could because you'd need your strength for tonight."

"Tonight? What did he mean?"

Tyler took the cup, sipping as Carlisle crossed the room to send one of the tasseled shades rolling up with a clacking snap. The room was immediately flooded with bright sunlight. Tyler blinked and quickly shut her eyes from the glare.

"I've really been dreading to tell you, but I guess it's better coming from me than Gray. They know all about Henry Hardcastle."

Tyler sat straight up in bed. "What do they know?"

"Oh, that you were fibbing about being married. But I thought you did a wonderful job of acting last night."

"How do they know?"

"Apparently Stone told Gray all about you and Mr. Hardcastle, and then later Gray did some checking on you in St. Louis. Anyway, believe me, they know."

Tyler flushed with anger. "Then why didn't they just say so last night?"

Carlisle sat down on the bed. "Brace yourself, Tyler. They didn't say anything because they wanted time to arrange the wedding." She paused sorrowfully. "It's this evening, I'm afraid."

Her remark brought Tyler out of the bed. "What? They can't!"

"They have."

"How? Why? I won't."

Carlisle shook her head. "I think it's terrible, too, but they won't listen to me. I've talked and argued until I'm hoarse."

"I've got to get out of here, Carlisle!" Tyler said, panic rising when she realized how quickly everything had changed. "You've got to help me escape!" She pulled Carlisle to her feet.

"They won't let you."

"They can't stop me!"

"They've told the entire household staff to keep an eye on you."

Tyler sank down on the bed, staring dismally at her friend.

Carlisle rounded the bedpost and sat beside her. "I know you don't want to marry Gray, but he really was an angel this morning. He sent me to the most exclusive couturiere in town and told me to get us both gowns for the wedding. He didn't even set a limit on how much I should spend, and I must say that's the first time that's ever happened! He's always scolding me for being too extravagant. The only bad thing was that your odious cousin insisted on accompanying me."

"Chase went with you to the dressmaker's?" Tyler asked suspiciously. She was beginning to think

Chase was odious, too, after what he had done to her. She had been relying on his help.

"Unfortunately. All he did was ogle the Parisian models. And they flirted shamelessly with him. It was disgusting. He even had the audacity to point out the dresses he thought unsuitable and tell me what shades wouldn't look good with my hair! Can you imagine such boorishness? So I told the oaf what colors he didn't look good in." She laughed, bringing over the dress boxes and placing them beside Tyler.

"While he was busy trying to seduce the models, I selected the gowns he didn't approve of, just for spite. See, here's the one I intend to wear to the ball tonight."

"What ball?" Tyler asked, her voice listless.

"It's a big diplomatic affair given by the governor. Javier and Arantxa will be there, and when they told the Mexican ambassador that Chase was here, he arranged for the governor to send us all a special invitation. Your cousin must be fairly important down in Mexico City. Why didn't you tell me?"

Tyler watched without answering as Carlisle pulled out a scarlet gown trimmed with gorgeous black lace, cut so low in the front that Tyler first thought she was looking at the back of the dress.

"I can see why Chase didn't like it," she ventured, but her head was spinning. Her Plan A lay in ruins around her feet, so her next option was to adopt Plan B—escape. Before the wedding, if possible.

"It's the latest style in Paris. Yours is similar. See?" Carlisle quickly untied the bindings on another long box and pulled a second satin gown from a cloud of crinkly white tissue paper. "I thought this golden color would look beautiful with your russet hair."

"What time did you say the wedding was?" Tyler asked, wishing she hadn't slept so long.

"In a couple of hours," Carlisle answered, laying

the dresses across the bed. ''The priest is already here with the license. Chase insisted on being the one to pick out your wedding gown, and he paid for it, too. As much as I hate to admit it, I do think it's perfect for you. If it needs fitting, Madame Broussard has agreed to come for alterations this afternoon.''

''How dare they! How dare they try to force me like this!''

Tyler began to prowl, hands balled in fists at her sides, until Carlisle went to her, wrapping her in a sisterly embrace. Her green eyes were dark with sympathy.

''I know you don't want to marry my brother, Tyler. And I know you have good reasons since he took your plantation and all. But you really don't have any choice. As awful as it is, they can make us wed whomever they choose.''

''Not me, they can't,'' Tyler replied between set teeth, resuming her pacing.

Carlisle trailed after her. ''Really, Tyler, Gray's not as bad as you think. I have to admit he's arrogant at times, and bossy, and domineering.'' She stopped suddenly, as if she'd just realized she wasn't painting a very good picture of her brother. ''But that's just with me. Most people like him and admire him for all his business accomplishments. Why, Charles Bond told me once that we were absolutely poor when we first went to Chicago. I was a baby then, because Gray and Stone have both been rich as long as I can remember.''

She turned Tyler around to face her. ''But really, Gray can be very sweet at times, and he mostly means well. You'll just have to learn to stand up to him, like I do, or convince him he's making the decisions when you've really put the ideas in his head. That always works for me. In fact, that's how I got us all these new clothes.'' She grinned smugly.

''But I hate him! Ever since I was little, when Un-

cle Burl told me he was the one who took Rose
Point!''

Tears welled up in Tyler's eyes, and she angrily
dashed them away.

''Oh, you poor darling. But listen, you must look
at this another way. You must be practical. I certainly learned to do that, living with Gray and Stone
all my life. Just think, Tyler, Gray still owns Rose
Point. It'll be yours, too, as his wife. I know it would
be better if you didn't have to marry him to get it,
but even so, you can go home again! I know you
can persuade Gray to fix it up, if it needs it. And if
you have children, they can grow up at Rose Point,
just like you did. You'd like that, wouldn't you?''

Tyler was silent.

''Don't you like Gray, even a tiny bit?'' Carlisle
asked, her serious gaze searching Tyler's face.

Tyler thought of the times he had held her so
gently and made her laugh, made her feel safe and
almost loved again.

''No,'' she said.

Carlisle sighed. ''You'll get used to him in time, I
suppose. And maybe tonight won't be so bad.''

They looked at each other, neither believing that.

''Do you know what it's like to be bedded by a
man?'' Tyler asked. Color flooded her face as she
realized that if she didn't get away, she might have
the experience herself that very evening.

Carlisle quickly shook her head. ''Only what the
Sisters told us.''

''What did they say?'' Tyler asked curiously. But
Carlisle's somber expression gave her pause.

''They said it was a deadly sin, and that a woman
should only do it with her husband when he insists,
so as to help propagate mankind by having children.
They said it was painful and awful, and that we'd
burn in hellfire if we did it with anyone but our husbands.''

''Oh.'' Tyler swallowed hard. The nuns' description closely paralleled Uncle Burl's account of the

marriage bed. He had told her it was painful for the woman but pleasurable for the man. As she had grown older, she had wondered if he had painted the experience with such cruel colors so she wouldn't be tempted to find out for herself. Now she feared he had told the truth. But the devil could take her, she vowed, before she'd suffer through such torment with Gray Kincaid.

"Don't worry so much," Carlisle told her. "Perhaps you'll get with child right off the cuff and Gray won't expect you to do it anymore. Wouldn't that be grand? Anyway, Arantxa told me a lot of men don't expect such sacrifices from their wives anyway, except for now and then to get them with child. She said her father has several mistresses in Mexico City for that sort of thing. I suppose loose women like it better than well-bred ones. That's it—Gray will probably get himself some mistresses and leave you alone. Or maybe he'll just keep the ones he already has. Now, doesn't that make you feel better?"

Tyler watched as Carlisle happily smoothed the fine fabric of the red gown before carefully hanging it on a pink padded hanger. She wasn't sure if the idea of Gray taking mistresses, new or old, made her feel better or not. But it did propel her to the window to check for a sturdy trellis in case worse came to worst.

Outside Tyler's bedchamber, Chase shifted the big white box under his arm, then tapped on the door. A moment later the portal swung open.

"What do you want, you cad?" Carlisle demanded. "Haven't you done enough to Tyler already?"

Chase stepped past her without comment. "I would like a word with my cousin alone, if you don't mind, Miss Kincaid."

"She doesn't want to talk to you, I'm quite sure," Carlisle replied icily. But across the room, Tyler turned and scowled at her cousin.

"No, let him come in," she said.

"Are you sure?" Carlisle asked as if she coveted the honor of throwing the man from the room. When Tyler nodded, Carlisle gave Chase one last glower.

"If you need me later to help you dress, just call," Carlisle told Tyler. "I'll be next door in my room."

As Carlisle departed, shutting the door behind her, Chase looked at Tyler, feeling absurdly sheepish now that he had to face her accusing glare.

"I thought you loved me! I trusted you!" she cried furiously, coming straight to the heart of the matter.

"Now, Ty, it's not so bad," he began. "Gray's a good man. He wants to marry you, and he promised he'll be good to you."

"Good to me? He's the blackguard who murdered Papa and took Rose Point!"

When he saw how Tyler was trembling with rage, Chase tossed the box atop the bed and walked toward her.

"I know he did that, but it was during the war. You have to take the facts into consideration. Men are called upon to do things in war whether they like it or not. God knows, I did things I wish I could forget. Gray only performed his duty. Now, I truly believe he cares for you."

"He doesn't. He thinks I'm a thief and a liar and lots of other terrible things. He hates me, almost as much as I hate him."

Chase couldn't fault Gray for thinking such things about Tyler; they were true. But he didn't say so to his cousin. She was upset enough already.

"He doesn't hate you. If he hated you, why would he ask to marry you? I think it's the best thing for you, or I wouldn't have agreed. You're old enough to be wed, past the age really, and I think that's what you need now—a husband and a home, and children."

"Children! With that monster? God forbid!" Tyler stormed across the floor in a dudgeon.

"I know Gray will take good care of you, and I'm

not sure I could find a better man for you to marry."
Chase hesitated, deciding to change tactics. "Besides, after the wedding he's taking you home to Rose Point."

"And that's supposed to make everything all right? I'm supposed to trade in my life and happiness, and then fall on grateful knees in front of you two lords of creation!"

"I'd say life with Gray is a damn sight better than the criminal one you've been leading!" Chase answered angrily, then quickly tamped down his ire. Tyler was upset. Yelling at her would only make it worse. "Look," he said as gently as he could, "I've brought your wedding gown."

"Oh, Cousin Chase, that makes everything, oh, so much better. I'll be eternally grateful." Her words oozed sarcasm.

Chase's jaw clenched. His patience was nearing its limit.

"Obviously, Tyler, you're not ready to listen to reason. But as your legal guardian, it's my decision to make, and mine alone. You'll just have to resign yourself to it. Arranged marriages are customary for most women, and you're no different. It's the way things are done, and the sooner you accept it, the better."

Tyler presented him with her back and a cold, stony silence.

Chase frowned, at a loss as to how to handle her.

"If you want my advice, you'll put on this beautiful gown I bought you and behave like a well-bred young lady instead of a spoiled child. Someday you'll look back on this day as one of the happiest of your life. You should try to make it pleasant and memorable. I know that's what Gray wants."

He turned and stopped with his hand on the doorknob. "Heed my words, Tyler, for your own good. I'll be back in an hour to escort you downstairs. I'm giving you away."

"As if I didn't know," Tyler flung at him bitterly.

After he had gone, Tyler moved back to her bed. She stared at the dress, loath to touch the ivory satin. The gown was magnificent, with a tight-fitting bodice and long, transparent Irish lace sleeves atop a slender white silk skirt. But in Tyler's eyes the expensive fabric and seed pearl trim were only decorations for the heavy yoke the wedding ceremony would place upon her shoulders for the rest of her life.

"So Gray Kincaid wants this wedding to be memorable, does he?" she muttered. "All right, dear cousin, I'll make it as unforgettable for him as I know how."

Gray glanced over to the lace-covered buffet table where Father Chevier was helping himself to yet another glass of champagne. He hoped the good priest would remember the vows after drinking so much wine. If they ever got Tyler downstairs, he didn't want anything to delay the ceremony.

Retrieving his gold pocket watch, he checked the time. Six o'clock. Tyler was procrastinating. Chase had gone upstairs to collect her nearly an hour ago. More than anything else, Gray was afraid she would simply refuse and force him to carry her to the altar bodily. He no longer underestimated Tyler. If she had been able to flee the house undetected, she would have been long gone.

"I do wish to emphasize again, Mr. Kincaid, how grateful I, and every member of my little flock, are." Father Chevier paused as a hiccup interrupted his speech, causing a raised brow from Gray. "Ah, pardon me, good sir. Now what was I saying? Oh, yes, how grateful we are for your generous contribution to our parish purse. God will notice, I assure you."

"I'll take your word on that, Father," Gray replied absently, glancing toward the door again. The offering had been more expedient than philanthropic. Such a rushed ceremony had required greasing a few palms, both religious and civil.

"I do hope your lovely bride isn't indisposed, my dear man," the priest went on, his slurred speech further demonstrating his lack of sobriety. "Ah, but there she is now. What a lovely creature."

Gray jerked his attention to the doorway, but saw only Carlisle crossing the room toward him. His grim expression deepened at the first words from his sister.

"I cannot fathom why you persist in this travesty of a wedding when the bride absolutely detests every single thing about you."

Father Chevier gasped, stared, then cleared his throat in embarrassment. Both Gray and Carlisle ignored him.

"Behave yourself, Carlisle, or I'll paddle your backside."

"My dear sir," blustered the priest, "I must say that is certainly no way to speak to your lovely young bride on your wedding day."

Gray and Carlisle stared at him blankly; then Gray shook his head.

"This is not my intended, Father. Allow me to present my sister, Miss Carlisle Kincaid."

"Oh, of course, I should have known. How do you do, Miss Kincaid? Are you to be the bride's attendant?" The priest presented her with a bleary-eyed smile.

"Yes, if her obnoxious cousin can drag her downstairs," Carlisle answered under her breath.

"Carly, you're beginning to irritate me—" Gray began, but a choked exclamation from the tipsy cleric brought him up short. He followed Father Chevier's bug-eyed stare, and even Carlisle gasped in dismay.

In the open doorway beside her apologetic-looking cousin stood Gray's long-awaited bride. A flush of embarrassed color overtook his face. She was dressed in the same outfit she had worn inside the casket the day she had left Chicago. Every article of her clothing was drab mourning black, from her high-necked silk dress and cascading widow's veil to her dangling jet earrings and onyx brooch. Fury ignited inside his soul, but he struggled to contain it. Her intent was to anger him; he wouldn't give her the satisfaction.

As the priest retrieved a large white handkerchief from under his robe and nervously swabbed his sweating brow, Gray crossed the floor to meet his bride.

"My, don't we look happy," he commented as he took her arm.

"I only chose the color I deemed suitable for the occasion, Mr. Kincaid," Tyler replied with a sweet smile.

Across the room, Gray saw the priest run his finger around the inside of his tight clerical collar, but Gray was determined not to be goaded.

"Unlike most people, I have no aversion to black, my dear," he told her calmly. "Come, before the priest gets too intoxicated to perform the ceremony."

Tyler grimaced, but Chase grinned, noticeably relieved to relinquish his willful cousin to her bridegroom.

Gray led Tyler across the room to Father Chevier.

"My dear, please accept my condolences," the priest said, patting Tyler's hand. "I was unaware you mourned a death in the family."

"Only my own, Father."

"Oh, my, I say. Mr. Kincaid, I do wonder if we shouldn't delay this—"

"No, we're ready now, Father Chevier. You may begin."

"I must say this is all rather unorthodox."

Gray stared at him until he opened his Bible. Chase and Carlisle moved into position at their sides, and the prelate peered dubiously at Tyler's white face, faintly visible beneath the black net draping her head. He swallowed hard.

"Dearly beloved—"

"Hmmph," came a low snort from beneath Ty-

ler's widow's veil, halting the priest's words for a
moment.

Gray frowned but said nothing, and Father Chevier began again, rushing and stumbling through the
vows as if afraid something dire would overtake him
before he could finish. Gray was just as eager to
have it done. He grasped Tyler's small hand firmly,
in case she tried to snatch it free, and slipped a narrow, diamond-studded gold band onto her slender
finger.

"I now pronounce you man and wife," the flustered clergyman finished hastily, darting a glance at
the bride as she tried to jerk her hand away from
the groom. He hesitated. "A kiss is customary at
this point, Mr. Kincaid, but if you wish to forgo it,
I'm sure no one will object."

"I have no intention of forgoing it," Gray informed him.

Tyler turned slightly and waited as Gray lifted her
veil, still disappointed that her intentional insult in
wearing black had been met with such indifference.
She had expected a more forceful response, perhaps
even postponement of the ceremony. She braced
herself to hide any unsettling reaction his kiss might
churn up inside her. She had not forgotten the one
in the sleigh.

Expecting him to grab her and punish her for humiliating him, she was surprised when, instead, he
merely lifted her chin with one finger and leaned
forward to press his lips briefly to hers. As he
straightened, their gazes locked, his azure eyes
glowing with an inner light.

Silence prevailed, for an embarrassingly long interval. No one in the wedding party seemed to know
what to say. Finally Carlisle stepped forward from
her place at Tyler's elbow.

"Best wishes, Tyler, and congratulations to you,
Gray," she said, forcing a bright smile, obviously
trying to lighten the oppressive atmosphere. Ignor-

ing Chase, she stood on her tiptoes to kiss her brother's lean brown cheek.

Tyler gazed longingly at the door as Chase crossed the room and brought back a tray filled with goblets of champagne.

"A toast to the bride and groom," he cried in a hearty voice that fell flat. Ignoring the dead silence that followed, he handed around the wineglasses.

"May all your days be as happy as"—he paused, having intended to finish with an allusion to their wedding day, then concluded lamely—"I know they eventually will be."

Everyone stared at him until Tyler set down her glass, untouched. Carlisle followed suit in a show of support. Chase and Father Chevier downed their wine in single draughts, as if seeking solace, and Gray absently tasted his, then placed his goblet beside his wife's brimming one.

"We really should be leaving for the ball soon," Carlisle said. "It starts in less than an hour."

"I prefer you change your gown before the ball," Gray said to Tyler, his tone low.

She stared defiantly at him. "I prefer not to. I hardly think my mourning period is over. In truth, it's only just begun."

"I'm afraid I'll have to insist."

"No."

Tyler met his eyes with studied challenge and was startled by his sudden smile, one tinged with mockery.

"As you wish, my dear. We'll send Carlisle and Chase to the hotel without us. I'm as eager as you to retire."

His subtle threat caught Tyler off guard. She certainly wasn't about to let herself be taken to that chamber of horrors. Besides, Plan B revolved around attending the ball. There, in all the excitement and crowds, she could give him the slip. Gray and Chase couldn't possibly watch her every minute at such a gala event. They might have forced her to recite vows with Gray Kincaid, but an annulment was still attainable, and she meant to have one.

"I'll change my gown," she said curtly, thoroughly nettled by the derisive look of satisfaction which appeared on Gray's face.

"Wait, Tyler, you haven't thrown your bouquet. Do it now, and I'll catch it," called Carlisle from her place near the buffet table.

Wanting only to be done with the distasteful ceremony, Tyler obediently flipped her nosegay of white rosebuds in Carlisle's direction. But as Gray turned Tyler to lead her toward the photographer waiting in the front hall, Chase darted out a quick hand, deftly snatching Carlisle's prize.

She whirled on him, eyes snapping like fire. "Why, you vile thing! What do you think you're doing? She threw the bouquet to me!"

"I don't think you're ready for marriage yet, love."

"I don't give a hang what you think! And don't call me love!"

"Chase, Carlisle, hurry up. The photographer's been waiting for hours," Gray called from across the room, effectively ending their quarrel.

Carlisle turned on her heel, teeth clamped tight enough to make her jaw jut out to an abnormal angle.

Thomas Link, the young photographer hired for the occasion, fussed with his hooded tripod camera for a long time, posing everyone around a small velvet sofa, while Father Chevier furtively helped himself to Tyler's and Carlisle's untasted wine.

When at last Mr. Link was satisfied and ducked beneath the heavy black canvas camera cover to capture the propitious moment, the wedding party looked none too happy. Tyler sat on the settee frowning darkly, swathed in deep black, with her husband beside her, appearing impatient and displeased. Behind them, Carlisle looked like a threatening thundercloud, while a step away, Chase stood grinning in obvious good humor and holding a dainty bouquet of white roses.

The reflector flared briefly as Mr. Link caught the two couples for posterity, after which Tyler shot to her feet.

"May I be excused now?" she asked with scorn.

"By all means," Gray answered calmly.

Tyler quickly left the room with Carlisle, still fuming. Now Gray Kincaid's my husband, she thought in revulsion. Husband, she repeated incredulously to herself as she clutched a handful of black silk and stomped up the stairs after Carlisle. She couldn't believe it! Why, her dear father would roll over in his grave! Her uncle Burl, too! And Harriet would surely have a real heart attack when she learned of this ridiculous marriage.

"Did you see Chase grab your bouquet just to spite me?" Carlisle said. "I think your cousin is touched in the head. He is just too loathsome a creature for words. Well, I'm not going to think about him again, not this whole night. I'll think about Javier instead." She suddenly beamed.

"I intend to dance until dawn, don't you, Tyler? I love these gay affairs so, and I haven't attended one since I was in Chicago. And we both have such beautiful new gowns! Arantxa says Javier waltzes divinely, so I'm going to write his name on every line of my dance book. Or perhaps I should dance with others to make him jealous. What do you think?"

Tyler barely listened to her friend's exuberant chatter. She had more pressing thoughts on her mind. Gray would be smugly overconfident now. But when he let down his guard, she would leap over it to freedom.

As they reached the second-floor landing, she contemplated whether or not to apprise Carlisle of her planned flight, and decided against it almost at once. Even under the best circumstances, Carlisle was excitable and not one to mind her tongue. Tyler couldn't take any chances. And if Carlisle did help her escape, she would be left behind to face the consequences. Tyler didn't want that.

"Madame Broussard told me all the French ladies are wearing this style," Carlisle was saying as they reached Tyler's bedchamber. "She said many of them tuck lace handkerchiefs or sweet-smelling flowers in their cleavages to tempt men. I got both for each of us. Which do you think you'll wear?" she asked, taking Tyler's dress from where it hung on the door of the wardrobe.

Tyler lifted the shimmering golden silk to examine the fine ivory lace that edged the neckline and basque. The décolletage was revealing, much more so than that of any gown she had ever worn.

"I can't wait to see it on you," came Carlisle's enthusiastic voice. "Let's see how we look."

Ten minutes later, Carlisle finished fastening the last button on the back of Tyler's tight bodice, then moved to the mirror to preen in her own creation of scarlet silk and black lace.

Tyler joined her, concerned over the way her dress barely covered her breasts. She envisioned Gray's blue eyes on the soft white skin displayed so wantonly, then grew hot all over at such thoughts. What if her plan failed? she thought suddenly. What if she was forced to spend the night in his bed?

Images of the time he'd attacked her in Chicago jolted across her mind. She remembered the way he had grabbed her so roughly, his mouth savaging hers as he'd pushed her against the wall. Sensual shivers swept over her flesh as she relived the strange weakness which had reduced her to quivering jelly. She shook herself mentally. It would never happen again, she vowed.

"I can't wait to see that abominable Chase's face when he sees me wearing the very dress he asked me not to choose." Carlisle smiled maliciously. "And Gray will be spellbound by you—even more than he already is. I've seen him eye his ladies' bosoms a thousand times. He never even bothers to hide it.''

Carlisle stuck a large white rose in her deep cleavage. ''There, see? Madame was right. It makes it look much more alluring. The models told me men are tempted nearly beyond control to pluck out such flowers or hankies so they can see more bare flesh. But they never do, of course. No gentleman would dare be so bold.''

Thoughts of Gray's eyes on her nearly naked breasts gave Tyler a perverse thrill. She hoped he was tempted beyond control, just so he would know what he had missed after she escaped his clutches. She picked up a transparent white lace handkerchief from the dresser top and tucked it into place, arranging it to tease a masculine eye as much as possible.

''Oh, yes, that will tempt any man,'' Carlisle declared when Tyler turned toward her, ''Especially Gray. Now come, we're late. The ball started nearly half an hour ago. Gray would be angry with us if he weren't so distracted with thoughts of tonight.''

Carlisle noticed Tyler's alarmed expression and went on quickly. ''Don't be so scared, Tyler, really. It can't be too horrible, or all the married women we know would be frightened out of their wits every time night fell. I don't remember seeing any wedded ladies looking distraught at bedtime, do you?''

Tyler shook her head, trying to remember. Carlisle's observation did make sense, and she scolded herself for never asking Harriet what lovemaking was like. But how could Tyler have known she would be forced into marriage so suddenly? Even so, she wished she had talked to Harriet about it. She had been married and widowed, and now that Tyler thought upon it, Harriet had had nothing but positive things to say about wedded life.

''I think I'll put on a bit more rouge,'' Tyler told Carlisle, who now waited impatiently by the door, her silk evening wrap in hand. Tyler had to pack a bag and hide it so she would be ready to run. "Go on down, Carly. I'll follow shortly."

Carlisle nodded and left her friend, wishing there were more she could do to calm Tyler's nerves. Downstairs, she found the formal parlor empty, and she walked to the huge oval mirror hanging over the mantel. She pivoted from side to side, regarding herself from every angle, pleased with her appearance. She froze as an amused masculine laugh came from behind her.

"I see I was wrong about the dress," Chase Lancaster said from the portal, his dark blue eyes gleaming. "Scarlet is the perfect color for you."

Something told Carlisle the compliment had a derogatory double meaning, but she decided that ignoring him was still the best way to handle his unbelievable bad manners. It was hard to do so, though, as he moved up behind her, close enough to loom over her in the mirror. He was very tall, as tall as Gray, and Gray was six feet four. Chase's gaze riveted in the rudest possible way on the delicate white rose anchored in her soft bosom. To her shock, he promptly reached to pluck it out—just as Madame Broussard's models said a man would never, ever do—and he did it so swiftly that Carlisle could only gasp.

"Except that you shouldn't hide your charms, *querida*. The rose should go behind your ear in that flaming hair of yours, the way the senoritas of my country wear them."

Chase proceeded to place it exactly where he wanted it, without hesitation and without asking her permission. Carlisle was so amazed by his audacity that she could only stare up into his dark, grinning face.

"Tell me, senor, were you born so crass and disgusting, or did someone teach you to be a boor?"

"I'd probably call you out for that if"—his gaze dropped impertinently to her heaving bosom—"you were a man."

"If I were a man, I would have called you out the first time we met," she snapped as her brother joined them from the hallway.

"Where's Tyler?" Gray asked without preamble, as if he feared she had fled.

Carlisle moved away from Chase, to a spot where Gray wouldn't notice the front of her gown. He wasn't looking at her anyway, she realized. All he thought about now was Tyler. And that would certainly keep him out of her hair. Poor Tyler, though. Now she would be the one to feel the brunt of his domineering ways.

Tyler chose that exact moment to appear on the threshold. Gray could only stare at her. He'd never seen her look so beautiful. He swallowed hard, sorely tempted to go to her, scoop her up in his arms, and carry her to his bed like some barbarian of old. With effort, he stopped himself from giving in to that fascinating urge, even though he knew he had every right to do just that. She was his wife now, under his care, protection, and authority. Blast the damned ball, he thought, irritated to have accepted an invitation on his wedding night.

He quickly crossed the room, his eyes lingering on his bride's low-cut golden gown. More than anything, he wanted to pull the hankie from between Tyler's tantalizing breasts and press his mouth to her smooth, fragrant flesh. His hands nearly trembled with desire.

"Does this dress meet with your approval?" Tyler asked coldly, her color heightened by his thorough and lengthy scrutiny of her bosom.

"Yes," he answered softly. "I'm pleased. You're more beautiful than I could ever have dreamed."

Something stirred in her cinnamon eyes, a softer expression perhaps. But his hopes for a smile were dashed by his sister's intruding voice.

"Well, come on, Gray! Javier and Arantxa will be wondering where I am!"

Tyler turned away from him, and Gray followed the women outside with Chase at his side, deciding then and there that he and his bride would not linger long at the ball.

14

An hour later, as Gray sat in the cavernous ball-room of the St. Charles Hotel, he was still thinking about his bride's smooth white flesh. He found it sheer torture to sit beside Tyler, especially when she was wearing that provocative dress, obviously worn with the sole intention of tormenting him. She to-tally ignored him, as she had done since they ar-rived, while he examined every inch of her lovely body—as yet unseen and untouched by any man. He shifted uneasily in his chair, thinking how it would be later that night when he would slowly un-dress her and make love to her for the first time.

A moment later he became so affected by his vis-ualizations of their lovemaking that he knew he ought to distract himself. Summoning up all his willpower, he pulled his gaze from Tyler and watched Carlisle, who was being swept gracefully around the floor by Javier Perez. The young Mexican had been her partner for nearly every dance.

"I believe I'll step outside for a breath of air," Tyler said abruptly.

Gray displayed no reaction, but he was immedi-ately wary. "I'll join you."

For a bare instant, Tyler's dismay showed clearly; then she glanced away.

"Never mind. The idea has suddenly lost its appeal."

Instinctively, Gray knew she had a trick in mind. She was just waiting for the right moment to implement it, which gave him even more reason not to let her out of his sight. There was no way she was going to evade him tonight. He had waited too long for the pleasure of having her in his bed. She was angry again, he thought, studying the rosy color staining her cheeks.

"You know, you really should smile once or twice this evening, Tyler, or someone might think you aren't exactly pleased to be my wife."

"Someone just might be right," Tyler snapped, but her sarcasm only brought a low, amused laugh from him.

"I don't know why you wanted to marry me anyway," she said, breaking her self-imposed silence. "You told me I was stupid and a liar. And a thief you wouldn't turn your back on."

Gray decided to see if he could bait her into a more communicative mood. "I never said you were stupid, Tyler."

Her fragile jaw clamped shut as he continued.

"I can't say I wanted to marry you because you're such a fine, honest lady, now can I, since we both know you're not."

Tyler turned her attention back to the swirling dancers without responding, and Gray gave in to his desire to touch her. He scraped back his chair and stood. "It's time we danced together, I suppose. For appearances. We'll be returning to the house soon."

His last words captured Tyler's undivided attention.

"But it's so early," she protested, her voice suddenly more civil. "The evening has barely begun."

"That, my dear," said Gray, lifting one dark brow in a significant way, "is why we're leaving."

Tyler could feel the heated blood rushing up her

neck into her cheeks. How she hated the way he could always make her blush! And his fingers holding lightly to her bare arm as he led her among the other couples sent chills over her skin.

She stared first at the buttons of his starched, ruffled shirtfront, and then at the other people around them while he led her in an expert waltz that circled the long, shiny floor.

"The way you're scanning faces leads me to believe you're afraid you'll discover another one of your victims here tonight, like poor John Mooney."

Tyler had been afraid of that very thing ever since they had entered the spacious hall with its polished oak floor and gleaming crystal chandeliers, and her guilty frown brought yet another low chuckle from her tall husband.

"I wonder how many duels I'll have to fight or bribes I'll have to pay defending your nonexistent honor, my love. How many men did you rob or seduce for your uncle anyway?"

"I seduced no one, and you know it!" Tyler retorted, then was furious at herself for letting him goad her into an argument. Every time he did, he bested her. She had learned that the hard way.

"Then perhaps tonight you will have an opportunity to try seduction for the first time," he whispered close to her ear.

Tyler wanted desperately to laugh contemptuously up at him, to tell him not to hold his breath on that count, but his mocking words brought home too sharply her own fear of the marriage bed. Plan B certainly was a dismal failure, since he refused to let her out of his sight. She bit her lip and looked away, and if Gray noticed her reaction, he made no comment.

Tyler was glad when the music died, and even more relieved when her handsome cousin appeared at her side to request the next dance. She smiled gratefully up at Chase as Gray handed her over.

"Are you still angry with me?" Chase asked, studying her flushed face.

"I'll never forgive you as long as I live, if that's what you mean," she returned bitterly. But as usual, Chase's wide, slow grin had a softening effect on her.

"Didn't Carlisle ever tell you that menfolk always know what's best for young female kin?" he asked, straight-faced.

Tyler relented enough to smile vaguely at the notion of those words coming from the lips of her flame-haired sister-in-law.

"Hardly. But she did say things would probably work out for the best."

"Indeed?" Chase remarked, his gaze finding Carlisle, where she stood in her bright red gown, sipping champagne with her Mexican friends and several other gentlemen admirers. "I have to admit I'm surprised. But she's right. Gray's a good man, whether you think so now or not. He won't mistreat you, so don't be afraid of him."

Tyler wished she could ask Chase exactly what would happen later if Gray did trap her in his bedchamber, but the idea of broaching such an intimate subject with a male made her cringe. Only a married woman could tell her what to expect, and even they would probably faint dead away before engaging in such an indelicate discussion. She wished again that Carlisle had been able to point out a few specifics of the act; then Tyler could at least prepare herself. It just wasn't fair! Girls had to go blindly to their wedding night, like lambs to the slaughter. But she was sure men knew all about it before they went. She bet someone had coached Chase and Gray most thoroughly their first time!

As the lilting strains of the orchestra faded and the hubbub of hundreds of voices mingled together beneath the high frescoed ceiling, she walked with Chase back to the table. Gray stood at once, as if ready to leave, and Tyler went rigid with dread.

"Oh, I'm having such a wonderful time," she gushed nervously. "I do believe I could dance all night."

"I'm sure you could," Gray said dryly, "but you're not going to." He turned to Chase. "Since we're leaving early, would you see that Carlisle gets home safely?"

"Nothing would give me greater pleasure," Chase said, and he again sought out a certain coppery head.

"Good. We'll see you in the morning, then," Gray said, taking a firm grip on Tyler's elbow. He led her outside, eager now to be home and alone with her.

Their carriage was waiting, and Gray sat across from her, content to look at her and savor the pleasures to come. The small lamp inside the coach sent a faint glow over her, making her diamond earrings twinkle. He disrobed her yet again in his mind, slowly unbuttoning the back of her gown, pushing it off her shoulders until it fell around her feet and he could finally see what he had wanted to possess for weeks. His gaze moved to her chignon, which was caught up with pins and glittering combs. He loved her hair, and mentally he pulled down the silky auburn softness and gathered the fragrant tresses in both his hands. Just a few minutes more, Tyler, he thought, and you'll be mine.

Just a few more minutes, Tyler was thinking, and I'll be gone. Plan C was nearing fruition. When he left her to prepare for bed, she would climb down the trellis outside her window. Often as a child at Rose Point she had climbed down the tree outside her bedroom window. Gray would never suspect such a ploy. Then she would catch a steamboat to St. Louis and go into hiding.

When they arrived home, only one lamp lit the foyer, and the silence between them drew out alarmingly as they climbed the staircase and walked to Tyler's bedroom door. She opened it quickly, ea-

ger to put her last plan into action. To her shocked
dismay, Gray made as if to follow her inside.

"You don't think you're coming into my bedchamber with me, do you?" she asked indignantly.

"Yes, I think maybe I am."

"But I'm not ready for bed yet. I can't—I won't
undress in front of you."

His voice was patient. "I believe you have a dressing screen to use, if you wish."

At that point, Tyler knew she was in trouble.
There was no Plan D, and Gray had just thrown the
bolt behind them in the most final way.

"I really prefer some time alone to prepare myself, if you don't mind," she said, hiding her desperation as he shrugged out of his dark frock coat
and tossed it over a chair.

"Alas, I'm afraid I do mind," he answered, unbuttoning his waistcoat.

Tyler's eyes grew wider, and she turned to hurry
toward the tall, louvered screen in the corner, but
was stopped abruptly by Gray's hand on her arm.

"Wait, there's something I've been wanting to do
for a long time."

She stood tense and wary as he reached out to
pull the pins and jeweled combs from her hair. He
dropped them carelessly to the floor, his eyes intent
on his task. His hands went to the heavy coil at her
nape and he threaded his fingers through the soft,
silky strands as if he derived immense pleasure from
simply touching it.

"You have beautiful hair, Tyler," he murmured
softly as he arranged it in shimmering waves around
her shoulders. "There, that's better. Now you can
undress."

Tyler fled behind the screen, putting trembling
hands over her mouth.

She couldn't go through with it, she thought
wildly, listening to the sounds he was making on
the other side of the barrier—shoes falling to the
floor, fabric fluttering. She swallowed hard, wishing

the windows weren't all the way across the room. But even if they were closer, he would stop her before she could reach the trellis. How could this be happening? She'd had three plans!

She struggled to pull herself together and muster what courage she could before *it* happened! She prided herself on her courage. Hadn't Uncle Burl called her his "brave little soldier"? She was caught fast, and there was no way to escape. At least, not until tomorrow.

Steeling herself, she unfastened the tiny row of buttons down her back, a difficult task without Carlisle's help; then she stepped out of the elegant gown and hung it carefully upon the hook on the back of the screen. She untied the satin ribbons holding her pannier around her waist, then removed several silk petticoats and pantalettes, until she stood in her thin chemise.

Slipping out of that, she pulled over her head the soft silk nightdress that Carlisle had chosen for her at Madame Broussard's. It was pure white with a modest scooped neckline trimmed with exquisite gossamer lace and narrow white satin ribbons. Then Tyler took a deep, fortifying breath and stepped outside to face her ordeal.

Gray was propped up in bed, the sheet covering him to his hard-muscled waist, but revealing his broad brown chest with its matting of black hair. All she could think was how big and manly he seemed in her delicate white four-poster bed with its pastel blue spread and canopy. She stood staring at him, rooted to the floor, not knowing what to do next.

"Come here, Tyler," he ordered.

She hesitated, then was afraid that if she didn't do what he said, he would stride unclothed across the room to get her. She moved slowly to the side of the mattress farthest away from him. She perched gingerly on the edge, her eyes averted from his very virile, very naked body; then, in one last-ditch attempt to stop whatever was about to happen, she launched desperately into a hastily concocted Plan D.

"If you touch me, I'll scream," she warned softly, not daring to look at him.

Gray only laughed. She didn't move, though, and his next words were tinged with impatience.

"Come over here right now, Tyler, and stop acting like a child. You're a grown woman, for God's sake."

Injured pride made her lift the satin-stitched comforter and slip into bed with him. One of his strong, sun-browned arms brought her quickly against him, and she lay stiffly in the curve of his arm, his long, hard body stretched out her entire length and well beyond.

Tyler's heart raced with terrified anticipation.

"Couldn't we at least douse the lamp?" she asked in a small voice after some time had passed. "I can't sleep with a light on."

She felt, rather than heard, Gray's chest rock with silent laughter.

"Not until I get my full of seeing you in bed with me."

"Well, I hope that's soon."

"Well, it won't be."

They lay quietly together, and Tyler waited and waited, terribly on edge as Gray's hand idly stroked her bare arm. Even after a quarter of an hour had passed with no threatening move on his part, Tyler remained so rigid and wary, she was afraid her muscles had turned to stone.

"Why are you so afraid?" he whispered at last, his lips moving atop her soft hair. "I intend to be very gentle with you."

So it *is* true—it *is* painful, she thought woefully. Gray's hand continued to caress her back. Tyler felt like a condemned prisoner.

"Do you know anything about what happens between a husband and a wife in bed, Tyler?"

She wet parched lips. "Only what Uncle Burl and Carlisle told me," she admitted reluctantly.

"Carlisle? What the devil does she know about it?"

"Only what the nuns taught her at the convent," Tyler murmured, filled with shame to be discussing it with him. "You know, about it being a terrible sin and all. And about submitting to your husband anyway."

"Submitting anyway?" Gray repeated almost angrily. "Good God, no wonder so many virgins feel as if they're laying themselves on a sacrificial altar."

Tyler looked up at him in surprise. "Shouldn't they?"

Gray's expression softened as he gazed deep into her wide, cinnamon-brown eyes. "No. Because it's not like that at all. It's sharing, between a man and a woman, not giving or taking. The marriage bed is just as pleasurable for a woman as it is for a man— or at least it's supposed to be," he amended. He smiled. "It will be for you. I promise you that."

Tyler was so relieved to hear this that she almost forgot how embarrassing the subject was. She relaxed a wee bit, not sure the languor overtaking her muscles was from his reassuring words or from the wonderful way his fingers were massaging her neck and shoulders.

"Then it won't hurt me as much as Uncle Burl said?" Tyler asked shyly, hiding her face against his smooth, broad shoulder.

Gray muttered what sounded like an oath. "I guess that's just one more thing I have to blame your uncle Burl for."

"What do you mean?"

"Never mind. It isn't painful for a woman, if that's what he told you, except perhaps for a few moments the very first time. And even that isn't very bad." He lifted himself on one elbow, turning so he could look down into her face. "Trust me, my love. I don't want you to be afraid of me, not ever. Do you understand?''

Tyler wasn't fearful anymore, not with his sweet words and the incredibly tender look he was bestowing upon her. This was a new Gray Kincaid, another facet of the man who seemed to have a thousand different sides.

She felt him leaning toward her, felt the hard muscles of his chest press against her breasts, but she forgot about that as his lips came down on her mouth, so nice and gentle that she felt no threat at all. She relaxed completely for the first time since she had awakened that morning, her mind reeling under his long, thorough exploration. He kissed her slowly and expertly with deep, draining kisses, the kind that melted her bones and made her as pliant as clay in a sculptor's hands. Her eyes fluttered and opened slightly as his dark head moved to the side of her throat, his mouth inching warmly and tenderly along her arched neck. She no longer thought of plans to escape him, or of fear, or her resistance to marrying the big, strong, handsome man who was touching her body so intimately.

Her long lashes came together again as he pulled her gown off one shoulder so his lips could settle lightly on her bare skin. He lingered there for a long time, then moved across the silken flesh of her collarbone to the other shoulder, then suddenly back to her mouth as if he hungered for her lips. His tongue found entrance there as his hands slid beneath the soft folds of her gown. The feel of his long fingers upon her naked thigh was a shock she could hardly withstand, but as she squirmed, uttering a weak protest, his mouth hushed her speech, his kisses growing deeper and more urgent, until she couldn't lie passive another moment. Unbidden, instinctively, her arms came up to encircle his neck, and she was surprised that even that small response brought a muffled groan of pleasure from him.

All thoughts were lost as his fingers pulled the

gown loose, and his dark curly head came down
upon her breasts, his lips closing gently over one
tender peak. She jerked as if touched by a fire that
shot into her very core.

Her fingers threaded into his thick dark hair,
tightening there as he continued to explore her quivering body, the gown slowly lowered inch by inch,
her flesh kissed and caressed until she felt herself
aglow with heat and need and never-ending waves
of pleasure. He moved atop her at last, bracing his
elbows on either side of her head, taking her lips
again, molding, tasting, tantalizing, until his mouth
pressed softly into her small, shell-like ear.

"I'll only hurt you this one time, my love, I swear
it," was his gruff whisper. But Tyler barely heard
him, thinking only of his heavy body pushing her
into the soft featherbed, and of the exquisite sensations he was arousing everywhere he placed his hot,
moist lips.

When he moved suddenly, pressing himself into
her, she stiffened in his arms, groaning from the stab
of pain, aware not only of the hurt but also that he
was inside her, that they were joined together as
one. The very magnitude of such intimacy frightened her, but as he thrust into her again, her fear
was quickly quelled, forgotten by his long, intoxicating kisses that numbed her mind and fired her
blood.

They moved together then, his fingers entangled
tightly in her flowing hair, and she found it not the
least uncomfortable or painful, but right and good,
as if they were created to fit together in such a close,
special way. She held tightly to him, feeling wanted
and needed and cherished as she never had before,
and he moved slowly above her, kissing her until
she felt his body go rigid, saw his lips open in a
groan against her temple, breathing her name and
words of love.

Great shivers of joy passed through her. It pleased
her that even in her innocence she was able to sat-

isfy a man as experienced and virile as her masculine, handsome husband.

For long moments they lay entwined, arms tight around each other, and Tyler felt as if the weight of the world had been lifted from her shoulders. She had survived her worst fears. Not only survived, but enjoyed and shared, just as Gray had told her.

He turned suddenly, holding her close, his whisper low in her ear.

"Was it so bad, sweet?"

"Not so bad at all," she murmured, her lips touching his chest. It surprised her that her kiss caused a quick intake of his breath. "In fact, I think Uncle Burl must have been quite ignorant about such things as this."

Gray laughed softly and put his lips on hers for several enjoyable moments.

"And there are many more pleasures for you, Tyler. More than you ever dreamed of."

"Oh, it can't be better than that," she returned without hesitation.

Gray lifted his head, smiling tenderly at her. "You have only taken the first taste of what I will show you."

"Show me now," she whispered, then was immediately appalled at her eagerness.

"I intend to," Gray assured her, taking her lips again.

And he did, all through the night, slowly, expertly, carrying her to the burning brink of her own sweet fulfillment and then beyond into ecstasy—over and over, until Tyler moaned and cried out in disbelief and wonder, as the sky slowly streaked red with the dawn of a bright new day.

15

Carlisle Kincaid lifted her foot to the tufted red velvet bench at the foot of the bed and quickly tied into a jaunty bow the lavender ribbon securing the top of her white silk stocking. She had overslept, of all things, and on the day of her voyage! It was little wonder, though, that she was exhausted; it had been nearly dawn when Chase had insisted she accompany him home.

She wrinkled her dainty nose at the thought of him, anger shooting through her at the way he had brazenly challenged her to kiss him in the carriage. The pompous wretch! And she was going to have to live at his hacienda for months while in Mexico.

Unbidden thoughts of that rather thorough kiss came with disconcerting clarity, but she quickly blocked out the memory. He had no doubt had a lot of practice. Now all she wanted was to find Tyler and make sure she was all right. Even more, she wanted to know the secrets of the marriage bed from someone with firsthand experience!

After pausing to give a few quick instructions to the maid packing her huge trunk for the sea journey, Carlisle hurried downstairs in search of her friend. She found Tyler sitting calmly at the dining room table, looking not at all as if she had just gone through the most frightening and momentous occasion in a young woman's life.

"Tyler!" Carlisle cried, rushing in with a swirl of lavender lace. "Where's Gray?" she asked, glancing quickly around the deserted room.

"He's instructing the staff about closing the house. We're leaving today, too, because he's decided to take me to Rose Point for our wedding trip. Isn't that wonderful? And Chase is—"

"I don't give a fig where that no-account blackguard is! I want to hear all about last night. Did Gray hurt you? Was it as bad as we thought? I got scared when I came home, because when I passed your door I heard you moaning and groaning like he was killing you!"

Tyler's eyes grew enormous and a surge of color darkened her cheeks to poppy red. Her gaze darted across the room just as Chase's deep voice floated to them.

"*Buenos días,* Senorita Kincaid."

Carlisle whirled as he rose from a chair half hidden by a potted fern. She nearly wilted beneath the amused smirk on his bronzed face.

"Why didn't you make yourself known?" Carlisle demanded.

"I guess because I'm a no-account blackguard," he replied evenly, obviously enjoying her plight.

"Excuse me, please, I've packing to finish," Tyler mumbled, so stricken with mortification that she fled the room.

Carlisle wanted to follow posthaste, but she knew if she did, Chase's mocking laughter would follow her. Her pride would not allow that. Instead, she proceeded with jerky steps to the sideboard to pour a cup of warm chocolate and was appalled at her scarlet face as she caught a glimpse of herself in the narrow mirror above the silver coffee urn. She had been so amused at the way Tyler was always blushing around Gray, and now she was doing the same thing around Chase! Although she couldn't see him now, and refused to look at him, she knew Chase was probably still wearing his infuriating crocodile grin.

"You know, Senorita Kincaid," he drawled as she sat down at the table, as far away from him as possible, "if you really want someone to explain the wedding night to you, I would be happy to volunteer. Now that I've taught you how to kiss, I could show you a few other things as well."

Carlisle leapt to her feet, nearly overturning her cup and saucer.

"When elephants roost in trees, Juarista," she gritted out harshly, then stalked furiously from the room.

His laughter followed her.

Headlong in flight from Carlisle and Chase's disconcerting conversation in the dining room, Tyler ran smack-dab into Gray, who was just coming from the servants' quarters in the back of the house.

"What's the matter?" he asked at once, grabbing her shoulders and eyeing her pinkened cheeks.

"Nothing," she said too quickly, embarrassed that she was embarrassed, and certainly not wanting Gray to know why.

He searched her face, but all she could think about was the night before in his bed and all the wonderful things he had done to her there. She swallowed hard as erotic shivers nearly overcame her.

"Good God, woman, you look like you're about to faint," he noted with concern. "Here, sit down."

His hand on her arm made her heart thud, and she began to wonder if every night of married life would be like the first. If that proved to be true, she wasn't sure she could bear it!

"Shall I get you a glass of water?"

"No, no, I'm fine, really. I was just going to finish packing my trunk."

"I've already had that done for you. Actually, I'm

ready to leave. Are you up to it, or would you like to rest awhile?''

She shook her head, thinking he was being much kinder than usual. Perhaps their night together had made a profound impression on him as well.

''All right, but you better sit here a moment while I round up Carly and Chase. We're to take them to the docks before we board the train.''

Tyler watched him walk away with long, graceful strides. He had moved like that the night before when he poured them both a glass of wine—except then he had not been dressed. More heated blushes warmed her face, and she wondered if she would wear such a revealing flush every time she looked at her husband, for the rest of her life.

By the time the foursome stepped down on the long wharf alongside the muddy Mississippi River, Tyler had managed to attain a certain degree of self-control. The thought of Carlisle leaving made her sad, and she embraced the other woman warmly. They stood at the base of the gangplank that led to the launch which would take the passengers to the *Mayan*. Gray and Chase conversed quietly several yards away.

''Oh, Carly, I wish I were coming with you and Chase,'' Tyler murmured.

''Me, too, but tell me quickly about last night while your hateful cousin isn't lurking behind some potted plant.''

''It wasn't''—Tyler hesitated, darting a quick look at Gray—''bad. Not bad at all. Actually, it was really, well, almost, quite nice.''

Carlisle smiled. ''Then you must love Gray a little after all. I'm so glad.'' She hugged her again. ''I think he loves you, too. I guess he'd have to—to want to marry you so fast. I might even be married next time you see me, if things go well. To Javier, I mean.''

''What? Are you really thinking of marrying him?''

"Oh, I don't know," Carlisle said airily. "He's desperate for me, and if the marriage act really isn't horrible like the nuns said, I might say yes. He's very charming, don't you think?"

"Yes, he is," Tyler agreed, but they had no more time for private conversation, as Chase drew Tyler aside.

"Gray has assured me he'll take good care of you," he told her, smiling, "but if things don't go well and you need me, send a telegraph message to the hacienda. But give yourself a chance to be happy. And no more tricks or swindles, you hear me?"

"Yes. Oh, Chase, I wish I were going to Mexico, too."

"Gray's already said he'll bring you down for a visit, perhaps when Carlisle's ready to return home. How's that sound?"

"Wonderful," she said wistfully, watching Gray give his sister an affectionate good-bye hug. Despite all their differences, she knew Gray and Carlisle were deeply fond of each other.

A moment later, Carlisle rushed up to embrace Tyler one last time.

"Oh, Tyler, I almost forgot," she whispered. "I've decided to send that letter to Emerson Clan's cousin in Alabama after all. I'm sure that if I do, Stone will be able to catch him."

"Wait, Carly, I don't think you should. Where will you tell him to collect the inheritance?"

"I don't know yet. Probably our house in Chicago. Remember? We discussed it."

"No, that's not a good idea," Tyler protested, but Carlisle's attention was drawn to the whistle calling passengers to board the waiting vessel.

"Well, maybe I won't, then, I don't know, but I still think it's a wonderful idea. Good-bye, Tyler. I'll miss you so much. I'm so glad you're my sister now!"

Another quick hug followed; then, after a scathing

look at Chase, Carlisle flounced down the gang-plank toward her adventure in Mexico.

Chase and Gray exchanged grins and clasped each other's hands in a warm handshake.

"Good luck, my friend," Gray said. "You'll need it."

Chase smiled, a glint in his eyes. "Lady Luck's always been my mistress," he said. "Don't worry about Carlisle. I can handle her. And besides, you haven't met the duenna I chose for her. They call Senora Alvarez *la aguila*—for her eagle-sharp eyes. She's known far and wide in Monterrey for her strict supervision of young unmarried girls like Carlisle. You can rest assured that no man will be able to get within a foot of your sister without incurring the senora's wrath."

"That's good to hear. Don't worry about Tyler, either. I can handle her."

Chase laughed at Tyler's indignant frown, then strode off quickly after Carlisle.

Tyler and Gray stood quietly watching the boat until it was rowed to midriver and brought up alongside the sleek sailing ship anchored in the mighty stream.

"Come along now, Tyler. Our train is due to leave shortly," Gray said, leading her away with him. Tyler gave one last, longing look after Carlisle's boat before she allowed her husband to assist her into their hired carriage.

Dusk had long since fallen when Tyler and Gray sat across the marble-topped table in his plush, private railway car. The familiar *clack-clacking* of the rails hummed in their ears, the water in their long-stemmed crystal goblets quivering from the constant motion.

Tyler watched Gray surreptitiously, amazed at how much everything had changed since the last time they had dined together at this table, only days ago. That first trip had been a silent, angry one, and now they were husband and wife and had shared the closest physical intimacy that could exist between a man and a woman.

Tyler looked down at her plate, appalled at how often she had thought about their lovemaking. It was just such a wondrous thing, a surprise she had not expected. She still couldn't believe such pleasures existed.

"What are you thinking about?" Gray asked suddenly.

Yet another blush began its incriminating path up her neck. She told her half lie quickly, almost guiltily.

"About how different things are now. I mean, since the last time we were on this train."

"Yes, very different."

He said nothing else, but he watched her closely, a slight smile on his lips.

"I think we'll have a better time this trip," he remarked as he leaned over, pulling open a hinged door on a nearby table.

Tyler watched him take out a small package wrapped in bright green tissue paper and secured with a red bow. He laid it on the table in front of her.

"What's this?" she asked, unable to hide her surprise and pleasure.

"Your wedding present."

Tyler met his azure eyes, took in his warm smile, then shivered. "You shouldn't have," she murmured, toying with the narrow ribbons.

"Why not?"

"Because I didn't give you anything."

"Yes, you did."

Although his answer was vague, she knew what he meant. He had already told her it pleased him greatly that she had not lain with any other man before him. Though, she thought wryly, if she had known how truly magical it was, she might have been sorely tempted. She suddenly wondered if it was always so good, or if it depended on the man and woman involved. It must be a natural thing, she decided, if even enemies like her and Gray could enjoy it so thoroughly.

"Open it."

Tyler obeyed, tugging the bow loose, then carefully folding back the fragile paper. A familiar drawstring bag lay there.

"Mother's jewels," she said softly, swallowing hard, her heart touched by the gesture. She raised her eyes to him. "Thank you. You don't know what this means to me."

"I think I do," Gray replied. "There's more."

Surprised, Tyler picked up the jewelry bag and found a paper lying there, folded in thirds like a legal document. At first not understanding what it was, she picked it up, her face paling slightly as she read the neatly penned words.

"It's the deed to Rose Point," she said, shocked. "You've put it in my name!" Tears came unbidden, and she blinked them back, her voice choked. "You're going to give it to me? Why?"

"Because you want it," he answered simply.

Tyler couldn't believe her ears or see how he could actually be handing the vast estate over to her, just like that.

"Even after all I've done to you? You're just giving it to me as a present?"

Gray smiled. "You should have asked me for it in the first place. It would have saved you and poor Mrs. Stokely a lot of time and trouble."

"Are you saying you would have agreed to sign it over to me, a complete stranger, when I first arrived in Chicago?"

"If I had known then everything I know now, I think I would have done just that."

"Father would be so pleased," she said, her emotions rising again.

"Do you still miss him?" Gray asked gently, and Tyler dabbed a tear from her eye.

"Yes. He was the kindest, most wonderful man who ever lived. And he loved me so much. More than anything else in the world."

Tyler looked at Gray, seeing him again as the man who had caused her beloved father to take his own life. An expression flitted across Gray's face, one she couldn't identify, but it made him rise abruptly and cross the room to the bellpull. He gave the tasseled gold cord a tug.

"We're done here, aren't we? I have to finish some correspondence, so why don't you go on to bed? It's growing late."

His mention of bed pushed away any other thoughts, and Tyler hesitated. But as Homer, the steward, came to clear away the dishes, toting his round silver tray, she rose from the chair. Gray was already seated at his desk, no longer paying any attention to her. So, clutching the jewels and the deed to her beloved home tightly against her breast, she parted the portiere that led to the bedroom.

Feeling lonely all of a sudden, she glanced around, then sighed, looking down at the land deed again, still finding it hard to comprehend that Gray Kincaid had actually signed her father's plantation over to her.

Smiling, she carefully placed the jewelry and the document inside the locked drawer of her trunk, then went behind the screen to disrobe. She slipped into her nightgown as she had the previous night, but this time there was no fear in her heart, only a thundering, quivering anticipation. Gray was being courteous by waiting outside, because she had asked him to let her undress in private. He was being nice again. And he was taking her home to Rose Point!

Crossing the soft carpet barefoot, she peeked through the curtains. He wasn't working anymore. He sat motionless in one of the deep armchairs by the windows, smoking his pipe, watching the darkness pass outside. His profile was as cleanly etched as those she had seen on ancient coins, and she realized again what a handsome man she had married.

Tiptoeing back to the wide bed, she pulled down the covers and snuggled under the downy comforter. She leaned back on the soft pillows to wait for him, turning her head to look at the lamp burning nearby. Her first impulse was to extinguish it, but he had not wanted her to do that the first night, so she only reached out to turn the wick very low. Then she waited.

Gray knocked his pipe on the ashtray at his side, then leaned back to contemplate the dark countryside rushing by. He wanted to give Tyler plenty of time to prepare herself, since he had not dared to leave her alone the previous evening.

Thinking of the blissful hours he had spent making love to his small wife made him want her again with a quiet desperation he had never before experienced. He glanced at the closed curtains, his blood quickening to think of her there, undressing for him. His pulse raced hotly through his veins as he thought how good it had been between them.

Never before had he lain with a woman he truly loved, and now he knew what a difference it made. He loved Tyler, and it had been blissful with her, so much so that he doubted he would ever desire another woman again. Grinning, he realized that, despite his experience, he was discovering the true wonder of lovemaking for the first time, just as she was. He'd never been hopelessly in love before—but now he was.

Closing his eyes, he leaned his head against the velvet chair. That was why he had decided to take her back to Rose Point. Under no other circumstances would he have ever set foot in that vile, evil place. Swallowing hard, he recalled the one occasion he had walked through the rooms—after the war, when he had first acquired the mansion. He could feel again the tremendous loathing that had possessed him in those dark, high-ceilinged chambers. Even the thought of entering the place filled him with hideous memories of the night his father had died, long before Tyler had been born.

Was it a kind of punishment? he wondered. God's way of teaching him right from wrong? What worse judgment could he receive than having Tyler—the woman he loved more than his own life—want to live in the very place he considered hell on earth? At times he wasn't sure he could go there, but then he would remember the way Tyler's face had looked in the throes of delirium, when she had begged to go home. Harriet had told him Tyler would never be happy until she returned to Rose Point, and he knew she was right. But would he be able to go through with it? Could he sit in those rooms where Colin MacKenzie had ordered Gray's father's death and listen to Tyler singing the praises of the man who had cruelly wielded a cane against his own back until he couldn't walk?

Suppressed rage flashed through him like a meteor, and Gray gripped the arms of the chair until his knuckles turned white. As quickly as the feeling had come, he willed it away.

None of it was Tyler's fault. She didn't know what had happened; nor did she understand what a perverted sadist her father had been. And now that Gray knew her better and sensed the fragility of her emotions, he couldn't even consider telling her the truth. He would not intentionally hurt her, not ever.

Nevertheless, with each mile eaten up by the chugging locomotive, dread filled him. But for Tyler's sake, he had no choice but to steel himself to accept his fate.

During the next few days, he would prepare himself for the visit to Rose Point. And who could say? Perhaps he would exorcise his own ghosts by going there. Perhaps he would finally be free of the past.

* * *

In the bedchamber, Tyler yawned sleepily, wishing Gray would come to her. It had been a very long time since she had climbed into the big empty bed to await him. He had certainly been eager enough the first time! What if he had already had enough of her? she thought suddenly. What if he didn't want to sleep with her anymore? What if he had compared her with his other women and found her wanting? Perhaps he was longing now for the woman to whom he had gone the first night they had arrived in New Orleans. That thought made her feel ill.

She worried for a time about Gray and his legion of former lovers, their ranks swelling and growing more beautiful with each passing minute. He would surely find her disappointing after the older, more sophisticated ladies he no doubt preferred. Then she began to feel silly for pining after him. Only last night she had not wanted him to touch her at all! Fuming inwardly at her own perversity and his sudden indifference, she impatiently threw back the covers and padded barefoot to the drapes. She hesitated there, debating what she should do. I should just go to sleep and forget all about him, she told herself crossly.

Instead, she parted the curtains. He still sat in the same place, deep in thought.

"Aren't you coming to bed?" she finally got up the nerve to ask.

At her soft voice, Gray turned to look in her direction. He grinned. "Are you so eager to have me there, Tyler?"

"No," she retorted, feeling angry and stupid. "I hope you never come."

Before she could slide beneath the sheets again, however, he had entered the bedroom. Tyler looked away as he began to undress. To her surprise, he turned down the lamp until the chamber was plunged into blackness, with only a wide band of misty moonlight slanting in from the open window on the far side of the bed.

"I thought you liked the light on," she whispered as he sat across from her.

"Perhaps I want to see you in the moonlight," he murmured, reaching out to lift a strand of her silky hair, his touch so soft she could hardly feel it. She sat still, her heart drumming in her breast.

"Where did you go that first night in New Orleans?" she chagrined herself by asking.

Gray seemed surprised by her unexpected question. "I went to see my lawyer about signing over the deed to Rose Point to you. Why?"

Relief nearly overwhelmed Tyler, astounding her. "Carlisle said you were with another woman."

"Would it bother you if I had been?"

Tyler could not admit it, not to him. She looked down without answering.

"Come here, Tyler," Gray ordered softly.

She obeyed at once, forgetting that she had been annoyed with him only moments ago. She moved across the bed on her knees until she sat facing him. He reached out, deftly pulling loose both her shoulder straps. Her gown fell to her waist, and his head dipped forward, his lips touching the smooth, satiny skin of her breasts.

Tyler could not stifle a gasp of pleasure or keep her head from falling back weakly, her soft russet tresses swinging against her bare back as his mouth inched with maddening slowness up the curve of her eagerly offered throat to just beneath her ear.

"Why won't you admit it? You love me, and you know it," he demanded gruffly, his lips moving atop the throbbing pulse of her neck.

"No, I don't. I hate you, and I will as long as I live," she answered automatically. But the breathless moan that followed her pronouncement belied her words, as did the quivering flesh his lips were caressing with such expertise.

Gray gave a low laugh, pressing her back on the

bed with the weight of his body, and Tyler moaned again as he took off her gown and tossed it carelessly aside.

"Yes, you do, Tyler, but you don't have to say the words if you don't want to. Not when you'll prove different to me every night in our bed, just as you're going to do right now." He took her lips then, tenderly, hungrily, and they began their long, slow ascent to the very gates of heaven.

16

Three days after they had left New Orleans, Tyler sat in a rented buggy in Natchez, waiting for Gray to finish his business at the Adams County Courthouse on Market Street. In the next block she could see the Presbyterian church on Pearl Street, and she sighed as she gazed around the familiar city, nostalgically reminded of childhood shopping excursions with her father.

She snapped open the small watch pinned to her waist. Three o'clock in the afternoon. She glanced up the steps of the courthouse again, wishing Gray would hurry. It was a surprisingly dry, warm day for early April. The dress she wore was rose silk, and it was already damp at the small of her back. She opened her parasol, watching a nattily dressed Negro man on the sidewalk beside her listening to a white businessman in a plaid suit. Even from her place in the carriage she could hear the Northerner's la-di-da Eastern accent. She frowned slightly, sizing the white man up as a carpetbagger. Troops of them had descended on the South at the end of the war, and they were apparently still in control.

Tyler's mood plummeted. She had dreamed a thousand times of coming home, and when the train had quivered to a standstill and Gray had helped her to the platform, she had been filled with exhilaration. But now, sitting alone, Tyler felt a deep, disturbing ache throb in her breast.

She mentally shook herself, inordinately pleased to see Gray descending the steps at last, looking tall and very important in his fine brown coat and trousers with a white double-breasted satin waistcoat. She continued to watch him as he moved toward her with his long, masculine strides. Another rich Yankee businessman claiming the spoils of war, she thought, then was immediately ashamed of her bitterness. He didn't deserve her contempt. He had given Rose Point back to her in good faith! She could no longer despise him for taking her home away. In truth, she wasn't sure she could hate him for anything anymore.

Guilt rose up, like a great, rolling wave, engulfing her, as Gray climbed to the seat beside her. He took the reins, giving her the easy smile he had worn so often of late. Some of Tyler's guilt disintegrated as he reached out to lift the back of her hand to his lips. That tender, affectionate gesture melted her heart like butter in a bake pan.

"Everything's ready now, love. The carpenters and household staff will be coming out tomorrow morning," Gray told her, slapping the reins lightly against the mare's back.

Tyler sat silently beside him, still thinking of the casual endearment he had spoken. Did he really love her? She swallowed convulsively, her pulse quickening again with pleasure. And did she love him? Was that the cause of all her hot and cold sensations, her quivers and long, hot blushes? It was all so strange and hard to accept. Gray Kincaid, of all people, the man she had vowed to hate forever. How could she have fallen in love with him? But at night in bed it was truly wonderful between them.

"I wired the caretaker yesterday to air out a couple of rooms so we wouldn't have to stay in town tonight. I hope he had time," Gray said as he turned the horse down Union Street past the front of St. Mary's Cathedral. "Remember now, Tyler, the house itself will probably be in some disrepair."

Gray glanced over at her as he spoke, and Tyler wondered if it could really be anxiety she heard in his voice. He had tried to prepare her for Rose Point's neglected condition more than once during the past few days.

"It's been six years. I know it won't look exactly the same," Tyler answered quietly, her gaze fastened on the road ahead.

Jefferson Street took them past one of the oldest buildings in Natchez, the half-brick, half-timbered King's Tavern, which sheltered travelers on the old Natchez Trace. When they turned onto Pine Ridge Road where tall evergreen trees cast spidery shadows over the buggy, Tyler welcomed the cool, dim shade.

They traveled in silence for a time, over a gradual rise to a ridge where well-tended cotton had once grown. But now the fields were choked with weeds, saplings, and yellow wildflowers. On the far side of the hill, the horse trotted past the blackened ruins of Hillcrest Manor, where Tyler's father had spent many nights at a chessboard opposite Owen Morton, the rotund master of that sprawling estate. Now the great house was gone, with only a skeleton of the pillared facade left. Vanished, with everything and everyone inside. Tyler wondered what had become of the Morton family with its six strapping sons and three married daughters. Had they been forced to survive the war in any way they could, as Tyler herself had done?

More unbidden, disconcerting emotions threatened her composure, and she felt nauseous, pressing herself backward into the worn leather seat as if her own unwillingness could delay the inevitable confrontation with her past.

Stop, stop, turn around! she wanted to cry out to Gray, but an inner voice mocked her cowardice.

Within her head, a chant sounded over and over in cadence with the clopping of the horse's hooves— going home, going home, just the way you wanted, just the way you wanted!

Inside her dainty rose silk gloves, Tyler's hands tightened upon the ivory handle of her matching lace parasol, and she sat ramrod straight, growing rigid with dread.

Gray guided the buggy down the last stretch of road, his eyes fastened inexorably on the entrance gates of Rose Point Plantation. He had passed beneath its fancy iron grillwork arch on only three other occasions. The first was the worst time—when he had stumbled up that long road, blinded by tears, rain, and a rage no child of eleven should ever have to feel. Then he had come as a grown man at the head of a mounted column to burn, plunder, and appease his thirst for vengeance. But even then he'd had no desire to live in the commandeered house. He'd set up his headquarters at a nearby plantation, leaving Rose Point's spacious rooms for his men.

On the third visit he had entered the hall and promptly vowed never to return. He cursed the irony of life as he slowed the mare and looked up the long line of thick, fragrant cedar trees over which he could just make out the green, Spanish-tiled roof. As he glanced at Tyler, he worried about her reaction and felt a sharp regret for allowing the house to fall into disrepair.

Tyler looked pale, her splendid eyes on the distant chimneys, but her face was so carefully expressionless that Gray suspected she was reining in her emotions as tightly as a prancing stallion. His gaze dropped to her hands, both of which were clenched around the handle of her parasol.

"Are you all right, Tyler?"

She nodded without speaking or looking at him, and a stronger wave of foreboding swept over Gray. Had it been a mistake to bring her to Rose Point now? Would the sight of her childhood home de-

stroy his efforts to win her to him? He urged the
horse forward, glancing up at the metal gate, now
rusty and in need of paint. As they rolled up the
avenue of cedars, Tyler remained stiff and silent beside him, until halfway up the hill. Just before the
point where the front of the house would come into
view, her slender hand gripped his forearm.

"Please stop."

Gray slowed the buggy at once, looking at her
as the wheels came to a standstill. He hoped she
had changed her mind. As much as he'd wanted
anything in his life, he wished to turn around and
return to Chicago.

"I'd rather go on alone this first time," she murmured, avoiding his eyes. "Just for a few minutes.
Please, Gray?"

Since he had secretly nurtured the hope that she
would want to share her homecoming with him—be
it painful or pleasant—her quiet rejection slashed a
gaping wound across his heart. Hiding his disappointment, he climbed out and quickly lifted her to
the ground. He had forced her to marry him, but he
couldn't make her share her feelings. She had to
give him her trust, and acknowledge her love, on
her own terms. He must be patient.

"Thank you, Gray, for understanding."

He nodded, and she hesitated, seeming small and
young beside him in her pink dress with layer upon
layer of frilly ruffles and her pert straw bonnet
bedecked with pink-and-white velvet ribbons. He realized with a pang that she was struggling to face
her past with dignity. He respected her for it.

Gray leaned against the wheel as she moved a few
steps up the road away from him, her dainty slippers crunching on the gravel. He heaved a heavy
sigh, appalled at his growing revulsion to Rose Point
and his intense reluctance to go any closer to the
house.

* * *

As Tyler moved up the road, she quickened her step to match the staccato beat of her heart. Everything was the same so far, the old split-log fence along the north side of the road, the great mimosa stump where she had often sat, waiting for her father to return from some journey.

Now honeysuckle vines ran rampant over the fencerow and ground, even creeping up into the branches of the great cedar trees. She would come upon the house any moment, she thought, increasing her pace and striving desperately to retain her composure. Her heart felt like thunder in her breast now, and her hands shook until she clenched them together to control their trembling.

But all her fear and foreboding fled when she saw her family's home; swirled away like leaves before a coming storm. She stopped dead still, drinking in every detail of the big, elegant estate, framed beautifully by familiar, beautiful magnolias and live oaks.

Home, home, home, her heart sang, and Tyler left the drive to run up through the weeds and tall grass choking the once immaculately manicured, velvet-turfed lawn. She didn't stop until she reached the spot where the entry road encircled the oval lily pond in front of the veranda. The water was gone now, the foundation bricks cracked by stubbornly encroaching grass. She sank down on one of the two decorative benches near the hitching rings. Another lay broken in half nearby, but both the giant flower urns, bleached and rusted by years of rain and neglect, were still in their rightful places at the corners of the house.

It didn't matter. To her long-starved eyes the house was home, despite the peeling white paint and boarded-up windows. Her gaze wandered over the curved portico, up the double Corinthian columns to the small railed balcony leading off the second-floor corridor. Higher still, in the uppermost eaves, a huge nest of wasps buzzed and swarmed, darkening the ornate cornice.

Glossy green ivy crawled over the front wall, obliterating several of the lower windows. Nevertheless, Rose Point stood before her, intact, beautiful, eliciting so many wonderful, bittersweet memories. Her father had loved it so much, and now, finally, she had gotten it back for him.

After ten minutes had passed, Gray slapped the reins and drove the carriage farther up the drive. When he saw Tyler sitting on a bench in front of the empty lily pool, he stopped the horse a good distance away. Not wanting to disturb her, he climbed down, his eyes sweeping over the big square house. He found himself loath to approach the stately facade. Against his will, his gaze settled on a ground-floor window behind one of the pillars. Now it was hidden by weathered boards, but on that summer night during his youth, it had been bright with lamplight—until he'd heaved a brick through its glittering panes.

Forcing the unwanted memory away, he transferred his attention to Tyler. She stood near the front steps now, and when he realized that she was crying, he went to her. He put his arms around her and drew her against him.

"We'll fix it up again, I promise," he whispered, his chin resting atop her head. "Just the way it used to be."

Tyler closed her eyes, leaning back against his wide chest. He lowered his head to kiss the side of her throat, and she raised her hand, sliding her fingers into his soft black hair.

"Thank you for bringing me home," she whispered, her voice gruff with emotion.

Gray turned her to face him, smiling as he smoothed away the wetness on her cheeks.

"Shall I go inside with you? Or would you rather go alone?"

"Yes, I want you with me," she murmured, completely unaware of how much she pleased her husband with that simple invitation.

Excited now, Tyler drew Gray with her up the wide, curving steps to the porch, where sodden leaves and other debris clogged the bases of the columns and the stone balustrades. Tyler didn't care. The workmen were coming in the morning. They would clean it up in no time! She would help them!

She waited impatiently as Gray retrieved the big iron key, and he laughed at the way she fidgeted while he worked to release the rusty padlock. Once the door was open, he stood back as Tyler rushed inside. Just within the wide front hall, however, she stopped.

Tyler stared around the dark, silent house, spooked by the dead quiet and misty gloom. Dust motes danced in front of her eyes, illuminated by the smoky light filtering from the grimy glass of the elaborate fanlight above the door.

Her gaze went to the back of the house, past the massive staircase, which curved to her right up behind the entrance. Down the hall stood the closed door of her father's library. For one awful moment, she was drenched with cold, uncanny fear. The unreasonable fright fled as Gray's strong hands settled lightly on her shoulders.

"The overseer was to have readied the front parlor for our stay."

Tyler followed him into the room to the left of the door, smiling when she saw the richly upholstered crimson damask couches and gold-striped chairs, all arranged in their places. Everything seemed the same as it had been the day her uncle Burl had pulled her out the door. She grew cold inside at the sheer pain of that recollection, but she crossed to a nearby table and picked up a fragile blue-flowered vase that had held hothouse roses every day of her childhood.

"I thought the furniture would have been sold a

long time ago," she murmured, glancing at Gray standing near the doorway.

"I ordered everything covered and left in place the day I boarded up the house," he said, turning away from the puzzled questions in her eyes. As he moved past her to open a window, Tyler glanced around, feeling peculiar, as if she had been transported back in time. Her gaze went to the fireplace, set in readiness with logs, then to the wall above the mantel where a magnificent, life-size portrait of her father had always hung.

"I had it taken down," Gray answered without being asked. "I'm afraid it was destroyed."

Tyler faced him quickly, surprised by the change in his voice. His words were clipped, very different from the tone he had used outside in the hall. She didn't know what to say, and Gray glanced around, his stance stiffly erect, his hands clasped tightly behind his back.

"I'd better bring the buggy up to the house. I need to unload our things."

Tyler nodded, but as he left the room, his footsteps a loud, hollow echo on the bare wooden floors, she felt an inexplicable desire to run after him. She fought down the urge, impatient with herself, then walked determinedly to the foyer.

Firmly keeping her eyes away from the back of the hall, she crossed to the dining room doors. The tall panels squeaked loudly as they slid apart, and inside, the drapes were drawn tight against the sun. Cobwebs hung from the ceiling and walls, giving the room a spooky look, as if evil ghosts crouched beneath the sheets covering the furniture.

Tyler bit her lip and hastily shut the doors. Suddenly the dark, empty rooms seemed frightening and malevolent. She jumped a foot and whirled around as Gray's voice came unexpectedly from behind her.

"Let's take these things upstairs. Then I'll see to

the horse.'' He stopped and regarded her with some surprise. ''Did I startle you?''

''I didn't hear you coming.''

For a moment he searched her white face, then started up the steps with their bags. He glanced around at his wife, who followed very close behind him. Once at the top, Gray surveyed the dim hall with its long row of closed doors. ''I ordered this bedroom at the top of the stairs prepared for us.''

''That's my old room,'' Tyler told him softly, pierced by the poignant sting of painful memories.

Gray looked at her for a moment. ''Well, it should be clean and aired out.''

Tyler glanced wistfully at the adjoining suite of rooms her parents had shared. She was drawn toward them, but at the same time strangely repulsed. Tomorrow it would be better, she thought, after they had opened all the windows and rid the place of the old, musty odors permeating the rooms. When the sun shone in again, the gloom would be dispelled for good. Then she would explore every room slowly and lovingly, all by herself.

But more shattering emotions flooded over her as she followed Gray into her childhood bedchamber. Like the parlor downstairs, it had been dusted and scrubbed. The scent of beeswax and lemon came from the tables and a tall wardrobe. The white linen hangings on the slim-posted rosewood bed had been freshly starched and blew in the breeze from the open window.

Memories stirred and swirled and hurt her and gave her pleasure, confusing her so much that she didn't know what to think. She walked to the high-backed white rocker in which her father had creaked back and forth while he sang her to sleep in his rich baritone voice. He had taken pleasure, too, in brushing her hair, she remembered, and she turned to look at the silver brush-and-comb set lying on the bedside stand.

It seemed as if her years of exile had never occurred. She touched the cleverly wrought angel on the brush handle. An elaborate, five-drawered music box sat on the table beside an oil lamp. She lifted the lid. The haunting strains of ''Greensleeves'' tinkled into the silence, making her feel so forlorn that she quickly closed the top to end the song and the pain it engendered. Her eyes filled, and she was grateful when Gray's arms came around her, pulling her close. She clung to him, wordlessly.

''It'll take some getting used to, my love. I know it's difficult for you.''

''Yes,'' was all the answer she could muster.

A moment later Gray released her, glancing toward the open windows. ''It'll be dark soon. I'll start the fire and light the lamps. Why don't you unpack the supper basket?''

Glad for something to do, Tyler unpinned her hat and laid it aside, then set out the cold roast beef and crusty bread that Gray's cook had prepared in the galley of the railway car before they had reached Natchez. She poured them each a glass of wine, pulling up chairs at either side of a small table near the window. As they sat down to dine, Tyler was finally able to relax, sipping her wine and listening to Gray's plans for returning Rose Point to its previous grandeur. The strange, eerie feelings faded and she began to enjoy being home with Gray across the table, his eyes warm and possessive. She smiled when he picked up a small piece of cloth lying on a nearby table.

'' 'Tyler MacKenzie is my name. Rose Point Plantation is my home. Adams County is my dwelling place and Christ is my salvation.' ''

Tyler laughed as he finished reading the embroidered words, then took the unframed needlework from him. ''I had forgotten all about this sampler.'' She smiled as she observed the crooked, uneven stitches. ''I wasn't very good with a needle then, was I? I'm better now.''

''When did you do it?''

"When I was eight or so, I guess. I lost interest in it, long before Uncle Burl took me away."

"You could finish it now," Gray murmured, taking her hand.

Tyler was touched by his gentle words. "No, I think I'll start a new one instead. One to hang in our parlor."

Gray looked pleased, but a moment later, he stood. "I'd better stable the horse for the night. After that we can go to bed."

Tyler nodded in agreement, growing warm from the promise in his voice. After he had gone, she unpacked their clothes, placing the folded garments in familiar old drawers and chests, vividly remembering when Mammy Rose Marie had done the same with Tyler's girlish frocks and starched pinafores. Such thoughts conjured up other fond recollections—the spirituals her old nurse had taught her and the thrilling tales her father had told her about faraway lands where knights rode gallant white steeds and rescued maidens from dragons.

Sighing, she disrobed and donned a soft white nightgown before sitting down before the dressing table with its round mirror and ten tiny drawers. She began to brush her hair, suddenly eager for Gray to return. She longed to be in bed with him again, lying close while he moved his hard palms over her bare skin.

Shaking her head at her own wanton thoughts, she let her gaze linger on the gently billowing curtains reflected in the mirror. The sight brought yet another favorite memory back to her, a childhood prank that had particularly annoyed poor Mammy Rose Marie.

Smiling, she walked to the window, parting the lacy drapes. Outside, a wide flat branch of a gigantic live oak nearly touched the house. On impulse, she lifted her gown high, then climbed atop the low windowsill and out onto the tree limb, holding tightly to the branch above.

Straddling the limb, she sat down and leaned back against the trunk. She peered up through the branches to see the stars gleaming like tiny silver lanterns. Although she suddenly found it hard to believe she was home at Rose Point and sitting in her favorite tree, pure happiness bubbled up deep inside her. She laughed out loud.

"Tyler? Where are you?"

She laughed again at the puzzlement in Gray's voice as he called from inside the room.

"Out here. In the tree."

An instant later, her husband appeared between the blowing curtains, the oil lamp in his hand clearly revealing the shocked expression on his face.

"What the hell are you doing?"

Amused, Tyler tried to explain. "I used to come out here nearly every night before I went to sleep. It's lovely. You can lie back and watch the stars."

"Tyler, come in here right now, before you kill yourself." Her husband's voice had taken on the authoritative tone he sometimes used with inattentive employees.

"That's exactly what Mammy Rose Marie used to say."

"I mean it! Tyler, for God's sake, you had wine tonight!"

"Don't be silly. I hardly drank any. You're the one who refilled your glass. Besides, it's perfectly safe out here. Why don't you join me?"

"Don't be ridiculous. Come in here at once."

"What's the matter? Do you suffer from vertigo?" She laughed at the notion.

Gray frowned darkly. "Tyler," he began in calm tones that clearly heralded underlying anger, "if I have to come out there, you won't care for what I do when I've got you."

A deliciously benign terror tingled through Tyler at his threat. When she climbed to the next limb with a challenging grin, he ducked back into the room and muttered a few choice oaths under his breath as he set the lamp on a nearby table.

Then he climbed out the window in pursuit of her, a feat difficult for a man his size. She gasped, wincing as his head hit the casement with an awful thud and another ungentlemanly epithet. Stifling her urge to giggle, she watched him wrathfully pull himself to a standing position atop the limb.

"See, Gray, it's wide and sturdy and as safe as can be." She smiled playfully, leaning down to plant a quick kiss on his cheek. "We could even sleep out here, if we wanted."

Gray looked down at the ground, twenty feet below. "Did you really come out here as a child?"

"Yes, but Mammy Rose Marie never worked up the courage to join me like you did. She was too scared to tell Papa either, so she just let me do it. Now I feel bad about misbehaving. She was such a dear."

"Why was she scared to tell your father? You were certainly endangering yourself."

His quiet question disconcerted Tyler for a moment. "I guess because he would punish her."

"Why would he punish her? You were the naughty one."

Tyler was quiet, thinking of one time when she had climbed outside her room. She had been nine years old, and her father had come early to put her to bed. When he'd seen her in the tree, he had slapped Mammy Rose Marie across the face. Tyler shivered, still able to recall the cracking sound the blow had made. She had been shocked and frightened to see him do such a cruel thing. But when he had coaxed her inside, he had been as kind and gentle as ever and had explained how terrified for her safety he'd been. But after that night, she'd never climbed out her window again, unless he was away from home. Troubled, she lifted her chin defensively, not wanting Gray to know of her father's one transgression.

"Well, didn't you ever climb trees or do naughty things when you were little?" she demanded.

Gray thought of the nights of his boyhood when, more often than not, he had gone to bed hungry, nursing fingers raw and bleeding from sharp cotton bolls. He changed the subject.

"Are you happy to be home? Is it turning out the way you thought?"

"Yes, I love it here. Papa always said this place was in his blood. I guess it's in mine, too." She looked down through the leaves at the dark lawns below their perch. "He said a man wasn't really a man if he didn't own land." She looked at Gray again. "I guess that can be true for a woman, too."

She couldn't see his face very well, since the light from the bedchamber was behind him. He stood very still, staring at her. She sensed intuitively that his mood had become serious.

"And my father always said it's not what a man has that makes him rich, but what he values."

Tyler was struck by the somber way he had uttered the words. Realizing the vast difference in their fathers' ideas, she couldn't think of anything to say in answer. Silence prevailed for a long moment, with only the croaking serenade of frogs and the chirping of crickets to disturb the quiet night.

"You know what I think?" Gray said at last. "I think you've played out here long enough. I want you inside in bed. Now."

He was teasing, but she decided that his last word had been too peremptory for her taste.

"How much do you want me there?" she asked mischievously, inching away from him.

"Quite a bit."

"Enough to come after me?"

"Tyler . . ." he warned.

Laughing, she took little heed and went higher. "I was going to climb down the trellis to escape you on our wedding night. Did I ever tell you that?"

"Dammit, woman, I'm not joking. You could fall."

Tyler watched him swing himself to the branch below her, and in turn she moved nimbly to the next leafy bower. She watched as he looked down at the ground again, then heard him groan as he laid his forehead against the tree trunk.

"What's the matter?" she asked, her smile fading.

"Nothing. I'm asking you nicely. Come down here. Please. This isn't funny anymore."

Realization dawned, and at once Tyler was contrite. "You're afraid of heights, aren't you?" She scrambled down to the limb just above him. "Are you dizzy? Oh, Gray, I'm sorry. I didn't know. Stay still and let me help you. Don't look down."

"I have no intention of looking down. Not with you here," he said, grasping her around the knees before she could get away.

"You tricked me!"

"Yes, for a change. You're entirely too gullible for a former thief."

As she squirmed and tried to free herself, he pulled her down until his face was level with her chest. "I think you need to be punished," he muttered, holding her tightly with one hand while he pulled loose the ribbons on her gown.

"Stop, Gray, we'll fall!"

His mouth was inside her bodice now, atop warm, velvety skin. "I'm beginning to like climbing trees." His lips closed over the tip of her breast.

"I thought you said I wouldn't like what you did when you got here," Tyler gasped weakly, her hands braced on his wide shoulders. "Oh, please, stop. I feel dizzy."

"Could be vertigo." His laugh was muffled against her naked flesh.

"No, it's you," she whispered, moaning again and wrapping both arms around his head.

Gray smiled, sliding his mouth up her arched throat until he could taste her lips.

"Are you willing to come quietly now?"

Her answer was a long erotic shiver and he held her tightly against him with one arm as he descended, entering the window, then hastily pulling Tyler in after him. He began to kiss her before her feet touched the floor, deftly stripped off her gown before they were halfway to the bed, and then for the next few hours subjected her to a dizzy, languorous kind of vertigo, the likes of which she'd never experienced in the tree outside her window.

17

The carpenters and servants arrived early the next morning with a great deal of noise and uproar as they unloaded boards, paint, and wall coverings from their wagons. Tyler lifted her head from soft, downy pillows, drowsily looking around for Gray, whom she found dressed in tan riding breeches and a blue work shirt, sitting in the chair beside the bed. He spoke while pulling on a tall brown leather boot.

"Go ahead and sleep awhile, if you want, sweetheart. I'll take care of things downstairs."

He leaned forward to give her a light kiss on the forehead, then strode away, leaving Tyler to close her eyes contentedly, fully intending to drift back into slumber.

Masculine shouting from outside continued nonstop, however, and eventually brought her out of bed to pad barefoot to the windowsill. She leaned out, and from her high vantage point was just able to see a portion of the front lawn, where several men were busily stacking fresh-sawed pine boards.

Gray walked among them, giving each man orders. He really was going to make Rose Point everything it once was, she thought. And he was doing it for her. Happiness made her shiver, and she hurried to the bowl and pitcher for her morning ablutions, wanting to join in the restoration as soon as she could.

She dressed quickly, eager to help, chose a plain morning dress of blue chambray, and left off all but one petticoat, thinking she would have to look for an apron in the kitchen linen closet. She tied her hair back at her nape with a bright yellow scarf, then ventured into the upstairs hall. She put her hand on the banister, looking around, and was appalled as a sudden sense of stifling doom spiraled down around her. The feeling was so strong that it sent her fleeing downstairs to where she could hear the babble of several female voices.

In the hall below, she found half a dozen Negro women with brooms, pails, and feather dusters. Upon seeing her, they quieted their lively chatter and dropped into curtsies.

"Do you be de missus?" one of the older ones asked her.

Tyler nodded, looking up at the sound of workmen wrenching boards off the front windows.

"Mistah Kincaid, he say we weren't 'posed to wake you."

"That's all right. You didn't. I was up already. Is he still outside?"

"Yes, missus, but he say to tell you he be ridin' down to de caretaker's place and dat he be back real soon."

"I see." Tyler looked around, not knowing exactly what to do.

The servants stood quietly, as if waiting for orders. Then their self-proclaimed leader spoke again. "Mistah Kincaid, he say we should do de downstairs here first off, then go up. Is dat what you be thinkin' us to do?"

"Yes, that's a good idea."

Tyler felt embarrassed. She really wasn't used to giving orders to other people, but she knew that Gray would expect her to run his household for him. The idea of being the mistress of his home gave her

pleasure, and she vowed she would learn her duties
well and make him proud of her. The cleaning
women dispersed, several of them disappearing into
the dining room while the others started down the
hall toward the kitchen and cook's quarters.

Left standing in the foyer, Tyler suddenly felt very
much alone. She glanced down the hall toward her
father's library, and deep inside, she imagined she
again heard the awful, final gunshot. She fought
against an overwhelming need to get out of the
house. She lost. Gray, she thought, hurrying for the
door. She had to find Gray!

Outside, in the deep, cool shade of the pillars,
Gray sat astride the big palomino stallion he had
purchased the day before in Natchez, listening to
the carpenter he had put in charge of the workers.
He barely heard the man's plans, so eager was he
to get away from the house. It was worse for him
than he had ever imagined it could be. He'd been
tormented every minute he'd spent in the rooms
where Colin MacKenzie had once lived.

From the first moment he'd set foot inside, the
old, vicious hatred had begun its insidious battle to
poison his mind. Yesterday in the parlor, he'd remembered with undiminished gratification the day
he had pulled down Colin MacKenzie's gilt-framed
portrait. The very day he had purchased Rose Point,
he'd taken great pleasure in stomping it to pieces
before burning it to a curling black crisp. That vicious act was one he could never relate to Tyler—
and only one of his horrible memories concerning
her detestable father. He'd been tormented by them
since their arrival.

When he had made love to Tyler the bitterness
had been forgotten momentarily, but afterward
when she'd slept peacefully in his arms, he had lain
awake for most of the night, staring at the ceiling
and detesting the bed in which he lay, the walls
around him, everything.

Each time Tyler mentioned her father—with her face softening in adoration and her tone growing almost reverent—he could hardly restrain the urge to tell her what a monster he really had been. Gray wanted to scream it out and destroy her false, idealized memory of Colin MacKenzie forever. But he couldn't—not without losing her. She would hate him if he shattered her sacred illusions. And it would be genuine hatred, not the memorized kind her uncle had taught her. His only hope was that someday, somehow, she would realize that the saint enshrined in her heart was nothing but a figment of her imagination.

Gray sighed deeply, glancing at the house and feeling a chill as tingling as a January dawn. How could he bear it? How could he live under that roof indefinitely when the first night he'd spent within its walls had brought to the surface powerful acidic emotions he'd long thought dead and buried?

His burgeoning antagonism melted away as the front door opened and Tyler rushed headlong onto the portico. She looked fresh and pretty, and more important, happy to see him. In that moment he knew he'd remain at Rose Point just as long as she wanted to live there. Her joy and contentment would soothe the venom of his contempt.

"There's my wife now, Mr. Boyer," he said, motioning for Tyler to join them. "Whenever you please her, you'll please me."

As Tyler reached the balustrade just above him, he said, "Tyler, Mr. Boyer here is taking care of all our repairs. If there's anything special you wish done, just tell him."

Tyler smiled at the thick, heavyset man, who immediately swept off his worn navy blue work cap and gave her a respectful nod. She descended the steps and waited while the two men conversed for another minute. When the carpenter departed to attend to his duties, Gray walked the big horse toward her.

"I thought you'd want to rest longer. Did the hammering disturb you?"

Tyler shook her head and reached up to clasp the hand he held down to her.

"I want to come with you. May I? Please?"

Her request surprised Gray, but it certainly didn't displease him. "Can you ride?"

"No," Tyler admitted reluctantly, "but I'm not scared of horses. I could ride with you, couldn't I?"

"You could," Gray answered, swinging to the ground beside her. "And you will."

He boosted her up into the saddle, then mounted behind her. Tyler leaned against the solid wall of his chest, content as his strong arms came around her to take the reins. She was not the least bit afraid. What woman would be with a man like Gray holding her?

"I figured you'd want to direct the housecleaning," he remarked as he urged the horse forward.

"I'd rather be with you," she answered simply.

"Glad to hear it," he replied, grinning as his mouth settled on her temple.

Birds sang all around them, happy, carefree chirps and warbles that echoed loudly in the serene green-and-gold-dappled morning sunshine. Huge magnolias shaded the south corner of the house where Gray headed them down the sloping east lawn to a path that Tyler knew led toward the old slave quarters, then on to Possum Creek and Township Line Road.

From infancy, her father had forbidden her to go farther than the fencerow nearest the house, but often she had disobeyed and sneaked closer to observe the cluster of small white houses where the Negroes had lived. They had fascinated her because, other than her mammy, the cook, and the housemaids, she'd not been allowed to speak to the slaves.

Once, when she had hidden behind the lilac hedge near where she and Gray now rode, she had heard the most horrible shrieks coming from the quarters.

Mammy had never told her what had happened, but
she'd seen her father striding away not long after,
angrily slapping his riding crop against his leg. For
days afterward, everyone had been very somber and
quiet. She hadn't thought about the incident in
years, but as she stared at the deserted, overgrown
dwellings, she felt sick inside, afraid to think what
her father had done that day. Upset by her own misgivings, she wondered what had happened to all the
black people who had congregated around the tiny
huts.

"Do you think we could find some of Father's former slaves to work for us, Gray? I'd love to see
Mammy Rose Marie again. She was like a mother to
me."

"I doubt if many are still in this area. But if you
wish, when we advertise for workers, we can give
Rose Point people first consideration."

"I'd like that very much," Tyler murmured, nest-
ling closer into Gray's arms as they left the open
fields near the outbuildings and entered a narrow
forest trail. She looked around the tall pine trees and
thick verdant vegetation, enjoying again the feel of
her husband's warm arms around her.

Farther along, the creek came into view, quick,
bubbling, and clear, rushing downhill to pool in a
deep, tree-canopied pond.

"It's so pretty, isn't it? I've never seen so much
moss, and the water's as green as Carly's eyes," she
said, turning slightly. "Could we stop for a moment?"

"If you like," he answered, guiding the palomino
down a rocky incline with one hand while he kept
the other securely around Tyler's small waist.

On the grassy bank overlooking the water, he dismounted and lifted her down, then flipped the reins
over a branch. Tyler moved to a spot where violets
flourished among graceful fern fronds, like sap-
phires in a waving green sea.

"It's so clean and clear," she said. Her eyes fastened momentarily on a frayed rope hanging from a big limb above their heads. "Look, someone used this place as a swimming hole."

Gray stopped beside her. "Didn't you ever swim here?"

"Oh, no, my father wouldn't let me. Actually, I don't know how to swim."

"You don't know how?"

"No," she answered, smiling at his obvious surprise. "No one ever taught me. I always wanted to, though. Chase liked this creek. He used to come down often when he visited us with his mother. I can remember him telling me how pretty it was, with all the tree limbs extending out over the water."

Gray sat down on a big rock nearby, pulling off his boots.

"What are you doing?" Tyler asked as he began to unbutton his blue linen shirt.

"I'm going to teach you how to swim," he told her, unbuckling his belt.

Tyler was startled. "What? Here?"

Gray grinned at her. "I think a swimming hole is a pretty good place." He shrugged out of his shirt, and Tyler's eyes went to his muscular chest with its furring of dark hair. She shook her head.

"But I can't. I don't have a swimming costume."

He stripped off his tan breeches, his grin as lazy as a Louisiana bayou. "You don't need one."

When he came to her, she stood docilely but with a shivery alarm as his fingers went to work on the small buttons of her basque.

"Really, Gray, we can't do this. I mean, just undress and parade around in broad daylight?"

"I wasn't planning on parading around much."

"But it's just not decent. I'm sorry, I just can't—"

"Oh, yes, you can."

He pulled loose her ribbons, parted her bodice, and dragged it down over her shoulders. When he tugged free the yellow scarf in her hair and sent it floating to the grass, she felt a streak of panic.

"Gray! I've never done anything like this before!"

"That's good."

"Someone will see!"

"No one will see."

Her merino skirt fluttered and fell to the ground, then his fingers went to work on her petticoat.

"But I'll drown!" was Tyler's last frantic squeal of protest, which only brought an amused laugh from Gray.

"Tyler, love, you'll be much too busy to drown."

Tyler felt the delicious sensation of being lifted easily into his arms. He waded out into the water with her, and she quickly looped her arms around his neck, gasping as the cold water invaded her sheer chemise.

"Is it very deep? Oooh, it's freezing," she managed shakily as her camisole came swirling up around her waist. Her husband's hands slid under her and held her tightly against him as he waded deeper, smiling wickedly into her eyes.

"It's not as cold as the Chicago River in February, now is it?"

"Oh, hush about that! I'm cold. Aren't you?"

"No, and I'm going to warm you up right now."

His lips nuzzled her mouth while his hands continued a bold and well-executed exploration beneath the surface of the water.

"I hope no one comes along," she gasped out, unable to say more as he stroked a particularly sensitive part of her. She laid her cheek against his bare chest, moaning weakly from what was going on under the water.

"How do you like swimming?" he wanted to know, his mouth moving atop hers.

Tyler's answer was another breathless sigh. The water sparkled all around them, but she could only think of what Gray's hands and lips were doing to her and how much she loved him—

At that realization, she started. Suddenly wanting to show him how she felt, she tightened her arms around his neck, eagerly pressing herself against his legs. It felt so good—the cool water sloshing over skin on fire from his caresses.

"Gray, please—"

Her whispered entreaty ignited his passion as nothing else could, but as he moved to pull off the clinging chemise, Tyler couldn't forget that they were in an open clearing, not far from a public road.

"We can't, not here. Someone will come along. Let's go back home!"

Gray was not to be dissuaded, and he clamped her bodily to him with one arm, sloshing out of the water with her, laughing at her protests.

"This is my property—your property, I mean. I want you here, and I want you now."

He dropped down over her on the bank, but Tyler was embarrassed at the way he was staring at her body through the wet shift, completely transparent where it was plastered against her aroused breasts.

"Please, Gray, not here."

"God, Tyler, you don't know what you're asking me," Gray groaned, but he stopped what he was doing, rolling onto his back and pulling her close.

"I can't believe you never came here as a child," he murmured a second later, his fingers splaying through her hair.

"Papa said white trash lived down on Township Line. He was afraid they might hurt me—"

She stopped in midsentence when she felt Gray's chest muscles tense hard beneath her cheek. When he suddenly withdrew his arm from around her, she lifted her head to look at him. He rose to his feet in one swift motion, and Tyler watched in surprise as he angrily jerked on his shirt, then put on his pants.

"What's wrong?" she asked, sitting up and crossing her hands over her chest. She looked around in alarm.

"I don't like people calling other people trash," he answered as he bent to snatch up her dress. He walked back, handing it to her. "Trash is something you dispose of. People are worth more than that."

He didn't seem the least bit angry now, just serious. Tyler looked down, hurt and showing it, but Gray didn't console her as he pulled her to her feet. He helped her dress, and while Tyler buttoned her bodice, he mounted the horse and gazed out over the creek while he waited for her.

"I'm—I'm sorry, Gray. I didn't mean anything by it," she said at last, upset and confused by his behavior.

Gray leaned down to lift her up in front of him. "Forget it. Right now, there's someone I want you to meet."

He pressed a kiss to the top of her head, as he did so often, and Tyler relaxed in the circle of his arms. But she was still puzzled about what had happened. He obviously wasn't angry at her any longer. She felt, instead, that he was disappointed in her, and she wasn't so sure that she wouldn't rather have been the object of his ire.

They rode in silence until they reached Township Line Road. About a mile down it, they came upon a small sharecropper's shack that had stood for years at the edge of Rose Point's cotton fields.

Gray walked his horse into the yard, and Tyler remained in the saddle as he dismounted. He stepped onto the rickety front porch and knocked, but when no one answered, he walked around, looking the place over.

Tyler watched him, unsure of his mood, but sensing a difference in him as he stared in silent contemplation at the ramshackle old place. Oblivious to her, he ran his hands through his hair in a distracted way, then shook his head mutely as he noticed a bucket placed on the porch to collect rainwater under a leak in the roof. A moment later, he mounted behind her.

"They must be in the field," he said, spurring the palomino.

Gray was right. As they crossed the rutted road and moved down a row of cotton plants, they saw several people beneath a solitary pecan tree at the far end of the field.

Gray prodded the stallion, and as they neared, a slender young man with a blond beard walked forward to meet them.

"Morning!" Gray called out. "You're Ben Rainey, aren't you?"

"Yes, sir, I am," came Ben's courteous reply. Gray swung to the ground and led the horse forward, his hand outstretched.

"I'm Gray Kincaid, and this is my wife, Tyler. We arrived at Rose Point last night."

"Welcome to you, sir. I hope everything was to your likin'. Bess and me, we done worked real hard on getting it right for you. We just ain't had no time to do the whole place, it bein' so big and all." He motioned to a woman, who had remained seated on the ground beneath the spreading tree. "This here's Bess, and that's my little Jake she's holdin' there. I'm a mite proud to say we's got another on the way."

Tyler watched the girl walk toward them. She looked about Tyler's age, or maybe younger, and her belly was distended with her unborn child. The little boy she held in her arms appeared to be about a year old.

"Good morning, Mrs. Rainey," Gray said politely, then smiled down at her son. "Hello, Jake. You're a fine-looking young man."

To Tyler's utter astonishment, her husband reached out and took the child from his mother, shifting the boy into one arm.

"I came to see you, Ben, because I need an overseer for my cotton pickers," Gray said. "I was hoping I could persuade you to take the job."

The young husband looked at his wife, and Bess beamed with pleasure.

"I have to say, Mr. Kincaid, that I ain't never had

no experience as an overseer afore. But I been a cotton farmer down south of here since I was sixteen, fourteen years now. And my pa was, too, afore me.''

"Well, that's good enough for me. If you're willing to give it a try, so am I.''

"Oh, Lord, yes, sir, I'd be more than just willin'. And I swear I'll give it ever' thing I got.''

"I know that.''

Tyler smiled at the happy look on young Bess's face and the way little Jake kept grabbing Gray's ears.

"We'd be right honored if you and your missus would join us for a bite to eat. It ain't much, but Bess can cook up vittles purty good.''

Gray flashed a smile at the young mother, then glanced at Tyler.

"We'd like that, wouldn't we, Tyler? Our cook hasn't come out from Natchez yet.''

He helped Tyler down from the horse as Bess knelt on a tattered brown wool blanket to unpack a small basket.

"When will your baby arrive?'' Tyler asked, sitting beside her.

Bess grinned shyly as she handed Tyler a piece of golden corn bread and an apple.

"Soon, I reckon. He's been kickin' up a fuss for sure.''

"Kicking up a fuss?'' Tyler repeated with a quizzical look.

"Why, yessum, Missus Kincaid, ma'am. Sometimes I think he's off runnin' a foot race inside me.'' Bess laughed as she put her hand to her rounded abdomen. "He's up to no good in there right now. You want to feel?''

Tyler was startled by the offer, but she tried not to show it. When she nodded, Bess guided Tyler's palm until it lay atop her hard belly. When Tyler felt the thumpings from inside, she was so awestruck that her eyes flew to Gray. In that one moment as their gazes locked, she knew she wanted to have a baby, too. She wanted to feel Gray's child kick and run races inside her.

"See, he's a-wantin' to be born in the worstest way."

"Yes, I can feel him. Does it hurt when he kicks so hard?" Tyler asked.

"Oh, lawsy, no. It makes me glad 'cause then I knows he's gonna be a fine healthy one. We already done lost a wee little girl. It near broke my heart. Her name was Sally Margaret."

"I'm very sorry," Tyler said, her eyes reflecting deep sympathy as she visualized a baby girl named Sally Margaret.

"Do you and Mr. Kincaid have any chillen, missus?"

Tyler shook her head at Bess's question, but Gray answered for her as he handed the chunky toddler into his mother's arms.

"We've not been married long enough yet, Mrs. Rainey. But we're hoping."

Tyler did not hide her happiness, glad to hear he wanted a child, too.

They ate together on the blanket, and Tyler realized she was very hungry. There wasn't much food, but what they had tasted delicious, and they washed it down with cool apple cider. The men talked about Gray's plans to replant the fields to full capacity, and Tyler played with the little boy, who had an impish smile that made her laugh.

"Well, we'd better be on our way," Gray said at length, assisting Tyler to her feet. "Thank you for your hospitality, ma'am."

Bess colored with pleasure, and Gray turned his attention to her husband again. "I couldn't help but notice that your roof is in pretty bad shape. I'll send my carpenters over to repair it, if you don't object."

"I'd be mighty obliged, sir. I been meanin' to get up there and patch it some, but I just ain't found no time."

"Then I'll send them over. You'll be busy enough with your new responsibilities at Rose Point."

"Thank you, Mr. Kincaid."

Gray bid them good-bye, and he didn't talk to Tyler until they had reached the road again.

"Do you still think people like Ben and Bess are trash, Tyler? To be disposed of, just because they're poor?"

Tyler stared down at her hands, which gripped the saddle horn. "No, of course not. I told you I was sorry for what I said. Papa called them that, but I've never even met any of them before—"

"Then maybe it's time you stop repeating things your father and uncle Burl told you, and start thinking for yourself. You've got a good head on your shoulders if you'd just use it."

If such words had been uttered in any other tone than the quiet, gentle way in which Gray had said them, Tyler might have taken offense. However, since they were not harsh, and since his cheek rested affectionately against her temple as they rode, Tyler only leaned back and pondered the wisdom of his advice.

18

April 15, 1871
Rose Point Plantation

Dearest Harriet,

I was so pleased to receive your letter in this afternoon's post! Your correspondence took a long time to reach me, since it had to be forwarded from Gray's house in New Orleans.

Please let me first congratulate you on your recent marriage to Charles. You must accept my sincere wishes for good fortune and happiness, which you certainly deserve more than anyone else I know. I am certain that he will be a wonderful husband and companion to you. I hope he has it in his heart to forgive me for what I did to him, and I do so much want the two of you to accept Gray's invitation and visit us here at Rose Point during your wedding trip. You really must see my home, Etty. We spent so many hours talking about it.

We have been in residence now for nearly a fortnight, and I have found it most strange, especially since I am with Gray. I must tell you in all honesty that he has been nothing but kind to me since we were wed. I do appreciate the cordial wishes you expressed in your letter concerning our happiness, and despite all that has happened between us, I feel Gray and I might find it most pleasant to live here together after all.

I was upset and angry at first, as you well know from that scathing letter I wrote to you just before my marriage. I do hope I didn't cause you too much worry or alarm, but I was experiencing the most terrible feelings the night I penned those passionate words.

However, I know you will be glad to learn that I am rapidly becoming a dutiful wife. Gray treats me as if I am special and beloved, and at times he makes me think seriously about what I've said and done. I've come to wonder if I was wrong about him from the beginning, as you have suggested on more than one occasion. When will I learn to listen to your wisdom? In truth, I am beginning to believe that Gray is a generous, agreeable man. He is restoring the house—did I tell you that in my last letter?

Tyler paused in her writing, tapping the pen beneath her chin. She stared over the flaming wick of the oil lamp atop her small escritoire to the windows across the room. The curtains were being whipped inward by a fierce night wind that carried the fresh, damp scent of impending rain.

Frowning, she contemplated the words she had written to her dear friend. All the affectionate remarks about her husband had come straight from her heart. Wedded life was turning into a wondrous adventure.

A dreamy expression overtook her features. It was quite splendid, actually, having someone to hold her and love her every night before she went to sleep. And Gray must love her. Why else would he have given her Rose Point and treated her so well? And why would he have married her in the first place?

She leaned back, recalling the afternoon when

Gray had waded with her in Possum Creek. But her thoughts soon shifted to later that day when he'd picked up little Jake. Gray liked children. He would want many of his own, and as Carlisle had once told her, they would grow up at Rose Point, happy and safe. No one would transplant them in the cruel way she had been uprooted during the war.

To banish such unpleasant thoughts, she dipped her pen into the inkstand again. She quickly finished her missive, begging in an earnest postscript that Harriet visit as soon as possible; then she sprinkled sand over the wet ink. Moments later, she had addressed the envelope and affixed the sealing wax. The letter was ready to post. She stood and picked up the lamp.

Gray was still downstairs in her father's library, working on a huge stack of letters and business papers which had been delivered to him earlier in the same postal bag that had brought Harriet's long-overdue letter. But it was growing late now. Perhaps she could entice him to quit his work and come to bed with her. Her growing self-confidence told her she would have no trouble persuading him to do that.

She smiled inwardly as she went into the upstairs hallway. It was pitch black, the lamps having been doused by the servants for fear of fire. The house was eerie and intimidating, alone in the dark as she was, and her nerves grew taut as she descended the front stairs. The flame of the lamp in her hand flickered and jumped in invisible air currents, causing grotesque shadows to dance on the wall beside her.

Downstairs, she stopped at the long, slender-legged table by the front door, depositing Harriet's letter in the silver correspondence tray. The fanlight above the door had been left open to dispel fumes from the freshly painted white walls, and Tyler stood motionless for a moment, looking down the hall toward the library.

Gray was working behind that closed door, she

knew, but even as she took her first step toward him, an inexplicable rush of fear rooted her to the spot. She stopped as wind gusted suddenly, howling through the transom and making her light cavort crazily. She tried desperately to shield the chimney top with her cupped hand, but the wick abruptly gave up its fight. The house was plunged into utter blackness.

Tyler couldn't move. Slow, awful, inescapable panic pushed against her chest. She felt as if she were in her worst nightmare, and her heart pounded so violently against her breast that she feared it would burst. Pressing back against the wall, she relived a night many years ago when she'd stood with a candle in the same dark hall. Again, endlessly, her mind reverberated with a single shot and the thump of her father's forehead against his desk.

"Gray! Gray!" she cried, her terrified voice echoing shrilly through the dark hall, until a light emerged from the back of the house and she heard the rapid click of Gray's boots as he ran across marble tiles. Then his arms were around her, his palm stroking her hair.

"What is it? What happened?" he whispered as he held her trembling body close. "Tyler? Tell me."

"My lamp blew out." Her quivery voice was barely audible against the soft fabric of his shirt.

"It's all right now. There's nothing to be afraid of. I'll put out the other lamp. Then we'll go upstairs."

He took her arm, but as he propelled her toward the library, she held back.

"I can't go there! Not in the library! Please don't make me!"

Instantly Gray understood her fright, mentally cursing his own stupidity. What in God's name was he thinking? No wonder she was terrified; her father had committed suicide only steps away.

"I'm sorry, sweetheart," he said soothingly. He

held her close for a long moment. "Wait here with the lamp. I'll be right back."

Tyler nodded, attempting to control her shaking as her fingers closed around the base of the lamp. But with each footstep Gray took away from her came a stronger wave of terrible, suffocating fear.

"Now," Gray said when he appeared seconds later, "let's go upstairs."

Once they reached the first landing, Tyler began to feel silly and embarrassed about her childish behavior. When they entered their bedchamber, she watched Gray place the lamp on the bedside table.

"I'm sorry. I don't usually act like such a coward."

"I know you don't. Forget about it and come to bed."

Instead, Tyler moved to the windows, and, sitting on the edge of the four-poster, Gray waited.

"Could we talk awhile?" she murmured. "I want to tell you something."

"Of course." Gray could tell she was troubled by thoughts of her father's death. He sat patiently as she toyed with the eyelet-edged ruffle at the bottom of the curtain, wind from the open window playing with her unbound hair and loose white nightgown.

"Gray, I—I just want to tell you that I've been considering what you said to me. You know, about me using my head and thinking for myself, and I know now that I've been wrong about you." She stopped, catching his eyes with her own somber gaze. "I'm sorry for all the terrible things I said about you, and I regret trying to rob you."

Pausing again, she endeavored to find appropriate words for the most difficult apology of all. "And I know that it wasn't your fault about—about Papa and Rose Point. It was war, just like you said. Chase told me the same thing, and so did Harriet, but now I'm sure you'd never deliberately hurt Papa and me." Tears stung her eyelids. "Uncle Burl must have been mistaken about you doing it on purpose. All

the problems between us have been my fault, because you've been kind and generous from the beginning.''

Gray watched her inner struggle with confused
feelings, knowing she could never piece together the
complete puzzle until she knew the truth. In the past
few weeks, she had gone through a metamorphosis
before his eyes. She'd grown more mature and self-
confident, both with him and with the servants. And
she loved him. He knew she did, though she'd never
once said the words. Perhaps she was ready now to
hear the facts about what had transpired between
him and her father.

''Quit blaming yourself, Tyler. None of what happened in the past, here or anywhere else, is your
fault. Maybe mine, maybe your father's or Burl Lancaster's, but never yours.''

When Tyler looked up, obviously surprised, Gray
hesitated, suddenly unsure he could bring himself
to tell her. He would be taking a terrible risk with
her fragile emotions. But he abhorred the continu-
ous deception into which he'd been forced. He
couldn't face any more lies between them.

''I don't understand what you mean,'' Tyler said
hesitantly.

''You will, because I'm going to tell you what really happened. Why don't you sit down? It might
take awhile.''

Tyler sank obediently into the chair beside the
window. Gray's eyes were intense; hers were be-
wildered.

''Tyler, I don't want any secrets between us. There
have been too many for too long. And I don't want
you to blame yourself anymore. You were the only
innocent one involved in the whole damned mess.''

He paused, his reluctance to hurt her again threatening his desire for honesty. ''Burl told you the
truth. I ruined your father. Intentionally.''

Tyler was so stunned she couldn't move. She began to shake her head as he went on, gently but with relentless determination.

"The day after the war was declared, I financed my own regiment of volunteers. I purposely requested to fight in Mississippi so I could destroy Rose Point." He hesitated, pained by the expression of betrayal overtaking Tyler's face. He forged on, wanting his confession to be over and done with. "I ordered your father's cotton burned, Tyler, knowing full well it would bankrupt him."

"Why?" Tyler's hurt whisper was full of agony. "Why would you want to hurt us? You didn't even know us."

Knots began to form in Gray's stomach. "Yes, I did. I knew your father better than you ever knew him." He turned away, then looked back at her. Anger, suppressed for two weeks of mental torture in Colin MacKenzie's house, rushed up in an appalling surge. His mouth twisted into an ugly line. "You see, I was born down on Township Line. In the very house where Ben and Bess live now. I was the white trash your father warned you about."

Tyler blanched, her fingers clenching around the carved arms of the chair.

"That's right. My family lived in that little shack for years. Mother and Father, and Stone, Carly, and I. Carly was just a baby, and your wonderful, gentle father"—he emphasized the words with grinding sarcasm—"treated all of us like garbage that threatened to soil those snow-white gloves he always wore."

His hateful words brought Tyler out of her shock. "No! You're lying! He wasn't like that!"

Vainly, Gray fought to control the fury Tyler's defense of her father ignited in his gut. He could not. His laugh was short and bone-chilling. "Oh, yes, he was. He destroyed my family, and I swore I'd return the favor when I got the chance. That's why I went after Rose Point, and that's why I boarded it up and let it rot. God, I despise every brick and board in this place! I've hated every minute of every day since we've been here!''

"It's not true! I'll never believe my father did those things to you!"

"Your father was a devil," Gray ground out viciously. His expression was so cold, so contemptuous, that Tyler was shaken.

"I was right to hate you!" she whispered brokenly. "I'll hate you as—"

"I know, you'll hate me as long as you live," Gray finished curtly. "Spare me that blasted little speech of yours. I've heard it too many goddamn times already." His eyes were as hard and blue as December ice. "So be it, then, Tyler. Go ahead, hate me forever, if that's what makes you happy. I don't care anymore. Just don't ever sing me praises about your rotten excuse for a father."

He stalked out of the room, slamming the door so violently that a picture fell from the wall. Tyler stared after him for a long moment, then sank weakly to her knees. She buried her face in her hands, hard sobs racking her body.

The ancient coach bumped and jerked through a dry, rock-strewn creek bed, then lurched sharply as the horses strained together to pull the carriage back up onto the roadway. Inside the bouncing conveyance, Harriet Stokely Bond hung tightly to the strap on the door. Her husband patted her knee.

"According to the directions Gray sent me, it shouldn't be too much longer now, my dear. I know you're tired. I daresay the springs on this confounded contraption wore out a decade ago."

Harriet smiled at Charles's observation, placing her hand on his arm. Sometimes it seemed she was living in a dream, a wonderful fantasy where everything was perfect. Never had she expected to love again, and though her feelings for Charles were different from those she'd felt for her beloved first husband, they nevertheless ran deep and true and grew stronger with each passing day.

"I'm just so eager to see Tyler again," she murmured, clutching the strap tighter as the coach plunged into another deep rut. "I've missed that child dreadfully."

"I know you have." Charles took her gloved hand between his palms. "Even so, I have half a mind to take Tyler over my knee the minute I lay eyes on her. Saints alive, when I think of the grief she put me through, I want to thrash her."

Harriet averted her eyes, guilt stinging her like a wasp. Beside her, Charles suddenly chuckled.

"I daresay, though, that Gray has taken over the task in my stead. If the look on his face that last day in Chicago was any indication of his intentions, I'm sure he dealt with Tyler accordingly."

"If he did, she has certainly forgiven him. Her last letter veritably glowed with marital contentment. She sounded absolutely ecstatic to be living at Rose Point again. That's one reason I was so eager to visit. She's desperately anxious for me to see her home."

"I've missed Gray as well. He's rarely been away from Chicago for this long in the past, except during the war, of course. Tyler certainly has beguiled him. Just as you have me."

Charles squeezed her fingers, and they exchanged loving glances before sitting back to enjoy a companionable silence. Soon the driver turned his team into newly repaired iron gates decorating the entrance to Rose Point Plantation.

Harriet immediately sat forward to look out the window, straining to see past the long row of gigantic cedar trees as they rounded a wide bend in the road. When the white-pillared house loomed up, immense against the blue sky, Harriet detected the couple standing on the shady front veranda.

"Look, Charles! They're waiting for us. See? There by the columns."

Charles peered over her shoulder as the coach

rolled to a halt, then smiled and quickly swung open the door. He called a hearty greeting to Gray and Tyler as he helped Harriet descend the carriage steps.

"Tyler, Tyler, dear Tyler," Harriet cried delightedly, embracing her friend, who had left her husband's side to rush down to her. But her glad expression died upon first sight of the violet smudges beneath Tyler's tearful eyes.

"Oh, Etty, I'm so glad you've come. I'm so miserable!"

"What on earth has happened, child?" Harriet asked in concern. But Tyler only hugged her again as Gray descended the steps more slowly and shook Charles's hand.

"Welcome to Rose Point, Charles. You've made it just in time for dinner. Mrs. Bond, I hope you're well? You certainly look wonderful."

"I'm fine. And you?" Harriet answered, noticing with alarm the extreme formality of Gray Kincaid's speech, and the way Tyler studiously avoided looking at her husband.

"Tyler and I both wish to extend our congratulations and best wishes upon your marriage."

"Thanks, old chap," Charles replied, slapping his host's shoulder. "And the same goes for you and Tyler, of course." He looked up at the house. "What a magnificent place. I see you're doing work on the facade."

The men discussed the newly repaired columns and upper balcony as they climbed the stairs. Harriet followed with Tyler, acutely aware that things were not going well between the younger couple.

She had no opportunity to question Tyler, however, since Gray hovered nearby. Instead, she attempted to draw Tyler into conversation.

"So this is Rose Point. It's beautiful, Tyler. I can't wait to see every room. Shall we have the grand tour?"

"Perhaps tomorrow," Tyler answered listlessly.

Then, as if she realized how rude she'd sounded, she quickly added, "Unless, of course, you'd rather see it now."

Harriet darted a worried glance at her husband as Gray silently took Tyler's arm and led her into the spacious gold-and-white dining room. Charles's answering frown alerted Harriet that he, too, had noticed the strain between their host and hostess.

Matters worsened during the meal. Long, awkward silences—which had no place between four good friends separated for so long—punctuated their desultory conversation.

"How is Betsy?" Gray asked during an uncomfortable lull.

Charles jumped at the chance to enliven their discourse. "She's fine, indeed. She's visiting with her cousins at Rock Island until our return. And I'm happy to report she already considers Harriet a mother."

"How nice," Gray said, politely killing yet another subject.

Neither Gray nor Tyler had spoken a word to each other. Tyler didn't even glance in her husband's direction, though Harriet had seen him furtively eye Tyler on more than one occasion. When Gray suggested that Charles join him in his study for cigars and brandy, Harriet was thoroughly relieved. A private, heart-to-heart conversation with Tyler was certainly in order.

As soon as the ladies had retired upstairs, Charles Bond seated himself in one of the comfortable leather chairs in Colin MacKenzie's library. Never one to beat around the bush, he turned his inquiring eyes on Gray.

"What in the deuce is going on between you two?"

"So you noticed? Well, Tyler and I have had a falling out."

"I must say it would've been hard not to notice."

Gray finished pouring French brandy into two snifters. He handed one to Charles without comment.

"Well? What happened, Gray? Your telegraph message suggested you were finding married life to your liking. And Harriet said Tyler absolutely glowed in her last letter."

His remark about Tyler brought Gray to full attention. "What did she say about me?"

"She said you were restoring the house and treating her well. For God's sake, man, what happened to ruin it all?"

Gray leaned an elbow on the mantelpiece and heaved a sigh of frustration. "I told her I went after Rose Point on purpose."

Charles stared at him. "Why in tarnation would you admit such a thing? Surely you knew she'd find it hard to forgive you."

"Of course I did," Gray answered, prowling restlessly behind the desk. "But she was blaming herself for everything. I wanted her to know the truth, dammit! Ever since we got to this goddamn place, I've thought about what a bastard her father was! I couldn't go on pretending he was the wonderful godlike creature she kept describing to me. I meant to tell her gently, but I ended up throwing it furiously in her face. God, I wish I'd never brought her here."

Charles took a sip of his brandy, thoughtfully shaking his head. "How did she react?"

"As always. She said she hated me."

"When did all this happen?"

"A week ago. Hell, it seems more like a month."

"You shouldn't have told her."

"I wish to God I hadn't."

Charles hesitated, knowing that Gray usually reacted adversely to the subject he was about to bring up. "Did you tell her how your father died?"

Gray stiffened, turned, and stared unseeingly at the lawn outside the window. "I told her what kind of man her father really was. I said he destroyed my family, but I couldn't bring myself to look her in the face and brand him a murderer. She'd never forgive me for that.''

Charles's compassion for his young friend swelled. ''Well, Gray, Harriet's always been a good influence on Tyler. Maybe she'll be able to help smooth things out for you.''

Upstairs, however, Tyler burst into tears the moment Harriet closed her bedchamber door.

''Now, now, dear, don't take on so,'' Harriet murmured soothingly, putting her arm around Tyler as they sat together on the upholstered sofa at the foot of the bed. When the young woman continued to cry against her shoulder, she tried again. ''Tell me what's wrong. I must say I'm shocked by all of this. In your last letter you sounded deliriously happy.''

''I know. I was then. I thought everything was going to be all right. He was so kind and fixing up the house and all.'' More sobs and sniffles followed, and Harriet waited patiently, never having seen Tyler so upset. When the girl finally quieted, she gently stroked her hair away from her face.

''Now, won't you please tell me exactly what happened?''

''He told me he ruined Papa on purpose. He called him a devil and said awful things about him.'' Tyler lifted long lashes, spiky with tears. ''But he wasn't, Etty. I remember him. He was good to me. He treated me like a princess, and during the war he gave nearly all his cash to the county regiment—more than any of the neighboring plantation owners. And he was always donating money and food to the poorhouse in Natchez. He might have had some faults, but he wasn't anything like Gray says he was. Gray's wrong! He has to be!''

''Perhaps there were things he did that you didn't know about. You were only a child then.''

"But Gray said he destroyed Rose Point intentionally. It wasn't an order he had to carry out. He picked Papa on purpose so he could bankrupt him. He wanted to hurt us. He admitted it."

Harriet frowned, trying to understand Gray's motives. "There has to be more to the story. Did he say why he chose Rose Point?"

"No, except that my father hurt his family and deserved to be ruined. You see, I was right all along about Gray being responsible for Papa's death."

Tyler's weeping began afresh, and Harriet patted her until the onslaught passed, then held Tyler away from her, drying the tears on her cheeks.

"Tyler, I know how you must feel, but you have to think this matter through more clearly, you really must. You have to remember that you went after vengeance from Gray, and saw nothing wrong with it. Yet, now you can't forgive him for doing the same thing. Even if Gray did set out to get Rose Point, how could he have known how your father would react over its loss?" She stopped momentarily, peering over her spectacles at Tyler. "You can't really believe Gray could have foreseen that your father would take his own life. Other men lost their land and wealth during the war—too many to count—but they survived it. I survived losing the farm, did I not? You may be right in blaming Gray for taking Rose Point, but you cannot lay your father's death at his door."

Her soothing kindness brought Tyler's gaze to her, and for the first time in her life, Tyler felt the truth pushing up from where she had kept it buried inside her heart. Gray had not been to blame for that terrible night downstairs in the library. Regardless of everything else he had done to her and her father, he hadn't killed her father.

"Oh, Etty, what am I to do?"

Tyler lay her head wearily against her friend's sturdy shoulder, glad for human contact. More than anything in the days since their quarrel, she missed the way Gray held her in his arms.

"Have you discussed your problems since your argument?"

"No. It's been six whole days and we've rarely even seen each other. He spends his time directing the workers or taking long rides. I think he avoids the house on purpose. He told me he hates living here. At night he stays in the library because he knows I won't go near it." She shivered.

Concerned, Harriet shook her head. "What have you been doing with all this solitary time?"

"I've been staying here in my room."

Tyler's answer startled Harriet. "Surely not all the time? Haven't you been working on the house? You've wanted to come home for so long."

Tyler didn't reply at first, intently examining the fine embroidery work on Harriet's handkerchief. "I don't know why, Etty, but sometimes the house frightens me." Her voice lowered. "Sometimes I'm afraid to walk through the rooms by myself, though I do try to oversee the servants and act as the mistress of the house the way I'm supposed to."

"Oh, you poor child. I'm glad I'm here with you now. Things will get better, you'll see. Charles and I will help you and Gray straighten out this misunderstanding."

Tyler's face remained troubled. "Sometimes I think Gray hates me," she whispered. "I've seen the most awful look in his eyes—one that makes me want to shrivel up and die."

"That's nonsense, Tyler. If he hated you, why would he have insisted that you marry him? Why would he bring you home and restore Rose Point—at very great expense, I should think, especially if he doesn't like it here. Has he ever said he hates you?"

"No." Tyler looked down at her lap. "I'm the one who says it to him. I told him I'd always hate him." Her words caught in her throat.

"Do you?"

"No. Oh, Etty, I think I've gone and fallen in love with him."

Harriet smiled. "Have you told him that?"

Tyler swung her head from side to side, and for the first time since they had begun to talk, Harriet assumed a stern expression.

"Then swallow your pride and tell him. Tonight, before it's too late."

Long after Harriet left Tyler's room to join Charles in their bedchamber, Tyler lay wide awake in her bed, agonizing over recent events. She was torn apart by strong, roiling emotions that urged her to blame Gray for everything that had happened, past and present. Somehow, though, the tears she had wept against Harriet's shoulder had been cleansing. Much of her anger and lingering torment were gone, and she wanted to talk to Gray. She wanted to ask him what her father had done to the Kincaid family.

She remembered the night her father had slapped Mammy, and the time she had heard the screams coming from the slave quarters. Had her father done something to Gray in a similar fit of anger? If so, it must have been a terrible deed to make Gray so angry and vindictive, even after this many years. It seemed strange that he had suffered the same thirst for revenge that she had. How queerly their lives were entangled, like two skeins of yarn thrown haphazardly into a sewing basket.

Restless and unhappy, she sat up in bed, wishing Gray would come to her. All week she had waited for him to make the first move at reconciliation, but she knew now he wouldn't beg forgiveness. *So be it*, he'd said when she had cried out her hatred. His face had been hard and unyielding. She swallowed convulsively, suddenly needing desperately to talk to him, to be in the same room with him. But what if she went to him and he sent her away? She couldn't bear that!

Upset with herself, she began to pace the carpet. Then, unable to help herself, she opened the door and peeked into the hall. It was dark and deserted, but she could see a crack of light coming from beneath the door of her husband's bedchamber.

Heart thudding, she tiptoed toward it, terrified at the prospect of facing him. She turned, poised to flee back to her own room, but her desire to see him won the battle. She resolutely stopped in front of his door, tapped lightly, and then stepped inside.

Gray was already undressed, but sat upright in bed, obviously shocked to see her. He didn't speak, and for a moment Tyler couldn't either. They stared at each other, then Tyler moistened dry lips, her words pouring from her heart.

"I love you. I can't bear for us to quarrel and be apart like this."

Her throat closed up, but no other words were necessary.

"Thank God," he said huskily. "Come here, Tyler."

Tyler went gladly, eagerly, sliding into bed with him and sighing with unabashed joy as he pulled the coverlet over them.

"I'm sorry I said I hated you," she murmured against his naked chest as he enclosed her tightly in his arms. "I don't, I really don't."

"Shh." Then Gray quieted her with his lips.

Tyler moaned with sheer, blissful pleasure at Gray's urgent desire to touch her.

"I don't understand why you hated Papa so much, but I want to. Please tell me, Gray; explain it to me—"

"I don't want to talk about it," he muttered, his fingers tearing loose the drawstring at the front of her gown.

"Please—" Tyler whispered as his arms slipped inside her gown and around her waist, violently clamping her body against his own nakedness.

"I said I don't want to talk about it," he repeated

hoarsely, his starving mouth moving over the silken flesh he had craved and denied himself for so long. He made Tyler gasp and groan, until very soon after, she didn't want to talk about it either.

19

"I'm so worried about Tyler. 'Tis dreadful, seeing her so unhappy," said Harriet the next morning as she and Charles descended the front stairs for breakfast.

"Gray's just as miserable. But that's a good sign, I believe," Charles told her with a sage nod.

His reassurance did not assuage her concern, but when her husband paused at the foot of the steps and looked past her, a smile overcame his face. Harriet quickly followed his gaze and found that Gray and Tyler had just rounded the banister above them, hand in hand. As they joined their house guests, Tyler beamed at Harriet.

"Good morning! I hope you haven't been waiting long?"

"Oh, no, we just came down, my dear," Charles replied. "May I have the honor of escorting you into the breakfast parlor, Mrs. Kincaid?" he asked formally, bowing with the utmost gallantry.

"Why, I would be delighted, sir."

Tyler glowed with happiness as she took Charles's elbow. Gray watched them move away, then tucked Harriet's small hand into the crook of his arm. He patted her fingers.

"I don't know what you said to Tyler last night, Harriet, but I'll be eternally grateful."

Harriet gazed up at him, relieved that Tyler had acted on her advice. "She loves you," she told him. "Very much."

"Yes. She told me that last night for the first time."

Harriet laughed softly. "Events are turning out very different than she expected, don't you agree? You'll have to be patient with her for a while longer."

"I pride myself on my patience, Mrs. Bond."

They joined Tyler and Charles at the long oak buffet in front of the windows, and Tyler wondered at the reason for their smiles. As Gray seated Harriet, then took his place beside his wife, Tyler was overwhelmingly happy they were no longer estranged. She watched him remove a crisp linen napkin from the engraved silver ring on the table before him, determined to find out more about his family when they had lived down on Township Line Road.

Surely there was more to Gray's hatred for her father than resentment over being a poor tenant farmer on a rich man's land. If she could learn exactly what had happened, perhaps she could convince Gray that Colin MacKenzie had not been an evil monster. Her father had no reason to intentionally harm anyone. He was too honorable a man— she just couldn't believe otherwise, no matter what Gray said. Someday soon, after the heat of their argument had cooled, she would persuade Gray to tell her about his childhood.

"Ben was here earlier this morning," Gray was saying. "Bess was delivered of another son last night."

"Are they both all right?" Tyler asked, delighted with the news. She leaned back as their new Irish maid named Molly filled her cup from an ornate silver coffeepot. "She told me she already lost one child."

"Ben said mother and baby are doing well. He's concerned about leaving them alone so soon. You see, I'd previously asked him to come into town with me to hire some field workers. When I told him to stay home with his wife, he wouldn't hear of it. As overseer, he feels obligated to come."

"Tell him I'll go and sit with Bess," she volunteered at once, eager to see the baby who had been kicking so hard to be born. "I'd like to help, and I could take them some food. Bess won't feel up to preparing meals for a while." Excited by her idea, she turned to Harriet. "You'll come with me, won't you, Etty? You'll adore their other son, little Jake. He's precious!"

"I'd love to," Harriet agreed at once, glad to see the sparkle back in Tyler's big cinnamon-brown eyes.

"We could walk there, since it's such a beautiful day. If we cut through the woods near the slave quarters like Gray and I did, it won't be tiring at all."

"I'd prefer you to take the phaeton," Gray interjected. "The walk is longer than you remember, and you'll have baskets to carry."

"Of course; you're right. We'll leave after breakfast, as soon as we can gather things together."

Gray lowered his cup to the saucer, glancing at Charles. "Since the ladies have plans, why don't you accompany Ben and me into Natchez? I have several telegraph messages to send, as well as some business at the bank."

"Sounds fine," Charles answered.

"Have any of Rose Point's people applied for employment?" Tyler asked.

"Not yet," Gray answered gently, recognizing the hope in her voice. "But maybe they will, in time. We put out the advertisements only a couple of weeks ago."

In truth, however, Gray wasn't the least bit surprised. After they had endured the cruelties of a narrow-minded and tyrannical master like Colin MacKenzie, he was certain that most of the man's former slaves had fled far away from Rose Point and its evil memories.

As Tyler related a story to Harriet about Ben Rainey's small son, he wondered yet again how she could be so completely blind to her father's true character. He hoped she would soon realize that her memories of MacKenzie were distorted. He'd told her enough to plant the seed of doubt in her mind. Perhaps she would eventually accept reality.

His jaw tensed as he envisioned the pain she would suffer when she did find out how mean and vicious her father had been. How had MacKenzie managed to hide his malicious character from her? Or had he changed drastically after Tyler's birth? Gray couldn't believe that—not the Colin MacKenzie who had callously beaten him and then tossed a bag of coins at his feet. Gray's face went livid, and he fought for self-control before he said or did something else to hurt Tyler. He would *not* drive her away from him again. But the raw emotions raging inside him took their toll. Once more he knew he had to get out of Colin MacKenzie's house before it destroyed him.

"I don't mean to rush you, Charles, but I should get into town early," he said abruptly, scraping back his chair. "I think I heard Ben's wagon a moment ago."

At once Charles laid his napkin aside. "That's quite all right. I'm finished."

Tyler blushed with pleasure as Gray leaned down to press a light kiss on her cheek, his lips raising all kinds of quivers.

"Take care today," he told her. "We'll be back in time for dinner."

Long before noon, Tyler and Harriet were ensconced in the brand-new, single-seat phaeton which Gray had ordered from New Orleans, the awning folded down so the large picnic hampers could fit behind the red-cushioned squabs. Tyler had ordered enough food prepared for the young family to last them a week. She had been delighted to include several bolts of pastel blue flannel she had discovered in one of the sewing chests. Bess would be able to make dozens of garments for her two sons from the soft fabric.

As they drove along, Tyler felt wonderful. She was reconciled with her handsome husband and in the company of her dearest friend. She handled the reins herself, though Gray had hired two young Negro drivers.

She glanced at Harriet, very pleased she had taken her friend's counsel last night, and even more grateful that Harriet had not mentioned their talk again. She remained in a quandary about her feelings for Gray and for Rose Point. There were so many emotions she had to deal with, but at the moment, she didn't want to worry about them. Today she intended to forget all the fears and problems plaguing her. She wanted to smile, and be happy, and pretend everything was all right.

The phaeton rolled smoothly along, and they reached Township Line Road very soon. As they drove beneath the tall pine trees that shaded Ben Rainey's house, Tyler stared in amazement at the transformation of the rickety structure. Gray had indeed been generous with his carpenter's service, she thought with pride, surveying the newly shingled roof and fresh coat of whitewash on the walls. The porch had been rebuilt with broad steps and sturdy vertical posts. Even the small shed at the side of the yard had been braced up and repainted. It was difficult to imagine Gray, Stone, and Carlisle being raised in such a wretched place as it had been before the repairs. They all seemed born to wealth and fine things—as she had been.

"Gray is very kind, Harriet. Did you know that?" she said, halting the buggy near the front porch.

"I'm beginning to admire him more and more," Harriet replied as she lifted her skirts and stepped down to the ground. She looked at Tyler. "You're lucky to have been forced to marry him."

Tyler flitted a quick glance at her, then laughed at Harriet's knowing smile.

"Baba, baba," warbled a tiny voice.

Both women turned and found an excited child standing in the open front door.

"What a little sweetheart you are!" Harriet crooned, climbing to the porch and lifting the toddler into her arms. "Oh, Tyler, he's just the age of poor little Cole. And he has the same curly hair."

Tyler's heart twisted when she heard the pain in her friend's voice, remembering how Harriet's frail grandson had looked in those days before he died of consumption. Tyler could also recall her own anger and frustration as she'd watched an innocent baby suffer and die before his life had really begun.

As Harriet snuggled the giggling boy, Tyler shook off her morose thoughts. Someday it would be Tyler's child whom Harriet would kiss and cuddle, she thought, her heart warming. Harriet and Charles could take the place of the grandparents her own children would never have.

Lifting down the hampers, Tyler joined Harriet on the stoop and knocked softly on the door. Bess's voice drifted to them from inside, and as they entered the one-room house, they saw a worn patchwork quilt had been hung to separate the bed area from the cookstove and an old, scarred kitchen table. Tyler put down the baskets, tiptoeing closer and pulling back the makeshift curtain. Bess lay in bed, her newborn son in her arms.

"He's beautiful," Tyler whispered. Wonderingly, she reached out and touched the babe. The infant immediately clutched her forefinger with his tiny fingers.

"Why, you're a strong little thing," she said as Harriet came up behind her. She still carried Jake, who had apparently recognized at once Harriet's grandmotherly attributes. He held her tightly around the neck, his curly head resting contentedly on her shoulder.

"Bess, this is my dearest friend, Harriet Bond. We've brought you some food and several bolts of flannel for baby clothes."

"Thank you kindly," Bess answered softly. "I weren't really expectin' nothin', but I sure be obliged. Ben, he been takin' good care of us since the midwife went back home. I'm feelin' a mite weaker than I did with Jake, but I mean to get up soon. Can I fetch you cider or something?"

"Oh, no, you shouldn't get up! Not yet!" Harriet interjected quickly, then blushed at herself for barking orders to a complete stranger. "I mean, with two little ones, you need to gather your strength. When I had my boys, I was sometimes abed for a week."

"You have sons, too?" Bess asked.

Harriet smoothed Jake's tousled curls. "Four, all grown to manhood. They were killed in the war."

"I'm very sorry, ma'am. I lost my two brothers, too. At Shiloh." Bess's eyes clouded, and she gazed at each of her sons in turn as if already fearing some future conflict that might take them from her.

Tyler smiled as the baby stretched his tiny mouth into a huge yawn. "Do you think I could hold him? Just for a minute?"

"Yes. He's a good 'un. He ain't cried much neither."

Tyler bent, terrified as she carefully took the tightly wrapped bundle from its mother. Never before had she held a newborn infant. She knew nothing about babies.

Bess chuckled at the way Tyler cradled the child gingerly in her arms as if afraid he'd break. "We named him Kincaid, ma'am, after your husband." When Tyler looked up in surprise, she went on shyly. "Mr. Kincaid's been like an angel come down to help us. You saw all he done to the house, ain't

you? And he got those men to build this here bed
for the birthing. We was usin' a pallet over there by
the stove, and he just say nobody ought to have to
sleep on the floor." She hesitated, her face earnest.
"We just don't know how to rightly thank you and
him, missus, 'cept that Ben's gonna do his most to
make the crops yield high for Mr. Kincaid."

"My husband is very kind," Tyler said for the second time that day. She looked at Harriet, expecting
to be teased, but Harriet was already busy unpack-
ing the hampers. She still held Jake in one arm and
was mesmerizing him with the most extraordinary
baby talk.

"If you want, I'll rock Kincaid for a while so you
can rest," Tyler offered, not yet ready to give up the
baby.

Bess nodded. Despite her talk of rising, she appeared exhausted. Tyler crossed the room and sat in
an old, cane-seated rocker. The baby gurgled and
squirmed, kicking and fussing inside the confines of
his swaddling blankets.

Tyler lay him on his back on her lap, then carefully unfolded the blanket so she could admire his
ten diminutive toes. Tender longings swept her as
she sat there, entranced by the newborn child. She
hoped she would conceive soon. She had never
thought much about bearing children until the past
few weeks, but now the idea took hold of her. She
rewrapped the quilt snugly and shifted little Kincaid
to her arm, content to hold him while Harriet finished putting away the food.

After a time, when Bess succumbed to a much-
needed sleep, Harriet carried Jake outside so as not
to disturb his mother. Tyler could hear her laughing
at the child's play, and, lulled by the sounds of the
rickety rocker, she leaned her head back and day-
dreamed about the time she and Gray would have
children. Their sons and daughters would laugh and
play in the halls of Rose Point, and their happy

voices would drive away the gloom and bad memories hovering in those elegant rooms.

As she cuddled the tiny, helpless human being, she realized with some awe what a tremendous responsibility she would face as a mother. Parenting would very likely be as frightening as it would be gratifying, because she and Gray would have to teach their children all they needed to know to survive in a hard, unfair world. But she knew Gray would be a good father, just as he was a good husband.

Not long after Harriet had gone into the yard, Tyler became conscious of a man's voice outside. She stood at once, hoping Gray and Ben had come back early. She wanted Gray to see the baby. Carefully laying Kincaid in a wicker basket which Harriet had lined with flannel, she moved quietly to the door.

"There's someone out here, Tyler," Harriet said from the portal, Jake still clinging possessively to her neck. "He's asking for you."

"For me? Who is it?"

"He didn't say," Harriet answered, standing aside with the child as Tyler stepped out onto the porch.

A tall Negro stood beside the phaeton, nervously twisting an ancient palm-leaf hat in his hands. Tyler stepped down to the ground, looking at him questioningly.

"I'm Tyler Kincaid. Did you want to see me?"

"Be you missus of the new master of Rose Point?"

"Yes, I am. Nothing's happened to Gray, has it?" she asked, suddenly alarmed.

"No, missus. I done saw de paper 'bout hirin' on de old workers at Rose Point. De man who read it to me say you be Master Colin's girl."

"Why, yes, I am," Tyler answered, excitement blossoming inside her. "Are you one of our people?"

"Yes, missus. I be Grady, Mammy Rose Marie's boy."

"Mammy?" Tyler gasped out the word, then glanced around. "Is she here? Can I see her?"

"Yes, missus. Dat be why I's here to fetch you. She be wantin' you to come see her afore she go to de Lord."

"She's ill?"

"She be nearly all de way blind now, missus. And she ain't well 'tall. But when she heards dat you come back to de old place, she talk 'bout nuthin' but you."

"Where is she?"

"Just down de road a spell, at my place. I walked it just now to fetch you."

"Of course I'll go to her. Maybe she can help me convince Gray about Papa."

The colored man only looked at her, but Tyler turned around as Harriet spoke from where she'd been listening to their conversation on the porch.

"Now wait, Tyler. I'm not sure we should just go flying off with this man. Bess is still asleep. Why don't you wait until the menfolk get back and let Gray take you to see her?"

"No, it's all right, truly, Etty. Mammy Rose Marie was my nurse when I was a baby. She took care of me after Mother died. I must go to her, especially if she's ill. You stay here with Bess and the babies, and I'll come back for you in an hour or so, I promise."

"I'm still not sure you should."

"Don't worry."

Harriet watched Tyler climb into the buggy with the big colored man. She felt uneasy, despite Tyler's reassurances, but just then the thin wail of little Kincaid Rainey erupted from inside the house. Harriet hurried to tend to his needs, thinking that Grady seemed like a nice, pleasant fellow. Tyler would surely be all right with him.

20

The deserted back road to which Grady directed Tyler was so overgrown that Tyler was forced to use both hands to control the reins. The light buggy dipped and swayed precariously, but Tyler barely noticed, so excited was she about seeing Mammy Rose Marie again. Many years had passed since the day her uncle Burl had forced her out of the arms of her dear old nurse. She glanced at the man beside her, estimating him to be in his late forties.

"I'm sorry, Grady, but I can't remember your face. Were you at Rose Point when Mammy took care of me?"

"Yes, missus. I wust just a field boy then. I neber came upwards to de big house."

"I see." She wished she had the hat she'd left at the Raineys' house. Squinting from the sun's glare, she peered down the road. "Is it much farther now?"

"No, missus. Just upwards to a mile."

They rode in silence for a few yards, but there were dozens of questions rolling around in Tyler's head.

"Has Mammy fared well since I left, Grady? I didn't want to leave her, you must believe that. I cried my heart out, but my uncle wouldn't let me bring her with us. Has she ever told you about the day I left?''

''Yes, missus. After we wust set free, she came to lib wid me and Lolly. Lolly be my woman. Mama been farin' poorly now. Her eyes all whited over now.''

''Did Lolly work for us, too?''

''Yes, missus. She tended the cow pen.'' He suddenly pointed his finger. ''Dar's my place, dar in de pines.''

Tyler transferred her gaze to the house in the distance, and as they drew near the tar-paper shack, she saw that it was shabby and crudely constructed. Inside a makeshift wire fence, dozens of chickens pecked and scratched around the front yard. Two girls sat on a broken cracker barrel while three other children played catch with a big pinecone. Several black-and-tan hounds lazed in the sun.

''Dos be my chillen,'' Grady told Tyler proudly as he climbed down. He removed his hat, then respectfully held out his hand to assist her.

''Mammy'll be eat up wid happy when she finds you be come see her.'' Grady grinned widely as he helped her to the ground.

Tyler lifted her full skirts, eagerly following him through the clucking, scattering chickens to the front stoop. When Grady opened the door and stood back, Tyler entered the house. The smell of bacon fat hung heavy in the air, and the room was so dim that it took a moment for Tyler's eyes to adjust to the gloom. Then she saw where a lean-to addition had been built against the back of the house.

Grady led her to the blanket-draped doorway, and behind the partition, Tyler found a young black woman tending Mammy Rose Marie, who sat propped with pillows in a bent willow rocking chair.

''Mama?'' Grady said, going to one knee beside his mother's chair. ''Missus Tyler be heres. I went and gots her like I tole you.''

The old woman sat straighter, blindly holding out her hands in front of her.

"Baby girl, baby girl, be dat really you my boy done fetched?"

Tyler's heart lurched at the sound of her voice. She knelt before the woman who'd been like a mother to her. She caught hold of Mammy's frail, wrinkled hands.

"Yes, Mammy, it's me. I've come back to see you." Her voice quivered. "I've missed you, Mammy. I thought about you so often. I even dream about you."

"Oh, lawsy, sweet Jesus bein' so good to dis ole woman. I been askin' him to bring you back just one more time afore I's dies."

"Don't say that, Mammy. You're not going to die." Tyler lifted Mammy's hand to her cheeks, tears welling as she gazed into eyes covered by a milky film. She bit her lip, remembering how black and lively they'd once been.

Mammy Rose Marie groped the air in front of her until she found Tyler's face, her bony fingers sliding slowly over Tyler's soft, smooth skin.

"You be a woman growed now, ain't you? I worried 'bout you all dese years, just like I worried 'bout yore mama afore she die." Her thin bottom lip trembled. "She brought me wid her from down dere in Cape Christian on de Gulf. Did you eber know 'bout dat? I took care of her 'til de day she die. You was just barely walkin' den. I look after you, chile, 'til dey came and gots you away from me. Oh, God in heaven, I wisht I could see dat purty face of yourn."

A tear rolled from a sightless eye, and Tyler felt raw pain cut through her. She could not speak. She glanced over at Grady and Lolly, standing silently in the doorway.

"Oh, Mammy, please don't cry," she begged, wiping at her own tears. "I'm here now, aren't I? I didn't think I would ever see you again."

"I just wisht I could see my lil' white chile again.

I 'member dat purty face, I 'member dos red-brown eyes of yourn. Purtiest lil' white chile in dis county, I always say dat to my boy dere. Ain't I say dat, boy?''

Behind them, Grady murmured agreement, and Tyler squeezed Mammy's hands tighter.

"I'm married, Mammy, to Gray Kincaid. He's the man who bought Rose Point after the war. He gave it back to me. It's mine now, and you can come there again if you want. You and Grady and all your family. Gray needs people for the house, and he'll give you wages. He'll pay you a lot of money to work for us.''

The old Negress furrowed her brows deeply as if she were trying to remember, her sightless gaze focused on the wall to the left of Tyler's head.

"Kincaid, you say? I don' know no Kincaids 'cept dat white trash down on the county road. But yore pa, he done run dem off long time back.''

Every muscle in Tyler's body tightened. She leaned forward, her whisper urgent.

"That was Gray's family! Did you know them? Did you know my husband's father?''

"Oh, chile, you don' want to know all dem old thangs—''

"Yes, I do. It's very important to me. What did you mean when you said Papa ran them off? Did Papa hurt them?''

As if suddenly weary, Mammy Rose Marie leaned her head against the back of the rocker. "Mebbe hit ain't nuthin' you want to be rememberin', chile.''

Tyler ran her tongue over her lips, a sense of foreboding welling up inside her. "Please, Mammy. Please tell me.''

Mammy's fingers tightened around Tyler's hands. Her voice came in a hoarse whisper. "Dat Kincaid man be a poacher. You pa done had him drugged.''

"Drugged?'' Surprised, Tyler glanced at Grady. The man lowered his eyes. His wife also shifted her gaze.

Tyler turned back to her nurse. "I don't understand, Mammy. How? With laudanum, or what? Why would he give him medicine?"

Mammy didn't speak, and in the ensuing silence, a child's laughter filtered in from the bright sunshine outside. Grady finally answered Tyler's questions.

"Mama doan mean no medicine, missus." He hesitated, looking down and twisting his hat. "She mean drugged like when dey gets a rope on him and drug him down on de road. Your pa punished his people dat way, too, if dey caused trubble."

Tyler could not move. The vivid, horrible image seared into her brain. "Papa did that to people? Papa? How could he do such a cruel thing, Mammy? He was kind to you, except for that one time, wasn't he? He couldn't have! Tell me he didn't do it!"

Teardrops ran in jagged rivulets down Mammy's dark, wrinkled cheeks. "Dat's right, chile. He be kind."

Tyler heard the pity in her mammy's voice, and she knew the old woman was no longer telling the truth. Her heart felt caught in a vise, squeezed so tightly she thought she would faint.

"Did Gray's father die? Did Papa kill him?"

Mammy nodded her grizzled head, her mouth drawn down with sorrow.

"Was he cruel to everyone?" Tyler's voice faltered; then she turned to Grady, desperate for an answer. "Grady! Was Papa cruel to you? And the others? Was he?"

Grady refused to look at her. His words were low and reluctant. "I wust scairt bad of de druggin's, missus."

Tyler felt physically ill, so sick at heart that she couldn't say another word. She stood jerkily, staring at Mammy, then at Grady and Lolly. She fought for control.

"I have to go now, Mammy," she choked out in a voice that sounded nothing like her own.

She whirled and fled the house, her face as white and set as a marble mask, leaving Grady to console his weeping mother.

"Gray! Thank goodness you're home! It's Tyler!"

At Harriet's distraught voice, Gray jerked his head around from where he had just dismounted on the front drive of Rose Point. Charles stood beside him, but Gray moved quickly toward Harriet as she ran down the steps.

"What is it? Where is she?"

"She's upstairs in her room. But something dreadful must have happened to make her behave this way!"

Harriet wrung her hands together, clearly agitated, until Charles took hold of them and tried to soothe her.

"Harriet, dear, calm yourself and tell us what she's done."

Gray frowned as Harriet clutched his arm, her alarm quickly communicating itself to him. "Did something happen to Bess?" he asked quickly.

"No. Tyler left with one of her father's slaves—"

"What? She went off with a stranger?"

"Yes, but she returned safely," Harriet hastily reassured him. "She was gone with him only an hour or so, but when she came back, she acted so queer! She wouldn't say a word, would barely even look at me. By the time we got home, she was crying as if her heart would break. She locked herself in her bedchamber and wouldn't admit me, no matter how much I begged."

"Who was this man? Where did he take her?"

Harriet shook her head distractedly, twisting her handkerchief. "His name was Grady, or Brady, or some such thing. He told us that her nurse wanted to see her."

"Mammy Rose Marie?"

"Yes! That was the name! He said she was dying and was calling for Tyler."

"Well, then, that surely explains it," Charles interjected, patting Harriet's shoulder. "Tyler's upset because her old nurse is ill."

Harriet was not pacified. "I don't think so. Gray, I wish you'd talk to her. I've never seen Tyler in such a state."

Gray left at once, entering the front hall and bounding up the stairs three at a time. Their bedchamber door was locked. He rattled the doorknob.

"Tyler? Let me in."

Leaden silence was his answer, and he clenched his jaw. "Dammit, Tyler, open the blasted door."

Seconds later, the bolt was pushed back. He opened the door and found Tyler in front of her wardrobe, holding several gowns on padded hangers.

"What's wrong?" he asked.

Her face wore a chilling, blank look. When she spoke, her voice sounded flat and mechanical.

"Nothing is wrong. Why?"

"Harriet's worried about you."

Tyler turned back to lift a yellow silk dress from the tall wardrobe. "There's no need."

She crossed the room, and Gray saw an embroidered traveling valise lying open across the bed.

"Where are you going?" he asked tightly, fists on his hips.

"I've decided to return to Chicago with Harriet and Charles."

A frown knitted Gray's black brows, but he forced himself to remain calm. "Then perhaps you should tell me why."

Tyler didn't reply, and when she retraced her steps to retrieve more clothes, Gray lost his temper. He reached her in two angry strides and jerked her around to face him.

"What the hell's going on? What did Mammy say?"

Tyler pulled away, avoiding his eyes, and Gray made no attempt to restrain her. For the first time, fear shuddered through him. He leaned against the bedpost as Tyler took her time folding a white satin waist.

"If you're ready to go home, we will," he said quietly. "I'm more than willing to get back. I've already left my business for too long. I thought you were happy here."

Tyler stopped packing, staring unseeingly at the garment in her hands.

"Did my father kill your father?" she muttered in a wooden voice.

Shocked, Gray stiffened, then felt an overpowering sense of relief. She knew. He remained silent. But as much as he wanted no lies between them, neither did he want to subject her to every sordid detail.

Tyler turned slowly to face him. "Tell me why he did it."

Gray still hesitated. "Are you sure you want to know? It's not pleasant."

"Yes. I want to know everything."

Gray stared at her, dismayed by the anguish in her eyes. He was gripped with a sudden rush of rage to think that even from the grave, Colin MacKenzie was able to hurt Tyler, able to make Gray's life miserable. Perhaps telling her the ugly truth was the only way to free them both.

"Then come and sit with me. We'll talk about it together."

She sat on the sofa at the foot of the bed. Gray settled beside her, taking her hand and pressing her fingers to his lips.

"I wanted to tell you before, but I was afraid I'd hurt you."

Tyler's eyes filled with tears. "Please, I'm so confused."

Gray took a long breath. He stared down at the back of her hand as he stroked it with his thumb.

"As I said before, we lived on Township Line Road. The winter had been bad. There was little work for anyone in the county, especially the tenant farmers. Carly was a baby, and when Mother became ill, Father couldn't bear to see us hungry anymore. He shot a deer." He paused, finding the story harder to relate than he had expected. "He shot it on Rose Point land, Tyler. And when your father found out, he rode up to our house with a dozen of his slaves. They kicked down our door and jerked Father out of bed. Then they strung a rope around his chest." The terrible memory came gushing up, a black nightmarish vision he had never been able to forget.

Tyler's features seemed carved in stone, and Gray ran a hand over his face. His voice was low, unnatural.

"They dragged him behind a horse, Tyler. I remember every detail. It was cold and dark, and pouring rain, and Mother was screaming. Then she wept and held Carly when they dragged him back into the yard on the end of that goddamn rope." He sighed shakily. "I'm the one who went for the sheriff. But he did nothing, because we were poor and MacKenzie was rich. That's when I ran all the way to Rose Point, so full of rage I thought I'd die from it. I threw a brick through the front window downstairs and called your father a murdering bastard."

Gray's teeth came together, his jaw clenched with hatred. "He tied me to the whipping post in the slave quarters and beat me with his walking cane. Then, with all his people watching, he tossed me a bag of coins and told me never to set foot on Rose Point again. He said he wouldn't tolerate white trash on his land."

Tyler's carefully controlled expression suddenly contorted with pain. "My God, Gray, how could he have been so cruel! You were just a little boy! How could I ever have loved him?"

"He was your father. You loved him the same way I loved my father."

Tyler lay her face against her knees and made

keening sounds. "Don't you see? I didn't love him! Not after he killed himself. I've never admitted it, but down deep in my heart, I knew it. I blamed him for leaving me all alone. I despised him for not loving me enough to care how I felt when I saw him put that gun in his mouth. Now I hate him even more for what he did to you."

"Don't, Tyler," Gray murmured soothingly, drawing her against his chest. "He's dead. Hating him won't punish him. You can't do anything about what he did to me or anyone else. You have to see him for what he was and accept it—and realize that none of it was your fault."

Tyler went limp against his chest, her shoulders racked by hard sobs. Gray held her tighter as she clutched the front of his shirt.

"I was so wrong about everything," she sobbed brokenly. "Mammy told me. She told me what he was really like. You were telling the truth."

Gray shut his eyes, sick at heart over her grief. "I'm sorry, sweetheart. I wish now I'd told you myself a long time ago."

Tyler put her arms around his neck, crying for him and his family's suffering, as well as for her own. After a long time, she quieted within her husband's strong arms, her head resting on his shoulder, feeling weak and drained of emotion.

When she leaned back to look at him, the candlelight illuminated her tear-ravaged, puffy eyes. "How could you bear to come back here and live in this house after all he did to you?"

"I wanted you to be happy. I was hoping you'd stop hating me, I guess. I never intended for you to be hurt this way." He pushed a damp curl off her cheek. "But now we have to start anew. We have to put all our memories and mistakes behind us. Let's go back to Chicago, where there won't be any ghosts to haunt us."

"Yes, take me home," she whispered, her wet cheek against his face. "I only want to be with you."

Gray held her close, hoping that nothing else would ever come between them. They'd both gone after retribution, sought it in their fathers' names. But in seeking vengeance, they'd only hurt each other. Perhaps, though, the final victory was theirs. They'd found each other. They loved each other. It was time to forget the past and look to the future.

21

Gray handed Harriet into the carriage as his driver shouldered a heavy trunk and then stowed it inside the boot, along with several large bandboxes. The master of Rose Point looked back toward the veranda as Charles climbed up to sit beside his wife. It had taken only two days to ready themselves for the journey home to Chicago, and Gray hadn't felt better about the course of his life in many a day. As he had told Tyler, he would be glad to escape the haunting old plantation house.

Now that Tyler knew the truth about her father, the place had become as repellent to her as it was to him. He resolved to help her as much as he could in the days ahead, keenly aware that she would be vulnerable until she resolved her confused feelings.

"She's still in the front hall, poor child," Harriet told him, as if divining his thoughts.

"I'd better go see her."

Gray mounted the steps to the open front door. Inside, Tyler stood motionless at the foot of the grand staircase, her palm resting on top of the carved newel-post. She turned when she heard his boots clicking across the tiles.

"Are you ready?" Gray asked, hesitant to rush her, yet eager to be away.

"Yes," she said quickly, coming into his arms and pressing close. Gray accommodated her embrace with the utmost pleasure.

"We'll return someday for a visit if you want," he said softly. "I've dismissed the staff, but Ben and Bess have promised to look after the house for us. I told them they can bring the boys and live here. Mammy and her family have also agreed to come. Lolly's to be the cook, so I offered them the rooms off the kitchen."

"I'm glad." Tyler looked down the hall toward her father's library. "But I don't think I'll want to come back," she whispered. "Not ever."

Gray put his palm atop the mass of silky curls hanging down her back, then led her by the hand to the waiting carriage. When the driver directed the horses down the lane toward Natchez, neither Tyler nor Gray looked back at the grand pillared facade of Rose Point Plantation.

Despite Gray's attention and obvious sensitivity to her inner dilemma, Tyler was plagued by deep remorse. As the train roared and smoked its way north, she agonized over her past misdeeds. Thoroughly miserable, she grappled incessantly with doubts concerning her own worth and apprehension about Gray's ability to truly forgive her for the crimes against him. She tried valiantly to hide her anguish from Gray and their friends, but each time she sat across the chessboard from Charles Bond, she remembered with cutting regret the pitiful sound of his heartsick weeping when she had faked her death. It appalled her to think that she could have done such a wicked thing to him.

And Harriet, poor, dear, sweet Harriet, who had gone against her principles to help with Tyler's schemes, only because Tyler had shamelessly persuaded her to do so. Worst of all and hardest to bear was the treachery she had perpetrated against Gray. When she lay nestled close in his arms at night, she would listen to his even breathing and wonder if he could actually love her—the woman who'd tricked him, lied to him. The mere fact that she was the daughter of his father's murderer was good enough reason for his disgust. What if someday he realized how awful she really was? What if he was only infatuated with her for the moment? Each time such thoughts spun through her head, Tyler would feel so low and unlovable that she wanted to flee the company of the people she had hurt so much—for their sakes.

As the days passed, she became convinced that she should go away before she hurt them any more. The thought of leaving Gray tortured her. She loved him so much. But if she returned to Chicago as his wife and her criminal past was uncovered, he would face humiliation and ruin. And he would become a laughingstock among his friends and associates.

On the evening before the Kincaid car was scheduled to reach Chicago, Tyler had arrived at no solution that would enable her to stay with Gray. Her heart was heavy as she sat at the dining table with him and the Bonds. Completely dejected, she drew in a long breath from a sore heart as the efficient, ever-smiling Homer hovered nearby with his wheeled serving cart.

Increasingly worried about Tyler, Gray studied her face from across the table. Since she had discovered the truth about her father, her behavior had changed drastically. More often than not, she sat silent and introspective, allowing the conversation to flow around her like a stream rushing past a boulder. Gone were her quick smiles and saucy retorts, which had always drawn him to her. She rarely laughed anymore, and when she did, it was fleeting and lacked real feeling. She was in the throes of an internal struggle, and he felt powerless to help her.

Harriet was concerned as well. They had discussed Tyler's low spirits at length the day before.

Even now, Charles and Harriet both strove to divert Tyler from her melancholy. Gray frowned and turned his attention to Charles when the older man addressed him.

"Gray, I believe your idea to conceal Tyler's past will work splendidly. I certainly intend to tell who-ever asks your story—that she grew up in Montgom-ery. And Harriet will do the same among her friends. Since our wedding, Harriet's been accepted most readily, I'm proud to say. Our tray is usually over-flowing with calling cards. No one should have any reason to doubt our version of the facts surrounding Tyler's past, especially since John Mooney and Betsy have agreed to keep mum about the incident aboard the *Lady Jane*."

"Good," Gray answered. "As long as John makes no accusations, we'll be able to hush it up. Then Tyler won't have to worry about the authorities. If anyone does recognize her, we'll simply pay them off."

He waited for Tyler's reaction, but she said noth-ing, listlessly pushing her untasted food around on her plate.

Harriet leaned closer and gently touched Tyler's shoulder. "It'll work out, dear. Please try to believe that."

"I appreciate everything the three of you are try-ing to do for me," Tyler murmured. But her tone was so disconsolate that her friends exchanged trou-bled glances.

After dinner, when they sat in comfortable, velvet-tufted swiveling chairs before the parlor windows, Tyler remained silent, deep in thought as Charles described in dazzling detail the construction of a pa-latial dry goods store on State Street, in Chicago's shopping district, which was partially owned by Marshall Field, a good friend of both Gray and Charles.

As the hour grew late, Charles stood and stifled a hearty yawn. "I suppose we should retire. Don't you think so, my heart?"

Harriet nodded, an anxious furrow between her brows as she pressed an affectionate kiss to Tyler's cheek. "Sleep well, dear."

Glancing at Gray with a nearly imperceptible shake of her head, she accompanied her husband to the luxurious guest accommodations at the other end of the car.

"Are you ready for bed?" Gray asked Tyler a few minutes later.

"Yes," Tyler replied quietly.

"I am, too. Go ahead. I'll turn down the wicks."

A perplexed frown remained on Gray's face as he put out the oil lamps one at a time. When he pulled back the portiere, Tyler was sitting on the edge of the bed, staring morosely out the window.

Aware that she was more distressed than usual, he crossed the room and sat beside her. "Tyler, what's troubling you tonight? Let's talk about it."

He studied her fine-boned profile, but her long dark lashes remained down. She stared at her clasped hands without answering. As he had since the first time he had seen her, Gray felt an overwhelming desire to touch her soft skin. He ran a knuckle over the elegant contour of her cheek.

"Let me help you," he said softly. "I don't like to see you so unhappy."

Tyler looked at him, her face sober, but silent distress darkened her eyes.

"I've done a lot of thinking since we left Rose Point, Gray. I've made a decision, and I want to explain it to you."

Gray waited, pleased she was finally ready to share her feelings with him. She went on, not looking at him.

"First, I want you to know that I love you, more than I can ever say." She stopped, fighting tears. When one rolled down her cheek, she impatiently wiped it away. "I can't go back to Chicago with you, Gray. And I can't stay married to you—"

"Now, wait a minute—" he began. But Tyler put her fingers to his lips.

"Please, listen to me. I've turned this over in my mind a thousand times. Don't you see? I can never make up for the suffering my father caused your family. I'd be a constant reminder to you, and to Stone and Carly. And no matter what Charles says, my past is bound to come out eventually, and when it does, there will be a terrible scandal. You'll be ruined, you know you will. I'd be hurting you even more than I already have, and I can't bear the thought of that. It's better for me to go away now and let you get on with your life. You don't need me around to cause you more trouble and pain . . ."

Her words dwindled away as Gray lifted her hand and pressed his lips to her palm.

"Listen to me, sweetheart," he whispered, cupping her chin until she was forced to meet his gaze. "There's only one thing wrong with your decision. I *do* need you. You're a part of me now. You can't leave me any more than I can leave you. Even if you did go, you wouldn't be making up for what your father did to me and my family. If you go away, you'll take my heart with you, and that will hurt me more than anything else ever could." As Gray went on softly, Tyler sobbed, leaning her cheek into his hand. "What you have to remember is that what you did to me is no worse than what I did to you. I, too, was obsessed with the need for revenge. That's why I can understand the guilt you're feeling. God knows, I was driven by the same devils you were. During all the years after Father died, I hated MacKenzie with such a passion that it ruled my whole life. When my mother saw what the bitterness was doing to me, she begged me to forgive him. She always said that hate is the poison of the spirit, and that forgiveness is the most beautiful form of love. She said that giving up vengeance would make me free and happy. She was right, Tyler." He paused, searching her face. "Remember, you were able to forgive me, weren't you? So now give me the same chance. I deserve that, don't you think?''

Tyler's voice was barely audible. "I don't see how you could possibly love me, not after all the awful things I've done. I think you only married me because you felt responsible for what I'd become."

Gray closed his eyes, a rueful expression curving his lips. "That's what I told myself at first, but it wasn't true. I wanted you since the first time I ever laid eyes on you, before I knew who you were or what you'd done. I was so intrigued that you rarely left my thoughts."

"Then you do love me? Despite everything?"

"I love you even more now than before. God knows, I haven't been myself since I met you. Ask Charles and Stone. Ask anybody. But don't ever try to leave me, because I'll find you—no matter where you go or how long it takes."

"But I feel so guilty sometimes, and so bad about my father that I don't think I can stand it."

Gray smoothed a soft auburn strand of Tyler's hair behind her small ear, his face serious.

"Tyler, you'll find, I think, that the guilt you're feeling is what will eventually set you free. You've done wrong and now you're suffering for it. If you were evil, you wouldn't care. So much of what you've done in the past was forced upon you by other people anyway, at a time when you were young and vulnerable. Tonight, you've proved that you care about me more than your own happiness. How could I not love you for that?"

Tyler smiled through her tears and believed him. He loved and wanted her, though she didn't deserve to be a part of his life. She would not leave him, now or ever, not as long as he needed her.

"Thank you for loving me anyway," she whispered, then closed her eyes as his lips touched hers.

Gray's gentle caresses proved beyond a doubt that he did love her as much as she loved him. She let remorse over her past and worry for their future fade beneath the sheer ecstasy of their exquisite lovemaking.

The next afternoon when they disembarked at the LaSalle Street Station in Chicago, Tyler felt secure in Gray's love, though inner peace still eluded her. When she stepped down to the platform and found Betsy Bond awaiting Charles and Harriet, she paled, aware of the girl's close friendship with John Mooney. Charles went forward at once, a delighted smile spreading across his face.

"Betsy! So you've missed your old father, have you?"

"Oh, yes, Papa, very much! I couldn't bear to wait back at the house for you, so I persuaded Aunt Georgia to let me bring the carriage to meet you!" Betsy embraced Harriet warmly and gave her a daughterly peck on the cheek. "Welcome home, Harriet. I missed you, too."

But when Betsy's gaze fell on Tyler, her eyes held icy contempt, and she glanced away without a word. Tyler decided to withdraw in order to forestall an embarrassing scene, but to her dismay, Gray's fingers closed tightly around her elbow and propelled her forward against her will.

"Hello, Betsy. It's good to see you," Gray cordially greeted the girl. "I guess you've heard that Tyler did me the honor of becoming my wife during our stay in New Orleans."

"I hardly think I would call it an honor," Betsy answered, her calm insult so unexpected that Harriet gasped in dismay.

Tyler's face burned scarlet with guilty color, and she was even more mortified when Charles rebuked his daughter in front of everyone.

"There's no call to be rude, Betsy."

"I think it's ruder to steal Johnny's money," Betsy replied. "Johnny says she's a common thief. I think all of you know it, too. I only feel sorry for you,

Gray, because someday you'll find out exactly what she really is. Then you'll rue the day you let her trick you into marriage.''

With that remark, she turned and walked away, but her words had cut a slice out of Tyler's already wounded heart, as precisely as if Betsy had wielded a surgeon's scalpel. She had articulated Tyler's own greatest fear—that Gray would someday see her for what she was and leave her.

Even Gray's supporting arm around her waist did not lessen her heartache, and Tyler hardly heard Harriet's words during their farewell embrace.

''Don't you worry, dear. Betsy's just grown so fond of John that she's forgotten her manners. I'll have a dinner party soon so she can see how wrong she is about you. Then I'm sure she'll feel dreadful about what she said.''

''Thank you, Etty,'' Tyler replied without believing a word of her friend's prediction, then watched forlornly as Charles and Harriet moved off with the angry young woman.

''Stone should be here somewhere,'' Gray said, and when Tyler didn't respond, he raised her chin with his forefinger. ''Don't look so sad, love. Betsy will come around in time, I promise. She's always been one to speak her mind. You know that yourself. Remember the night you overheard her say she loved me?''

Smiling, he squeezed her gloved hand. Tyler desperately wanted to believe that things would really get better so the terrible heaviness in her chest would go away. Would she ever be able to breathe normally again? She pressed herself into Gray's side, and he leaned down to kiss her, despite the disapproving glare of a black-cloaked lady standing nearby.

''You'd better save that sort of thing for later, brother, unless you want to spend your first night down at the Des Plaines Police Station.''

At the sound of the man's voice, Tyler whirled around and found Stone Kincaid just behind them.

"Welcome home," he said as he clasped Gray's hand. "You certainly took your time getting back. I thought I was the wanderer of the family."

"I kept busy," Gray responded, drawing Tyler closer with an arm around her shoulders.

When Stone's gaze rested on Tyler's face, she braced herself for an attack similar to Betsy's.

"Hello, Tyler. Gray's always had good taste, and now he's proven that beyond a doubt by marrying such a beautiful lady."

Pleasantly surprised by his reception, Tyler vowed never to forget his kindness. As the two men conversed about the trip for a moment, she wondered if he had ever caught up with Emerson Clan, but more important, if Carlisle had decided to mail her letter to Clan's cousin.

"Let's go, Tyler," Gray said. "I know you're tired."

Not until later, after they had arrived at their home on Lincoln Avenue, did Gray have a chance to talk privately with Stone. They sat together in Gray's office. Stone watched his brother flip distractedly through the hefty stack of correspondence awaiting his attention after such a long absence.

"I guess I should belatedly congratulate you on your marriage. Actually, I would have appreciated an invitation to the wedding, since I'm the only brother you have."

"I'm sorry. It was sudden."

"So I heard." There was a short silence. "Any particular reason for that?"

Gray looked annoyed and dropped the letter he held to the desktop. "If you're asking me if Tyler is pregnant, she's not. I wish to God everybody would stop treating her like a vulture about to pick my bones!"

Stone said nothing as his older brother walked with agitated strides to the liquor cabinet. Gray poured himself a stiff shot of whiskey and drained it with one toss of his head. Afterward, he stared down at the empty glass in his hand.

"I'm sorry, Stone," he said, not looking at him. "She's having a hard time right now, and there's not a hell of a lot I can do to help her through it."

Stone waited a moment, pausing to light a cheroot. "I don't want to make you angry, Gray, but you have to know it's going to get a lot worse for her if anyone finds out about her past."

"I've already taken care of that problem." Gray sat down behind his desk and massaged the nape of his neck. "We've decided to spread the story that Harriet is her aunt, and that they both lived in Alabama before they came to Chicago." He looked up suddenly. "You haven't told anyone the truth about her, have you?"

"Of course not. I only got back from Denver a few days ago," Stone answered, propping a booted foot on his opposite knee. "But it might have been better if you'd stayed in Mississippi for a while."

"It was worse there for both of us. You should know that. You remember the night Colin MacKenzie killed Father as well as I do." Gray saw Stone's mouth tighten, and he looked away. "Anyway, I want her here with me. If the truth *does* come out, the two of us will face it together."

"No, you won't," Stone said, bringing Gray's gaze back to him. "The three of us will."

The brothers exchanged smiles.

"Thanks. Tyler's not really a bad person. I daresay you'll find that out soon enough." Gray caught himself up short at his own remark, giving a self-deprecating laugh.

"What's the matter?"

"When I first found out about Tyler and was so angry with her, two different people told me the very thing I just told you—in almost the same words. Now I've assumed the role of defending her, too. It's ironic."

"Do you love her?"

Gray shut his eyes. His sigh was deep. "You know, Stone, I used to find it amusing when people used the word *besotted* to describe a man's feelings for a woman. It doesn't make me laugh anymore."

Stone grinned, but Gray knew that the first weeks in Chicago would be difficult for Tyler. Now she had Stone and him to stand beside her. She would weather the days ahead just fine. He would make sure of it.

22

A fortnight after his brother's return to Chicago, Stone Kincaid strode into the dining parlor, knowing in advance the breakfast table would be deserted. Gray preferred to keep his young bride to himself before he went to work at his downtown office. They always took their morning meal in their bedchamber. *Besotted* was the word that Gray had used to describe his feelings for Tyler, and after having witnessed the couple's behavior firsthand, Stone was inclined to agree with his brother's assessment.

Stone smiled as he circled the long damask-covered table, amazed at Gray's behavior. His brother had been famous as a womanizer, both in Chicago and other cities, with only the loveliest and most accomplished ladies finding their way into his bed. Now all Gray thought about was Tyler. Stone shook his head. She was beautiful, but he couldn't see why a man would let a woman control him in such a way. It would certainly never happen to him.

Lifting the silver warming dome, he took several blueberry muffins, then poured himself a cup of steaming coffee. He picked up the stack of newspapers he had ordered delivered to the house first thing every morning.

The *Chicago Tribune* lay on top, the *Times* just beneath it, and the Kincaid railway expresses came in daily with editions from every large city in the country—from New York to Charleston. Someday he would find the name he was looking for in one of them.

Emerson Clan's face rose up in Stone's mind, as if seared there by a red-hot poker. He visualized the man's mane of wavy white hair, white eyebrows and lashes, which were a stark contrast to his ruddy complexion. He had the palest eyes Stone had ever seen on a human being, so ice-blue that they were almost white—and cruel beyond belief.

God, he could see him at the court-martial, standing at attention in his Union uniform. When Stone had stripped the bastard of his rank, Clan had laughed contemptuously in Stone's face. Clamping his jaw, he sat down and spread a New York daily on the table in front of him. He took a drink of his coffee, methodically scanning the front page, column by column.

Clan had been elusive since the war, and as clever at avoiding capture as he'd been when a Confederate spy in Stone's unit. Someday, though, he would make a mistake. When he did, Stone would repay him for every goddamn, hell-on-earth torture Clan had subjected him to while in Andersonville.

Every muscle in his body flexed hard, and he willed his mind away from gruesome thoughts of the prison camp and the horrible abuses perpetrated there. After the war had ended, he had preserved his sanity only by forcing the grisly memories out of his mind. He exerted that willpower again, concentrating solely on the newpapers before him.

For nearly an hour, the only sound was the crinkle of turning pages. Outside the dining room, a large gold mirror hung upon the foyer wall, and when Stone heard voices and glanced up from his reading, he saw a clear reflection of his older brother engrossed in an intimate farewell with his young wife. It was so enthusiastic, as a matter of fact, that Tyler was pressed against the wall. Stone shook his head again and turned away.

The front door closed behind Gray about ten minutes later, and Stone was surprised when Tyler appeared in the portal. She had been shy and retiring around him since her arrival in Chicago and had spent most of her time upstairs in Gray's private suite. She certainly had never sought him out before.

"Good morning," she said, her greeting followed by a lovely smile which made him understand to a degree his older brother's unbalanced state of mind.

Stone rose and returned her pleasant greeting with a polite nod. "Good morning, Tyler. Would you care to join me?"

"Yes, but I'll just have a cup of chocolate, if there's any left."

Stone watched as she picked up a cup and saucer from the sideboard. When she came back, she surprised him again by choosing the chair adjacent to him. She watched him as she sipped her chocolate, and Stone began to feel apprehensive.

"You have trouble sleeping, don't you?" she said suddenly, surveying him from large reddish-brown eyes. She did have an unusually beautiful face, he had to admit.

"Yes. I don't need much sleep, but I'm sorry if I've disturbed you and Gray."

"Oh, no, you haven't disturbed us. I haven't slept well either lately, and it's so quiet in the house that I can hear you prowling around in your room. When I'm awake before dawn, I like to watch the sun come up. Do you?"

Stone had never given the sunrise much thought, but to be courteous, he nodded. Again his instincts told him she had sought him out for a particular reason.

"I hope I'm not disturbing your reading," she said, glancing down at the newspapers littering the tabletop.

"No, I'm almost finished."

She fiddled with the handle of her teacup as if she was nervous, then looked him straight in the eye.

"Forgive me for bothering you with this problem, but I need your help. I really have no one else to turn to."

Stone wondered briefly at that statement. She certainly could go to Gray. "I'll be happy to help you, Tyler. How can I be of assistance?"

Tyler looked around in a furtive manner, and again Stone felt uneasy about her motives. He watched her withdraw a black velvet drawstring bag from her skirt pocket.

"I . . . well . . . I would appreciate it if you would take me to a reputable jeweler's shop. I would like to sell these jewels."

Stone's gaze dropped to the glittering strands of gold and silver studded with diamonds, rubies, and emeralds, which she had poured out into her palm. He shook his head.

"I'm sure Gray would rather take care of this for you himself, Tyler. I don't really think it's my place—"

"Please. I can't ask Gray."

"Why?"

"Because I don't want him to know about it."

Stone held up his hands, palms out as if to ward her off. "Oh, no. I'm not doing anything he doesn't know about. I won't go behind his back on this or anything else."

"But I didn't steal this jewelry, I give you my word! It belonged to my mother. Gray gave it to me for a wedding present."

Stone smiled faintly. "I didn't accuse you of theft, Tyler. It didn't even occur to me. I just don't think Gray would like you selling off your possessions when he has enough money to buy you anything you want. All you have to do is ask him."

"I can't do that."

Stone waited for her to elaborate, but Tyler hesitated, fingering a large ruby rose on a slender gold chain.

"You know that I robbed John Mooney, don't you?"

"Yes."

"There are many things I've done in the past I can't make recompense for, but I can give back John's money. That's why I need to sell my jewelry. It's very valuable. I'm sure it would bring enough cash to repay him."

Her big cinnamon-colored eyes implored him, and Stone found that wordless appeal much harder to resist than her spoken request.

"You don't have to sell your mother's jewelry," he told her gently. "I know Gray would want to give you the money. If you can't bring yourself to ask him, then I'll give it to you. Or I'll lend it to you, if that would make you feel better."

Tyler shook her head. "Don't you see, Stone? If I take the cash from someone else, I won't be giving up anything I care about. I won't be atoning for what I did. I love this jewelry. It's the only thing I have that belonged to my mother." She bit her lip, unable to meet his eyes. "But I can't hold up my head around the people who know about my past. If Gray just pays him for me, how will that change the way I feel?" Her smile was very sad and sweet. "Sometimes it seems I've been rewarded instead of punished. Few women have husbands as wonderful as your brother."

Stone hesitated. He couldn't help but admire her intentions. A moment later, he made up his mind. "You know, don't you, that if Gray finds out about my part in this, he's going to have my hide?" He grinned. "When do you want to go?"

Pleasure lighted her extraordinary face. "Could we go now? So Gray won't know."

"If you want to. Get your wrap and meet me out front."

When Tyler reached the front porch a short time

later, a carriage was waiting. Stone stood beside it, idly holding the reins of his saddled horse.

"Aren't you going with me?" Tyler asked in surprise.

"Yes, but I don't like carriages. I'll ride alongside you."

As he assisted her inside, Tyler remembered Carlisle's remark that he didn't like to be shut up in small places. Tyler shivered as she watched him mount his horse. He was tall and handsome, but so much more remote and unapproachable than Gray or Carly. When he paced the floor of his bedchamber at night, as she'd heard him do at times, was he thinking about what had happened to him in that terrible prison? She could understand now why Carlisle was so anxious to help him find Emerson Clan.

Stone kept his horse at a trot beside her door as they rode along the shoreline past Lincoln Park, and Tyler gazed out past him to the vast blue-gray waters of Lake Michigan. It looked beautiful in the morning, with the sun sparkling off the surface. She was finally doing something to make up for her crimes—at least one of them—and she felt better about herself than she had in a long time. Stone had no idea how much his help meant to her. Gray would never have allowed her to sell her jewels. Although her heart cried out at the loss of the heirlooms, perversely, she welcomed the pain.

The shop to which Stone escorted her was located in a busy, store-lined section of Randolph Street.

"Would you like me to make the deal for you? I know the proprietor," Stone offered as they paused before the small, twin-windowed establishment.

"Thank you, Stone, but I prefer to do it myself."

"If you should need me, I'll be waiting at the carriage."

Tyler watched him stroll away, then opened the glass door on which the words DAVID COHEN, JEWELER were spelled out in fancy gold script. A small silver bell tinkled, announcing her arrival. A bent, wizened old man soon appeared from behind a doorway curtained with royal blue silk. He wore a dark green visor and black sleeve protectors, and he squinted myopically out of dark eyes.

"Good day, madam. I am Mr. Cohen. How may I be of service to you?"

"I'm interested in selling a few pieces of jewelry. Are you buying at the moment?"

"Indeed, I am. Please, come this way."

He held aside the curtain, and Tyler entered the back room, a cluttered office with a musty smell. She sat down in the worn, overstuffed armchair that the jeweler pulled out for her. Mr. Cohen seated himself opposite her, watching as she opened her velvet reticule and pulled out the jewelry bag.

"These jewels belonged to my mother," she said briskly, trying not to think about what she was doing. "They are of exceptional quality. I know what they're worth. I tell you that, sir, with all due respect."

Her polite warning brought a chuckle from the old man. He tugged at his thin gray mustache. "You're very young to be so knowledgeable about precious stones."

"My uncle saw to my education," she said with not a little irony. "He could appraise a diamond to within a hundred dollars at a mere glance, and so can I."

"Extraordinary," Mr. Cohen murmured, taking the rose necklace and putting his eyepiece to his right eye. He leaned back and scrutinized the ruby for several minutes under the light of the desk lamp.

"Exquisite," he murmured, half to himself. He emptied the remainder of the jewelry onto a piece of black velvet which he had spread out on the desk. Neither of them spoke during his lengthy examination of each piece. When he had finished, he swiveled his stool around to face her.

"Are you quite sure you wish to sell these ornaments, madam?"

"Sometimes one must do things one doesn't particularly want to do. I'm sure you know that, Mr. Cohen."

"Indeed, I do, madam."

He picked up a pen and jotted down a few notations on a piece of paper. At length, he looked at her. "Eighteen thousand dollars for the entire lot."

Tyler only laughed. "Thirty thousand," she countered immediately, bringing a smile from the grizzled old man.

"Twenty."

Tyler shook her head. "Twenty-eight."

"Madam, please, I must be able to regain my purchase price. Twenty-two thousand." His earnest plea was lost on Tyler.

"Twenty-five thousand, Mr. Cohen, or I'll have my brother-in-law take me to another jeweler. I don't think you want me to do that. The rose designs are one of a kind."

"You are a thief, madam."

"If you only knew, Mr. Cohen."

The old man studied her for a long moment, then nodded. "Done, then. Wait here, and I'll get the money for you."

A quarter of an hour later, Tyler bade Mr. Cohen good-bye, clutching her purse tightly as she left his shop. Stone was leaning indolently against the lamppost, but he stood as she came toward him.

"I got enough cash to pay John back, with interest," she said, smiling. "And perhaps others who my uncle and I robbed, if I should ever meet up with them."

Suddenly her face grew worried. "You won't tell Gray about this, will you, Stone? Please, you must give me your word on that."

"You have it. I won't tell him. And, Tyler," he added as he opened the carriage door, "I think you've done the right thing."

"Thank you, Stone," she said, her heart warming

toward him. "I can only pray that it will repay John Mooney for all he has suffered this past year."

Outside the open bay windows of the front parlor, Tyler heard the throaty cooing of pigeons roosting in the eaves. The faint essence of the aromatic lilac potpourri she had set on the windowsill wafted to her in the breeze, and in the distance she could hear the laughter and cries of children rolling hoops in the park. She lifted her gaze from the sampler held in a wooden frame in front of her and caught a glimpse of a carriage rattling over the bricks of Lincoln Avenue.

The only sounds were those of Joyce and Sally leaving the house for their daily trip to market and Hildie's off-key humming as she trundled the carpet sweeper past the open parlor door.

Tyler knotted a piece of gold embroidery thread, then carefully snipped it free with her sewing scissors. Her needle remained idle in her fingers for a moment, as she realized how utterly content she felt. After long years of traipsing around the country with her uncle, Tyler knew her life was peaceful and serene at last.

Sometimes when she thought of Burl Lancaster, bitter feelings threatened, but mostly she remembered him with affection. He had certainly not been a good influence, but he had kept her with him when no one else had wanted her. She would always be grateful to him for raising her. Despite his obvious faults, she had loved him—in fact, more than she had loved her father. And now, she loved Gray more than anyone in the world.

Smiling dreamily, she laid her head against the chair pillow. It was hard to believe how happy they were. She loved being mistress of his home. Bless Harriet for teaching her what she needed to know about running a large household. Bless Harriet for being such a good friend—even in past days when Tyler was bent on Gray's destruction.

Harriet had made sure her new Chicago friends accepted Tyler as well. Many ladies had begun to visit Tyler or leave their calling cards in the silver tray in the entry hall. Gray had given Tyler her own beautifully designed silver card case, and she was filled with pride each time she presented one of the fine white vellum cards with MRS. GRAY KINCAID imprinted in gold.

Tyler paused in choosing a shade of blue floss from her wicker sewing basket. It seemed inconceivable now to think that only months ago she and Harriet had entered this very house and done such horrid things to Gray and Charles. A surge of shame darkened her cheeks, as it usually did when she remembered her past treachery.

In the last few weeks, however, she had begun to lay aside some of her guilt. With Gray's help, she'd learned that blaming herself accomplished nothing. She had done wrong, but as Gray had said, she must learn from those mistakes and never make the same ones again.

Within a fortnight, Harriet would again become her accomplice. But this time she would help Tyler perpetrate a more admirable ruse. Harriet had already invited John Mooney to a family dinner party at the Bond house, in order to give Tyler an opportunity to repay him in person. When that debt was discharged, perhaps Tyler would find peace of mind.

She had already decided to use the painful lessons life had taught her. She planned to raise her children to revere truth and honesty, and to show them how much she cherished Gray's love. He'd given it to her despite her faults. Surely heaven had a hand in bringing them together.

She resumed her sewing, deciding her husband was certainly the most magnanimous, magnificent man to ever walk the earth. She loved everything about him, she thought, drawing her needle through the fine damask—the way he furrowed his brow when he was absorbed in his work, smiled at her when he undressed at night, threaded his fingers through her hair and held her head while he kissed her so long and fiercely.

Her passionate thoughts caused her to prick her finger painfully, so she focused her attention back on her embroidery. Gray had spent the day downtown at the Kincaid building, but he would be home soon. She wished he would hurry. She missed him.

At quarter past five, Gray stopped in the doorway of the front parlor, in search of Tyler. She was sitting in her favorite place near the windows, a sweet, tranquil expression softening her face as she stared out at the street, her needle forgotten in her hand. Tender feelings assailed him as he gazed fondly at her exquisite face. God, what had he ever done to deserve her? At times he was uncomfortable with his own powerful feelings. Never in his life could he have imagined the emotion she could call up inside him with a single look or touch. How had he managed before she had entered his life? What had the days held for him?

While he watched, her lips curved into the most beautiful expression, and he was suddenly compelled to take her in his arms and find out what had caused the happy smile.

"Hello, my love."

Tyler looked up as he joined her on the camel-backed sofa. "I'm glad you're home. I was just thinking about you."

"Is that why you were grinning?"

"Yes." She gave him another brilliant smile just to prove it, then threaded her fingers through his long brown ones and lifted his hand to kiss his knuckles.

"We can do better than that, I think, since I've been gone all day," Gray murmured. The long, thorough mingling of their lips that followed left them both a little breathless and desperate for more. Tyler cuddled closer as Gray looked at his wife's embroidery frame. He had never noticed it before, but now he saw that she had stitched it beautifully in rich shades of gold and royal blue.

" 'Home is where the heart is,' " he read aloud, kissing the top of her head. He was pleased at the sentiment. "Is that true for you?"

Tyler nodded and leaned back to look at him.

"And is your heart here in Chicago, or do you still long sometimes for Rose Point?" he asked gently.

"You are my heart," she murmured, and Gray found the most curious, unlikely lump rising in his throat. There was a time, not long ago, when he had despaired of ever hearing such loving words from Tyler.

Again, as always, he sought her lips, her soft skin, her fragrant, silky hair, and their embrace quickly grew passionate, until the exaggerated sound of a throat being cleared pierced the fog of their desire.

"Pardon me," Stone said from the portal.

Gray laughed at Tyler's dark blush and attempts to straighten her disheveled chignon as Stone walked toward them. "Sorry to disturb you," he said, though his blue-gray eyes were more amused than regretful.

"Not as sorry as I am," Gray muttered.

"I have a letter I thought Tyler would want to see right away. It's from Carly."

"Really? Oh, splendid—I've been thinking about her so much lately! And Chase, too."

As she quickly took the sealed envelope from Stone, Gray focused on his brother. "I don't suppose our sister deemed it necessary to pen a note to either of us?"

Stone shrugged. "She's never been a prolific correspondent. What news does she have, Tyler?"

"Here, I'll read it to you, if you like," Tyler offered as she broke the wax seal. She withdrew the single sheet of vellum as Stone lounged on the armchair across from them and positioned his suede boots on a fringed Chinese hassock.

" 'My dear Tyler,' " she began eagerly. " 'By now I hope you have further resigned yourself to marrying Gray.' " Tyler paused and lifted her gaze to her husband with a trace of apology. "I guess she hasn't received my last letter yet," she suggested. Gray nodded, but as Tyler looked down again, he noted with some annoyance that Stone had an amused smirk on his face.

Tyler hesitated for a moment, glancing up again. "Perhaps I shouldn't read it aloud, after all. It's really just girl talk."

Gray looked more interested. "Go on. We'll try not to be too bored."

Tyler continued, reading with obvious reluctance. " 'Gray's really not so terrible as I told you. I realize I informed you of a good many of his faults in New Orleans, but once you learn to overlook his overbearing ways, he can be agreeable enough.' "

Gray frowned when Stone grinned. "I'll have to remember to thank my sister for her vote of confidence," he muttered sourly.

Tyler's eyes returned quickly to the long-awaited letter. " 'As for me, I am not making much headway in handling your oafish cousin. Chase Lancaster is certainly the most arrogant, annoying, and conceited of all God's creatures.' "

"Do you think Carly likes him or not?" Stone asked Gray.

"I'm more of the mind to pity poor Chase. But I did warn him of Carlisle's temperament before they set sail," Gray replied, grinning until Tyler glared.

"Do you two want to hear Carly's letter or not?" she asked sternly.

"Sorry, go ahead."

" 'The voyage to Matamoros was enjoyable, despite the horrid duenna Chase chose for me. Senora Alvarez is like a big, black-gowned parasite which I cannot pry off me, and your cousin only laughs at my complaints about her constant proximity. He keeps very close himself, just to annoy me, I believe.

But Arantxa and Javier's companionship made up for his boorish ways. We have grown very close— the Perezes and I, I mean—and I was grieved to have to lose their company when they sailed on to Veracruz, where they intend to disembark for their overland journey to Mexico City.' ''

Tyler paused in her reading. ''She must be going to the hacienda first,'' she said. ''Oh, yes, she goes on to say that. Listen. 'Tomorrow, I will be forced to accompany Chase Lancaster to his hacienda in Monterrey, thanks to Gray's interference. I cannot state emphatically enough how much I dread that long, isolated carriage ride with only him and my dragon duenna for company. He can be so disagreeable that I find myself on the brink of wrathful explosions nearly every waking moment.' ''

Tyler frowned as Carlisle's two brothers enjoyed a hearty laugh. She looked at Stone in some surprise, however, because he rarely even smiled.

''Methinks she doth protest too much,'' Gray quoted, but Tyler looked more concerned.

''I don't understand why she dislikes Chase so much. Most women find him wonderfully charming. Why, even when he was a boy visiting us at Rose Point, women noticed him. Older women, too.''

''She probably does like him. She's just too stubborn to admit it,'' Gray said. ''Regardless of what she thinks about him, though, I feel better knowing she's under his protection. At least she's not being taken advantage of by Javier Perez. Frankly, I didn't care much for the fellow.''

Tyler stared at him for a moment, vacillating about whether or not to tell him what Carlisle had intimated to her when they had said farewell. It was meant to be confidential, but if Gray was concerned about his sister, perhaps she should tell him. Tyler herself had been rather shocked at Carlisle's intentions. After another moment, she decided Gray did have a right to know.

"Carly told me she was thinking of marrying Javier—" she began hesitantly, but she got no further as Gray shot to his feet.

"What? When?" he demanded, glaring down at her with his hands on his hips.

"Just before they took the launch out to the *Mayan*. She said he was crazy for her."

"Good God, why didn't you tell me sooner? She wasn't planning an elopement, was she?"

"I don't know, and I didn't tell you because I didn't think she'd want you to know."

"Well, of course she didn't want me to know! She knew I'd put a stop to it!"

Gray turned a worried look to Stone, and his younger brother lifted one shoulder in a gesture of indifference.

"Carly isn't stupid," he said. "I don't think she'd go through with a wedding without our permission. She hasn't married him yet. She just said he's gone on to Mexico City without her."

Stone's reassurance made sense, and Gray resumed his place beside Tyler. "In any case, I'd better telegraph Chase and apprise him of the situation. I'll tell him to keep even closer tabs on her from now on."

"It sounds to me as if he's staying pretty close," Stone observed.

"Carly won't like him interfering between Javier and her," Tyler predicted.

"That's just too damn bad," Gray said. "Now I regret I consented to the trip in the first place. I should have known she'd find a way to worry me. She's too young to go gallivanting around in a foreign country by herself, especially one with an unstable government."

"She's a grown woman, Gray," Tyler reminded him. "She's my age, and I'm married."

"But you're not so apt to get yourself in trouble," he said, and as Stone's face indicated more amusement, Gray realized how untrue that observation was in light of Tyler's criminal past. "At least, not anymore," he amended, but he was more concerned with Carlisle's plans. "I'd better write Chase tonight."

"Oh, no!"

Gray turned to Tyler in time to see the color drain from her face as she stared down at the letter.

"Is she already married?" he asked, a sick sensation rising from the pit of his stomach.

"No, worse than that. And it's all my fault."

Gray moved closer to her, concerned by her obvious distress. "What is it, Tyler?"

"In her postscript, she says she had Javier word a letter for her to Emerson Clan's cousin in Alabama."

Stone's feet hit the floor, his face hard and alert. "Clan? Why?"

Tyler hesitated. "Oh, Gray, I told her not to do it. I told her it would take more planning—"

"Confound it, Tyler, do what?"

Tyler sucked in a shaky breath, then hurriedly explained her scheme to entice Clan to Chicago.

Gray looked furious, and as she finished, Stone began to pace the floor like a caged lion.

"She says she gave him my maiden name so he wouldn't suspect that Stone lives here," Tyler added miserably.

"Damn!" Gray growled. "What was that girl thinking of, giving him this address?"

"Maybe he won't receive it," Tyler suggested, hope flooding through her. "Clan's cousin might not know where he is. Stone hasn't been able to find him, has he?"

Stone stopped his agitated footsteps in front of the windows. Tyler was appalled at the way he kept clenching and unclenching his fists. The anger and frustration emanating from him went straight to her heart, but when he turned, she was surprised that his face was calm and composed.

"Perhaps it isn't such a bad idea. Not if we're ready and waiting for him."

Gray immediately disagreed. "It's too dangerous."

"It's also too late to stop it. Tyler"—Stone swung his attention around to her—"can your plan work?"

"Yes. If he gets the letter and he's the kind of man I think he is, I believe he'll come here as soon as he can."

Gray shook his head. "Damn! It's a good thing Carly's out of my reach right now." He frowned. "If the letter has already been sent, there's nothing we can do. One of us will have to be here at home with Tyler all the time. And maybe we should hire a guard, just to be safe."

Tyler listened as the two men discussed what precautions to take, sincerely hoping Carlisle's letter would go astray. She prayed it wouldn't reach Emerson Clan, but if he did come, she would have no one to blame but herself. Oh, why in thunder had she ever mentioned the trick to Carlisle in the first place?

23

As the next two weeks progressed peacefully, with no indication that Emerson Clan had received Carlisle's letter, Tyler became optimistic that their fears were for naught. The only positive outcome of the threat was her husband's presence at home nearly all the time. Stone, too, kept close to the house, and she often saw him peering out the windows or haunting the halls like a man possessed. He was determined to be on hand if his enemy took the bait.

On the warm June night of Harriet's dinner party, however, thoughts of Emerson Clan were far from Tyler's mind as she gazed out the coach window at the tall brownstones lining Madison Street, just west of the Chicago River. She and Gray were on their way to Number 42 near the east edge of Central Park, and as they drew up in front of the sandstone steps edged by gracefully curved green railings, she endeavored to bolster her courage.

When the driver opened the door and pulled down the steps, she gathered her skirts and descended, looking up at the second and third floors, which blazed with the amber glow of gaslights. She smoothed a wrinkle from the brown velvet sash draping her yellow silk skirt. Gray had picked the sunny color himself because it reminded him of jonquils. But Tyler's appearance mattered little to her, not with a small fortune tucked into her matching silk purse.

"Don't fret about John being here tonight, love. He's much too well mannered to be rude, and he's the only other guest except for ourselves and Stone. And Betsy, of course."

"I'm looking forward to this evening," Tyler told him as he led her up the steps. And it was the truth. By inviting John Mooney to dine, Harriet had given her the chance to apologize to her former victim with no one but trusted family members present.

"Are you sure you're all right? You've been awfully quiet tonight," Gray asked.

"I've just been thinking," she answered, entwining her fingers with his long ones.

"And should that worry me?"

Tyler laughed. "No. Most of the time I've been thinking about how much I love you."

"Sounds good," Gray answered, grinning at her as he lifted the ornate door knocker shaped like a pineapple and let it clang against its brass doorplate. A moment later, Harriet herself opened the door, a wide, welcoming smile on her face.

"Oh, I'm glad you're finally here! I was afraid you weren't coming! I'm so happy to see you!"

She drew them inside, beaming at Tyler while Charles's formally attired butler stood nearby to take Tyler's short black satin cape and Gray's top hat and cane.

"Oh, my, but you do look beautiful in yellow, dear," Harriet said approvingly, looping her arm through Tyler's. She guided her down the cream-and-rose brocade foyer, lowering her voice as they approached the open dining room doors. "Now don't you worry about tonight. Charles and I have already talked to Betsy and Johnny. They'll behave themselves and soon see how much you've changed, mark my words."

Tyler glanced at Gray, wanting very much to believe her good-hearted friend, but the moment she stepped through the threshold, the two young people froze where they stood talking with Charles and Stone near the fireplace. Their pleasant expressions gave way to icy distaste, and Tyler knew with a sinking heart that her task would not be easy. Gray's palm settled possessively at the small of her back, and she felt grateful for his presence.

John and Betsy gave Tyler a wide berth as Gray led her toward the table, but Tyler set her chin to a stubborn slant. Despite their unfriendliness, she would offer her apology immediately and be done with the dreaded task. She might never get another opportunity, because both John and Betsy had avoided her since she had arrived in Chicago. She turned and moved forward until she was face-to-face with John Mooney. He stood very erect before her, his face turning as red as his hair, while Betsy appeared ready to defend her wronged friend to the death. Tyler ignored the girl, gazing instead at John.

"I know you have every reason to detest me," she began, annoyed at the way her voice was trembling. "And I don't blame you in the least. But please hear what I have to say."

Beside her, Gray stiffened, but Tyler pushed on, her earnest eyes beseeching John Mooney. The young man looked unwilling to comply. For a moment Tyler wondered whether he might thrust her aside, though it seemed unlikely, given the presence of her big, protective husband.

Tyler breathed easier when he acquiesced with a slight nod, though a glance told her Betsy looked angry enough to erupt.

"I know I was wrong to do the things I did," she said, determined nothing would deter her from repaying John Mooney. "I also know there's no way I can possibly make up to you for the humiliation you've suffered because of me."

John Mooney's expression did not change. It was as if he were forcibly holding every facial muscle in check; but contempt smoldered in his eyes. Tyler saw it and felt hurt, though she knew she deserved his disdain.

"But I can give back the money I took from you. I have it here in my purse, in cash—please, accept it with my sincere regret. If I could, I would undo everything I've done to you and others, but since that's impossible, this is the only way I know to make amends."

She fumbled in her purse while she spoke, finally retrieving the currency, which she thrust into his hands. John Mooney stared down at the thick stack of bills, disbelief spreading over his face.

"It's all there, and more for interest," Tyler continued hopefully. "I only pray that returning the money will redeem you in your father's eyes."

As Tyler waited with bated breath for him to speak, John Mooney stood mutely before her. The moments lengthened to an embarrassing interval, until Gray was unable to bear the stricken expression on his wife's face.

"Tyler, I believe Harriet's ready to serve dinner. Where would you like for us to sit, Harriet?"

Tyler forced a shield over her hurt as John Mooney and Betsy left the room, apparently unaffected by her sincere efforts to right past mistakes. As Gray seated her at the table, she forced a wan smile, but a nauseous feeling swam around in her stomach. She had so hoped the money would make a difference. But it hadn't. Nothing would. They would never forgive her.

Stone took his place across from her and gave her one of his infrequent smiles. "Don't look so sad. You did everything you could."

"That's right, sweetheart," Gray agreed as he sat down beside Tyler. "If John can't relent now, then it's his fault, not yours."

Tyler nodded and was silent. Gray and Charles carried on a desultory conversation with Stone as

Harriet rang a gold bell to summon the maids with the first course.

All talk stopped, however, when Betsy reentered the dining room, John at her side.

"Johnny has decided to stay for dinner after all," she announced, leading him forward to join them.

"Wonderful," Harriet said, presenting them with a gracious, highly relieved smile. "You're certainly more than welcome, John."

Tyler's smile was tentative, but the great heaviness inside her chest lifted, allowing her heart to soar. John Mooney studiously averted his eyes from her, but Tyler didn't care. They might never become friends, but by accepting her money, he had given Tyler back the first brick with which to build the foundation of her self-esteem. She needed that more than anything else.

She smiled at Gray as he found her hand beneath the table and pressed it in a way that told her how much he shared her happiness.

Later that night in the privacy of their bedchamber, Gray lounged in a big wing chair in front of the hearth and watched his wife struggle with the buttons at the back of her yellow gown.

"Here, love, let me help you."

Tyler came immediately to where he sat. "You really shouldn't dismiss Hildie so early every night," she told him. "Then she could assist me."

Gray drew her between his knees, then turned her around. "But that would deny me the pleasure of undressing you," he replied, his fingers making short work of the tiny hooks and pearl buttons.

Tyler suffered an involuntary shiver as he pulled the dress down and let it fall around her ankles in a voluminous mountain of shimmering silk.

"I never could understand why women want to torture themselves with all these unnecessary clothes," he muttered, untying her padded pannier and tossing it into the chair opposite him.

340 Linda Ladd

"Would you rather we wear trousers like men?" Tyler teased, chuckling at such a preposterous thought.

"Pants would be easier to undo," he answered as he tugged impatiently at the ribbons holding her petticoats.

He stood when she was naked but for a pair of gold wrist bracelets. Eyes smoldering, he suddenly swooped her up into his arms, strode across the room, and deposited her in the bed. Tyler became warm and aroused as he slowly stripped off his clothes, his blue eyes never leaving her body. She was eager to demonstrate how much she appreciated him, and Gray laughed at the ferocious way she came to him when he joined her beneath the soft covers.

As his arms went around her and pulled her close, Tyler smiled, kissing a meandering path along the smooth skin of his broad shoulder.

"Thank you for being so good to me," she murmured, disappointed when Gray pushed her back so he could look into her eyes.

"Aren't you going to tell me where you got the money to repay John?" he asked, picking pearl-studded pins from her hair. He combed his fingers through the thick waves until they fell like a silken cloud over his chest.

"Oh, that. It doesn't really matter, does it?"

Something glinted deep in Gray's eyes. "Should I check my safe downstairs?"

"Oh, no, Gray, I didn't steal it, I promise! Please don't think that!"

Gray quickly put his finger to her lips. "Tyler, Tyler, it was only a joke." He smiled. "I know you would never take anything of mine again, even though now everything I have is yours."

Tyler relaxed, laying her cheek contentedly against his bare chest. "Do you think John will forgive me? He never said a word during dinner."

"He will, given time. He's a fine boy, but he has

gone through some hard trials this past year. Once his father absolves him, which he will if John returns the company's money, then John will be all right.''

Tyler ran her hand idly over the bulging muscles and crisp dark hair of her husband's chest, secretly thrilled at the obvious pleasure he was deriving each time her lips brushed lightly against his warm skin.

''I had better get your present,'' he groaned, ''while I still can. Don't look.''

Tyler sat up as he leaned toward the bedside table, smiling in delight as she obediently shut her eyes. She was used to his surprises; he often brought home gifts for her. ''What present? And what for?''

''For becoming such an honest woman,'' he answered with a laugh.

Tyler laughed, too, as he positioned her hands palm up. A moment later, he filled them with something cold and heavy. She opened her eyes and stared down at her mother's rose jewels. The rubies and emeralds winked and sparkled as the candle beside the bed flickered, and Tyler's throat clogged as her first thrill faded into disappointment.

''Stone promised me he wouldn't tell you,'' she managed after a moment.

''Stone didn't tell me.'' Gray propped his head in his palm, watching her. She wasn't smiling. ''Aren't you pleased to have them back?''

Their eyes locked. ''Of course, but I don't understand.''

''Mr. Cohen knows Stone. When you left with him, he thought I ought to know what my wife was up to, I suppose, so he came to see me at my office. I believe he was rather taken with you. He complained you attempted to make a pauper of him.''

Tyler smiled vaguely, but with Gray's act of kindness, her valiant sacrifice had been reduced to ashes, and that made her sad.

''I appreciate what you did, Gray, I really do. It's kind and generous.'' She stopped, picking at one of the tassels edging the silk comforter, not wanting to hurt his feelings or appear ungrateful. "But don't you see, I wanted to do something myself, to give up something of my own so I could atone for what I did to John."

"To rid yourself of guilt?"

Tyler lifted his hand, stroking his long fingers. "Partly, but more to give John back his father's respect. Having a family to love you is so important."

She remained somber, glad for an opportunity to tell him what her days of soul-searching had taught her.

"I think that's why I hated my father so much when he"—she paused, still finding it painful to discuss—"committed suicide. You don't know how badly he hurt me when he did that."

Gray pulled her down into his embrace, but Tyler continued to speak.

"I wanted to die, too. I wanted to put a gun to my head like he did. I thought about taking my life lots of times."

"Thank God, you didn't," Gray whispered. "I wish I'd been there to help you."

"You're here now, and I feel so blessed to have found you. It's hard to believe that I ever hated you. But I think I know why I did."

When she grew quiet, Gray spoke. "You had good reasons to hate me, sweetheart."

"No, it wasn't that. I think that deep inside I felt so guilty about despising my own father that I was happy when Uncle Burl told me you caused all our problems. So I loaded all my bitterness and anger on you instead of him, and I told myself I didn't really hate Papa. That's why I did all those terrible crimes that Uncle Burl taught me. I was determined to hurt you." Her voice caught pitifully as she choked on tears.

"Oh, Gray, I loved him so much when I was little. How could he have left me like that? I didn't have anyone but him."

Gray hugged her closer. "He was lost in despair,

I guess, and not thinking straight. No one knows what drives a man to take his own life.''

"I thought it was me. I was afraid I'd done something wrong that made him want to die. That's why I worked so hard to please Uncle Burl, so he wouldn't go away and leave me, too.''

Gray sighed, stroking her soft hair. "I know how you felt. I blamed myself for what happened to my family. I can remember thinking that if I hadn't complained about being hungry, my father wouldn't have gone after the venison. But we were all hungry and had no money for food. He had no choice. If it were you and our children, I'd do the same thing. That's why I took your father's bag of coins and moved us all to Chicago. I was determined that no one in my family would ever again be abused or hungry. I guess that's why I've worked so hard to acquire my wealth.''

They lay quiet for a moment, their hearts beating as one.

"Let's give the jewels away to one of the charities that feeds the poor,'' Tyler whispered softly. "I believe that would be the right thing to do. But I'll choose one special piece to give to our son or daughter in memory of my mother. She was good, even if my father wasn't.''

"All right, sweetheart, if that's what you want. I'm very proud of you, Tyler; have I ever told you that?''

Tyler went into his arms with a quiet desperation, oblivious now to the gems glittering around them on the coverlet.

"Oh, Gray, I love you so much. I'll love you as long as I live.''

Gray turned over and pressed her back into the soft pillows, their lips hungrily seeking each other. Inside he was smiling because she had reversed the words she had uttered so often as a child. She had turned her hatred into love, and he had waited what seemed an eternity for that. Then and there, he vowed that his beloved wife would have other jewels in place of those she had given up so unselfishly. He would bedeck her with strands of diamonds, pearls, and emeralds, rings, bracelets, necklaces—a collection of gems the likes of which Chicago had never before seen.

Later, when their passion was spent and they were content to lie close in each other's arms, Tyler's drowsy murmur came softly and sleepily against his shoulder.

"How much did you pay Mr. Cohen for Mother's jewels?"

"Thirty thousand."

"Why, that old thief! He cheated you!"

Gray gave a low laugh. "He predicted you'd say that."

They were quiet then, drifting off to sleep together, their bed still carelessly sprinkled with thousands of dollars' worth of precious jewels.

One pleasant afternoon in September, Tyler leaned across the marble-topped table in her parlor to pour tea for her guests. As she handed the first servings of jasmine brew to Betsy and Harriet, she admired anew the exquisitely wrought silver tea service which Stone had given them as a wedding present.

Smiling, she picked up a costly Sevres plate that sat on the epergne of rose-patterned china, offering Betsy a selection of cinnamon oatmeal cookies and ginger pumpkin bread. She had been astounded, but even more pleased, when Betsy had arrived unexpectedly with Harriet. It was the first friendly overture from Charles's hostile daughter since Betsy had agreed to sit down at the same table with Tyler at Harriet's dinner party three months ago.

"I'm so pleased you decided to come, Betsy," Tyler told her.

Betsy looked embarrassed. Flushing, she glanced at her stepmother as if for encouragement.

"Harriet told me . . . well, she told me about that night last February when you fell through the ice and I followed Gray up to your room." The blush turned deep, darkening her pretty face. "I know now, of course, how silly I was to blurt out all those things to Gray. Papa always told me I should think before I speak, and I'm trying hard to remember that. Now that I've come out and Johnny's been calling on me, I realize it was just an infatuation. I want you to know that." She had been carefully examining the roses on her plate as she spoke.

"You were loyal to John when he needed a friend," Tyler answered. "I hope someday you both will consider me a friend as well."

"Johnny's already forgiven you, now that he's reconciled with his father," Betsy said. She hesitated, glancing at Harriet. "Tyler, I know you weren't asleep that night. I can't tell you how embarrassed I am that you heard all those stupid things I said to Gray."

"You only said what you felt," Tyler protested. "I've done and said much more embarrassing things."

"I can attest to that," Harriet said drolly.

Betsy's eyes twinkled. "Like when you got under Harriet's hoop?"

Tyler jerked her attention to the girl. "You know about that, too?"

Betsy nodded, then burst out laughing. "Every time I think of it, I can't believe it truly happened."

Tyler chuckled. "It's true, all right, but don't tell Gray. He'd tease me to distraction!"

"Tease *you!*" Harriet exclaimed. "It was my hoop you were under! That's one reason I gave up wearing the things!"

The two girls laughed, then settled into a comfortable conversation about the dry fall weather and the frequent fires springing up sporadically around the city.

Finally Harriet picked up her reticule and parasol.

"We really must be leaving, Tyler. Charles will worry if we're late."

Tyler walked with them to the foyer and was giving each woman an affectionate hug when the door knocker banged.

Hildie hurried past them to admit the caller, and Tyler glanced toward the door as a man's voice drifted inside.

"Please inform Mrs. MacKenzie that Mr. Emerson Clan is here to see her."

Tyler froze, then spun around as Hildie darted frightened eyes to her mistress, having been warned long ago of Emerson Clan's possible arrival. Tyler's thoughts raced, and she realized she must take charge of the situation before something disastrous happened. Emerson Clan was a cruel, hardened criminal. Her first priority was to get Harriet and Betsy out of harm's way. She walked to where Emerson Clan stood, a carefully delighted smile on her face.

"Mr. Clan! How very nice to meet you at last! I was afraid you hadn't received my letter concerning Grandfather's will. When we found your cousin's address, it was absolutely our last hope. Did they forward our notification to you?"

Emerson Clan was above average height, dressed immaculately in an expensive tan frock coat and dark brown vest and trousers. He held a small bowler hat in one hand and appeared to be much younger than Tyler had expected. The infamous and elusive traitor certainly looked nothing like her image of him. In fact, he was handsome in a rather boyish way, with white-blond hair and a thick mustache. But his pale blue eyes unsettled her.

"Yes, ma'am. They forwarded the notice posthaste, as a matter of fact. I travel a good bit, you understand, so I have no permanent address."

"I see. But you've come now, and we can finally comply with the final tenet of my grandfather's will.

Your great-uncle was a dear friend to him for many years, you know.''

"Actually, ma'am, I never had the opportunity to meet him. Our kinship was quite distant. My cousin wasn't familiar with that branch of the family either.''

"Oh, how strange. But here, I'm forgetting my manners. Please come and meet my friends. They're just leaving, I'm afraid. Then we'll summon my solicitor to finish the affair.''

Tyler drew him by the arm to where Betsy and Harriet stood listening to their conversation. "Please let me present my dear friend, Harriet Bond, and her stepdaughter, Betsy. Etty, Betsy, this is Mr. Emerson Clan.''

"How do you do?'' Harriet said pleasantly, inclining her head. Betsy nodded politely.

"I'm honored to make your acquaintances, ma'am, Betsy,'' Emerson Clan said in his deep Alabama drawl.

"I'm so sorry you must go now,'' Tyler said pointedly.

Harriet adeptly handled the exit cue. "Yes, we really should be leaving. Thank you, dear. We had a most agreeable afternoon.''

At the door, Harriet leaned close on the pretext of a hug and whispered in Tyler's ear. "You don't have a grandfather, Tyler. What is going on? You're not up to your old tricks, are you?''

"Oh, Etty, you're so amusing! You must come again soon!''

Harriet's eyes narrowed suspiciously, and Tyler breathed much easier when she closed the door behind her friends. Taking a deep breath to fortify her jittery nerves, she turned and said, "You will join me for a cup of tea while we wait for my husband, won't you? You'll hurt my feelings if you don't.''

She flashed a brilliant smile, an enticement Emerson Clan obviously had no intention of resisting.

"Madam, how can I refuse to join such a lovely lady?"

"Oh, you're too kind," Tyler replied, glancing at Hildie, who still stood mute and wide-eyed beside the front door.

"Hildie, run and tell my husband Mr. Clan has finally come. He should be working in his office. We'll be in the parlor." She stopped in the doorway. "Oh, yes, and, Hildie, please fetch my brother-in-law as well."

She made sure the maid was off and running before she slid the doors together.

Emerson Clan smiled warmly at his hostess as she led the way to the tea table. God, what a beauty she was, he thought. Her skin looked as soft as satin, and she was interested in him already, perhaps even nervous in his presence. He wasn't surprised. Women always found him attractive. His gaze went to the wide diamond-studded wedding band on her left hand. It was unfortunate that she was married, and to a wealthy man, judging by the size and lavishness of her home. She would be interesting to try to seduce, and if necessary, husbands could be eliminated. He hadn't come halfway across the country for nothing.

The solicitor's letter had arrived at the best possible time. He'd been ready to move on after having killed a man in Savannah for a small fortune in gold. Chicago was on his way to California anyway. Why not add his great-uncle's inheritance to his stash? The law was after him, but this stop would allow him to arrive in San Francisco an extremely wealthy man. He smiled at the beautiful Mrs. MacKenzie as he took the teacup she offered him.

"Is your husband a solicitor?" he asked casually. Perhaps he'd strike it lucky, and the man would be old and feeble.

"He knows a good deal about the law," she answered. "I suspect he'll be coming any time now. He'll be glad to meet you."

Emerson Clan admired her lovely face, then noticed the cups and saucers scattered upon the table between them.

"I do hope I didn't spoil your tea party," he said, wondering if he could persuade the auburn-haired beauty to meet him someplace away from the house. He did find her extraordinarily desirable.

"Would you care for a cookie, Mr. Clan? Or perhaps a piece of homemade pumpkin bread? It's freshly baked."

"They look delicious," he answered, examining her soft lips.

He took a thin slice of iced cake. She placed the serving plate back on the table, and a short silence followed. Something about the woman began to make him wary. She was chatting on about the weather now, and he nodded politely until a deep voice outside in the hall caught his full attention.

"Why, that must be my husband—" Tyler began, nervously looking toward the door. To her relief, Gray entered and quickly strode the length of the room to join them.

"Mr. Clan," he said, extending his hand. "We've been waiting for you."

The two men clasped hands, and when Gray looked at Tyler, his eyes held a definite warning.

"Thank you for entertaining Mr. Clan for me, my dear, but if you'll excuse us now, we have business to discuss."

"Of course," she said, relieved at an opportunity to escape the room and find Stone. "Good afternoon, Mr. Clan."

She hurried for the hallway, but before she could reach the door, she heard a shout and running feet. She gasped when Stone unexpectedly burst into the room, savage fury twisting his face.

Emerson Clan jumped to his feet, overturning the tea cart as Gray attempted to rush him. Dishes and trays crashed to the floor as Clan pulled a derringer from the inside pocket of his vest.

Stone ran straight for his nemesis and Tyler screamed, pressing herself against the wall. Before Clan could get off a shot, Stone had him by the throat, his other hand locked in an iron vise on his gun hand. He squeezed his wrist until the weapon fell free. As Clan tried to jerk away, they went down together, overturning another table holding books and Chinese porcelain.

"You bastard!" Stone yelled into Clan's face while they grappled on the floor. He drove his doubled fist down into the smaller man's face, over and over again, until blood covered them both.

Appalled by the vicious fight, Tyler watched Gray use every ounce of his strength to pull his enraged brother off the man he was intent on killing with his bare hands.

"Stop it, Stone, it's over! We've got him! He'll hang for what he's done! I've already sent Hildie for the authorities!"

Gray's voice finally penetrated Stone's bloodlust, and he let go of Emerson Clan's throat, his hands still shaking with fury as he jerked his foe to his feet. Clan's face was covered with blood, his pale blue eyes already beginning to swell and blacken as they found Tyler where she cowered against the wall.

"You bitch. You tricked me," he mumbled thickly through cut, bloodied lips. But further words were stopped when Stone backhanded him savagely across the face, hard enough to send him to his knees.

Several policemen burst through the door with Hildie in their wake, and Gray shoved Clan toward them.

"Get him out of here," Gray said tightly. He tried to restrain Stone from following. Still livid, Stone jerked free.

"I'm going with them. I'll be damned if he'll get away this time."

Gray watched Stone move out the door after the knot of men dragging Clan; then he turned slowly to Tyler. She ran to him and he gathered her close, relieved the uncertain waiting was over and his brother's tormenter was safely captured.

"Are you all right, sweetheart?"

"Yes."

"I was terrified he'd hurt you before we could get him," he muttered gruffly. "Thank God, he didn't suspect anything."

Tyler let him seat her in a nearby chair. "Did you see the look on Stone's face?" she whispered, shuddering. She'd never seen anyone so enraged.

"My God, he would have killed him if I hadn't stopped him."

"Do you think Stone will be all right now?"

"I don't know, but I hope to God it's over. Stone's suffered too much already."

Tyler could see the worry on her husband's face, and she prayed Stone would be freed from his torment. Perhaps he could live with all the terrible things Emerson Clan had done to him now that Clan would be punished for his crimes. She hoped he would be happy now and find a wife to love him as much as she loved Gray.

24

Several weeks after Emerson Clan had been jailed, Gray stood among a group of gentlemen at the lavish mansion of Roswell Mason, the esteemed mayor of Chicago. He listened with half an ear to the excited discussion about the latest fire raging on the West Side, but his primary interest remained on his small wife, who stood with Harriet and a few other ladies near the buffet table. He had squired Tyler to three other parties before they'd arrived at the mayor's soiree, and now it was near dawn. He smiled to himself when he saw Tyler stifle a yawn.

She had been fatigued frequently of late, and although she hadn't complained, he knew she had also suffered bouts of early morning queasiness—all of which made him fairly sure she was with child. He was just as certain she didn't have the faintest inkling of her condition.

Gray grinned, pleased with himself. He wanted a child, almost as much as Tyler did. Son, daughter, or both, he didn't care. He had been waiting for Tyler to realize she was going to have a baby and tell him. But apparently it just hadn't occurred to her. She was very naive in some ways. He remembered her endearing innocence on their wedding night. Since then, however, she had become most adept at lovemaking. Of course, he had given her plenty of instruction.

After months of marriage, Gray still found it hard to be away from her for any length of time. Even now, that desire impelled him to cross the room and revel in her company. He nodded to his host as he passed, thinking Roswell looked tired and harried over the rash of fires. But his invitation for the night's festivities had delighted Tyler, who was becoming as popular as Harriet. He wondered what the people in the room would do if they knew the truth about her past.

"I was wondering where you went," Tyler whispered as he reached her. "I almost fell asleep a moment ago listening to Harriet and Mrs. Marpole discuss the fires. Where have you been?"

Gray drew her down beside him on a small settee. "Charles and the other men are concerned because the firemen can't seem to get this last one under control. The winds are whipping it, and it's spreading down De Koven toward the river."

"Is that near our house?" Tyler asked in alarm, not yet familiar with the streets of Chicago.

"Not really, but it's not too far from here, directly across the river and a few blocks down. Roswell's wired St. Louis, Milwaukee, and Cincinnati for more equipment. Apparently, the fires this summer took their toll on the condition of our own fire department." He draped an arm around her, resting it on the back of the sofa. "We ought to leave now, just in case. I wouldn't want to get trapped here."

"It's just so dry. If only it would rain, all these fires would stop, wouldn't they?"

"I don't know, my love, but there hasn't been a drop since July first, and Stone said that when he came back from Denver last week, the prairies were ablaze for miles at a stretch. The woods up north in Michigan and Wisconsin are burning as well. You've seen the soot floating on the lake winds. Thank God, our country estate is too far up the lake to be endangered." At her worried look, he smiled and pressed her fingers to his lips. "How are you feeling?"

Tyler shook her head. "Not very well, I'm afraid. I just don't know what's wrong with me." She paused, her serious eyes meeting his azure gaze. "I haven't said much until now, but I really haven't been myself for the past few weeks. I'm afraid I'm coming down with influenza or something."

She tipped her head to one side, narrowing her eyes. "What are you grinning about? Tell me."

He reached up to caress her face with his fingertips, the urge to touch her as irresistible as ever. "Perhaps you should make an appointment with Charles. He can tell you for sure, but I think we're finally going to have a use for that cradle you were admiring last week."

Cinnamon eyes grew huge. "Are you telling me I'm with child?" she whispered softly.

Gray laughed. "I think you probably are."

"But how on earth could you possibly know that?"

"Stranger things have happened, sweetheart. If you'll remember, we've been working on it rather diligently."

"Shh," Tyler scolded, looking around to see if anyone had heard his outrageous remark. She laid both palms against her flat stomach. "I've been praying every day for a baby." She studied his face anxiously. "Do you really think I am?"

"You show all the signs—being tired and sleepy, and unwell in the morning. Pregnant women usually feel that way."

"Oh, Gray, you should have told me sooner!"

Tyler's exclamation brought another low laugh from her husband, and he pulled her close so he could whisper in her ear. "Aren't you ready to go home?"

Tyler nodded at once, agreeable to the idea of being alone with him so they could further discuss the wonderful news. Before she could speak, however,

a commotion caught their attention near the front
door. The formally dressed men congregated there
were gesturing and talking loudly.

Gray frowned. "We'd better see what's going on.
The fire must have changed course."

Tyler followed him across the room, glad they
were going home. She was too caught up in excitement over her possible pregnancy to think of anything else. Why, she should have had sense enough
to know without being told! Of course she was with
child! She would go to Charles's office tomorrow
morning, as early as she could persuade Gray to take
her!

Gray caught sight of Charles Bond on the outer
perimeter of the excited throng and veered Tyler toward him.

"What's going on?" he asked as soon as they
reached earshot.

"The fire is totally out of control. My God, they
say the wind's whipping the flames along the street
as fast as a man can run!"

Gray's face took on somber lines. "What direction
is it heading in now?"

"This way. It's jumped the Chicago River and entered the South Side. It's already consumed Frank
Parlee's Bus Lines, and now Conley Patch and Shin-
bone Alley are in flames. It's nearing the business
district and the courthouse, and they're releasing the
prisoners, of all things. I'm taking Harriet and Betsy
home. You and Tyler better go, too."

"We are. Your house sounds fairly safe, but if you
feel you're in danger, bring what you can and come
to us. If worse comes to worst, we can evacuate to
our country place."

Charles agreed distractedly, hurrying off to collect
his wife and daughter. Tyler gasped in horror as they
exited the building and saw for the first time the great
orange-red cloud glowing eerily against the dark night
sky.

"My Lord, I've never seen anything like it!" she

exclaimed. "None of the others were so big. How did it start?"

"No one knows for sure, but it was down on De Koven Street. The firemen seem to think it started at a house owned by a family named O'Leary. Come on, we'd better hurry."

"It'll reach our office building before dawn," Gray said a moment later in the carriage, his eyes grim as he watched two men smash the plate-glass windows of a milliner's shop, then climb through the broken panes to scavenge for whatever they could steal.

Oblivious to the looters, soot-begrimed refugees with bundles and boxes of possessions in their arms crowded through the street beside their carriage. A great pall of smoke hung low over the rooftops, with the hot, acrid smell of burning pine lumber and tar roofs scorching their nostrils. Tyler held her handkerchief to her nose when she caught a whiff of burning animal flesh. In the distance, the cacophony of shouts, brays of trapped horses and mules, shrill whistles, and discordant clang of fire bells pierced the night.

"You aren't thinking of going back downtown by yourself, are you, Gray?" Tyler asked worriedly, already afraid to hear his answer.

Gray squeezed her hand reassuringly. "I have to, sweetheart. There are important papers at the office, and a good deal of cash in the safe."

"But what if you get caught there? Charles said the fire keeps changing direction!"

"I'll be careful, I promise, but I don't want you to take any chances. If you even think the fire's turning toward our house, I want you to go to the country estate, whether I'm back or not. Jonah and Hildie can take you. I gave the other servants leave to help their families escape the fire, so they probably won't be back until morning, if they come at all. Half the town's evacuating."

"No! I won't go anywhere without you."

Gray turned her to face him. "In all likelihood

you're carrying our baby, Tyler. Do you want to endanger it?"

"Of course not, but—"

"So you'll do as I say. I'll probably be back in plenty of time to leave with you anyway."

Tyler felt better, but her fears increased when they found Stone in the driveway, his horse ready to ride.

"They need men to build barricades around the Union National Bank. They're going to try to blow it up with dynamite. They hope the explosion will create a firebreak. It's their last hope," he shouted as he jerked open the carriage door. "I'm going down to see if I can help."

"I'll go with you. I've got to go to the offices, too. Have my horse saddled while I take Tyler inside. And, Stone, we'd better arm ourselves. Looters are having a heyday on the streets."

"Right. Hurry, Gray!"

Gray hastened up the front walk with Tyler. He went first to his office and removed several guns from his weapons cabinet. Tyler followed, afraid for him as he quickly loaded both rifles.

"Don't worry about us," he told her a few minutes later at the front door. "We'll be back soon."

"Please be careful!"

"I will. Now, you stay here, and I'll either come back or send word to you as soon as I can. You might want to pack some of our clothes and belongings, just in case we have to go to the country."

Tyler nodded, her heart frozen with fear as she stood on the porch as Gray ran down and swung up into the saddle, still wearing his black evening jacket and ruffled white shirt. Paralyzed with apprehension, she watched the brothers canter off into the night. Their silhouettes were dark shadows against the great crimson glow of the hellish inferno burning out of control below a pale, ghostly moon shrouded in wispy veils of smoke.

When Gray and Stone were out of sight, Tyler went back into the house, realizing she must pack as much as she could. She now feared that they would be forced to flee. Without Gray and Stone, the rooms were unusually quiet and lonely.

"Hildie!" she called, frowning when there was no answer. She looked into the parlor and dining room. Both chambers were deserted, so she climbed the stairs in search of her maid.

"Hildie? Where are you?"

She walked alongside the banister to her bedroom and found the door ajar. As she stopped in the portal, she was drawn up short by the sight of Hildie sprawled on the floor by the bed.

"Hildie!" she cried, running to her. She knelt and turned the girl onto her back. Then she saw the pool of dark blood beneath her head.

Before she could scream, a hand clamped over her mouth and she was jerked to her feet. She stared into the black muzzle of a pistol, groaning in terror as her gaze found the man holding the gun.

Emerson Clan smiled, his teeth white against his singed, smoke-colored face. His tan coat and trousers were wet and filthy, and his awful pale eyes chilled Tyler to the bone.

"So we meet again, Mrs. Kincaid," he murmured, his voice brutal with sarcasm. "You really didn't expect me to leave town without paying my respects, did you?"

Tyler gasped in pain as he suddenly grabbed her by the hair. Remembering that he had done horrible, grisly things to Stone and other people, Tyler didn't dare struggle.

"How did you get here?" she whispered hoarsely.

"Why, my dear, I was rescued by the fire," he replied. "You see, my jailer was thoughtful enough to let us poor sinners out so we could burn in hell instead of in our cells." He threw back his head and released a short maniacal laugh. "I was supposed to sit in the lake with irons on my wrists like a goddamn fish and watch the city burn." He grinned again, his eyes cruel. "But you know what I decided to do instead, Mrs.

Kincaid? I decided to drown my jailer and steal his gun." He stopped, encircling her throat with his hands. "I could kill you, too, the very same way. You know that, don't you, Mrs. Kincaid?"

"Please," Tyler muttered, horrified by the insane look in his eyes, "please don't hurt me."

"You ought to plead for your life after tricking me the way you did. You think you're quite clever, don't you?" Rage suddenly engulfed him. His fingers tightened on her neck. "I don't like being made a fool, especially by Stone Kincaid's wife."

"I'm not Stone's wife," Tyler croaked out of her constricted throat. "I'm his brother's wife."

Her revelation obviously surprised him. He released his stranglehold, but his anger didn't diminish. "Stone won't like what I'm going to do to you, no matter who you are. I owe him, wouldn't you say?"

"Servants are here in the house. They'll stop you," Tyler cried desperately as he jerked her out into the upstairs hall. "You'll never get away!"

He took her wrist and brutally twisted her arm behind her back. "You don't understand, do you? There's no one here anymore but you and me."

"What do you mean?"

Tyler's question was answered after he dragged her down the back stairs to where Jonah lay unconscious in the open kitchen door. A butcher knife protruded from his back, and Tyler moaned and tried to go to the injured man.

"Leave him alone, damn you," Clan growled, shoving her before him down the hall. He wrenched her head back and glared into her face.

"Where's your husband's safe?"

"In his office," Tyler managed weakly.

"Then you better take me there," he snarled, giving her a violent shove.

Tyler broke her fall against the wall with both hands and stumbled, terrified, into Gray's office.

"Where the hell is it?"

"There, behind the picture."

"Open it, damn you!"

Tyler fumbled at the dial with trembling fingers. When the safe was open, Clan thrust her aside and held her throat pinned to the wall with one hand while he pulled out the contents.

"Very good. Thank you kindly, Mrs. Kincaid."

He spoke with the utmost courtesy, and a chill rippled over Tyler's flesh as he turned frozen pale eyes on her. She flinched when he put his gun to her belly, then slid it slowly over her ribcage until it rested between her breasts.

"You know what, Mrs. Kincaid? I want you. I wanted you from the first moment I saw you." He smiled, his gaze moving to Tyler's heaving chest as he slowly pushed down the bodice and chemise until the gun muzzle lay cold and hard against her bare skin.

Tyler squeezed her eyes shut, and he put his mouth against her ear. His tongue intruded there, wet and repulsive, while his body pressed her against the wall. "I was going to kill you, my dear, but now I think I'll take you with me." His lips moved down her throat to the exposed swells of her breasts. "Stone and his brother were most obliging to leave you here alone for me."

Tyler bit her lip as his hand left her throat to fondle her breast. Her every muscle went slack with relief when he suddenly let her go and reached inside the safe again.

"We'll make a hell of a good team out west where no one knows us," he told her, slipping several bundles of banded currency into his coat pockets. "I like smart women like you, always have. After you help me with a few swindles, perhaps I'll let your husband ransom you. But only if you cooperate with me, Mrs. Kincaid, and only if I get tired of all your"—he rubbed the gun over her breast again—"attributes."

Tyler stared at him, sensing the brutal savagery

just beneath the surface of his polite veneer. He was capable of anything; he would kill her if she looked at him wrong. With that realization, Tyler knew she would have to do whatever he told her. She didn't want to die. She didn't want her baby to die.

"I'll go with you," she muttered hoarsely. "I'll do whatever you say."

"What an agreeable little thing you are, my dear. Now it's time to fetch my stash from the hotel. Your clever plot to get me here almost lost me all my hard-earned savings. I killed a man for that gold. I don't intend to leave it behind."

Tyler didn't attempt to break free as he pulled her outside the house. She would wait until a good chance came; then she would escape. Oh, God, please let Gray come back, she prayed as Emerson Clan thrust her down the back steps into an early dawn light darkened by ashes and billowing black clouds.

Clan pushed her into the carriage house and stopped in front of the first stall. Tyler stifled a sob. He yanked her around, belting his pistol long enough to take a leather bridle from a hook on the wall.

"I'm going to have my gun on you all the time. And you better remember it. If you yell for help or try to get away, I'll shoot you point-blank. I will, my dear. Don't be so foolish as to underestimate me. I've killed a woman before, Mrs. Kincaid, and it's no different than killing a man."

Tyler stared at him, so frightened she could barely breathe. He bridled the mare and led her out of the stall, then boosted Tyler up onto the horse's back. She sat stiffly as he mounted behind her, aware of the pistol pressing painfully into her ribs. All the while her eyes desperately sought some avenue of escape, or someone, anyone, who could help her.

As Clan calmly walked the horse along Lincoln Avenue, few of the passersby even looked at them.

Everyone was busy with his own troubles, packing to leave before being consumed by the fire.

Near the Clark Street Bridge, the smoke and streams of refugees filled Wabash Street from curb to curb. Tyler went rigid as Emerson Clan blithely turned the horse against the flow of rowdy, shouting pedestrians, directly into the path of the fire.

"Wait! We can't go that way! That's where the fire is!"

The nose of the pistol jabbed so deep into Tyler's side that she cried out in pain.

"Ten thousand dollars is worth the risk. Now shut up, or you won't be around to worry about it."

Tyler was too scared to utter another word, but her hopes rose as she saw several volunteer firemen standing guard alongside a high dirt barrier at the perimeter of the fire zone. Two blocks down from them, the fire burned unrestrained.

"Whoa there, mister, we ain't lettin' you through this here gate. See the Star Hotel down there a ways? It's already burning, and the one next to it is about to be blown up. We're thinkin' to stop the spread that way. Nobody's going any closer than those blokes building the breastworks on the other side of the bridge."

Tyler felt Clan increase the pressure of the gun as she glanced toward the high earthwork where hundreds of men were laboring to erect a wall against the ravaging fire. Maybe Gray was somewhere among them!

"It's an emergency," Clan insisted. "I've got to get to that hotel before it goes up. I'll take my chances."

The fireman spat a wad of tobacco on the ground, resolutely shaking his head. "Nope. Nobody goes past me. I don't give a hot damn about your emergency."

He got no further. Before Tyler could move, Clan suddenly pointed his pistol toward the man. She screamed as he pulled the trigger with cold-blooded deliberation, the bullet slamming into the man's chest.

Just as quickly, Clan shot the other two guards on duty, then spurred the horse forward in a wild dash. Tyler held on to the saddle horn with all her strength, leaning forward in terror as workmen on the bridge tried to stop them and more shots rang out.

Near the center of the bulwark, Gray straightened from the backbreaking labor of shoveling dirt, his attention arrested by the sound of gunfire. Stone leaned on his pick, wiping the sweat from his brow. A horse raced past them, scattering workers and the last evacuees from the buildings across the bridge.

"Good God, that's Clan!" Stone yelled.

"Tyler!" Gray shouted, "My God, he's got Tyler!" He grabbed his rifle, roughly pushing his way through the crowd as he ran after them. Once on the bridge, he knelt and aimed at Clan's horse.

The bullet took the mare down to her knees, and Clan scrambled off, then jerked Tyler after him. Gray sprinted down the center of the bridge with Stone at his heels, but both were forced to duck as Clan let loose several shots in their direction. The people on the bridge panicked when they realized they were in the midst of a gun battle, screaming and fleeing for safety. Clan backed away, holding Tyler in front of him like a shield.

"Don't shoot, Stone! You'll hit Tyler!" Gray yelled, pulling down Stone's arm as Clan dragged Tyler backward into the entrance of the flaming Star Hotel.

Tyler stumbled to her knees when Clan yanked her through the blazing lobby toward the staircase, her skirt brushing up against a smoldering sofa. She slapped at the burning fabric and tried to pull away from Clan's hold.

"Let me go!" she cried. "It's on fire up there! We'll never get out!"

"Shut up and move," he yelled, prodding her up the steps with his gun.

Halfway to the top, Tyler quailed as a pair of smoking curtains burst into flame in the archway at the top of the stairs. She dropped to her knees, her arm protecting her face from the terrible heat.

"Hold it, you bastard!"

Tyler whirled at the sound of Gray's voice, her heart leaping when she saw her husband running across the lobby. Clan fired at him, and to Tyler's horror, Gray fell, clutching his side. Before Clan could shoot again, Tyler grabbed his arm and struggled desperately for the gun.

"Get out of the way, Tyler!" Stone yelled from the floor below.

As soon as Tyler dropped to her knees, a shot rang out. The impact of the bullet sent Clan staggering backward. He held his thigh, viciously cursing Stone as he limped along the upstairs corridor, dragging his wounded leg. Stone sprang past Tyler in pursuit of Clan, and she ran to her husband, who was trying to pull himself to his feet.

"Gray, how bad is it?"

"It's my side. Help me up! We've got to get out of here!" he rasped. "They're going to blow this hotel any minute! Get Stone down here!"

Tyler draped Gray's arm around her neck and tried to brace him. He groaned in agony.

"Stone! You've got to help me!" she screamed desperately. "Gray's hurt!"

Upstairs, Stone looked down at them from where he was crouched beside the banister. He hesitated, peering through the smoke-filled corridor where Clan had disappeared seconds earlier, then turned and vaulted down the steps to where Tyler was

struggling to support Gray's weight. Stone got an
arm around his brother's waist and, with Tyler's
help, quickly forged a path through the burning
lobby.

Outside, fire swept the rooftops, engulfing every
building around. As they fought their way toward
the earthwork, coughing and choking on the thick
black smoke, the first explosion went off with a deaf-
ening roar. All three were hurled to the ground by
the blast, fiery debris raining down around them.
Stone's sleeve caught fire, and Tyler screamed as
flames were kindled in her hair. She beat at them
frantically while Stone jerked off his burning shirt.

"We can't make it to the bridge, Gray! The river's
our only chance!"

Gray gritted his teeth against the pain as Stone
hoisted him to his feet again, and Tyler dragged his
other arm around her shoulders. They stumbled
blindly toward the riverbank, pulling Gray into the
warm, ash-coated water only seconds before another blast rocked the area.

She desperately attempted to hold Gray's head
out of the water as Stone frantically towed them both
deeper into the stream. It seemed an eternity before
they reached the opposite shore, and Tyler helped
drag Gray onto the bank. A third explosion sent
burning boards, bricks, and roof tiles plummeting
into the river.

"Gray, we've got to get you to a doctor," Stone
said. "Can you make it any farther?"

"Yes, so let's get out of here before the fire jumps
the river," Gray mumbled, stifling his cry of pain as
he forced himself to stand.

Stone held him up as Tyler pulled off her sodden
sash, wrapping it around his torso and temporarily
binding the wound as best she could. Then she and
Stone made their way to the street, bracing Gray
between them. She didn't even glance across the
river to where the fire stubbornly refused to die. At

that moment, she didn't care if the whole city went up, if they lost everything they had. They were safe from Emerson Clan and the fire, and that was all that mattered.

Epilogue

November 10, 1871

Tyler stood at the end of the busy train depot, looking toward the tall Water Tower at Michigan and Chicago avenues that had somehow managed to escape the fire. Across the street, she could hear the incessant tap of hammers on fresh-cut boards. Nearly every street in the city was filled with similar sounds of construction.

Only one month had passed since October eighth, the terrible day of flame and red devastation which had destroyed three and a half square miles of the city and over seventeen thousand homes and businesses. She shuddered to think what would have happened if Providence had not sent the light rain which had finally put out the fire when it was just blocks from their own home on Lincoln Avenue.

She turned her attention to Gray, who had walked ahead with Stone after Tyler had bade her brother-in-law good-bye. For a moment she admired the two men, both so tall and handsome. Gray made an emphatic gesture with his hand, his brows drawn down; she knew what they were arguing about. Gray had tried every conceivable method at his dis-

posal to dissuade Stone from going after Emerson
Clan again—all to no avail. Apparently Stone was
still ignoring Gray's arguments, as he'd done from
the moment he'd learned that Clan had been seen
alive and well in San Francisco.

Tyler wasn't sure which side she should take in
their disagreement—not that her opinion mattered.
Stone was going, regardless of what anyone said.
Clan was so evil, she thought, shivering at the memory of the way he had treated her. He deserved to
be caught and punished for his terrible crimes.

Poor Jonah lay dead because of him, and Hildie
was still weak from a concussion. And Gray. Gray
had been very lucky. He still could not move as easily as he once had, but his flesh wound was healing
well. Charles said he would soon be as good as ever.
But what if he'd died from the injury? What if the
gunshot had pierced his heart? She couldn't bear
the thought.

Tyler was momentarily distracted by a black-
garbed nun, peering around the platform. As she
looked in Tyler's direction, Tyler was taken aback
by the beauty of the small face with sapphire eyes
beneath the dreary black wimple. She had never
seen such a young, pretty nun.

Tyler suddenly thought of the first day she had
met Carly, when she'd worn her chaste white wimple. She smiled as the young Catholic Sister glided
off toward Gray and Stone, a bamboo suitcase in
one hand and her black skirt swirling out behind her
like the robe of a medieval magician. Tyler hadn't
heard from Carlisle in a long time, but perhaps she
could persuade her to come home for the baby's
birth. She put her hand to her stomach, wishing her
confinement was at hand. Six more months seemed
an eternity to wait for such a precious gift.

Her eyes widened as the nun made a direct path
for Stone, bumping into him hard enough to knock
herself down. Stone immediately bent and assisted

her to her feet, then shook hands with Gray before escorting the nun toward the waiting train.

Hating good-byes, Tyler blinked back her tears as Gray joined her. He reached for his handkerchief.

"Gray, did you see what that nun did to Stone?" Tyler asked, sniffling as she dabbed at her tears.

"You mean when she ran into him?"

Tyler nodded, and he shrugged. "She didn't mean to. She apologized."

"But she did it on purpose."

Gray's eyes left his brother to dwell on her face. He laughed. "I doubt that. She nearly got the breath knocked out of her when she fell."

"But I *saw* her do it on purpose," Tyler insisted, her eyes narrowing distrustfully as Stone helped the nun onto the outside platform of the passenger car. "Why, I've just had the most awful thought! What if she's out to swindle him? Uncle Burl used to dress as a priest on occasion. What if she's what I used to be!"

Gray laughed again. "If she's like you, which I doubt, then Stone's a lucky man." He reached out to caress a wispy tendril of her hair, admiring the way it had curled since he had helped her shear off the burned parts. "But if you want my honest opinion, I think she's just clumsy."

"No, Gray, I'm telling you she's too young and pretty to be a nun. You didn't see her face like I did."

"Even if she is, Stone's too obsessed with finding Clan to have his head turned by a nun, no matter how pretty she is." He shook his head, realizing how absurd his words sounded.

Tyler knew he thought her suspicions ridiculous, but, worried, she looked at Stone, who stood waving at them from the observation platform. The nun had already disappeared inside.

"Gray, you know how good my instincts are about things like this," she insisted. "I hope Stone won't be fooled by her. I was in the business a long time. I can nearly always trust my first impressions.''

Gray slid his fingers through hers. ''You were wrong about me,'' he reminded her.

''Well, that's the only time.''

''Then tell me your predictions concerning our baby. Will we have a son or a daughter in the spring?''

''Oh, it's going to be a boy—a big, healthy boy.''

''What? No girl?''

''Next time.''

Gray put his arms around her and watched his brother's train roll away, a surge of tenderness filling him as Tyler smiled at him, her big cinnamon eyes full of warmth and love.

''Let's go home,'' he whispered.

Desire darkened her eyes and made her blood flow warm and eager. ''Yes, let's do.''

The following is a selection from
MIDNIGHT FIRE,
featuring Carlisle's story,
the second book in Linda Ladd's
"Fire" Trilogy
coming in February 1991
from Avon Books

"In my country, young marriageable girls such as yourself are required to have a female chaperone to accompany them everywhere they go. At least, until they're safely married and have a husband to protect them." One corner of his mouth curved into a smile. "The custom prevents unsavory scandals and assures a man that his bride is virtuous."

Carlisle was outraged. "Are you insinuating that I am, that I would—"

"No need to take offense, Senorita Kincaid. But I did happen to see the Perez boy kissing you out on the balcony. I'm afraid I just can't let anything like that happen again. I'd have failed miserably in my duty if I had to telegraph Gray someday and invite him to your hastily arranged wedding. So you'll just have to put up with a duenna while you're in my care.''

Incredulous, Carlisle stared at him. ''You were spying on us!''

''Gray told me to keep an eye on you. Otherwise, I wouldn't have bothered.'' His smile appeared again. ''Actually, by the look of Javier's kiss, I doubt if you were very much impressed, one way or another.''

Carlisle's fingers curled into fists. ''And what does your kiss do to women? Turn them to mush?''

He laughed. ''Sometimes.''

Carlisle looked at his handsome face, wondering if there really was a difference in the way men kissed. Perhaps she should find out. Why not flirt a bit, sample the kiss of a man known for his philandering? It would be an intriguing experiment.

''I daresay kissing you wouldn't affect me one whit. After all, you have to like someone a little before you can enjoy kissing them.''

''Shall we find out, Senorita Kincaid?''

His challenge hung between them for an instant.

''Don't get your hopes up, Senor Lancaster,'' she warned, but her heart skipped a beat as Chase moved toward her, his thumb and fingers gently bracketing her jaw. He held her firmly, capturing her gaze before his lips came down on hers—soft, warm, undemanding. He began to taste her mouth, molding his lips to hers, and Carlisle was swiftly flooded with peculiar, weak, fluttery sensations in the pit of her stomach, as if dozens of canaries were trapped there. Her reeling senses settled when he paused momentarily to look into her eyes. But then he began again, more intensely, hard and insistent, compelling her to respond. When his tongue found its way to hers, she moaned and clung weakly to his shoulders. He released her then, leaning back against the squabs.

Carlisle stared at him, her fingers on her throbbing lips.

"Do you call that a kiss?" she managed shakily, determined to act as indifferent to the experience as he had.

"You mean it didn't turn you to mush?"

His description was not far from the truth, but Carlisle remained silent, striving to regain her composure.

"You're really an awful man," she finally managed to say, her voice husky. "Gray would never let you escort me to Mexico if he knew you had kissed me like that."

"True, he probably wouldn't. But we don't have to worry about him finding out, do we? Because you're not about to tell him or he'll put a stop to your little trip, and then you'd see even less of your precious Javier than you will with your duenna in tow."

His voice was so openly scornful that Carlisle was shocked.

"You're every bit as bad as they say, aren't you? You're *worse* than they say."

"They?" he said casually, but a different, dangerous note had crept into his voice. "Who?"

At once Carlisle realized she'd made a mistake. Javier and Arantxa wouldn't want him to know they disliked him.

"Why, everyone, of course," she answered lightly. "Even Tyler. She thought you were wonderful until you showed up here and made her marry Gray against her will. I think it's disgraceful the way you treated her. She's your own flesh and blood."

"You seem to think your own brother will be a very disagreeable husband, Carlisle. Do you expect him to treat Tyler cruelly?"

"No, of course not! Gray will be good to her, but that's not the point. The point—"

"The point," he interrupted, "is that Gray is probably the best thing ever to happen to my cousin. She's lucky he even wants to marry her after she tried to swindle ten thousand dollars out of him back in Chicago. She's behaved like a common criminal all her life, due to my own thieving father. He was nothing but a gambler and a confidence man who taught her all his crooked games. I'd probably be as dishonest as Tyler if my mother hadn't left him when I was young. I'm just thankful Gray's willing to take her to hand."

Chase paused, his eyes pinning her. "But you, Carlisle, you're just the opposite, aren't you? You've been sheltered and pampered like a little queen by your brothers ever since you were a baby. You've gone to all the best schools, met all the right people, which probably bored you to tears. So now you're ripe to run wild and entice every man you see with those incredible big green eyes of yours."

Suddenly his voice took on an angry edge. "Unfortunately, in a moment of weakness I was thoughtless enough to offer you the hospitality of my ranch, a stupid blunder on my part, which I heartily regret but can hardly take back now. So, what it all boils down to is this: Whether you like it or not, you'll have a duenna to keep you in line while you're under my supervision in Mexico, because I'm already damn sick and tired of your spoiled tantrums."

Carlisle was completely taken aback. This was hardly the first time they'd quarreled, but always before he'd shown no emotion other than amused indifference. What had made him so furious all of a sudden?

"Actually, I'll welcome a duenna," she said quietly, slightly subdued by his attack. "If for no other reason than to protect me from any further unwelcome advances from you."

His eyes grew hooded, and she knew before he spoke that his anger would be gone, or well hidden.

"No need to worry about me, Senorita Kincaid. I kissed you only to prove a point. Now maybe you'll think twice before teasing a man you hardly know.

If not, one of these days you might find yourself in a very serious predicament. All men aren't as gentlemanly as I am.''

''You know,'' she answered furiously, ''this is just what I'd expect from you. Placing the blame for your own ill-mannered behavior on me!''

The coach stopped in the driveway of her brother's house on Third Street, and without replying to her denouncement, Chase climbed out, then politely lifted her to the ground.

''Sleep well, Senorita Kincaid. Our ship sails at noon.''

Carlisle gritted her teeth, raised her chin, and left him where he stood. She stalked to the front door, her full skirts bunched in her hands, her whole evening ruined by his boorish behavior and unkind accusations on the ride home. How on earth was she going to stand his irritating, chafing, disagreeable presence long enough to find out the information Javier Perez needed for his revolution?

A YEAR'S SUPPLY OF AVON ROMANCES FREE!

Dear Reader,

Here's your chance to tell us what *you* think about romance! Which celebrity would you most like to see in a romance novel? What is the most romantic thing about a man? What is the most romantic gift to receive?

Just take a few brief moments to answer the following questions. If your response is among the first 50 *completed* forms received by Avon Books, you will receive…

Enough Avon Romances to keep your life full of love for one year!

That's two books per month commencing in August 1990!

Limit one completed survey per person.

LOOK FOR THE POLL RESULTS
IN AN UPCOMING ISSUE OF
GOOD HOUSEKEEPING MAGAZINE!

Avon Romance Survey

Please circle the <u>one answer to each question</u> which you feel is the best choice.

1. *Which celebrity would make the sexiest romance novel hero?*
   a. Mel Gibson
   b. Sean Connery
   c. John F. Kennedy, Jr.
   d. Tom Cruise
   e. Arnold Schwarzenegger
   f. Dennis Quaid
   g. Joe Montana
   h. Eddie Murphy
   i. your husband/boyfriend

2. *Which celebrity would make the sexiest romance novel heroine?*
   a. Jaclyn Smith
   b. Meryl Streep
   c. Candice Bergen
   d. Cher
   e. Madonna
   f. Diana Ross
   g. Princess Diana
   h. Elizabeth Taylor

3. *Which is the most romantic gift to receive?*
   a. perfume
   b. jewelry
   c. dinner out
   d. flowers
   e. cash
   f. lingerie
   g. weekend off from housework

4. *Which is the most romantic sign of affection a man can give?*
   a. a kiss b. a hug c. a gift
   d. holding hands
   e. saying I love you

5. *Which clothes do you find the sexiest on a man?*
   a. pajamas
   b. a dinner jacket
   c. bathing trunks
   d. jeans
   e. a bath towel
   f. a robe
   g. a service uniform

6. *Which is the most romantic thing about a man?*
   a. money
   b. humor
   c. faithfulness
   d. looks
   e. kindness
   f. intelligence

7. *Which is the least romantic habit or characteristic in a man?*
   a. bad table manners
   b. snoring
   c. nail biting
   d. sloppy at-home appearance
   e. cheapness
   f. taking me for granted

8. *Which is the most romantic time of the year?*
   a. summer
   b. fall
   c. winter
   d. spring

QUESTIONS CONTINUE...

9. **Which sport is responsible for the greatest decline in romance?**
   a. football
   b. baseball
   c. basketball
   d. hockey
   e. golf

10. **Which is a man's sexiest feature?**
    a. cute dimples
    b. chiseled lips
    c. strong eyebrows
    d. wavy hair
    e. piercing eyes
    f. towering stature
    g. muscular chest

11. **If you could be a character in a romance novel, which would you most like to be?**
    a. a feisty spitfire
    b. a sweet innocent
    c. a worldly temptress
    d. a virtuous woman
    e. an intrepid adventurer

12. **What is your marital status?**
    a. married
    b. single
    c. divorced
    d. separated
    e. widowed

13. **Do you have children?**
    a. yes
    b. no

14. **What is your age?**
    a. under 18
    b. 18 - 29
    c. 30 - 39
    d. 40 - 49
    e. 50 - 64
    f. 65 or over

15. **Do you work outside the home?**
    a. yes
    b. no

Optional Question: Your form will still be considered complete if you elect not to answer this question. (Write answer on a separate sheet of paper.)

What is your favorite romantic fantasy?

The following information is required only if you wish to qualify for the year's supply of Avon Romances:

Name _____

Address _____

Phone _____

Please return to: Avon Romance Survey
c/o Publicity Department
Avon Books
105 Madison Ave.
New York, NY 10016